DRAGON'S
JUSTICE 8

Cover by Yanaidraws

CONTENTS

Chapter 1

Music thumped in the distance. Even in the limo, we could hear the music. Chloe had the biggest grin on her face as she sat next to me.

I took a moment to soak up the blue dragon in her human form. Her straight, black hair was pulled back but still loose as it cascaded down her back heavy enough that it wasn't all over the place despite the kissing we'd been doing.

Her lips were a little redder than normal as she bit them, made only more obvious with her pale skin. "Thank you for this, I know the concert isn't exactly your scene." Chloe searched my eyes.

I kissed her again. "Pretty sure I was the one to get the tickets. This was my idea."

Chloe was in a torn, white shirt with 'One-Two Shockers' stretched across her chest, and jeans that had more holes than fabric. To complete the look for the concert, she had on a pair of chunky studded bracelets.

She was the youngest of the dragons that made up my honor guard. The dragons at the conclave had wanted them to guard me, but also to join my harem and hopefully speed up the potential repopulating of dragons. Their numbers were still sorely low from a war that had spread across Europe hundreds of years ago.

The honor guard became my dragonettes, originally six, joined by Regina to make seven. They still stuck largely to their goals of protecting me, yet increasingly they were joining my bed, and the dragon part of me preened at having a harem of dragons to go home to every night.

As the youngest of them, Chloe was all spunk and, apparently, more than a little punk as I'd come to figure out her love of heavy metal concerts. Though, young was an interesting qualifier when it came to dragons. Chloe was in her eighties even though she had the body of a young twenty something.

Older than me by a long shot. I had only come into my dragon heritage recently and hadn't even finished college. Though, I was getting over the whole age things. Among paranormals, it was more how you acted rather than the number. Morgana was a testament to that.

My thoughts switched to one of my pregnant wives, and my dragon instincts craved to be back home, wrapping her and all of my other wives up in my hoard before snuggling them to death.

"Zach?" Chloe was still staring into my eyes and sensed my mind drifting off.

"Sorry. Tonight is your night." I blinked and refocused on her, letting my hands wander down her curves and pull her off her leather seat next to me and into my lap.

There was a particular hole in her jeans that I thought if I worked hard enough, I could go through and have a little fun here without needing to strip.

Well, besides my own jeans.

She kissed my neck and whispered into my ear. "Yes, it is my night. So let's go have fun." She pulled back with a grin, getting to her feet.

My eyes flickered to Pixie who sat with her legs crossed, a relaxed vigilance, and a placid smile on her face as she watched. The nymph might have been dressed like a secretary that was all business, but when she wanted to be, she was all nymph.

"Have a good night you two. I'll stay with the limo. Text me when you want to be picked up." She waved her fingers, and her eyes danced with delight.

Chloe pulled me out of the limo and took a deep breath of the smoke-filled air. "Yes, I love concerts."

My draconic senses picked up the smoke and everything else, parsing through the scents and finding nothing wrong. It was a strangely inhuman experience even if I was in my human form. I had accepted that I was a dragon, a part of the secret paranormal society.

Sarisha and Poly slipped out of the car behind us, but then disappeared into the crowd to avoid disturbing me and Chloe any more than they had to. The dragonettes had a small sisterhood even among the rest of my harem.

Chloe pulled me forward as I pulled the tickets out and made straight for the ticket counter.

"Two," I said, holding a possessive arm around the beautiful Chloe and handing him the tickets with the other.

He looked us both up and down, lingering far longer on Chloe before scanning the tickets and handing them back to us. "Have fun," he said largely to Chloe.

As soon as we stepped away from the booth, she rolled her eyes. "He thinks you are only here because I'm hot."

I raised an eyebrow. "He's quite insightful."

She couldn't help the smile that blossomed on her face before she nudged me forward.

The crowd was an eclectic blend of people. Some more normally dressed like me, others covered in tattoos with more than a few mohawks rising prominently above the crowd. Oddly enough, the stranger they appeared, the friendlier they turned out to be. Bodies were pressed together and conversations were short. Thankfully, the outdoor venue had open sky above that kept me from feeling claustrophobic.

Chloe chatted with people as we moved through the crowd. She was quite the extrovert. She finally got to an area that seemed perfect to her and grabbed my hand to pull me behind her. "Thank you for this."

The music had died down, and a band on stage was doing a little last-minute tuning.

"It's my pleasure, and more so to see you in your element." I ran my hands along her hips, and she pressed her rear into me and gave me a tantalizing sway.

"Oh you haven't seen me in my element just yet." She put my hands on her belt and pushed my fingers to grip it firmly. "Just make sure to hold on tight."

There was a heavily modified strum of an electric guitar that was far louder than all the tuning. It got everyone's attention, and the singer spoke into the microphone.

"Thank you everyone for coming out tonight. We are going to have a blast. This is Reckless Despair opening up the night. A 1... A 2... A 1. 2. 3."

There was almost a physical force as the band kicked off, and the speakers everywhere in the outdoor venue blasted out rough yet harmonic music.

Everyone cheered, and I joined Chloe as the music kicked off, feeling like part of the crowd. Bodies slammed into me, and I stumbled, still holding onto Chloe's belt.

"Don't be too rough," she said with a smile over her shoulder, and we pushed back against those that had pushed. We were pressed together, and she wiggled herself against me as we pushed back and forth as a team.

The concert fell into a rhythm only for the song to hit a point, and people purposefully broke the beat and slammed into each other. Chloe whooped and pressed herself to me grinding a little as we were pressed together by people on all sides.

Despite the music and the moshing, she glanced over her shoulder at me and grabbed my collar to pull me down for a rough kiss before we went right back to it.

***

I blew out a breath as we stumbled along with all the other concert-goers in the dim light; the city was never really dark.

Chloe had my hand in a death grip as she pulled me along out of the park to the nearby streets that were suddenly flooded with people searching for food or another adventure for their night.

"Did you have fun?" she asked, her blue eyes bright with excitement.

"You know, I really started to get into it after a few songs. There's just a..." I searched for the word and came up short.

"The rowdy energy is infectious, isn't it? Makes you feel alive." She couldn't stop her smile from growing, knowing that I felt it too.

"Feels like I'm high on life." It was a cheesy line, but that was the most honest description I had.

She nodded along. "Yeah. It's fun. As I outlive normal people, have to move around and remake myself, there's always these concerts, a particular crowd that I can go to, get lost in and just feel alive."

I squeezed her hand. "Sounds like a wonderful thing. Especially since we are going to be alive a long time. We might need something like this to make us remember."

My mind drifted off to some of the stiff members of the Philly council or what I almost thought of as my previous life going to school, then grinding my way up to a career where I'd planned to push myself up the medical specialist hierarchy.

Coming down from the high of the concert gave me perspective.

My life was fantastic. I was an immortal dragon, a king among dragons which made me important enough that I was drowning in administrative tasks thanks to the local paranormal council here in Philly. A few urgent dragon political items had been filtering my way as well. Even though I 'had people for that', somehow, it kept me all quite busy.

I wasn't making it easy for myself when I had broken some rules and looped in the DC Associate Director of the FBI who had come to plug the holes that Norton had made in Philly's field office. It had been necessary. I knew after Norton that I had to tell someone in the FBI, or there would always be someone either too curious or too stupid poking around.

"Come on. That pizza looks sooo good." Chloe pulled me into a store that sold pizza by the slice and distracted me from my thoughts.

A beautiful woman, who I hoped would officially elevate to my mate tonight, was a welcome distraction.

She got two slices and handed me a paper plate that was rapidly soaking up grease from the pizza and losing its form. But Chloe didn't care and pulled me over to the curb where we sat with a number of other concert goers who were recharging with grease ladened carbs for what promised to be a slew of afterparties.

"Oh. This is so good." She had grease lingering on her lips, and I ignored my pizza for a second to kiss it off her.

"It is." I feigned shock.

She was blushing. "Eat your pizza, my king."

I hummed, and it rumbled in my chest more than it would a normal human. "We need to change your address." Though I let them all call me king while they worked as my honor guard, she was off duty tonight, and I wanted something more personable.

"You are my king."

"Tonight, I'm hoping you'll be my mate." I kept my voice low, though I doubted any of the people at the concert would have minded if I said some strange things.

Chloe took another bite of her pizza in an attempt to hide her nerves, but her blush deepened. "I'd like that," she said around her mouthful when it was clear that I wasn't going to just move on.

"Me too." I took a bite of my own pizza. "Which afterparty sounded most interesting to you?" Even if the concert was over, I had the strong feeling the night wasn't.

"There's a place called Dark Alleys that has what I wanted." She couldn't meet my eyes, and I was eager to see what this was.

"Then let's finish up and see this place." I took a huge bite of my pizza.

She nudged me with her hip. "Get up—we'll walk and eat."

We were being a little weird with our slices of pizza, but in the crowd after the concert, there was a freedom to be as odd as you wanted. Tonight, Philly's night life was suborned by the weird.

Chloe pulled me into an alley where a queue was slowly being accepted into a back-alley entrance.

The bouncer looked Chloe up and down and smiled. "How was the concert?"

"Fantastic," Chloe blurted like she'd been waiting all night to say it. "But too short."

"Not The Shockers, but we got a good band tonight. Enjoy." He gave me one of those bro-nods that said I was in good company.

Chloe pulled me down a set of stairs as more heavy metal blasted through the halls. The place was thick with smoke and the floors sticky with spilled drink as she pulled me back to the dance floor to reignite that high on life.

Though, there wasn't as much shoving here, and she ground herself against me with smiles over her shoulder that told me she knew exactly what she was doing.

It was another half an hour of dancing that had my heart thumping in my chest before she pulled me out and down a back hall. No one paid us any attention as they were all over their prospective partners. People made out pressed against the walls.

Chloe stepped around people with the ease and grace of a battle-trained dragon. The deeper we got in the hallway, the more the acts shifted from innocent kissing to sloppy kissing and lascivious blow jobs.

Chloe found an empty space and turned around to kiss me. I wasn't stupid, and pressed her against the wall as she smiled into the kiss.

CHAPTER 2

I woke up in my bed, with Chloe pressed up against me. After a little fun, I had portaled us back to the manor and continued the night.

She was beautiful and very naked with a faint scar that hid well against her pale shoulder. Compared to Polydora, the marking had been tame, but no less fun.

Chloe cracked an eye open to find me watching. "Hello, my mate."

"Hello." I stopped holding back and ran a hand through her hair. "Just enjoying a little quiet before the day starts."

She squinted out the window that had bright light streaming in. "Pretty sure the day is well underway."

As if agreeing with her, there was a knock on the door.

"Come in," I called.

Pixie stepped in, her pink curls bouncing with each step. She was the picture of professionalism which only made me suddenly eager to make her anything but. There was a sparkle in her eyes as she saw my hunger. She was a constant tease.

"I cleared what I could this morning so that you could enjoy your new mate, but the Associate Director isn't something we can cancel. You'll have to make it up to Summer for missing another Summer Court meeting."

I groaned.

"Go. Last night was wonderful. I know that my mate will be busy." Chloe pushed me towards the edge of the bed and snuggled back into it herself.

"Not even fair." I slid to a sitting position. "What do I need to know?" I asked Pixie.

She put down her folio and moved to the closet, swiftly picking out an outfit, like she knew where every article of clothing would be before she even got there.

Which she probably did.

With everything that came with being the Dragon King, I had three nymphs. Well, two and a part. I laid claim to Evelyn, even if she was always with Maeve. The fae believed strongly in balance, so I needed one of each court even if I had enough women by my side. Pixie and Nyske were all mine, though. The greedy part of my giant lizard brain loved that word.

"Stand, please." Pixie motioned for me to stand and then flicked her wrist, a warm summer breeze blew over me, leaving me refreshed before the clothes jumped from where they were to my body. "Thank you. Come on. You can't be late here or everything will be behind."

I followed after Pixie, who strutted ahead of me in a pencil skirt that was tight enough that I was positive she was using her magic to move as fast as she was.

"Associate Director, that's an easy one. What's after?"

"Council meeting, then a quick fifteen-minute lunch. Nyske will bring it, and then we have a meeting with Amara and Herm, followed by one with Mrs. Wallachia, then a few prominent out-of-towners. Rupert's party through the night and then tail brushing to cap the night out."

Pixie rattled off without looking at her folio tucked into her arm.

"Tail brushing?" My mind stuck on the last one.

She gave me a sultry smile. "Yes. Scarlett insists."

"I don't mind tail brushing. We could skip the rest though," I sighed.

"You can't skip these things. As the Dragon King, there are a lot of expectations. Besides, you need to get ahead before your trip to Hell," she insisted, not for the first time.

"Thank you for everything. I know there's no small amount of pressure on you."

She shrugged. "I have access to the Dragon King's seed." Her tongue ran across her lips, and it felt extremely out of place given the rest of her mannerism. "Nymphs serve. There is great comfort in serving you in any way I can. Though, you could get a third nymph if you want to make it easier on me."

"I have Evelyn." That had been a crutch I had been leaning heavily on.

Pixie narrowed her eyes at me. "She doesn't count, only because of who you are and who you associate with has held the winter nymphs back."

"Do you really need another nymph?" I squinted my eyes at her, unable to really understand the nymphs.

They were wired differently than humans or dragons for that matter. Fae felt emotions far more powerfully, yet they always seemed so rigid having learned to control them better. It made reading them hard. Nymphs were even stranger, putting getting a powerful partner's seed as their top priority to have a strong child. They often made contracts with fae nobility in order to share the noble's partner.

I had recently learned that they were muses 2.0 made by a titan, which I knew mostly as The Dreamer.

"Yes," Pixie said after a moment of silence. "I'm working hard, and so is Nyske. If either or both of us get pregnant, you'll need a third. We can't do this level of work and be mothers."

Pixie had had plenty of opportunities in the last week to get pregnant. Now it was a waiting game. With the blessing from The Dreamer that I had, there was a lot of speculation that we'd be about to have a whole gaggle of pregnant nymphs.

A Dragon King might be busy, but at times, I could have a lot of fun.

"Okay. Give me options tomorrow."

She handed me a sheaf of paper from her folio. "Here, read them on the way."

I smirked. Damn, she was good. But if she needed another, I wasn't going to say no.

Pixie and I reached the parking garage where my limo sat idling. Well, it was Morgana's parking garage and technically Jadelyn's limo, but she had several, and this one had been co-opted by me quite thoroughly lately.

Larisa opened the door for me and Pixie, revealing Nyske inside tapping away at her phone before tucking it away with my entrance.

"Hello, Zach." She smiled, and her hair shifted colors as my shadow flowed over her and I sat next to her.

"Hello, Nyske." I ran my hand along her thigh, feeling her and a sense of familiarity. We had a complex history, especially since she had dated me with a different face freshman year.

Besides putting up with her pickle juice drinking habit, there had always been a layer of secrecy between us. But with it gone, it felt like I was falling back into a familiar rhythm.

Pixie found herself on my other side, the three of us pushed together in the large limo, leaving the rest of the space empty. Regina was up front as Larisa joined us all in the limo and rolled it out of the parking garage.

"Okay, so these are the winter nymph candidates. I assume you've looked them over, Nyske? Got a pick yourself?" I asked.

"Fiona is a favorite." She pointed to the first page.

It was a picture of yet another beautiful nymph. With my house full of them, it didn't quite hit me the same as the nymphs did at first. That and a glamor didn't come through a picture.

My eyes trailed down the descriptions. "She left Winter's employ? No detail as to why?"

"Rumor is Fiona left when Winter used Iapetus' power to restore herself. She saw it as the beginning of Winter's end and left. Besides, her contract was unlikely to be fulfilled anytime soon," Pixie pointed out. "But that's just rumors. She's about as good as they come. Probably a little stiffer than you'd like. With winter nymphs, you are going to find a lot of that."

"Evelyn isn't stiff," I shot back.

Nyske frowned at me. "Not for you. These will take a little adjustment. They are all good, but it is always meeting them in person that really lets you know if they are a good fit."

I nodded and looked through the other two. "So, when are they coming by?" I asked Pixie with a smile, guessing that she already arranged something.

"They are already in the manor; you'll meet with them tomorrow." She wasn't even abashed that she had already planned it.

Some might balk at these two women planning things for me, but that was their job, and they did it perfectly. There was no reason to complain.

"Okay. Can you refresh me on this before then? Let's focus on the Associate Director. What does she want?" I moved on; they were a well-oiled machine.

"She's got a job for you. The Associate Director is back in DC, but she said they have a problem that she wanted your expertise on. Potentially a contract for Silverwing Mercenaries," Nyske explained.

I nodded. "Okay, and she didn't run it by either of you, so it's sensitive. That's fine, I'd welcome a job. Wonderful excuse to get out of council meetings. I hope it's urgent. Have either of you checked on Sabrina?"

She wasn't exactly under house watch, but I had my nymphs checking on her regularly. Now that she couldn't hold back her succubus nature, it was going to gnaw at her and apparently turn her back into a vapid, lust-craven, lower succubus eventually.

Which I wouldn't let happen.

"Fine. But she was having trouble focusing on an enchantment today. It was frustrating her quite a bit," Nyske said with a sadness painting her face. "We are going to discuss it during the Golden Plushie Society tonight. I think we should pull up the departure date."

"Oh." I was not quite sure what to say about any of that.

The Golden Plushie Society was where my harem and harem potentials met up and discussed their plans for world domination. Or at least that was my favorite description, courtesy of Summer. It wasn't really my place, despite it being made up entirely of my harem.

"We don't know how long it's going to take for Zach to weed out Beelzebub," Pixie pointed out. "Hell is not an easy place. So, I agree that the sooner he goes and helps Sabrina, the better chances of it going smoothly."

I crossed my arms thinking about the trip. "Has the GPS decided who's coming?"

"Ikta and Summer actually are very interested in going," Nyske said while trying to keep a neutral face.

But that was a big deal. "Two fae queens? That's... a lot of fire power. Not to mention that Summer is coming down from the height of her power. She can't leave." She had just lost her daughter; I didn't want her making a rash decision.

"It's come up. Apparently, we don't have to worry right now. Something about the spear you destroyed." Pixie shrugged. "I understand most fae magic, but no one really understands the queens. Maeve agreed with Summer that she could step away if that makes a difference."

"Huh. That would be an interesting group," I said.

"Helena wanted to come and wipe the floor with Beelzebub. But I think the new changes happening at the FBI are going to keep her from going. She's going to be pissed. She would have loved to rip Beelzebub into pieces with her own hands after what he did to her." Nyske clicked her tongue.

"The girl can hold a grudge." I winced, my hips feeling sore at the thought of one of our rougher times together.

Pixie chuckled. "Still pretending like you two aren't fucking each other raw every chance you get?"

"Huh?" I blinked innocently. "Me and Helena?" I said in mock surprise.

"Stop it. She doesn't want people to know," Nyske played along, running her hands through her hair. It looked black, but as it moved, each strand seemed to have color that bled out of it as it moved, making it shimmer like a rainbow bleeding out of her black hair.

"Oh, Right," Pixie played along before returning to the topic of teammates for the trip to Hell. "Kelly really wants to go, but Trina shot her down. If the baby turns out to be a dragon, she could lose all her wolf powers during the trip."

"We don't know what's going to happen with her, especially since she's the only female alpha. Will she be able to handle the strain of the whelp? We just don't know. Either way, separating her from the pack is also not her strong suit. And we stick to that reasoning so that Morgana Stubornwing doesn't get to come," I said.

Both of my nymphs giggled.

I had tried to treat my vampire wife with kid gloves now that she was pregnant. Saying it went poorly was the understatement of the year. Now she was dead set on proving that she was not hindered in any way, shape, or form with her pregnancy.

"We did get the Council to start running their jobs for her past us first," Pixie confirmed.

"Good. If she gets something dangerous, she's going to go run off and do it herself just to prove how wrong I was." I shook my head. My protective instincts had flared up knowing that they were pregnant, yet they were all individually powerful and independent women. Trying to change that was not going to do more than blow up in my face.

Thus, I had to focus upfield and try to keep anything too dangerous from coming down.

"Things are still pretty quiet on that front. Even the vampires are behaving themselves." Nyske was running through something on her phone.

"Mrs. Wallachia is too enamored with our king. She wants to impress him with her control over the vampires. If we aren't careful, she's going to piss Morgana off and push too far," Pixie reminded Nyske, yet it sounded like she was talking to me.

"I have no interest in her. Morgana is my only and the best vampire," I repeated for the thousandth time.

"We have a tight rope to walk there," Pixie continued. "Because I don't think she's going to take rejection well."

"I don't think she'd take any rejection seriously." The woman was a few cards short of a deck. "Besides, she is keeping a lid on the vampires. So, we keep meeting with her, keeping things polite."

"Even if she wants your babies, madly," Nyske chuckled. "It takes a really high mana paranormal to get a vamp pregnant. They then are also drinking for two. Which I'm sure Mrs. Wallachia wouldn't mind."

I groaned. "Only one pregnant vampire, please. The barrels we are preparing for Morgana while I'm off to Hell are ridiculous. I'm not sure I could survive two."

CHAPTER 3

Pixie's curls bounced as she walked through the portal into the Associate Director's waiting room. I noticed that the way she was setting up meetings was giving me an excuse to practice my fae magic more, which was coming along quite well.

Regina went through next. "Clear."

She stood tall with broad shoulders. The Amazonian woman was only dwarfed by Polydora. Her messy red hair was pulled back but refused to be contained by hair bands, so she had a metal clasp that looked like it might be sturdy enough to strangle someone. Or knowing the hunter nature within her, could probably double as a weapon.

I stepped through the portal next, and then reached back to help Nyske and Larisa through. "Ladies." I smiled at each of them in turn.

Larisa swayed her hips and kept eye contact with me, a smug smile on her face. Her mating mark was clearly displayed on her shoulder, and with it had come enough confidence to strut into my room when I wasn't busy for a little fun.

The petite woman taught me that I really should have taken the study abroad program in France I had once considered. French ladies turned out to be a lot of fun.

I looked over, catching Nyske's eye. Nyske and I hadn't physically reconnected yet. But there was a deeper connection between us than ever before, a feeling of familiarity.

Pixie was already moving forward and knocking on the Associate Director's door before we'd all settled into the space. "Hello. Zach Pendragon has arrived."

There was the sound of someone walking up to the doors, before they opened up wider. The Associate Director raised an eyebrow as she spotted the portal. "Welcome. Not entirely sure how I feel about the protocol for you to appear here. Can you make a portal whenever you want?"

"If you want to defeat it, you can change up the furniture more often," I told her. "Then I can't pop in so easily."

"Might not be a bad thing." The Associate Director of the DC FBI field office had read into information on paranormals, but she was still learning quite a bit. Helena and Agent Tills' files were her learning ground.

She scanned my entourage. "You always have such different and beautiful women surrounding you. Pixie." She nodded to my assistant in respect.

"Thank you for the compliment, but I am nothing but a tool for my king." She bowed politely, and I tried not to laugh at the startled look on the Associate Director's face.

"Sometimes, I find it more helpful to make friends with people's assistants than the person themselves." She gave Pixie a light smile.

I snorted.

Pixie flashed a look at me that dared me to argue.

The Associate Director broke the tension with a laugh. "Sit. Well, those of you that will. Red doesn't appear to be the sitting type. She's the red dragon, right? I get the sense that she could break half my agents in half."

"Yes. But so could Larisa." I hooked a thumb at the petite woman that didn't have the same level of dominance radiating off of her as Regina. "Both of them could curl a loaded semi-trailer. Larisa just comes in a smaller package."

"Some might say that makes me better." Larisa stuck her nose up while taking a position behind me as my guard.

The Associate Director shook her head. "This whole paranormal business is still hard to wrap my head around. We do have a short list now for the Philly office. I hope when the selection is made that you can help me do their induction?"

"Sure. Care to make sure they don't run?" I smirked. When I had brought the Associate Director into the Faerie for her introduction, she had bolted.

"No promises. But I think it's less likely with me there." She settled in behind her desk while I took a seat in front of it, my nymphs on either side of me.

Nyske had her phone out to take notes, while Pixie seemed to be taking a moment to rest. I wondered if I was pushing them too hard. They seemed able to handle anything, but I knew everybody had their limits.

"Helena and Tills dug up something that they think is paranormal, but it seems that it's an issue that involved other planes. That is to say, they suggested that I include you to help manage the problem." She slid a folder across her desk for me.

I flipped open the folder. Inside were aerial images of a large compound. "What's this?" I flipped through a few pages.

"Religious cult. You know the kind. People go in, give all their savings over, and then live their lives out under some overly charismatic knob. We sent two agents undercover, and they went native on us." She gave a pained frown. "If something's been done to the two agents, can you fix it?"

"Me? Oh, you don't want me doing complex magic on someone. But some of my people? Sure. If magic did something to them, magic can probably fix it. My best magic user is under some pretty harsh constraints right now. In fact, I'm on a tight timeline myself because I need to go to Hell to help her." I glanced over the contents of the folder and lifted the pages to see the photos.

I realized after a few moments that the room had gotten strangely quiet. I stopped in my flipping and returned my attention to the Associate Director.

"Hell?" she asked.

"Yeah. You know, fire and brimstone? Surprisingly, I've heard it's a pretty variable environment. There's only really one area that's actually like the stereotype." I smiled, trying to give a disarming smile, but the Associate Director still looked shaken.

The Associate Director was having a little more trouble. "Then who is your magic expert that they need you to go to Hell?"

I leaned back in my chair. "Sabrina. She's a succubus. Well, sort of. She came to earth, and used magic to suppress her succubus nature. There she found a love of studying magic, but now her succubus nature is breaking the bonds she's had on it. She's struggling with its return."

"A demon? I'm sorry. I know they were mentioned in the report with the Representative's death this spring. But can they be trusted?" She frowned like she was holding back a tidal wave of bias.

I respected that she was trying, but she needed to try harder if she ever saw Sabrina.

"The lower order demons, as I understand it, are fairly dominated by their nature. Each demon is bound to one of the seven sins. Their nature relies on that sin to feed. They specialize in drawing out and feeding on a particular emotion. Angels are actually the same way, but they feed off different emotions. Each basically has a huge drive to draw out and feed, a hunger that makes them more animalistic than human," I rambled on.

The Associate Director's brows slowly crept upwards. "Like Helena?"

"No. She's— actually, I don't know where on the order of angels she is. But she's also an angel bound to earth, a nephilim. Not really a half angel, technically. There aren't half-breeds in the paranormal world." I glanced at Nyske. "Not naturally occurring ones anyway."

I was drowning the AD in new information.

"But she's not a lower order?" she surmised.

"Nope. The higher order you go, the more they act with a will like humans. Their nature still drives them a little, though. Beelzebub was the one working with the vampires that killed the DC Representative. I'm going to go kill him and feed his essence to my wife to make sure she retains herself now that the suppression on her nature is broken."

A dark smile grew on the AD's face. "I wish you could bring him to our justice, yet I understand this is the paranormal world's sense of justice."

"A dragon's justice if you would." I tried not to smile too wide. "It might seem barbaric to you, but these are our rules. I don't really think putting people in prison for life is any better, especially now that it's basically become a form of slavery."

Her glower told me to move on from that particular topic.

"But that's all more information than you need. I bring up angels and demons because this case might very well be an angel based on the situation. If I had to guess, that's why Helena wants to bring me in. Morgana sealed the celestial plane, so to see an angel running around raises questions." I frowned.

We always knew they'd find a way back, but I wasn't happy to see it actually happen.

The Associate Director slapped down five more folders in front of me. "The overarching case was to explore a number of these cults popping up at the same time. Not just here. We've found several large cults operating across South America for a while. There were some blips from our friends at the DEA, and they pulled us in to help. Then I lost two agents. I've come to learn that the DEA has lost four."

I let out a soft whistle. "That's a problem."

"Hence me asking Agent Tills to explore the case. And then her recommendation was to involve you. You said you had a tight timeline. I'd like you to explore the cult that absorbed our agents and help them. Maybe when you are back, we can work on the larger problem." She pursed her lips.

I snagged up one of the new folders and started flipping through, moving on to the next. "This is a huge operation. Now I'm wondering why I haven't heard about this deal in South America. The Brazil cult has tens of thousands."

"It's been growing rapidly. Do you have global authority over the paranormal?" the AD asked, curiosity sparking in her eyes.

"Over dragons," I replied quickly. "Not all paranormal. I have some authority over all paranormal here in Philly, and it reaches out over the eastern half of the US since we are the largest collection on the east coast." Turning to Larisa, I asked with a glance about South America.

"El Dorado," she said quickly. "Well, it's seven cities actually. El Dorado is just the famous one that the Spanish named and were searching for."

"Seven cities of gold?" I perked in my seat.

"We are... not welcome guests," Larisa chuckled.

The Associate Director frowned. "I'm missing something."

I turned back to her. "Dragons love gold. I can only assume we've gotten in trouble for being in one of the gold cities. Who runs them?"

"A paranormal similar to the medusas. They called themselves basilisks. That part of human myth vs paranormal reality is very murky, especially when you realize that basilisks and cockatrices are the same myth." Nyske sighed. "Their imagination really got away from them on that one. It's related to the Quetzalcoatl in reality."

I blinked as my mind tried to stuff all three myths into one. "Wait, but the Quetzalcoatl is real. I watched my mother fight it in Faerie."

"Yes, it is—it was their god. But the basilisk/cockatrice myth is a cobra born from a rooster egg because it was incubated by a toad. Even if modern TV likes to make one a big serpent and the other a chicken with snake tails." Nyske let out a sigh of pure exasperation. "Really, it's a paranormal that has feathered wings and a serpent's tail. And they can turn stones into gold. They built really secluded cities because they can't fake being human at all."

I licked my lips. "Oh really? Human torso?"

Pixie chuckled. "I thought your harem was filled up? Apparently, you'll make room for a woman that turns things to gold?"

Even Regina was chuckling now as she tried to maintain her professional bodyguard glare.

"You know, if I need to help the FBI go down to South America for this cult business, maybe I should visit one of the cities and try to repair dragon/basilisk relations. You know, for the good of paranormal kind." The dragon part of my mind was fairly fixated on this idea of basilisks.

"Unfortunately, it's their blood that turns stone to gold," Nyske informed me. "But they can turn objects to stone with their eyes like a medusa. So, I'd be willing to bet that any basilisk is very wary of becoming a dragon's mate, for fear that said dragon would bleed them dry. And they have some reason to believe it. Dragons have attacked their cities many many times before things got civilized. The grudge runs deep."

The Associate Director took the folders away from me. "The last thing I need is for you to kick a hornet's nest. Just focus on the cult in North Carolina. If you can get the agents out of the situation, that would be wonderful."

"If it is an angel, it would be great practice for you too," Pixie pointed out.

Larisa shook her head. "Careful. We need to be sure of who we send down there. Also, success will depend on what kind of angel it is."

"Alright, Silverwing Mercenaries will take the case. I'll have to fly down tomorrow and get a visual on the area so that I can portal back and forth for it. But it shouldn't be too big of an issue to pull your people out and magically undo whatever whammy was done to them. Do you want me to do anything with the cult itself?" I asked.

"Helena and Tills will probably step in to deal with it. Your support there would be all we need." The Associate Director gave me a polite smile that felt like a dismissal.

"Wonderful. It'll be the normal price. Let's go, ladies." I stood up and snapped my fingers, opening a portal back into the limo, which was parked near the Council Chambers. Pixie had me busy with meetings.

My honor guard performed their duties, exiting the limo first and checking before waving me forward to the nondescript building that was the Philly Paranormal Council.

"Clear," Larisa called back, making room for the rest of us.

"What's on the council docket today?" I asked Pixie as we kept moving. It was already close to noon, and my stomach was rumbling. "Actually, do you think I could eat during the council meeting?"

Pixie gave me a flat stare.

"That's a no," Nyske translated for me.

"Fine. But make it good. Could you get tacos?" I asked, suddenly having a craving. "I've been giving Morgana a lot of blood lately, and I'm just wanting something to refill the tank, you know?"

Nyske rolled her eyes. "Sure. How many?"

I hesitated. "Four."

"Four dozen it is." Nyske scribbled down. "I'll just get a good variety and order plenty more for Regina and Larisa."

"Plenty of fish tacos, please!" Regina smiled politely at my nymphs. "We need to find a place with magical food here."

She wasn't wrong, but the only steady source of meat with mana would be in Faerie.

"Well, I don't know if we really need to get any bigger. For me, I'm focusing on my magic for now. Besides, the biggest problem I'm going to have in Hell is going to be stopping the intrusions on my emotions."

Sabrina had been working with me on enchantments, while Ikta and Summer worked with me on my magic. Unfortunately, the recurring theme was that I needed focus and control, both of which weren't my strongest characteristics.

"That's why you'll have two fae queens." Larisa gave me a smile as she held the door and we walked into the council proper. The place was filled with big, ornate stone decorations and a giant pit surrounded by stone chairs.

They liked to put on a show.

"Son-in-law!" Rupert Scalewright greeted me with a giant grin as he stepped out of his chair to wrap me in a hug. "Every day, I'm so happy that my daughter found you."

"Dad." Jadelyn sighed his name. "You don't have to do this every time you see him."

"I love my son-in-law," he shot back.

"Husband, come sit." Jadelyn patted the stone throne next to her. She used to sit next to her father, who ran the council, but now she sat with me.

"Sorry, Rupert, but I do have a slight preference for your daughter. I married her after all." I patted him on the shoulder and made my way over to Jadelyn, who promptly looped her arm in mine.

Rupert made a playful expression of hurt before snapping right back into business mode and talking with Detective Fox.

Jadelyn leaned in for a peck on the lips. "Glad you still prefer me."

"It isn't even a contest, but don't tell your father," I whispered conspiratorially.

The smile that blossomed on her face made my heart swell. Damn, I was one lucky dragon.

CHAPTER 4

I ran the brush along one of Scarlett's tails. There was a small arsenal of oils and lotions near me on the counter.

My first mate leaned against me, still wrapped in her towel from the shower. Soft sighs of pleasure escaped her mouth every time I ran the brush along her tail, and the white tips on her tails wiggled happily. She seemed to be trying to keep them still for the brushing, but she couldn't help the little wiggle at the end.

"Okay, I think this one is done." I moved her tail gently to the side and reached for the oils, hesitating on the right one.

"Blue bottle," she helped me. "It's chamomile oil. Then we'll rotate through for it to soak in, brush it out. Then almond oil, then the scented oils."

I quickly rotated the bottles so that they were in order. "Good thing I like your tails." I put a little oil on my hand and started running my fingers through the tail.

Scarlett's tails were extraordinarily soft, and I knew that it made her feel loved. My first mate blushed heavily and bit her lip to keep herself from moaning as I ran my hands along her tail. Finally, she broke and let out a mewl of pleasure before grabbing my head and kissing me.

"I like tail brushing." I gave her a smile.

"Of course you do. It always ends quite nicely for you, my husband." Scarlett gasped as I went back to brushing, picking up the second tail.

"But we can't stop there, can we? We aren't even finished with the first tail." I ran the brush through with an impish grin.

"No." Scarlett shuddered and clung to me. "But you should hurry."

***

Summer lounged across my lap as summer fae filed out the door.

"So, you are running off today?" She had a playful pout on her face as she teased my chest.

Ever since Summer's daughter had died, I had been regularly attending her court sessions. It was her one request, and it did help me get a better idea for fae politics. She was insistent that I learn about how to handle a court.

Each time we were in her court, Summer would sit me down on her throne and then drape herself over my lap. The fae woman enjoyed teasing me, yet I suspected it was a facade to hide some of her inner turmoil. Even if she was an ancient fae queen, losing a daughter wasn't easy. She was dealing with the loss in her own way.

"Hopefully not for long, because you are coming with me to Hell it seems. I would have thrown in for a place with a beach, but I guess you wanted somewhere warmer?" I teased her right back.

Summer pursed her lips. "Yes, the Golden Plushie Society has agreed that we need to speed up our timeline. As soon as you are back from your case, we are preparing to head out."

"That bad?" I asked.

Summer's playful smile dimmed. "Sabrina is getting increasingly frustrated at her inability to focus. We should have left yesterday, but you've promised the FBI."

"Fuck the FBI. Sabrina is more important than that," I growled, feeling protective of my mate.

"It'll be fine. Just don't dally." Summer lifted my hand and kissed the back of it, leaving a warmth like the kiss of sun through shady leaves. "Or maybe you can dally a little?" She looked up at me with half-lidded eyes.

I knew she was just teasing, so I served it right back.

"Oh, maybe I should dally here a little more? Maybe you'll tell me more about what's going on with my fae magic?" My hands roamed her body. She was wearing a soft, white and gold dress that sheathed her like a second skin.

Summer might be an ancient fae queen, but she was still in the prime of her beauty. Her eyes were the only part of her that showed her true maturity.

"Careful, I'm pretty sure that with The Dreamer's blessings, you are quite potent." She dared me with her eyes. "How many nymphs are pregnant?"

"Too early," I growled as I planted her in my lap. She ran soft hands over my shoulders and dragged her nails along my scalp. "Careful."

"Oh. Don't you remember what I offered the first time we were here?" She laid the softest of kisses on my neck making me shiver with delight. "Too bad you didn't take me up on that." Summer slid off my lap with the grace that defied gravity.

"Tease." I smiled.

"Shoo. Go have your trip and deal with whatever you need to. Then we'll go off on our own," she replied.

"That one will have Ikta, though." I still wasn't entirely sure how well that fact was going to go over.

"So it will." Summer tapped her lips thoughtfully. "We'll have to figure it out, I suppose." She glided out of the room. With her legs hidden below the dress, it seemed like she was floating away.

I let out a sigh. "Really worked me up. Tease."

Focusing was harder than I wanted to admit as I drew several breaths. I tried to draw the image of the manor back into my mind and solidify it along with the portal that I wanted to create. Reality crackled and a portal with a faint magical glow around the edges popped into place.

I stepped through into my office.

"How'd the court session go?" Pixie asked.

I entered to find her bent over my desk, arranging the objects on top of it and not turning around at my entrance. I let out a growl of sexual frustration and put a hand on her hip.

She glanced over her shoulder, raising an eyebrow. "Oh, she really worked you up this time. You need a release before you fly." She pushed herself back into me. "I should really thank Summer for all of the teasing she does."

"Less talking," I growled, working her tight skirt up over her butt.

***

My powerful wings beat as I flew above the clouds. My dragon form was a swirl of red and gold.

"You know, I could get used to having my own private jet," Morgana teased.

"Not a jet. Besides, once we are there, I can use portals in the future." I glanced down at the clouds, and the breaks in them revealed the green countryside. The landscape was a hell of a lot greener than Philly.

With my renewed focus on magic, the invisibility spell had been at the top of my list. Staying out of eyesight meant more freedom to use my dragon abilities. I'd cloaked myself before taking off, flying faster than a plane towards the location of the cult's compound.

"Portals have been making me a little ill lately." Morgana rubbed her belly.

"No portals for you then," I replied hastily. "We'll have you walk back."

"Hey." She smacked my scales. "I'd be without your blood for too long."

"That's the part you are worried about?" I sighed. "Besides, how much of my blood do you have stashed on your person right now?"

"Eighteen barrels," Morgana admitted.

I let out a whistle. But in my dragon form, the noise sounded more like a high-pitched hiss.

Morgana chuckled. "It's not that much."

"Eighteen barrels is a lot of blood for a single being, and that's just what you saved. You've been bleeding me dry," I grumbled.

"Don't pretend you don't like it." Morgana patted my head. "Besides, you put this baby in me. Take some responsibility."

"Can you take out your phone? How are we looking?" I asked, feeling like we should be getting close.

Morgana was busy for a moment on my back. "Still on target, but we should head down closer. You can land and I'll infiltrate. Your invisibility spell might work on normal people, but if there's something in there, it'll be blatantly obvious."

I grunted. "I'm plenty fine at stealth."

"No, you aren't. Last time you tried to be stealthy, you knocked a wall down. I'll go in, locate these agents, and we'll figure out how to get them out after." She crossed her arms defiantly.

Given her reaction the previous time I'd tried to shield her from the dangers of the world, I knew that it was best if I just let her do her thing. She wasn't exactly wrong about the difference in our ability to be stealthy.

"There's the compound." I pointed off into the distance with my snout.

Down below, nestled within the green hills, was an almost entirely white village. What little wood existed was bleached white by the sun. Nearly every surface had white cloth draped over it and white banners hanging from flagpoles.

"They really like white," I commented. "It's going to be hard for you to blend in."

"At least I won't break everything. Land over that hill. It should be far enough away that no one will feel your magic." Morgana was already scanning the surroundings.

"Not much in the way of places to hide." Between the hill and the compound, there were some sparse trees and bushes, but not nearly enough to hide Morgana creeping up.

"I'll manage. The place does seem nice." Morgana jumped off my back as I landed on the ground and shifted back.

"It does have a nice tranquil vibe to it." I pulled out clothes from the bracer on my arm. The bracer had been enchanted by Morgana to have a magical storage space and resize with my shifting. And the titan Typhon had added his own blessing to it as well, allowing me to devour the energy from other titans.

On my other arm, Goldie mimicked the bracer, only in gold. Goldie was an elemental that had formed from hunks of gold I had dug up as a child. Apparently as a dragon, I'd been feeding it mana until it took on an elemental form.

"Yeah, tranquil. I don't see it, especially if there's a celestial in there." She narrowed her red eyes. Morgana did not have a good history with the celestials; part of me worried that she'd find one inside and try to take it on.

I'd bubble wrap her if I could, but Morgana would never stand for that, pregnant or not.

"If there is, just shoot a flare up. I'll be there in a second," I promised, pinching my eyes as I narrowed them on my dark-elf-turned-vampire wife. She had a soft blue skin tone, silver hair, and red eyes. The latter, along with the fangs, marked her vampiric nature.

Morgana shot me a smile and slapped her leather clad thighs before zipping off with vampiric speed, weaving between what little cover existed. It wasn't long before she was slipping over the fence that marked the edge of the compound.

I laid down on the hill and pulled out an enchanted set of binoculars, courtesy of Sabrina. Morgana was hard to track, but against the light wood and cloth draped everywhere, her blurring form stuck out like a sore thumb to someone who knew what to look for.

While she was hunting through the compound, I shifted my focus, trying to get an idea of who was in charge.

People came and went from the area with stupidly large smiles on their faces, like they were high as they milled about with simple tasks. All of them were working. Some were tending to a garden, others were making pews out of rough wood with simple tools.

In all honesty, it painted a very pretty picture. But I refused to believe that it was all sunshine, smiles, and white cloth.

"We always have some curious folks," a voice snuck up on me.

"Huh?" I turned to see a guy in white linens holding out a flower with the same big stupid smile on his face. "If you are so curious, you can just join us for the afternoon."

"Is that so?" Wanting to test a theory, I shifted my eye in front of him.

He didn't even react. With my vision, I confirmed there was barely a trickle of mana within him. He wasn't a paranormal.

"Come on. Even if your eyes are a little funny. We have a few people who don't quite fit in normally either. All are welcome in Charity, though." The man pushed the flower he was holding further towards me.

I took it sensing no mana from the flower or him. And he didn't seem deceptive. "You came out here to pick flowers?"

"Of course. I've given up all my material possessions and found that God really does provide. I live a simple life. If I want to pick flowers, I pick flowers." The man pulled a flower wreath from behind his back and reached up to put it on my head.

I felt so incredibly stupid, but I couldn't bring myself to say anything. The man was too cheery. Somehow, it felt like punching an innocent baby as he stared at me with big brown eyes.

"Come, our place is a delight. Share in the glory." He held an arm out for me to hook my own into.

But that was where I drew the line. I crossed my arms. "Sure, lead on."

If the man wanted to walk me directly into their compound, who was I to say no? And then I could be a better backup for Morgana. I'd be right there if something went wrong.

I walked with the man as he strolled forward in a pleasant silence. My eyes were still shifted as I scanned for paranormals. There were multiple spots of mana in the compound, and the entrance had a few simple enchantments carved into it. It seemed that most of the enchantments were to drive people subconsciously away, likely intended for cops.

"This is Susan. She's the best gardener that we could ever hope for," the man introduced the first person we came upon.

"Tom here just picks flowers and women." She batted her lashes at Tom. "Are you going to introduce me to this man though?"

"Where are my manners?" Tom chuckled. "This is my new friend. He was watching from the hill. I've invited him in to see just how wonderful Charity is."

They were all so smiley that it was making my skin crawl.

"So, Tom has a way with the ladies?" I tried to make conversation.

"Oh, we all share our bodies. Everything we have has been given over to Charity. In return, Charity provides. If I'm feeling a little... excited, then Tom can provide in the same way he's free to pick my tomatoes if the urge strikes him. It goes for all of us. We all give what we have." Susan was fairly focused on Tom.

I had a feeling she was feeling a little excited at that exact moment.

The idea of sharing rankled my dragon instincts.

"It was lovely seeing you, Susan. I should bring him around to Cari." Tom handed Susan some of the flowers before shifting his focus back to me. "We are open, but Cari would want to know if we have an outsider walking around."

"Oh yes. Please bring me to him." I smiled, letting my eyes flit over the crowd near some garden patches.

There were two paranormals that I could see. I was pretty sure one was a werewolf of some sort. The other felt like some species of troll. The troll might be a pain in the ass, but both should be easy enough.

"This way." Tom led me down a path to the largest building present.

I did my best to not roll my eyes and failed. Of course the guy who runs a cult called 'Charity' is going to put himself in the biggest house. Tom came up to the front door and knocked before opening the door.

I already knew there was a paranormal on the other side.

CHAPTER 5

I studied the paranormal in the room on the other side of the door. A man with a pair of giant angel wings had his head back in pleasure as a woman knelt before him.

Thankfully, his pants were still on.

"Cari, we have a new friend," Tom introduced me.

The woman didn't stop kissing his exposed pelvis as she tried to tug his pants lower, but the man focused on me.

"Well, hello. Charity is welcome to all. Here we give up our mortal possessions and let God provide."

"Yeah. Like her?" I raised a brow at the woman who looked like she was about to start gnawing through Cari's pants.

"Sex is freely given and taken." Tom smiled. "It's an act of charity to help others when they desire it."

"Uh huh. Sure it is." I focused back on Cari's wings. "So, you are an angel?"

"I prefer Messenger of God. Come here and join us. Revel in the sensations of joyous Charity." The angel stared into my eyes, and I felt a familiar sensation run through me.

Having a succubus wife and an angel of love as an angry sex partner had made me familiar with what it was like to have someone magically tug on my emotions.

Cari's power drilled into me, and was the opposite of greed. His power tried to overcome any possessiveness, greed, or any hunger for more. I was sure it was very effective on humans, but he was messing with a dragon.

The wave of emotional magic tried to make me want to give up my harem, share them with him. It wanted me to dig deep into my hoard and hand over all my gold for him. To him.

He really picked the wrong emotions to push on me. My dragon instincts roared in response. It felt like a giant mental claw slammed down on Cari's power as anger and primal rage flooded me as he tried to push me to something anathema to everything a dragon stood for.

Cari attempted to push me harder, so I met his eyes and stepped forward. I was officially pissed off. I threw a bolt of lightning from my hand.

The bolt hit Cari in the chest and threw him across the room.

The woman screamed and Tom ran.

I took a deep breath, trying to get my mind back into a state where I could think more clearly, but my entire body was seething. He dared to try to manipulate me and make me something I wasn't.

It was one of the most violating experiences of my life.

Cari shot back to his feet. His feathers were now blackened at the tips, but it would take far more than a lightning bolt to take the angel down. Space warped around him and his wounds healed up.

Morgana appeared behind him a moment later, her sword swinging clean through his neck like it was butter. Morgana had become fairly skilled in killing angels.

I didn't miss the tell-tale blur of spatial magic on the edge of her weapon. She shared the same type of magic with celestials because her family's tree was currently supporting a portal to the celestial plane.

Cari collapsed to the floor before her like a marionette with its strings cut.

"I thought you were going to stay back." Morgana put her hands on her hips. "I had this under control. You didn't need to come barging in."

"The guy picking flowers spotted me and invited me in. I figured I'd just investigate with that opportunity." I gestured at the dead angel. "I wasn't expecting this guy to try to get me to give him my hoard and harem. Maybe I got a little worked up."

"Mhmm." Morgana rolled her eyes. "You're so good at subtlety, my love."

I went to defend myself, but stopped as screaming picked up outside the door. I had a feeling Tom and the woman were working everybody up into a panic.

"Look what you did." Morgana pursed her lips. "I could have done this very simply."

"Well, I can't fix it now. Guess we need to get out there and pick our agents up before they get hurt in that mess." I shrugged and stepped up to the angel's corpse, stuffing it into the spatial pocket in my bracer.

"Make sure no one goes running off, and if you can, portal the paranormals to the bar. I can get some specialists to work on them." Morgana frowned over my shoulder.

I turned around as the troll I'd seen earlier came barreling through the door, his body expanding. Rather than the swampy green I had seen far too much of, he had a craggy brown and gray of a mountain troll.

"Night night." A right hook took the mountain troll in the jaw, and his neck bent at an angle that was certainly not healthy. Thankfully, it would take a lot more to do any permanent harm to a troll.

Despite the hit, he lay on the floor peacefully. His healing started to kick in and he shrank back to his human form.

"Great. I'm going to make a call." Morgana disappeared in a blur.

I looked down at the spot the angel had been. "You got me in trouble."

Stepping over the troll, I opened a portal back to Bumps in the Night and threw him inside.

Maddie was on the other side sipping from Frank. "Oh. Look, you got us a present." She stared down at the troll with a frown. "Ugly one."

"Morgana says she has some people to help. He's been whammied by an angel." I shrugged and closed the portal before heading out of Cari's place.

The people of Charity were gathering in a main building with the big cross on top. I figured it was a church. Several stood with crosses held out against me.

"Begone demon!" one shouted.

I sighed. I wasn't demonic, and even if Sabrina was here, I'm pretty sure crosses, churches, and holy water did nothing to her unless the person using them actually had mana and access to magic.

"Not a demon. I need..." I paused and pulled out a notebook before rattling off the six names. "...out here."

There was a shuffling inside the church as an argument broke out.

"You've already given yourselves over wholly for Charity. What is your body but a mortal vessel?" someone argued.

"Yes, give everything and Charity will provide a way," another agreed.

Personally, I smelled too much smoke that had already been blown up their asses. But the group apparently came together to agree to turn over the names I'd spoken. The crowd pushed out the six agents, who looked shellshocked.

"Come here. Please step into the portal." I waved my hand and a portal appeared to the manor.

They balked at the giant swirling vortex and tried to retreat, but the rest of their cult pushed them back.

"Okay. The local police are going to come crashing down on this place soon. I told the Associate Director that we had her people. What are you waiting for?" Morgana frowned at the six when she reappeared. "Chop chop! Go through the portal or I start killing."

I wasn't sure which was stranger to them, Morgana's appearance or the casual threat of violence. But they were spurred into action as the six walked warily towards the portal.

I shook my head at Morgana who simply waved away my unspoken comment. After we stepped through, the portal closed behind us. Morgana moved to stand in front of the door with her arms crossed while Helena and Tills greeted the agents. They were all shaking like leaves in a storm.

The rest of the people in the compound the local authorities could handle. I'd considered if we needed to involve any more of the paranormals given the exposure, but that entire group seemed off their rockers. It was unlikely anybody gave credibility to their stories; they would probably assume drugs were involved.

"Are they going to be okay?" I asked, watching the federal agents cowering.

"No." Helena frowned at them. "They've been repeatedly subjected to emotional tampering."

"It never seems to bother me…" I trailed off at the glare she gave me.

"Is this where you finally admit the two of you have been bumping uglies?" Agent Tills asked. "There's a bet going around."

"There's nothing ugly about Helena," I chuckled and earned an even angrier glare from the angel.

"Morgana, Rebecca, take them upstairs. Sabrina was preparing something." Helena jerked her head, and her sharp bob of white hair swished like a knife through the air.

Morgana snorted. She rarely took commands. She and Helena seemed to tolerate each other, but that was about it.

For an angel, Helena had a lot of sharp edges. Helena rejected her angelic powers most of the time, but after I'd seen inside her soul and what her mother, the Archangel of Love had done to her with the power of love, it made sense.

Helena was still rebuilding trust with the world around her, especially those who claimed to love her.

I looked over, letting my eyes linger on the navy suit and a pencil skirt that attempted and failed to hide Helena's lovely curves.

"Stop staring. You're the reason everyone knows." Her eyes flicked back to me as Tills led the six agents out.

"Sorry?" I shrugged. To me, she already carried my mark. She was my mate, even if she rejected the idea wholesale because she didn't believe in love. "Not sure what you want me to do, unless you need another go to scratch an itch." I wiggled my eyebrows, smiling bigger as she frowned.

The way she glared at me told me that she did, but she would wait until she was absolutely exploding to come and get the relief now. And I was okay with that. I had grown somewhat to enjoy our rough time together.

"Those agents are broken." Helena frowned at the now closed door.

"What do you mean? I'm about to go to Hell. Any more insight into this would be welcome." I took a seat, expecting a little longer of a conversation.

"You remember Beelzebub? How his hosts were dying?" Helena asked.

"The vampires he was taking." I remembered the unusually gaunt vampires that the prince of gluttony had inhabited. "He was feeding on the body's soul, even as he fed on everything else through it."

"The soul is tricky magic." Helena leaned against the wall. "Gets trickier if you don't have mana flowing through you naturally. Think of it as a bowl of water. Gluttony, or the angel that did this..."

"Cari? Seemed like he was pushing the idea of Charity on me." I filled in some details for her.

Helena wrinkled her nose at the name. "Asshole. All of the Charity angels are hypocrites. Giving to them is Charity because they'll put it to better use. They warp the idea of giving to paying and live it up high."

"Not ideal," I agreed. "Didn't realize you could twist them quite so much." As I spoke, I remembered just how badly her mother had twisted love. Angels and demons both used their emotional magic to feed and to sway.

"So. Back to the bowl of water and this angel?" I pushed to get back to the topic.

"So, normally this bowl is murky. There are lots of emotions, lots of conflicting emotions, in the natural human or paranormal mind. But Cari needs his subjects to feel and express charity, even twisted as it may be for him to feed off them." Helena frowned at the idea of feeding. She was lucky in that she was born on Earth and basked in its mana naturally.

"Okay, so the bowl becomes less complex, and he pushes the idea of charity forward." I knew how their magic worked.

"Yes. The murky bowl goes from a murky mix of emotions to just one. It's like putting a drop of strong dye in water." Her face scrunched ever so slightly as she tried to figure out the best way to describe the manipulation.

I tried not to smile at how cute her thinking face could be; she hated when I complimented her.

"You or anyone in your harem collects enough mana that you could dilute that dye when you are removed from the angel."

"Ah, but normal humans have a very limited amount of mana. It doesn't really come and go very steadily. So they are stuck with the strongly dyed water that Cari put on them. Can we just flush them out?" I understood enough about magic to know that there should be a way.

"Sure. But then what do we do about what they saw? Chalk it up to drugs? The damage to their minds is going to be far longer lasting than what happened to their souls. More of the paranormal reality is bleeding through to the normal people. I don't like it, and I don't like what the angels are doing. It smells like they are preparing for something to establish these cults openly. Or worse, they already have." She scowled, but I knew it wasn't directed at me.

Getting up, I grabbed her and pulled her to me. She gave a token resistance, but she let me pull her into an embrace. "It'll be fine. They'll get therapy from the FBI, I'm sure. Their ramblings won't go far with the help we now have in the bureau. As for your extended family, we'll deal with them when we have to."

"I dread what happens if my mother returns." Helena shuddered in my arms.

The only reason she had even switched sides in the conflict of Sentarshaden was that the portal to the celestial plane had been severed. She'd been a tool of the Church, and her mother remained in the celestial plane.

"It's okay. You are mine. I learned today that not even the manipulated emotional magic from the angels could make me consider letting go of my harem or gold." I smirked. "You should have seen what I did when he tried to push the idea of charity on my mind."

Helena snorted. "It's true. You are a greedy dragon."

"I am." Pressing her hips up against the wall, I prepared to show her just how greedy.

Pixie opened the door, ignoring the position we were in. "Ah. Figured you'd be back given that Morgana is leading around six shellshocked agents. The winter nymphs are waiting for you in your office, and you might need to help with the enchantment to help the agents."

"Sabrina busy?" I asked thinking she had it covered.

Pixie's perpetual smile became troubled.

"Right." I knew what that look meant. "I'm on it. Rain check, Helena. Pixie, if you could squeeze some time with Helena in before I go to Hell, it's probably best for everybody. Don't want her pent up the whole time I'm gone."

Helena snorted, but she didn't argue.

"Of course, my king." Pixie nodded. "If you'll follow me to your office. We'll deal with the nymphs and then we can shift our focus to Sabrina after. Have a wonderful day, Helena." Pixie turned and left.

Helena pushed me away. "Go. I'll find you later."

"Promises, promises," I teased and ducked out the door before something heavy thunked into the wood of the frame.

Pixie strode through the mansion that was far bigger on the inside than it had any right to be.

Other nymphs did tasks about the mansion. Each of my harem had a nymph attached to them. Even Agent Tills had one; she had managed to root out a summer nymph that was magic with coffee.

I went through the kitchen, waving at nymphs preparing food for themselves or for one of my harem members. They all waved salaciously at me, but I knew that that was just their general nature, and I seemed to be extra susceptible to that pull.

"Don't get distracted," Pixie admonished me as I slowed down a little as we walked through. I sped back up my steps, entering the library before heading up the stairs to my office.

I followed after Pixie, seeing three nymphs poking around my office as she threw open the door and marched in. All three of them jumped to stand in front of my desk. Although nymphs moved gracefully, their movement was more like gliding into place.

My eyes raked over all three.

They all had the classic blue skin that I associated with the winter fae, but each shade was slightly different. It was a sharp contrast to the tan of the summer fae like Pixie or Summer. The wild fae tended to be pale.

Another contrast among the fae was their hair color. While Pixie's bright pink was among the colorful hair of the summer fae, the winter fae tended to have more sub-dued colors yet still with a startling sheen. I often thought of Maeve and Evelyn's hair as silver.

Two of the nymphs here had soft golden hair, almost a platinum blonde. The last one had a washed-out bronze.

Immediately, my dragon latched onto the two with golden hair.

"Out." Pixie nodded to the third.

"What?" I jerked towards her.

"It's clear to all of us which you prefer. They are nymphs; that's part of the job." Pixie looked at me over the edge of her glasses. She only wore them to enhance the sexy secretary vibe she enjoyed. Her vision was perfect.

The third nymph bowed. "Thank you for the opportunity." She hurried out.

The other two nymphs were looking at Pixie, as if waiting for her head to roll.

"Don't look at her like that. She's my nymph and I place a lot of trust in her. If she says something, it should be followed as if I'd made the ask. I want someone I can trust to take care of things *for* me. Not someone to make things more complex," I told the two remaining nymphs.

Pixie had a smug smile across her face, one that she had earned through her hard work.

Nyske moved into the room, looking over her shoulder. "One down. Hello, you two." She waved. Nyske was a wild fae. They had pale skin and jet-black hair, but there was always something a little extra about their hair. Hers changed colors as it moved, like there was an opalescent light that shone from within each strand.

"Hello." One of the two remaining nymphs bowed to Nyske, quickly followed by the other.

"Okay, let's settle in and get some questions out of the way." I leaned against my desk as Pixie slid me a sheet of interview questions.

I glanced at the first few questions and pressed my eyes closed while I let out a heavy breath. I was fairly certain that, in a normal corporation, I was not allowed to ask the type of questions I was reading.

I gave Pixie a look, but she stood her ground, motioning for me to continue.

CHAPTER 6

F iona strode behind me with a purpose. Her pale blonde hair cascaded like a wave behind her, roiling with each step. Her heels managed to not make a sound as she walked.

Pixie and Nyske were chatting in hushed tones with my newest nymph assistant.

The interview had been interesting. After the first few questions about sex, and my confusion as to several of their own questions in that regard, they promptly offered a 'test drive'.

That had been about the point that I threw Pixie's well intended interview questions out and just talked to the two nymphs.

Both were remarkably capable, with literally hundreds of years of experience in administrative and service tasks. At one point in both of their careers, they had spent time serving prominent nobles in the Winter Court. They mentioned the names, and I knew I had likely interacted with them in court, but I'd tried to keep out of the politics.

They were just too much for me with everything else going on.

Either way, Fiona had cared little for the politics and left, having worked for a prominent martial trainer for the last fifty or so years. Her contract with that trainer was up, and she had put herself forward to become one of my personal nymphs.

I wasn't sure if it was the way she held herself or something else that drew me to her, but she pulled ahead of the other candidate. She had a fighter's grace. I was learning that I was a sucker for powerful women. Soon it was obvious to everyone in the room that Fiona was the right nymph for the job, and Nyske had promptly dismissed the other candidate.

Once we were done with the selection, we headed to one of the work rooms where Sabrina was supposed to be working on the magical flush enchantment so that we could get rid of the Federal Agents we'd rescued.

Before I reached the doors, I was able to make out a frustrated shout from inside, followed by the crack of wood.

I opened them to find Sabrina on the ground with several boards arranged in a three-by-three grid. She had most of them done. It looked like she was creating a complex magical enchantment.

"Everything okay?" I asked as Sabrina tossed the broken board onto a decent sized pile that had accumulated on the side.

Enchantments could be difficult in the best of times. I had broken my own share of materials when making a new enchantment, but I rarely saw Sabrina struggle so much.

"I'm fine. Don't distract me." Sabrina didn't even glance up. Her succubus nature was on full display. Soft pink skin poked through a lacy nightgown while a pair of dark horns curled over her head.

If she looked up, her eyes, once pink, would be full of grain-like specks of gold. The change was a result of her constant feeding on me. I didn't mind at all; I had plenty of mana to spare.

Unlike the agents, my mana would flush out any influence her succubus nature had on me naturally. I smiled as I took in the thin scar on her shoulder. She wore my mark on her skin as one of my mates and wives.

Given that she asked that I not distract her, I sat down, waiting in silence and watching her. My nymphs hung by the doorway chatting. But no sound was reaching me, so they had clearly used magic to prevent themselves from disturbing Sabrina.

I watched Sabrina as she waved a finger over the wood, burning more of the pattern into the plank.

She was incredible with enchantments. That path to magic that had been taught to her by one of the greatest magi of this generation. Sir Benifolt had taken her in, knowing her nature and helping her keep it sealed.

However, now that it was unsealed, I had been told that she'd grow far more like the stereotypical succubus rather than the nerdy girl I'd come to know for almost a year.

Sabrina had made enough enchantments in front of me that I was startled with her current one and the difficulty she was having. It was more complex of an enchantment for me, but for Sabrina, it shouldn't have been difficult.

Yet multiple times while she was creating an element of the design, she had to pause, hesitating and glancing at the surrounding planks of wood to recenter her design and continue again. The Sabrina of a few weeks ago would have worked through the process, laying out this enchantment in half an hour flat with barely a mistake.

I could see her concentration slip again, and she pulled back to look at the other planks. Frustration grew on her face. Her succubus nature was enough of a pull on her focus; it wouldn't be wrong to compare it to being drunk.

At that moment, her nature was the difference between doing a puzzle sober and buzzed. She was understandably frustrated at the haze that stopped her from concentrating and doing simple tasks she easily could have done before.

"Is there anything I can do to help?" I asked, seeing that she had paused again.

"No." There was a defiance in her voice. I knew Sabrina could be persistent. It wasn't possible to get so good with enchantments without being willing to practice and sometimes fail.

"Yes." Her voice came out weaker. "I don't know if I can do this."

"Explain it to me. I'll be your hands." Getting down on the floor with her, I gave her a gentle smile.

She let out a sigh and went into the explanation of the parts of the enchantment. She broke it down into simple enough elements that I could piece it together and complete it in a few passes.

Despite her struggle to focus, she still knew all the information. Unfortunately, she only seemed more frustrated when we finished.

"Thank you. Put the pieces together and then we can help these people." Sabrina had a frown on her face as I put the pieces of wood back in order.

I nodded to my nymphs and Fiona broke off to get the agents. Pixie and Nyske read the room and stepped out while I shifted my focus back to Sabrina.

"We are going to Hell, tomorrow at the latest," I updated her. There was no room for argument in my tone.

She paused before looking down at the floor. "I'm fine."

"No, you aren't, and it's okay not to be. Sabrina, something is happening to you, and I can fix it. So I damn well will go down to Hell with you and tear the place apart if that's what I have to do."

Sabrina went from looking at the floor to swaying into me. "Thank you."

"Of course. You're my mate."

Those words led to a lusty aura from her that had significant draw. I was already in love with my mate, and that included the physical intimacy we often shared.

Her nature was like a heady perfume, giving me ideas.

"I'm not sure that's such a great idea right now. Somehow, I don't think that'd help your situation; you are rather ravenous." I tousled her hair.

"But I want to." She looked up at me with her golden flecked eyes. "I love how you taste." She licked her lips.

It wasn't an 'I love you', and something about that rankled me. It was like someone had done something to my mate.

"Not now. We have these agents to fix up. Maybe later," I deflected.

Sabrina saw through me easily. "You don't like what I'm becoming?"

"I'll remind you that you don't like your succubus nature taking over," I pointed out. "So, yes, seeing it peek through is not ideal."

Sabrina hit her head against my chest, her horn brushing my shoulder. "Sorry. I'm not the woman you mated right now."

"She's there. Just something is covering up her normal cuteness," I teased.

There was a knock on the door.

"Come in," I called and pulled Sabrina to her feet. "You okay to activate this?"

She nodded and paused to scan the enchantment. "It looks good, even if it was made by two people."

Squeezing her hand, I gave her what reassurance I could in that moment. "Alright, who's first?"

The agents were confused and backed away from the enchanted boards in the middle of the room. But Morgana pushed them through and Helena came up behind her.

"Move," the angel scowled at the agents that were acting more like sheeple. "Just get them in there?" Helena asked.

"Pretty much," I told her.

Helena grabbed one of them and lifted them like they were a child. She carried the worried woman into the circle, planting her hand on the woman's shoulder to keep her from moving. "Do it."

Sabrina touched the edge of the enchantment. There was a faint pink magic suffusing the enchantment for a moment and a few motes of magic floated up.

"That's it?" Agent Till asked as she closed the door and leaned on it. "I kind of expected... I don't know... some big magic display." She splayed out her hands with a mock look of wonder.

"They have enough mana to maybe cast one or two spells in their bodies, having not trained at all," I explained. "That's about how much you have. Though, flushing them like this actually might improve their capacity a small amount."

"Magi use these for their children," Sabrina explained. "Helps a little at the early stages."

"So, it might help me?" Agent Tills asked, a sudden interest entering her eyes.

Morgana snorted. "Sucking Zach's dick will do way more. This is like a trickle; he's basically a mana geyser."

"Is this really an appropriate conversation..." My eyes raked over the agents who'd been part of the cult. "Given they are going back to working for the FBI?"

"The Associate Director didn't tell you?" Helena shifted her focus from holding the woman in the circle.

"No?"

Helena had a wry smile on her face. "They are going to be in a new division. Rebecca is leading them after this."

"Congratulations!" I whirled on Agent Tills, who stood a little taller. I could tell she was proud.

"About time. That and we can do some real good with some paranormal knowledge." Her eyes floated about the room where there was a drow vampire, an angel, a succubus, and then me. Finally, her eyes settled on the six agents. "But we need to get them fixed up. Then I probably need to find a few therapists for them. Either way, it's going to be a few weeks before anything is up and running. Getting a security clearance for my nymph is proving to be a pain in the ass."

"Why does your nymph need security clearance?" Sabrina frowned.

"Because she's amazing." Rebecca smiled.

Helena coughed. "Coffee."

"That makes more sense," I muttered.

"Hush you. You are trying to get your nymph clearance as well." Agent Tills rolled her eyes and pushed the next agent clear as Helena pulled the first out of the enchantment. There was a heavy daze in the agent's eyes, but she seemed to be in possession of her mind more and more with each blink.

"My nymph won't stop stalking me," Helena sighed. "If I don't get her clearance, she's going to cause a very real problem when she sneaks in."

"Don't think I missed you letting her organize your work calendar." Agent Till smirked. "Because nymphs talk. I know you did."

"Stop teasing her. She'll pretend to not like her nymph the same way she's totally not sleeping with Zach on the regular. As if we don't all know that his nymphs have to fix the furniture after every time the two of them are in a locked room together," Morgana joined in the teasing.

Helena crossed her arms, but I smiled. Her rough edges had been largely smoothed out—or maybe fucked out would be more correct. In the past, she would have drawn her spear and pointed it in someone's face half a dozen times by that point in the conversation.

"What are you looking at?" Helena turned to me.

"Just a beautiful angel." I grinned.

Her spear appeared, pointing at me. "Well stop it."

"Uh. What's happening?" The first agent to go through the magic was regaining some clarity. "Where did that come from?"

"Now look at what you did." I shifted my focus to the agent and pushed the spear away, not even concerned that she'd do something with it. "Magic is real. Monsters are real. You were magicked by a monster, and we fixed it. Now sit quietly while we fix the rest of the agents caught up in this, and then Helena and Rebecca are going to give you 'the talk'."

"You make it sound like we are going to explain the birds and bees." Rebecca rolled her eyes. "Zach here is a dragon. My partner is an angel. And I understand that may come with complex emotions for you because the monster that messed with your head was also an angel." She clasped her hands in front of her, bracing a little as she had to share the remaining news. "Unfortunately, you also gave that other angel everything you own."

"Everything?" The agent latched onto that part of the information.

"401k, retirement, savings. You even sold your house to one of those 'we'll buy anything' people and gave that up." Rebecca gave the agent a sad smile.

"I what?!" The agent jumped to her feet.

"Magic," Rebecca said. "Just—"

"Give me your phone," the woman demanded.

Agent Tills raised an eyebrow at me as if asking if this was my fault for opening the can of worms. "No. You need to—"

The agent began becoming frantic. She was like a cornered animal searching for an exit as she glanced around, clearly about to bolt.

"Hi there," Morgana broke the tension.

The agent turned, her focus shifting to the blue woman with fangs and red eyes staring at her. Her eyes seemed to cross then refocus as she tried to understand what she was seeing. A few indistinct babbles exited her mouth, but she stayed put.

"Works every time," Morgana chuckled. "Now, look at her." Morgana pointed to Sabrina who was still very much a succubus. "Now back at Helena."

Helena cooperated, knowing what Morgana needed. Helena's wings flared into existence. The agent's eyes rolled up into her head and she dropped like a sack of bricks.

"Maybe we should just use a stick to put them to sleep," Helena suggested.

"I don't have a stick enchanted to..." Sabrina trailed off. "Oh, you mean hit them." She sounded sorely disappointed in the angel.

"Not all of us are giant repositories of magical knowledge." Helena shrugged. "I have my own ways to achieve the same ends."

Sabrina rolled her eyes, but as she turned away, I saw her starting to smile. She was getting along with the angel in her own way. They were more alike than either of them were willing to admit.

"Okay. So, let's get something to put them to sleep. Sabrina, can you lead the charge on that? I'd like to get the Associate Director in here for the real conversation. I want to wrap this up and go storm Hell." A growl entered my voice at the end. After watching Sabrina, I was more committed than ever to going down and killing whoever I needed to for her to stay my Sabrina.

CHAPTER 7

I portaled in the Associate Director and several staff. The staff immediately moved quickly to the six agents, beginning their examinations.

"Thank you for returning them so quickly." The Associate Director looked over her shoulder at the staff. "I wasn't sure that you could do it so quickly. I've heard authorities down there are struggling with the cult. Is there anything you can do?"

"Without overtly showing off magic?" I asked, frowning at the six who were being poked and prodded. "Not a ton. The people should return to their normal faculties over the course of a year or two without intervention. It's not the best thing for them, but to protect the secrecy of the paranormal, it is better than going in and starting to wave around magic."

"About that," she began.

"You have a new division," I jumped ahead. "Rebecca Tills told me."

"Right, she's part of the Plushies." The Associate Director raised an eyebrow, as if daring me to deny the group's existence. "The Bureau might not give out favors, but we prioritize protecting our own. Thank you for returning these six agents."

I gave her a smile and headed out. I was happy to bank the future favor, and I needed to keep on top of my next trip. Thinking about the Spider Queen, I wanted to find her and discuss the trip to Hell.

She was... difficult.

Jadelyn had finally forgiven Ikta for sending people to skin her alive, all a part of a crazy plan Ikta had to win me over by pretending to be Jadelyn. It had taken a lot of groveling and servitude before Ikta had been able to make amends, and I couldn't blame Jadelyn.

The entire concept had been twisted, but after getting to know Ikta, it also almost seemed reasonable in the context of the one forming the plan.

Ikta had been sealed in the void between my world and the existing planes for tens of thousands of years. She was beyond ancient, and at one point, she had been so powerful that both my parents and the fae queens of the time had to join forces to seal her away.

I hadn't seen anything even close to that sort of power, some of which I had inside of myself; I suspected that a large portion of her previous power had been forces that she commanded.

Still, her individual power was a little of a mystery besides her signature portal powers that I had taken to using. We had fought, but she hadn't been trying to do more than make me submit.

Her power thrummed inside of me, and with my manor now being a chunk of Faerie made by all three factions, it gave me power that I still didn't understand. Ikta, Summer, and Maeve had been quiet in explaining what exactly was happening.

But with Jadelyn having forgiven Ikta and the deal with The Dreamer looming in the future, I also had a bargain with Ikta about her and a hot spring full of her nymphs on the horizon. The Dreamer had wanted balance to save Winter. That meant adding Ikta and Summer to my harem.

I knew I needed to spend more time with Ikta. Or else I was going to run against the clock and wind up in a position I didn't want to be in.

Walking into my office, I waved at Nyske. "Any idea where Ikta is?"

She pointed at the corner of the office, and I stepped over, seeing the pinhole portal neatly placed next to the bookshelf. Getting close and peering through, I didn't see Ikta, but there was a drider watching.

"Forgive me, my king." The woman's voice shifted like she had ducked her head. "I am only a scout for my queen."

"Is she there?" I asked, having never really visited her realm before.

"I believe so, but she comes and goes often."

Focusing on the small portal, I pushed my wild fae magic into it and the portal swelled, growing in size until I could fit my hands in. I used them to pull and open it wider.

The drider moved back.

She was a pale fae woman from the waist up, and a dark spider from the waist down. A sheer cloth made of silk was draped around her chest before flowing over her hips. It covered all the most important bits.

She skittered back and bowed low, a cascade of dark hair pooling on the webbed floor. "My king." Even her spider half bowed until her head nearly touched the ground.

"Please. I don't really love the big bowing show." I motioned for her to rise. "Got a name?"

"Selidrax. I would be honored if you remembered it."

"Zach. Please don't make too much of a fuss. I'm just here to find Ikta and discuss something for tonight."

Nyske poked her head through. "Need me?"

"No. Send help if I'm not back in an hour, though." It started as a joke, but if I was honest with myself, it was also partially for backup.

The drider gave me a strange look before she led me down a passage. The spider woman deftly moved along the webbing that was so dense that it was like walking on carpet. "I will keep in mind your one-hour limit."

"It isn't sticky," I commented as we walked, studying the material with each step.

"Of course not. We have many kinds of silk, as do most spiders," the woman commented over her shoulder as she continued walking. "Only one kind is sticky."

"Huh." I walked behind her a few steps further before the tunnel began to open up. There was a giant central chamber with a large structural column in the middle, and branching pathways out in every direction with hallways similar to the one we had just exited.

"Are we in Faerie?" I asked as I looked around.

"Yes, most of the fortresses have been moved to Faerie. Our queen expended no small effort to keep us alive in the void," Selidrax explained.

"Right. She was sealed out there. You all survived in the void between planes?"

"It can be done. She built fortresses, and we were safe within them. However, our people and she were prevented from breaching any of the world's barriers. We could only stick to the side as she might describe."

"Sounds like a lot of magic that might be out of my current understanding. But I like that Ikta worked hard to save all of you." I thought about something that had been bothering me. "Is she the only one that has the spider limbs coming out of her back?" I asked.

Selidrax stopped and turned. "You know nothing of our people?"

"Afraid I've been running around and... uh... no?" I actually felt a little guilty. Here I had come to meet Ikta, and I was just starting to realize how little I knew about her culture. "Mind giving me a tour as we take the long way to Ikta?"

Selidrax frowned. "You are my queen's chosen consort and you are the Dragon King, son of two dragon deities. I can sense the growing fae powers that place you as some sort of... fae king?" She said the last with a sort of confusion as if the concept was so foreign that she struggled with it. "But you should understand my queen's people."

"You're right. I should. So, tour?" I stared at the giant central chamber. "Not really sure how to navigate this anyway."

Selidrax held out her hand, and I took it.

She pulled me close, and I felt the very human warmth from her upper half as her lower half crawled over the lip. We dangled upside down before going horizontal and moving straight down the wall. I tried not to react, coaching my body that I could fly if it became necessary.

"Our fortresses are divided into three layers. You have seen driders such as me. We are the warriors and labor castes. There are others among the fortresses that are elites;

they possess similarities to our queen's appearance and can pass for a normal fae if they so wish. Most of the nobles in her court have such an appearance. And then there are others, like the nymphs, but they serve and do not vie for power." Selidrax finished her explanation as she set me down in a new tunnel. "This way. We will wind ourselves through to Ikta's court where I believe she may currently be."

The tunnel we entered had the trickle of water within it. As we walked, the silk gave way to a rocky pool where nymphs scrubbed the back of a contingent of driders. The one up front had naturally sharp features. She looked like a beautiful bird of prey. There were also plenty of male driders in the group, which made me do a double take.

The closest drider rose from the pool naked as we passed, before bowing low.

"Do not deny her," Selidrax hissed in my ear. "Accept her bow and move on."

"Thank you." I nodded to the drider. "Please continue."

The nymphs in the pool all were beaming at me and posing, as if beckoning me to join them.

"It is my honor, my king," the drider intoned as she stepped back into the pool. Her fellow driders seemed to be congratulating her as we moved on.

I let us pass far enough away to turn back to Selidrax. "Did it upset you when I told you to stop bowing?"

"Somewhat, but I have been guarding the looking portals for some time. I understand your nature more than most of our people," she replied.

"Ah. So you weren't surprised, but it was still rude. Understood. You guys are even more formal than the other fae," I observed.

"We spent an eternity in the void. It is a harsh environment that allows for no questioning of a superior's orders," she reminded me.

"Fair enough. So, you have a lot of chambers like that in here?"

"Many. To relax in them is a privilege for those who have succeeded in their tasks. Come, the court is this way." She brought me down a steep tunnel to a pair of stone doors with two guards.

They glanced up.

"Halt. You must be announced, Dragon King." A male drider bowed his head, and I waited for him to move.

"Please, by all means." I turned to Selidrax. "If you'd do me a favor, I'd ask that you come get me if we get close to that hour."

"Of course." She bowed low in a sweeping gesture that ended with her hair touching the ground.

After our discussion, I was assuming that it was more for the guards than for me.

"Alright, let's go jump into Ikta's court." I grinned, and the other drider opened the doors. There was a discussion inside the doors that quickly shushed itself out.

"Announcing the Dragon King," the drider spoke softly, yet it carried through the chamber.

"We welcome him," Ikta gleefully called back. She stood from her throne as I walked in.

I looked around. The space wasn't that different from Summer's Court, but Summer's had far better lighting. Ikta's Court was a stone chamber with the seats heavily covered in silk to make them more comfortable. Twinkling purple light permeated the court from magic above. It was bright enough to see, but it made all the pale-skinned fae seem almost purple.

Most of them seemed like normal fae, but I knew that they likely could pop out a set of spider legs if they wanted. Of the fifty or so fae present, there were a handful that were driders and a few that were bizarre enough that I didn't have a name for what they were.

"Thank you for having me, Ikta," I replied formally, but a nearby fae hissed and moved away.

"Oh dear," Ikta giggled. "You can call me our love or Love here." She didn't move an inch, and I realized she enforced the 'my queen' quite heavily based on the closest noble's reaction.

I rolled my eyes, and she pouted in return.

Ikta's personality took up a lot of space in the room, making her seem large, but she was a petite woman. In many ways, she was more Summer's opposite than Winter. Where Summer was tan, Ikta was pale. All of the fae had sharp features, but while Summer's contained a nobility, Ikta's had a hint of sinister beauty.

"Come. Sit." She tapped on her throne. "I've heard of how you enjoy Summer's Court sessions."

Taking a seat on her throne, she draped herself over me.

Her starry purple silks covered my legs, and her leggings of loose spiderweb lace kicked off the side of her throne. In her court, she wore a crown, further cementing just how she liked to rule.

"I'm so very glad you came," she whispered. "Did you get lost on the way here? Fall into any pools of nymphs?"

"No, Selidrax led me. She was very helpful. Give her a reward."

"Already in the plan. Now she will get two." Ikta shifted her focus from me, and I could feel the change in her body language.

Ikta went from languid and teasing to a strange rigidity that somehow reminded me of broken glass. "Everyone. This is the Dragon King, but soon he'll be your king as well. Treat him with the utmost respect. Even more than you give me, for crossing him will be worse than crossing me," she threatened in a voice that sounded more like she was celebrating. "Now, let us return to the matter of the third fortress."

"Preparations are ongoing. The tree for the third fortress is complete, and we can begin to cocoon it and build out. The Raxlebir clan is awaiting your approval of the project. We will need considerable food allocated to a team of that magnitude." The noble bowed and resumed.

My interest was piqued. The fortresses started with a tree. That meant they made up the central part of the shaft that Selidrax had walked me through. When I had been traveling through Faerie, there were certainly trees large enough. Wrapping it in spider silk would probably kill the tree, but with enough of the silk, it would be reinforced and provide the structure that they needed to build the complex fortress.

"You'll have it. The Grasdril Clan will provide it." Ikta shifted her gaze to another noble who shrank in on themselves before managing to squeeze out a tiny squeak of an answer.

"Yes, we will."

"Good, then we'll move on with the plans for the next two weeks. With my soon-to-be husband joining us, that means he's going to take me away and do naughty things to me for a long while." Ikta smiled so wide it was a little creepy. "Thus we need to make plans for a period of my absence. Dramasa, how go the tunnels?"

Dramasa apparently was one of the driders present.

She rose slightly on her spider legs as she gave her report. "They are expanding within the root structure, but are still incomplete for the moss fields to begin. We encountered difficulties with a purple worm's hive."

I frowned. I'd never heard of a purple worm, but that didn't sound too dire. Actually, it sounded cute.

The rest of the court seemed to disagree. They all shifted around at the news, but they didn't blame her for the delay.

"Do you need aid?" Ikta asked.

"It has been dealt with. However, the delay was substantial, and much of our tunnels collapsed as part of the conflict. We do hope that when we finish digging them back out that the purple worm's nest could be used rather than the existing plans. With your permission, of course, to alter the plans." Dramasa bowed low to Ikta.

"What do you think?" Ikta put me on the spot.

I had no idea what a purple worm was or what their tunnels looked like. But I didn't have to. Leadership wasn't about knowing the details. "How expansive are these purple worm tunnels?"

"Very." Dramasa frowned at the question but didn't say more.

"Then as long as your builders can prevent them from collapsing on your people later, they are usable. If they are under the fortress, the worst thing that could occur is a potential collapse that could destabilize the fortress. If you are unable to ensure they won't collapse, seal them off and alter your plans. Have plans for both contingencies ready and move forward as I have suggested in your queen's absence." It wasn't my job to make the decisions, just to provide structure in which those who had the knowledge to make decisions.

"Understood." Dramasa bowed low and then raised herself.

Ikta patted my leg with a smile on her face. She was pleased with me giving orders in her court. "Next order of business."

CHAPTER 8

The nobles retired from Ikta's court, streaming out. Ikta waited for a good portion of them to leave before she stood, took my hand, and led me down a quiet passageway.

"What do you think?" Ikta turned to me, her eyes sparkling. Her hips sashayed down the hallway; she was in her element within her own domain.

"About?" I wanted her to drive the conversation.

"Well, do I have some big bad villain group that's aiming to take over the world?" She threw out her arms, doing a little twirl before stopping and batting her eyelashes.

"No, it seemed pretty normal. But there are plenty of webs to make it look sinister, or like it's some haunted house."

She laughed, stepping over and poking one of the webs. "Webs to us are normal, they've simply been portrayed as evil, just like spiders. Have a little venom and people get freaked out. Every paranormal has their own weapons. Spiders play an important role in the ecosystem, feeding on insects and helping prevent the spread of disease. And it's not like they're at the top of the food chain."

"So are you telling me that your people fill a role in the magical ecosystem?" I asked.

Ikta grinned. "Dragons used to eat a lot of my people. We in turn multiplied quickly and took territory from some of the unsavory paranormals like vampires."

"Wait, the wild fae were dragon food?" I asked, failing to keep the shock out of my tone.

"Yes." Ikta moved through the passage, and it opened up into what I expected were many bathing pools in her domain.

A bevy of nymphs played in the pool, each more beautiful than the last. They turned almost as one at Ikta's approach.

"Getting me in a pool of nymphs already?" I teased.

"You get to decide when to fulfill your promise. I'm just taking a bath." She tugged at her collar, and her silk wrap became loose before it fell to the floor.

"No glamors?" I asked.

"I wouldn't dare." Ikta didn't look at me as she sashayed over to the hot spring, slipping into the steamy water and letting out a soft moan.

She turned back to me, her hair slicked back from the water and the top of her breasts swelling just over the water line. The nymphs moved to her immediately, bringing soaps and cloths which they began to run over her body as she watched me, waiting to see my decision.

After a moment of pause, I shucked my clothes and tossed them into my bracer. Taking a few long strides forward, I waded into the pool of nymphs.

A cute nymph with dark blue hair came up to me. She pulled me to sit by Ikta before another nymph with purple hair handed her a basket and slipped up on my other side. The two of them giggled as they started to rub soap all over me, using any part of their body they wished to lather me.

I paid attention, making sure none of them used glamor as they worked. But they didn't; they treated me with the most respect that one could expect from a pair of nymphs in a hot spring.

"This is nice," I admitted.

"Then you'll have to come back and enjoy it often," Ikta replied, her eyes closed. "Or never. If you need my help, we can find a way around The Dreamer's bargain."

I sighed. "You aren't pushing me. Would you really help me out of the bargain? Doesn't it get you exactly what you wanted?"

Ikta opened her eyes lazily and stared at me through the steam. "You've made it clear that you won't let me force you into anything. Besides, I'm understanding my errors in my prior approach. But that can all be rectified." She let out a sigh as she waved away any concerns.

"Errors?" I asked.

She peeked an eye open again. "Like trying to become Jadelyn, or tricking you into devouring some of my power so that I could control you."

Something told me that Ikta still thought those were perfectly normal approaches, just not ones that worked on me. In a very real sense, she was the most alien of my ladies being thousands upon thousands of years old. It changed the way she thought.

"Why were those your first choices?" I was curious what she'd say in response.

"I've been alone for a very very long time, leading and trying to keep my people alive any way I could. I've made many choices I am not proud of, but they were the right decisions for my people. Making that many hard decisions, alone... it does things to the mind." She let the nymphs lift her arm and start working on her hands.

"You never developed a companion?" I frowned, her palace was expansive and she had an army at her back.

"Do you ever wonder why Summer and Winter are close?" Ikta asked. "There's a certain level of power and influence that becomes isolating. To be a being of power, having the power to change things makes you alone."

"A rival, even if you are against them, is at least an equal who understands the choices you make," I said, understanding Ikta a little more.

"Yes. An equal. I had nothing but subordinates for a very long time. Don't get me wrong, I love these nymphs, and I take great care of them. But they are not my equals." She shrugged.

The nymphs listened, but they showed no real reaction.

"My queen exaggerates. Her nymphs and direct workers are treated beyond excellently, to the point that there has been bloodshed as people try and get into these positions," the blue-haired nymph explained. "She's being modest."

"I treat them well, as anyone should those that work for them. But even if I treat them as a friend, they are still not my equal. They do not decide the fates of thousands every day." She leaned further into the water. "I moved quickly and harshly to try to gain your seed, because it felt like the right course of action for saving the fae."

"How'd that go?"

"I understand what it is like to stub a toe now." She smiled.

"Wait, you don't stub your toes?" I asked incredulously.

The nymphs laughed like a display of wind chimes. The purple-haired one was the first to recover. "No, we are too graceful for that. I certainly never stubbed my toe, and I doubt my queen has."

"That's just not fair," I chuckled. "Fae are incredibly graceful, though. I could see it."

As if to make the point, the two nymphs washing me flowed around me like a dance as they worked to scrub me clean.

"But you are surrounded by my equals," Ikta continued. "It has... helped. Rather than any trickery, I wish for you to accept me simply because your carnal nature can no longer resist my beauty."

Her eye cracked open as she watched me, interested in my reaction.

I laughed. It came out a little forced at first but more genuine after a moment. "Well, you are beautiful. But I'm surrounded by so many lovely ladies. Take these two nymphs for instance." I gestured to them, the nymphs instantly preening at the attention.

"Lorina," the purple-haired one said.

"Gresha," the blue-haired nymph's hand 'slipped' down my chest and brushed my cock. "Whoops," she giggled.

Ikta laughed. "Take them if you want. Henceforth, you two shall be my permanent attendants. Anytime your king is here, prioritize him over me."

"As you wish!" Gresha bowed over me toward Ikta.

"You really can do just about anything here, can't you?" I asked.

"So can Summer and Maeve to a slightly lesser extent. Summer just doesn't show it to you while you are with her. She plays the benevolent mother who cares for everyone in her domain. Do not let that fool you. She has led armies and will draw a sword to slay a thousand for a scrap of land." Her eyes were sharp. "We are as much queens as we are generals. In the void, there were times where one small act of rebellion would doom my entire court. I've had to bear that and ensure that decisions were followed."

I didn't think Summer was quite as ruthless as Ikta was describing. But she did always drive towards the greater good of her people. If saving a thousand meant killing one, I could see her taking care of it with a stony face, only to falter in private.

"You called me their king." I nodded at Lorina, who was still bowing.

Ikta smiled like she knew something that I didn't. "Maybe king is the wrong word. But you have your own little slice of Faerie that you rule."

"So did Nat'alet. He stole a piece from Winter," I pointed out. "Was he a king?"

"Stealing and accepting are very different when it comes to Faerie magic."

"Very different," Gresha echoed. "If this man stole a piece of Faerie, he had its magic but not its control. Only as good as a lump of iron compared to a forged sword." She suddenly ducked her head. "I'm sorry."

"Please correct my ignorance on these things as much as you want. What is different about this piece that I hold?" I asked Gresha rather than Ikta.

She glanced between us, unsure if she should speak.

"If you don't answer him, I look like an iron-handed queen. Zach, knowing is a power in and of itself. Truthfully, we don't know. This is a unique situation. But we can feel the flow of magic in our domains," Ikta half-warned me.

Gresha swallowed. "If you were given a piece of Faerie, then you are at least a queen. The fae queens hold the land and loan it and its power out to the nobles. So, what queen gave you a piece of Faerie?"

"All three of them. They made it together," I replied as Ikta floated in the water nearby, seeming to think nothing of it.

Gresha's face went pale and cast a glance between Ikta and me.

Clearly, I was missing something, and Ikta didn't seem to feel the need to say more. "So, that means what?" I asked Gresha.

"You are thrice king?" Gresha hazarded. "To have all three, it is a new domain. But one that contains everything. Have you given anyone a piece of it?"

I tapped my chin. "I gave everyone bedrooms."

"So, you gave the queens a piece too?" She glanced at Ikta who was still relaxing but obviously listening.

"Yes. That would make them nobles of my land?" I hazarded, starting to piece it together.

"They are already queens," Lorina blurted. "Only an emperor gives a queen her land." The nymph's eyes were growing wider by the minute.

"But we have our own domains still." Ikta seemed to wave away the concern. "So, we don't know what he is. But he can give us a piece of his land. We are happy to continue our relationships with him and let the result be what it may be. This, here now, is me courting the Dragon King. Calling him a king is already part of his title."

I thought back to my father saying that because of my birth I had the ability to change the patterns of fate. "So,

I'm going to change things and you all are buckled in for the ride?"

"Something like that." The water swished as Ikta moved over and climbed on top of me. "Kiss me."

I didn't hesitate, pulling her close and sharing a kiss, feeling a wave of mana pass between us as she tugged at my lips with hers.

"What was that?" It felt like she'd just hooked my fae magic to a car battery and let it rip as my magic swelled.

She pressed her forehead to me. "You have part of my magic. Why shouldn't I be able to exchange mana with you? Can you give it back?"

I kissed her again, sensing for the tingle. I found it and tried to flow back along the thread to her, but she didn't take it all.

It was more like she took the energy, but not the battery itself.

"You just gave me a piece of your Faerie, didn't you?" I asked incredulously.

"Maybe." Ikta batted her eyes. "I could give it all to you."

"Why?" I frowned, searching her eyes for answers.

"When I first approached you, it was through tricks and being superior to you. I know that is not the way now. So instead, I choose to lay myself bare for you and let you take what you wish. You are a dragon and a king. Either use me or don't, that is your choice. And I hope in the end that I will get what I wish for." She kissed me again and fed me more.

I had to put a hand on her chest and push her off. "Stop. That's... that's a lot. I feel like I'm going to explode if you keep it up."

"Then loan me some of the power." She came back and we traded tingling kisses as I worked to control the pieces of Faerie she had just given me. It was odd to try to retain control of them and give her the power within.

By the time I gave it all to her, I was left panting. And I felt a little strange, like I had a shit ton of potential, but it was empty.

"That feels strange," I said aloud.

"Yes, your dick is supposed to be inside of her," Gresha added helpfully.

Ikta laughed against me. "No. He's just becoming more aware of what magic lies within him. You took a good portion of my land and gave it all back to me. Summer is going to be jealous." That only made her smile wider.

"You gave me all of that." I was still a little dumbfounded at the level of trust that Ikta had shown. She had given me a huge chunk of her power, not anything that would fade either. The core and the source of much of her power was now mine.

"I said I'd open myself up and lay myself bare." Ikta bowed to me in the water. "My emperor. If you believe that someone else should be the Queen of the Wild Fae, it is now in your power to bestow it on someone else. When you are ready, I will give you the rest."

"What then?" I frowned.

"Then you may fuck me all you like." Ikta laughed and rolled off of me. "But I don't think we have time for how long I will occupy you once you start. I believe an entire week in a spring with me and the nymphs was promised. And I believe you came here to get me to head to Hell, which is rather time sensitive, did you not?"

I was surprised she knew. "Yes. Sabrina is getting worse. Pixie and Nyske brought it up during the Golden Plushie Society last night?"

"They did. But I would have known either way. Sorry for the delay, but selfishly, I wanted you to experience my court the same as you had Summer's." Ikta had a guilty smile on her face.

I wondered just how much of the time in the spring was planned by her, from me coming to look for her, to having a guide ready and for her to show me off to the court.

Ikta had experience on a scale I couldn't really even pretend to comprehend, and she had her little peep holes all over.

"No. It's fine. I was long overdue to visit you. Gresha, let's finish up. Ikta will come with me after this. That means you get to kick back and relax for a little." I smirked and felt the two nymphs redouble their efforts on giving me a soapy massage.

CHAPTER 9

By the time I dragged Ikta back to the manor, it was already time for dinner.

"I heard you had an exciting trip today. Apparently, you punched an angel. At least, that's the way Blueberry is telling the story." Kelly happily carried a tray of steaks to the table.

Her head bitch, Taylor, floated along behind her. Taylor was using the excuse of Kelly's pregnancy to follow her around and join in on family affairs.

Paranormal children were a coin toss as to which parent they would take after. There was no mixing except in extreme examples, and those tended to be later in life such as Morgana or Nyske where magic turned them into hybrids. Dragons were giant batteries of mana once they were born, but during the pregnancy, they consumed much of their mother's mana. Few paranormals could withstand the mana drain of a dragon in the womb easily.

Morgana was close to becoming a bloodlord, while Kelly was the first ever female alpha. Both of them were strong, but we weren't sure if their babies would sap their paranormal strength if either were dragons.

"I hit him with a bolt of lightning. Two actually," I told Kelly.

"One-two shocker!" Chloe overheard and giggled.

I smiled at the reference to the band. "Guess I better pick up the guitar."

"Nope. Work on your magic." Kelly put the tray of steaks down on the large table. Taylor came up behind her and put a second tray next to the first.

"Y'all eat more steak than a pack." Taylor shook her head, making her orange curls bounce around. She was taller than Kelly and generally dressed casually. She currently had on a plaid shirt tied over a t-shirt with torn jean shorts. And no outfit of Taylor's was complete without the cowboy boots. She had on a bright blue pair today. "Though you can take a bite out of me, Alpha-alpha."

Kelly rolled her eyes. "Down. You are here in case I'm suddenly struck with weakness from carrying this man's whelp." Despite her casual nature on the subject, I knew that the fact that Kelly was letting Taylor hover so much meant she was concerned as well.

"You could get a little weak in the knees if you like. I'd be happy to help you and Alpha-alpha work that out." Taylor shamelessly pushed.

Kelly flicked her nose. "Stop slobbering all over my man. You could have your pick of the pack."

Taylor escaped Kelly's flicks and grabbed my arm to hide behind me. "She's bullying me, Alpha-alpha. Maybe you could help a girl out?"

The helpless damsel act was comical because Taylor was a solid head and a half taller than Kelly and looked tough enough to beat Kelly to a pulp. But I also knew that wasn't the only dynamic at play. Kelly's shifted form was a giant alpha werewolf.

"Why don't you pick from the pack?" I asked.

"'Cause they are all wusses. I'm head bitch for a reason, and the betas just don't measure up." Taylor clung to my arm.

Kelly glared around me as Yev was walking past.

Yev picked Taylor up by the collar of her shirt, carrying her away like a naughty pup. "I don't know what's happening, but Kelly is pregnant. Stop teasing her so much."

In Yev's grip, Taylor played her part and gave me a pair of puppy dog eyes. Yev dropped off Taylor near the table and made her way over to her spot. She sat on her egg, which had been placed at the table like one of the chairs and heavily wrapped in furs.

"Damn. Why is everyone so strong here?" Taylor didn't have a hint of remorse in her voice.

"Because he is the Dragon King," Tyrande replied as she entered, taking the seat on the other side of Yev.

The two of them were sisters, both raised by the Highaen family, which was the ruling family of the elves in Sentarshaden. Both of them had blonde hair like spun gold with thin elven frames and sharp features. They shared bright purple eyes that swirled with blue magic of the Highaen family.

The biggest difference between the two was that Yev had a slightly larger frame and more curves. But they weren't biological sisters. The Highaen family had adopted Yev when her father had died, and her mother had died in childbirth; bearing a dragon child hadn't been easy for the elf.

"He's the Alpha-alpha. Nothing else really matters." Taylor shrugged.

Tyrande frowned and Kelly answered, "It's a werewolf thing. The hierarchy is absolute. And he's at the top. There are always some bitches like her that just want the big dog."

"I keep the others in line and push them to the betas so I can have a go at Alpha-alpha by myself," Taylor replied happily.

But her comment only made Kelly sigh deeply. "She's not wrong. Half the pack is smitten with the Alpha-alpha. Damnit, I'm saying it again."

I kissed Kelly's cheek. "It's okay. I kind of like it."

"Alpha-alpha says it's okay. So it's stuck. Besides, the pack loves chanting it when he's around." Taylor settled into the chair she had claimed as everyone found their seats.

I moved away from the group, taking my spot at the head of the table with Scarlett to my right and Nyske on my left.

"Evening, everyone." I smiled around the table, looking at all of my wives gathered and our added guest. There was a cheer of response with all the names they had for me.

Nymphs paraded around the table, filling our cups and refilling the steak platters as we quickly emptied them, passing the meat around. There were enough dragons present that we could put down a plate of meat in a blink of an eye.

"I'm going to miss you while you are on your trip." Scarlett carefully portioned her food, keeping an eye on what she ate.

"If only we could portal back and forth so easily," I replied, thinking about what they'd already explained to me about Hell.

Morgana had rolled her eyes more than once, asking me why I thought that I could portal back and forth. She had a fair point. If portals were easy to use to cross between Hell and Earth, wild fae would have released them all at some point. It turned out that both the Celestial plane and Hell were partially sealed. It took significant effort to pop between them.

Sabrina had been working on the trip to and from Hell. And Maeve was vetting the work. We'd be cut off and alone in the small group, which made the current dinner feel so much more meaningful. It was my last night with my mates who were staying behind.

"My father's been put on notice that he can't just summon you for golf games or whatever other nonsense he comes up with at the last minute." Jadelyn dabbed at her lips with a napkin. "Really, that old man of mine is taking up too much of your time."

"He has done me some solids, and he continues to help me in the council meetings. All I have to do is show up to a nice party he throws and let him introduce his son-in-law around." It really wasn't that big of a deal. That and all my mates came with me, dressed up and wearing some of my gold.

"You are, by nature of knowing you, a big bonus to his operations. Suddenly having the Dragon King as a son-in-law and letting him call you that publicly does wonders for his business," Jadelyn pointed out.

"Who's going to fuck with the Dragon King, and then who's going to fuck with his father-in-law's business? You add a lot of security. Threats against the Scalewrights are down like 75% since word of you marrying Jadelyn spread." Scarlett pointed at me with a carrot at the end of her fork before she flipped it back around and bit it.

"I didn't realize knowing me was that big of a deal."

Nyske sighed. "Your word carried heavy weight. This is why we work so hard to make sure you have everything laid out for you." Pixie and Fiona nodded along with her.

"I like your nymphs." Jadelyn smiled. "They really know how to be helpful. My own is great, don't get me wrong. But Tulip isn't Pixie or Nyske level." Jadelyn paused as she noticed the new addition. "Hi, I'm Jadelyn. I'm pretty sure you aren't Evelyn in a glamor."

"Fiona." The nymph did a small bow while sitting. "Is it all right if I'm here?"

"He considers you three his mates, or at least soon-to-be-mates," Scarlett told her. "So you get to sit with the wives. The other nymphs may get a nice little scar to match, but I don't think he'll include them very much." Scarlett pulled her shirt aside to show the scar on her shoulder; Jadelyn's wasn't covered and just pointed to hers.

Fiona's head was a swivel as she looked down the table, picking out all the visible scars that marked the ladies as my mates. "Ah. I see. What about you two?"

Pixie shook her head, making the pink curls bounce. "I'm sticking to conservative nymph rules. He doesn't get to mark me until I'm pregnant." She rubbed her stomach. "Hopefully, it will happen soon if he can get it in the right hole."

"He gets the wrong hole?" Fiona's brow curled curiously, seeming to shift a little more away from me.

"She's joking. Pixie likes to get him riled up and take it wherever she wants. Then she complains that he got it wrong," Nyske explained. "Besides, he's a dragon. His stamina is enough that even his succubus cannot keep up."

"Oh?" Fiona perked up.

Scarlett chuckled from across the table. "Careful what you wish for. Pixie tried to get him real riled up and came begging for healing from Trina."

Pixie scowled. "You weren't supposed to let him know that." She glanced at me, seeming concerned that it might ruin our future interactions.

"This was the time when you handcuffed yourself?" I asked.

"Yes." She frowned. "We should probably have you learn some healing magic. Just to be on the safe side."

Jadelyn smiled around her food. "Scarlett would love that too, and it would be smart for everyone's safety."

"Safety?" Fiona asked. "Was it that bad?" She turned to Pixie.

"Oh it wasn't—"

"She crawled down the hall until Kelly picked her up and carried her to the hoard where Trina was monitoring Yev," Nyske added.

Pixie snorted and tossed her hair. "I was performing my duties for my king. You should both be so thorough."

"I wouldn't mind being so thorough." Fiona turned to me with her eyes gleaming like two gems. "As your nymph, I must remind you that *all* of my services are available whenever you wish."

"Stop pawing at my man." Taylor jeered from the other side.

"Your man?" Fiona asked, confused. She glanced at Taylor's shoulder where there should have been a scar.

"Don't listen to her," Kelly sighed. "I'm sure you'll get your chance. He doesn't really keep it in his pants for very long."

"Hey," I protested weakly, my protest quickly being covered by laughter around the table.

"It got worse after he got the dragonettes. They opened the floodgates," Scarlett added amidst a wide number of head nods in agreement.

"Getting a bevy of dragons batting their lashes at him really went to his head. That and apparently pheromones," Larisa joined the teasing. "Then shortly after that, he attracted three fae queens into his orbit. You ladies really showed us up, and you had to bring an army of nymphs into the bed— Hey! I was eating that." Larisa started arguing with a nymph that took away her food as she started to bad mouth the fae.

"Careful, the nymphs are in charge now. You just don't know it." Summer smiled. "Welcome to the life of fae queens. If the nymphs ever rioted, we'd be done for."

"A stuffed nymph leads to a happy..." Kelly trailed off.

"Nymphs is hard to rhyme," I agreed. "Might have to work on that one."

"Furball has a lot of things to work on," Morgana took the moment to tease Kelly.

"Shut up, Blueberry. You have barrels of his blood. Barrels," Kelly huffed.

"I'm drinking for two. A lady has her needs." Morgana turned her nose away from Kelly and the two broke into laughter.

Fiona turned to me. "Your harem is very harmonious."

"Yes, it is," Pixie agreed. "It is our job to help him maintain that harmony. It is one of his top requests. We need to help balance out his time so that each of them get quality time with him on top of all of his duties."

"Oh." Fiona was wide eyed. "That's difficult. There are so many, and we have to balance the time?"

"More or less," I told her. "After dinner I'm pretty sure the whole family is going to retire together."

"The baths are being prepared," Jadelyn interjected. "Tulip and a few of the others have already snuck away to prepare them."

"And lots of 'cleaning' oil, I'm sure." Scarlett rolled her eyes but a smile crept up on her face.

"Before we get to that, how do we all feel about the readiness of our trip to Hell? I want to leave as soon as I can. The team is finalized?" I knew the Golden Plushie Society had been reserving no small amount of their meeting time for the topic.

My harem shifted their focus to Scarlett to be the bearer of the news.

"Fine." Scarlett put down her fork. "Summer, Ikta, Amira, Regina, and of course Sabrina, will be going with you."

"I knew Summer and Ikta. Talk about firepower. But why Regina? I would think fire would be the least effective?" My focus shifted down to Polydora who led the dragonettes.

"Demons are at least somewhat resistant to fire, but they aren't resistant to blunt force trauma."

The table laughed at her joke.

"But, seriously, it is a double-edged sword. They also use fire fairly often. Regina is the most durable in Hell. She can withstand attacks and just break anyone's face if they cause too much trouble. Of course, Amira is going because you need someone with healing magic," Polydora finished.

Amira had been in the background for some time. She was a black dragon which meant that she had death magic. I'd been surprised when I'd learned that death magic was also the best at *preventing* death and in turn provide healing.

But Trina was the best healer by far, having spent centuries as a doctor using her magic alongside actual medical knowledge. Of course, she was on call to monitor the pregnancies since there wasn't a whole lot of medical knowledge around them.

That had pushed Amira from the limelight along with my own challenging of her reasons to be here. She had come to my harem out of a sense of duty, not any sense of romance or attraction.

The same reasons that her parents had wanted a meeting with me yesterday. They were concerned that I hadn't mated with their daughter yet. That she hadn't performed her duties and something was wrong.

Amira was tense, watching me and waiting for a reaction.

"Of course. Amira, Regina, Summer, Ikta and Sabrina. Sounds like anyone causing trouble for us is going to be dead several times over," I added with confidence.

"Now, finish up dinner so that we can all get our dose of our husband before he absconds with five beautiful women and leaves us to knit socks," Morgana sighed and stared at my neck like it was an open liquor bottle and she was mighty thirsty.

I had eaten enough. "Let's go." I pushed off the table and stood.

The girls scrambled, but the first to reach me was Sarisha. "My king, if I could have your attention for a moment. It's about your investments."

Sarisha was a caramel-skinned beauty with exotic blue eyes. She had also stolen most of my hoard and put it in investment vehicles. The dragon in me wasn't happy.

I narrowed my eyes as she pulled up an app. Thankfully, when she showed me the screen, I noticed lovely green arrows. "Oh. That's not much. Two?"

"That's the percent. Multiply that by total invested and..." She punched it into a calculator app.

My eyes popped out at the number. "Already?!"

"Yes. If we divide that by the value of gold, you've made enough that you'd have trouble finding a car that could handle the weight." She smiled, clearly proud.

I was already sweeping her off her feet and cradling her in my arms. "Have I mentioned how beautiful you are?"

"It couldn't hurt to tell me a few more times, and maybe show me." Sarisha bit at my neck teasingly, but the move made my dragon instincts perk up and want to bite and mark her back.

"Oh. I think you've earned that."

"That's it. I'm switching my major to finance," Taylor shouted from behind me as I carried Sarisha off.

CHAPTER 10

The night had gone well. My mates were all exhausted and sleeping when dawn cracked its too bright head through the window.

Ikta was standing in my room with a big grin on her face. "We are ready. Let's go."

I blinked and slid my arm out from under a clingy Kelly. "The others?" I whispered.

"Slipped out earlier in the evening and got some rest, unlike you." She smirked as Fiona came out of the closet holding up a set of clothes before longingly looking over the giant bed.

I put a finger to my lips to tell both of them to be quiet and padded out of the master bedroom. Fiona's eyes tracked me hungrily, but she didn't make a move, following behind me with the stack of clothes.

It wasn't until we left the room and closed the door that I spoke. "Thank you for the wake up and the clothes." Slipping into the clothes, I got ready for a hike through Hell by putting on a T-shirt and jeans.

"The ladies of the house have been preparing. This way." Fiona waved down the hall before marching ahead.

"I like the new one. Not nearly as fun as Evelyn, but she'll relax here shortly. If you give her a good workout, she'll be downright cheerful, I suspect." Ikta smirked.

"It isn't fair to compare her to Maeve's nymph. Also, she is doing great. It's only her second day."

Fiona led us to Sabrina's room, where all the furniture had been pushed to the side. Sabrina had burned a big diagram into the floor of the room, and her stone tablet was in the center of the diagram. When she had been summoned to the world, she'd made the stone tablet to anchor herself so that she wouldn't have to return to Hell.

Along with Sabrina, the others coming on the trip were all standing around the edge of the room or sitting on the bed. Pixie and Nyske had carts of steaming food ready.

Nyske looked up first as I entered. "Come here and give me your storage bracelet. You are a hungry dragon, and some parts of Hell can be scarce with food. You need to have some home cooked food ready." She fussed over me like a girlfriend about to send her boyfriend off on a long trip.

It made me smile as she took my bracer in hand and started stuffing plate after plate of food into it before she pulled a large tray from the bottom of the cart and piled sandwiches into the storage space.

Pixie stood nearby with a smile as she continued.

"Remember not to pick up too many succubi while you are down there. The lower order ones just want sex. Honestly, besides rare cases like Sabrina, they are just mindless thots. I packed some sunscreen and some magical insect repellant. I'm told that mosquitoes were once a torture mechanism in Hell, but then some escaped. Apparently, they are even worse down there." Nyske continued to stuff item after item into my bracer until she looked up into my smiling face.

Really, the grin was giant at that point.

"Hush you." She looked off to the side, a little self-conscious.

"You care a lot about him," Fiona pointed out.

"Of course I do. He's my king now," Nyske said defensively.

"At this point, I expect a goodbye kiss," I teased her.

The nymph-dragon blushed. "Stop it. We haven't had a chance to reconnect. You've been busy, and it's understandable. We tried to cram in everything before you went on this trip."

I grabbed her shoulder and stopped her. "I'll miss you too, but I'll be back soon."

Nyske threw the sunhat she'd been holding onto the ground and grabbed the back of my head, pulling me down for a fierce kiss full of passion that she didn't always show. "Be safe." She straightened her clothing as she pulled back.

"Of course. I have so many beautiful women waiting for me. How could I not come back in one piece?" I teased.

Pixie had a broad smile on her face. "Yes. Maybe you'll come back to a few surprises. I know we've kept Sabrina busy with making enchantments for us to test ourselves."

Sabrina rolled her eyes. "Pregnancy tests. Come on. Let's get this done before I lose focus."

I wasn't surprised by the pregnancy tests. Given everything the nymphs did for us, I'd given them what they asked for.

"You'll look even prettier with my mark on you," I told Pixie.

"That's the plan. Just gotta get the right hole a little more often. Now, shoo. Sabrina is working her magic, and she will only be able to provide a short window to stuff you all through." Pixie was all business.

I remembered the magic that would be needed to get us back. "You have the tablet that Sabrina magicked to show her new—"

Pixie gave me a stare that could strip paint. "I organize your everything. Yes, I have the items needed to get you all back." She let out a sigh. "Nyske, when the portal opens, just kick him through. Maybe give him a big kiss on the way out."

A large crack of Sabrina's tablet splitting sounded. I turned abruptly, watching as a portal ripped open. The sound of a huge suction deafened me, tugging me towards it. The portal was like someone had opened the emergency door on a plane.

Ikta stepped forward and her six spider limbs shot out, latching onto the edge of the portal. "In!" she screamed over the noise.

I didn't hesitate, rushing through the portal behind Regina. As soon as I was through, I was ejected onto a field of pink grass. Someone landed on my back, and the sound cut off.

"Well that was fun." Ikta pulled herself off me with her spider limbs. "If I knew jumping through hijacked Hell portals was like that, I'd have done it centuries ago."

I ran my hands through the pink grass. The plant felt just like ordinary grass, but it was throwing off my senses that it was pink.

"Welcome to Hell." Sabrina looked around. "We are in the Pits of Lust."

"I expected more pits and less grass." I pushed off the ground and checked to make sure we had the whole party.

Regina and Amira were dusting themselves off while Summer stood proudly to the side, as if she'd never fallen in the first place.

"Enchanting really." Summer smiled and gazed out. "I'm quite excited. I don't get to travel very often."

Her smile was a little forced. She was still grieving the loss of her daughter. It didn't help that she'd been forced to be a part of her daughter losing her life, killing the thing that had taken over her body.

Following Summer's gaze, I saw the brightly colored world before us. The pink grass had small bursts of blue color that wove forward until it hit a town in the distance, which was a mashup of brightly colored buildings.

"We draw souls filled with lust here and then continue to pump them with lust. Tinting all the mana in a single direction has a profound effect on the world," Sabrina explained. Her eyes lost focus for a moment, and she licked her lips while looking at me.

"Then let's hurry." I recognized the signs of her nature poking through. "Any idea where exactly we are?"

"No, we'll have to check the town. I'll have a better idea from there." Sabrina took the lead, marching towards the town we could see in the distance.

Summer and Ikta chatted as we walked, as if we were out for a simple stroll through the park. But Regina was on high alert, her head swiveling back and forth, tossing her unruly red curls each time.

Amira came up beside me during the walk. "My king." She dipped her head towards me.

"Amira. I met your parents earlier this week."

She ducked her chin to her chest. "I've told my mother not to. She's been threatening for a while. Since the wedding, really."

"Ah. She was upset that you weren't among those married?" I asked.

Her mother had pushed several times before. Amira had even pushed, and I had posed a question to Amira that had made her pause. She was a dutiful daughter and had largely joined my honor guard because her mother was now the first female leader of a flight. Her mother wanted a deeper connection to me to help her in dragon politics.

Thus, her daughter was sent to be my guard and hopefully my mate in time. A relationship born entirely from her mother's ambitions rather than any of her own.

So, I had posed a question for her mother and told her that until Amira was the one with the interest in the relationship, then there was no point. While I might be a greedy dragon with a harem, I loved each one of them. There was a relationship with each woman I had marked as my mate, and I wasn't about to do it just for her mother's ambitions.

"Yes. She's been pushing, and I know you have some friendship with my father," she replied.

Herm and I had fought together during the dragon conclave. It had surprised me how quickly trust was built with somebody who literally had your back in a fight.

"What do you want?" I asked her.

"A whelp." She looked up to face me. "Every day I see Yev parading around with her egg, and I'm jealous. Something in me aches and yearns to be a mother like her."

"Okay. But any man could help you with that," I challenged.

She frowned again. "No. I want what you have with her. When you shifted and crawled over her after she laid the egg... I want that comfort and warmth between the two of you."

I grabbed the black dragon's hand. "That's something."

"I'm aware that I'm not exactly the most emotionally expressive woman." Amira stared at me like a knight waiting for marching orders. "But I still want to find that feeling."

"Then I think something can begin." I hugged Amira; the smaller woman fit nicely against my chest.

She was stiff at first, but she softened after a moment, murmuring something against my chest.

"What was that?" I pulled away to see her green eyes.

"Don't stop." She shoved herself against my chest again.

Sabrina had stopped, and Summer was turned back, smiling at us. "Don't get left behind, or you could just do it down in the grass. When in Rome, right?" She pointed off into the distance where there was a writhing mass.

I had to shift my eyes to see clearly. The mass was a pile of demons and more than a few human souls among them.

The succubus in the group slapped her hand against her face. "Come on."

Amira, blushing, moved away from me to catch up to Regina. Ikta and Summer let the dragons overtake them in the marching order and came back on either side of me.

"Lucky dragon. We are here, in the Pits of Lust, and you have two beautiful fae queens at your beck and call," Summer teased. "Whatever shall we do, Ikta?"

"Probably fuck our brains out," she chirped happily. "Or, at least, that would be my preference. Maybe the Pits of Lust are getting to me." She frowned for a moment before she shrugged it off. "Doesn't matter."

"Then what does matter?" I asked the capricious fae queen.

"That we are with you, and that all three of us are about to walk into a town of lust demons looking like the tastiest snack on Earth... well, in Hell too." She blinked and paused before turning to Summer. "Do I need to say tastiest snack on Earth and Hell or just Hell?"

"I think you are a delicious snack in both." I jumped in to stop her from going off track. "Do you have a recommendation about how to fix being too appetizing?"

"Did you see those souls?" Summer pointed back to where there had been an orgy.

"Yeah. Looked like normal people, but they were faint, like they were a little transparent and tinted pink." I realized what they were immediately after realizing they didn't have demon horns.

Summer nodded. "Have you ever wondered about how succubi are made?"

"Is this really the time for the birds and the bees?" I asked.

She snorted. "That is just one way. There had to be the first demons after all. Souls were siphoned off of their path to Tartarus to dwell here for the titan that made Hell to eat."

I had been to Tartarus, where the giant funnel of souls was surrounded by giant ghostly titans picking from the stream and devouring them. "So, this was his own buffet?"

"Yes. He wanted those with strong emotions and created the first demons from remnant souls and the overwhelming abundance of a certain emotion," Summer explained.

I glanced back in the direction of the orgy. "These souls are being drained, but also further pushed towards said emotion."

"Correct. They'll wink out eventually after having so much mana drained from them. Then they'll coalesce again and again only to be drained further until they become something so hungry for more lust that they'll draw it out of others," Summer explained.

"Shit... Does that mean..." I glanced further ahead at Sabrina.

"Once long ago," Ikta answered. "She has no memories, though. They would have been washed out by enough lust. But she became a succubus through the same process most of them have."

"Can you explain what the deal is with 'lesser' succubus, while Beelzebub is a 'prince'?" I asked.

"Beelzebub became more powerful having eaten enough lesser demons to form a more full and stable soul. One that can resist the base instincts that were imparted by the souls that make up a demon like Sabrina," Summer answered.

"So Hell is basically one giant marinade bowl for some titan, and Sabrina needs to become a bigger chunk of seasoning," I tried to understand.

"See? He gets it." Ikta smiled and nodded along. "Pretty much. That and she needs to not get eaten while we are here. The three of us are going to draw a lot of attention. We need to not become food for those that dwell here."

"We might have bodies, but we still have souls that these demons can feed off. Think of Beelzebub. He was hijacking souls in Philly, using them to feed on lesser people and then devouring the soul of his host," Summer warned.

I sighed. "And that was just a fragment of his soul." Yet it had been hard enough to take him down.

"Good news is that you are much stronger as well." Summer smiled like a concerned mother. "But there is a reason that Ikta and I joined you for this trip. If Hell were ever to spill into the normal world, it wouldn't even be a contest. They'd strip bare all of humanity and paranormals alike. It is a good thing that they are sealed down here." Her eyes fixed on the town that we were approaching. "You give off a lot of mana. Use your fae magic as much as you can to turn people's attention away from you."

CHAPTER 11

Following Summer and Ikta's example, I shifted people's attention away from me by pushing out a bit of fae magic.

Compared to the two fae queens, it felt like I was running around with a wooden club and knocking people's attention away rather than the more subtle approach they were using. And the move still didn't stop many of the demons in the town from looking up at the approach of Sabrina with the two dragons.

Sabrina felt like a pot of mana about to boil over compared to the other succubi I could see, but somehow that seemed to help. Demons rushed to get out of her path.

"In Hell, strength is everything. A demon prince, for example, could come in and just suck the life out of all the lower order demons here," Sabrina explained as we walked. "The fact that I have some clarity left from feeding on you for months gives me the power to back it up."

"So they think you are a higher order of demon?" I asked, looking around.

The buildings were made of stone or wood. It reminded me of a hamlet in some fantasy show, except washed out in neon colors. Lust demons watched as we passed, with hungry expressions on their faces even if they restrained themselves. It felt like we were giant hunks of meat and they were a starving pack of dogs.

"But I'm not." Sabrina's voice was soft as she watched the other demons. "That's what I really am, husband." Sabrina's eyes filled with sadness as she watched the hungry succubi act like animals.

succubi saw me looking, and they began posing, trying to steal my attention away. They flaunted their bodies and stared into my eyes as if asking if I wanted to come play.

I put an arm around Sabrina. "Not for long. Come on. You wanted to get an idea of where we were?"

The others trailing after us were getting similar treatment, though it was incubi that were strutting their stuff in front of my mates. I wanted to punch a few of them out when they got too close.

"Focus, my king," Regina instructed. "If one of them touches me, I'll turn them into ash or a bloody pulp, whichever suits me at the moment."

A low growl rumbled from my chest. "Fine."

"Think he'll be jealous of me too?" Ikta playfully asked Summer who just rolled her eyes.

"Don't cause more trouble than you have to."

Sabrina found the largest building in the town and walked in through the double doors.

"Guests?" A succubus looked up from the ledger in front of her. "Ah. Forgive me." She bowed low. "I didn't realize someone as esteemed as you was visiting."

The woman had no idea who Sabrina was, but she felt her mana. The hierarchy in Hell was clearly centered around power.

"I just returned and came... here." Sabrina put a tone of distaste into her voice that wasn't entirely faked as she stood up straight. She was in her element, and she was going to use it. "Where am I? I don't recognize it." Sabrina frowned.

"Of course you wouldn't. This is just a small town without a proper name. We are two days on foot north from The Vale," the woman at the counter replied quickly.

"Ah. Thank you." Sabrina patted the counter. "My guests and I will be heading out shortly."

"Lady, returning to Hell is an ordeal. Would you like to stay the night? Your... guests..." Her eyes roamed over me hungrily. "...would be welcome to stay as long as they'd like."

"I don't like what you are suggesting." Sabrina was fast, her hand finding the woman's neck in the blink of an eye before Sabrina pulled her half over the counter. "Do you think that you deserve even a piece of my spoils? I've tricked these fools into coming to Hell as a bargaining chip for my Lady. You think to spoil them?" She slapped the woman hard enough that the woman flew back into her seat.

"No— Never," her voice warbled. "Of course such treats are for the higher order demons."

"Yes. And don't forget it," Sabrina scowled, but I could tell that the scowl wasn't only caused by her act. "You five. Sit while I discuss things."

I was pretty sure that her current demeanor was all an act, but it was pretty convincing. I had no idea that Sabrina was such a good actress.

"She can be downright scary." Ikta looked at Sabrina with a new appreciation in her eyes as she sat in my lap.

"I... I think this has always been inside of her. She never really talked about Hell." I watched Sabrina arguing with the woman at the counter.

"It is a brutal place. Even the kindest of souls need to learn to be tough." Summer watched with nothing more than curiosity. "She's yours through and through. This is an act," Summer spoke softly enough that nobody else heard.

My attention shifted from watching Sabrina to the windows of the building. There were several succubi pressing their bodies up against the window, leaving large imprints of their chests before another pulled them away to give it a try.

"Is the lady at the counter a lower order?" I asked the group.

"Yes. But more satiated than those... things." Summer watched the windows. "They are hungry and young."

As we talked, several of the succubi turned to something else that caught their attention before abandoning the window. Screams filled the air and rattled the windows.

Before I knew it, I was on my feet. "What is that?"

Sabrina looked away from the counter and narrowed her eyes. "A monster."

"Please, lady, can you or one of your lust slaves deal with it?" the woman at the counter asked.

Sabrina stayed turned away from the counter so that the woman couldn't see her face as she raised a brow in question towards me.

I gave a slight nod, feeling a moment of relief at the confirmation that Sabrina was still in control of herself.

"Zach. Go deal with it." She dismissed me with a wave of her hand as she held her head high.

Regina coughed and glared at Sabrina, but my wife simply turned back to the counter. To change her orders would be a sign of weakness.

"My lady, can he deal with it himself?" the woman at the counter asked.

"Of course he can. He's a dragon." She waved away her concern. "As we were saying, I'm looking for the best route from here to Gluttony."

I pushed her comment aside, starting to walk towards the doors. I heard a scooting of a chair and looked back to see Ikta now sitting near a window so that she could watch the show, her eyes full of anticipation.

"Good luck." She waved as I stepped out.

I rolled my eyes, focusing my attention on whatever was causing the chaos. Another roar filled the air as I stepped outside, making the windows rattle through the street. I could have only missed the source if I'd been blind, deaf, and without a lick of sense.

Something taller than the buildings lowered its head, which was mounted on a neck so thick that it was hard to determine where its body started.

I tried to place the monster, but I couldn't think of anything that exactly matched. I could have called it a boar just based on shape, but it was half plated in black carapace armor. What little of its body was showing had thick skin and even thicker muscles bulging underneath.

"Come here, boy." I coiled a large cluster of mana in my hand before letting it loose and sending a bolt of lightning over the town and into the creature's face.

The monster reeled, but largely in surprise rather than pain. The lightning hadn't done more than add a scorch mark to the armor. The demon boar stomped its feet, and

I realized that it was going to charge. And I wasn't where I would want to be for that fight.

Throwing up a portal in front of me, I jumped through it onto a roof of one of the houses that the boar could see and ran along it, waving my arms to get its attention. Then I made another portal back the way we'd come into town, turning the boar almost a full one eighty.

It took a moment for the monster to readjust, but once it had, it charged once more. While it moved, I worked to pack on mass and shift as well. The beast was too big for me to beat using portals, and I had to admit that going toe to toe with it sounded a little fun.

By the time the armored boar hit me, I was equal to its size and still growing bigger. I went down in a tumble with the giant boar, continuing to grow until I had enough mass to toss it around and pin it on its back. Then I wrapped my jaw around the chitinous armor and squeezed.

The demon boar thrashed, fire pouring out between the armor plates and trying to scorch me. Unfortunately for the beast, I wasn't affected by the fire. I ignored the squirting liquid and flames as I increased the pressure. A few moments later, the boar went limp and my jaw finally tore through and took a huge chunk out of it.

I chewed. The boar was richer in mana than anything I'd tasted since the fae wilds, and I loved it. Interestingly, the demon boar seemed to be made up of a particular flavor of mana. I could feel my body warm up and my blood flow, rapidly diverting itself as I chewed.

Tossing my head, I tried to throw off the growing sense of lust that was inflaming my body. Movement caught my eye, and succubi came out of their homes. Only a few exited at first, then a flood of them charged. They all raced towards me with hearts in their eyes.

"Oh. Big daddy dragon, come here!" One landed on my head and laid a big kiss between my horns while they clung to my scales.

I tried to toss her off, but she was strong, clinging to my scales and riding me like a surfboard. She laughed, her chest bouncing right in my face.

More and more of them swarmed me, and I felt the tingle of each time they kissed my scales. They drew more lustful mana from me while tainting my reserves even more. I groaned with a different kind of need and rammed the crown of my head to the ground in frustration.

"Oh baby, don't worry. We'll take good care of yo—"

"Off!" A blast of warm light turned the succubus into ash, along with dozens more. Summer had her hip cocked to the side. "Really, Zach?"

I shook off the remaining succubi who weren't smart enough to run as Summer continued to turn more and more to ash.

"They mobbed me." I put up a weak defense.

"Uh huh." Summer smiled as she shook her head. "Just too tasty a treat? What happened to trying to keep them away?"

"He failed at that rather impressively," Ikta laughed as she walked up with Regina and Amira in tow. Sabrina was trailing after them, glaring at me too.

"Well, Sabrina sent me out after a giant boar demon." I glanced down at the shriveled corpse that was now devoid of mana. While they had mobbed me, the other demons had drained the corpse.

"I don't think I've ever seen a chastised Dragon King before."

I turned towards the voice. One succubus remained nearby, even though the others had all departed. She didn't have the same feral edge the rest of them did. In fact, she was far more put together than any of the others. She wore jeans and a skin-tight t-shirt, yet something about her was very very wrong.

Ikta took a step back, which put me on edge, but something about the succubus was keeping my attention.

Summer glanced over, noting the woman and frowning. "Zach, shift back. We need to get going. Putting on a show like that is going to cause ripples."

My bones crackled, and I returned to my human form, slipping on a pair of jeans as the succubus strutted forward, not seeming at all concerned with my mates as she teased her pink lips with a finger.

"My oh my. Aren't you just a walking treat."

For whatever reason, I couldn't stop staring at her as she came up and snuggled up against my chest.

"Protect me, big bad Dragon King?" She pulled my arms to wrap around her.

I had no idea who she was, and I wanted to stop myself, but she was completely in control of the situation and wiggled her rear against my hips.

"Who are you?" I eked out through my mind that was screaming to mark her as my mate.

The rest of my party was watching with various levels of concern. Regina and Amira seemed exasperated more than anything. Meanwhile, Sabrina was frowning heavily.

I could tell that Summer was concerned, as if she had a puzzle she was working out, but Ikta had already solved whatever the mystery was. She looked moments away from making a portal and disappearing.

"That's rude. But the one with the giant tits was right. You should probably stop making ripples. Although, this wasn't the only one you've caused. You made a big one when you popped into my domain." She looked up at me, wrapped in my arms.

"Your domain?" I asked, and Sabrina went rigid as Summer sighed and put her head into her hands.

"She's Lilith, or rather the current Lilith," Summer groaned. "It's more of a title."

I froze. The woman in my arms was a prince of Hell or maybe princess was more correct. Based on the sense I was getting from her and Ikta's current terror, I didn't want to fight with her.

But she didn't seem particularly interested in fighting at the moment.

"Oh. Sorry for barging in. We used Sabrina to hitch a ride." I smiled down at the lovely woman who was hopefully not going to start breaking necks.

"Yes, I assume you've to come kill Beelzebub and stuff his essence into your little succubus before she rejoins the lower succubi in their unfortunate mentality." Lilith's accuracy made me uncomfortable. Nobody should have known about our plan.

"Don't be like that. Information is of the highest value in Hell. A number of demons in Hell make a healthy living by knowing all that happens on Earth. We know about your fight with Beelzebub, and the trouble he caused you along with knowledge that the Dragon King has a lesser succubus in his harem with her nature sealed. It was simple deduction to put together your plan... unless... you wouldn't be here for poor little me... would you?" She turned in my arms and bit her plump lips, making me hungry in dangerous ways.

All I wanted to do was wrap her tighter and protect the woman in my arms. But something about it felt unnatural as well.

"Oh good. You didn't come here for me. I do like the feeling of your big arms, though" Lilith smiled and wrapped herself in me. "So. I'm afraid I'll have to break the bad news. You can't stuff Beelzebub's essence in your little succubus. The majority of her soul would then be Gluttony, and she'd become a gluttony demon, unless that's what you want in your harem?"

Given what I'd seen of Beelzebub's form before, there was a sudden revulsion to the idea. I liked Sabrina the way she was. My dragon roared that she might want to come after my gold, but I tried to push that aside and let Sabrina lead.

"It's up to her. Sabrina, do you want to become a gluttony demon?"

"Fuck no." Sabrina wrinkled her nose.

"I like you more." Lilith ran her hand along my arm sending a wave of pleasant tingles all the way down my body to my groin. "Glad you popped in for a visit. So, that's the first bit of bad news. But I have good news to wash it away. I'll make a trade. You kill Beelzebub, and I'll help Sabrina—cute name by the way—become one of my handmaidens."

"Handmaiden?" I narrowed my eyes at the idea of her making Sabrina subservient to her.

"Husband. It's a title. They are her direct subordinates in Hell, the second highest order," Sabrina was quick to inform me. "Why?"

"Because I have a few more pieces of news for you. Asmodia and Lucifer are aware of your arrival and..." She sighed like she was exhausted. "They have their own reasons to come cause problems. Yet I need you to survive and return because there's more at stake."

"And you aren't going to tell me everything?" I growled.

"Oh. Do that again. I liked it." She wiggled herself into my embrace again. "No, I'll tell you. I want to use you to bind Hell back to Earth. The plane is shifting, and the buildup of souls is causing issues. Originally, there was a sort of... release valve if it built up too much. But it's dead now, and we need solutions. You provide those."

"That sounds not great for Earth," I pointed out.

She nodded. "You'll have to figure that part out. You are in charge of Earth, I'm just looking out for Hell. Heaven might be a nice balancing act if you wanted my advice."

I scowled, not liking having to deal with the Celestial plane at all. After what they had done to the Servile—the silver dragon that they had controlled with runes branded into each of its scales—I hated to think what they'd do to me.

"Unfortunately, I'm going to play a little hardball with you. It's all a package deal. I'll give you something you didn't know you needed, play a little game with Lucifer so you only have to deal with Asmodia, and you kill Beelzebub. I'll make Sabrina here a handmaiden and visit me when you are done. Deal?" She smiled.

I'd barely followed everything she had said, but it was clear she was a few steps ahead of me. And if her information was correct, which based on the look on Sabrina's face was likely, I was going to need allies.

Part of me wanted to say fuck it and fight Lilith or go for her current handmaidens, but based on the way Ikta looked like a serious flight risk, I figured that was probably a terrible idea.

"Deal." I held out my hand.

Lilith grabbed my face and brought my lips down for a kiss that completely drowned me in lust, turning my insides out. I would have given up everything for her in that moment before she broke the kiss far too soon for my liking.

After the kiss broke, there was something that snapped into place, and it took me a moment before my head cleared and I recognized what it was. "Are you a fae? Why is there a fae agreement between us?"

She laughed. "That was all you. Seems that things are well on their way. Now, hold still." Lilith kissed my chest and left a lip stamp before she slipped out of my arms. "If you don't mind, I'm going to borrow Sabrina. Go kill Beelzebub, and avoid Asmodia if you can. She's not as strong as me, but you probably don't want to get all hopped up on Wrath. The world doesn't need you like that."

Lilith walked over, taking Sabrina's hand and disappearing in a blur before I could get my head on right.

"Uh. I'm not sure what just happened." I blinked.

"She just stole our guide is what happened," Regina grumbled, crossing her arms.

CHAPTER 12

"This way." Ikta pointed with one of her spider limbs. "And I think we should move quickly. Get some space between us and her. I got enough information from Sabrina talking to the other demon to know the general direction."

"She scared you," I commented, referring to Lilith.

Summer nodded. "Lilith should scare you too. She was too powerful. The titan here in Hell is dead."

Ikta nodded in agreement.

"Wait, how does her being powerful mean the titan is dead?" I was missing pieces of the puzzle.

"Remember how Hell was a place for the titan to create souls more to its liking? You said it's a giant seasoning bowl. Well, that includes the more powerful demons here. She's strong enough to threaten a titan. Yet she not only lives, but thrives," Ikta answered.

I wrinkled my nose at Ikta's explanation. "So, this place is just a farm?"

"One where the cattle has potentially revolted," Summer sighed. "We are lucky that she wants to help us."

Glancing at where Sabrina used to be standing, I truly hoped that was the case.

"So, we push forward to kill Beelzebub. If Lilith is as strong as you suggest, I'm not entirely sure I want to pick a fight with her, which means this trip just got a whole hell of a lot more dangerous, didn't it? Beelzebub is the same level as Lilith; this just got a lot harder."

Summer shrugged. "There was a reason that Ikta and I came along."

"You knew?" I frowned.

"Not entirely," Ikta hastily answered. "There was a potential concern. If I had said something, would it have stopped you?"

I thought about that for a moment. "Absolutely not. Probably would have made me stubborn enough to do this on my own."

Ikta gestured like I had proved her own point. "Exactly."

"Still, the whole soul eating is a little much." I frowned.

"You eat monsters," Amira spoke up. "All beings eat. All that differs is their choice of food. We cannot begrudge anything for trying to survive."

"She's not wrong." Ikta shrugged. "I like her."

Not wanting to talk about that topic any longer, I set off in the direction that Ikta had indicated. "Might be best to keep the fact that we are dragons quiet for now." After having been swarmed by the succubi, I was wary about drawing too much attention.

"For the best," Ikta agreed. "So, who wants to play i-spy? I'll go first. I spy something pink."

I glanced over the field of pink grass before us. "The grass?"

"Yes, but which one?" Ikta asked excitedly.

***

The trek across land was unfortunately necessary. Ikta hadn't been to Hell in a very very long time, making her unable to simply portal us as everything had changed.

"I spy something green," Summer called out.

"Oh! Oh pick me." Ikta jumped a little while she held a piece of paper and a paintbrush. I wasn't entirely sure where either of them came from.

"No. You are banned from the game," Regina grumbled. "Twice."

"This game is important though. The topography of Hell hasn't changed drastically, and I doubt the seats of the rulers have either. So, we know Gluttony is this way, Lust is that way." Ikta pointed with her spider limbs. "Then that way has to be the center. We spotted the pale mounds. Those are my favorite."

I snickered. The mountains had looked just like a pair of breasts, but that was to be expected in the lust domain of Hell.

Summer rolled her eyes. "Mine are better."

"Anyway. So. This is the rough map, and we are here." Ikta finished with the paintbrush and flipped around an extremely detailed map of Hell.

I wasn't sure what I'd been expecting, but it hadn't been something with the level of detail I expected from a printer. "Wow."

Ikta shrugged. "We fae are often artists. I've had a lot of time to work on my craft."

I stared at the photo-like quality, feeling like she was discounting her skill.

"Okay. We are headed this way?" I oriented myself based on where we'd been heading when we passed the mountains.

"Yep." She nodded. "So if we keep going far enough in that direction, we should see the border of the domain with Wrath."

"Why not just go through the center?" The Lust and Gluttony domains were on opposite sides of Hell. There were seven clearly marked domains. In the center, Ikta had just drawn a crown.

"Lucifer," Summer answered. "All of the other leaders of hell situate their domains around it. He put his right in the center of Hell. Lilith said she would distract him, and I think it's wise to give him a wide berth."

"Something's been bothering me. With Lilith leading Lust, and Lucifer leading Hell, that means Beelzebub is the strongest in Gluttony, correct?" I may not have read the bible, but I knew the name from other material.

"He's the demon prince of Gluttony," Summer explained. "Someone like Lilith is too powerful to be summoned by a mortal." Her eyes slid to me with a thought. "It would take someone like you to summon Lilith to Earth, at least in her current state."

"So, Beelzebub's power is about the limit for a human to summon?" I asked, ignoring the connotation in her last words.

"He sent a fragment. Apparently, he's broken himself up into numerous pieces so that he can gallivant around Earth devouring human souls," Summer pointed out.

"He's greedy. Greedy enough to keep himself at a point where he can continue to go to Earth and devour mortals." Ikta shrugged. "Don't underestimate him, though;

120

he may be stronger than your previous encounter suggests. Besides, we have to go through greed and wrath."

Asmodia was the second demon prince that Lilith had warned me about.

"Why not go around the other way?" I asked.

"Sloth," the two dragons and two fae queens said at the same time.

"Wait, Sloth is that big of a deal?" I frowned.

"It is by far the hardest to shake off if it overwhelms you. Belphegore is the strongest demon in Hell; stronger than Lucifer. But he rarely wakes up." Ikta seemed knowledge-able enough. "Everyone knows you don't go to Sloth if you enter Hell unless you want to stay there."

I held up my hands, acknowledging they'd thought through the route pretty thoroughly. "Got it. Wrath is first. Which means we have Asmodia to deal with."

"First we have other problems. I spy something big and black," Ikta giggled.

A large behemoth was rising up over a set of hills in the distance.

"Hmm. Wonder what it could be." Summer tapped her lips.

"This isn't a joke," I grumbled, realizing the scale of the creature up ahead.

The distance could make things look small, but the crea-ture looked like... well... like some monster from Hell. Its black carapace reflected spots of pink amid the Pits of Lust and the pink grass.

The creature was a quadruped, with several long serpent heads coming off in different directions. The monster sort of resembled a hydra in that it had multiple serpentine heads, but it was like someone had put one together without even glancing at the instruction manual.

"There's good news." Ikta hummed with a smile. "There's probably not any succubi for miles and miles with that thing around."

"I will handle it, my king." Amira stepped forward, dropping her pants and throwing off her jacket as her bones crackled and she began to grow.

Amira wasn't that big compared to the other dragonettes. Only Trina and Chloe were smaller. Yet she was a dragon, and as soon as she started shifting, the behemoth charged out from the hills it had been resting in, clearly looking for a snack.

"Regina. Please go help her." I realized just how big of a size difference there was as Amira got closer.

Regina didn't say anything, throwing her clothes in a pile and rushing forward. She shifted into a giant red dragon that dwarfed Amira.

"Just sending those two ladies into battle." Ikta propped herself up on her spider legs to rest her chin on my shoulder. "You are a big bad Dragon King."

"A king should use his people from time to time. Besides, we brought them for a reason. No need to exhaust myself with every monster." I shrugged.

"Now you are starting to think like a king." Summer sounded satisfied. "It's good practice for them either way. Amira, as small as she is, probably hasn't seen that much combat. At least, not real combat."

I knew what she meant. Amira fought like she had been trained within an inch of her life. She was all rigid rules, with none of the flexibility of experience.

Amira did several passes over the behemoth, spraying her death breath over it while trying to stay out of reach. I watched, surprised as the behemoth stretched its neck out far past what appeared its natural limit, snagging her and pulling the black dragon out of the sky.

I wasn't going to make it in time to help her, but Regina was there. She crashed down with enough bulk to topple over the behemoth, and the three stirred up debris over the hill.

"Shall we?" Ikta held out her arm.

Feeling odd given the battle of two dragons and the behemoth just ahead, I still took her arm. Summer moved to my other side, and I found myself walking arm in arm with the two fae queens like we were out for a casual stroll.

"You know. This is kind of nice." Summer held my arm up against the softness of her chest as a red dragon tail slapped the top of a hill and sent chunks flying.

"I feel odd not being the one jumping into danger," I muttered honestly.

"They can handle it," Ikta replied without worry. "Besides, you brought a healer."

"One that we just threw into the fight," I pointed out.

"Healing her would give you practice. Much needed practice." Ikta shrugged. "Besides, we get some time together. In the Pits of Lust."

"You two can't see a single problem here, can you?" I asked.

"Nope." Summer ran her hand up and down my arm as she walked through the grass. "Besides, your succubus is off getting fixed and upgraded."

"She's not getting fixed," I retorted quickly, not loving the terms.

"She's getting her soul juiced by Lilith herself." Summer rolled her eyes. "Which means you should be able to relax, and we should start talking about the next step of Faerie."

I frowned. "Ikta said she didn't know what was happening."

"Technically correct. It's like we put the ingredients into a blender and are waiting to see what comes out. But three fae aspects have gone in, so one thing it will be is fae. So, my question is, when will you start holding court?" Summer asked.

"Now? This is what you are focusing on now?" I looked over towards the fight, wanting to make sure my dragons were okay.

One of the behemoth's heads bounced off a hill as the two dragons roared on the other side. It was still hard to not want to jump into the fighting directly.

"Yes." Summer shrugged. "War is a constant in Faerie. Or at least, it has been up until now."

"Tea on a warfront can be very relaxing," Ikta added, causing Summer to nod in agreement.

"You two," I sighed. "Fine. You want me to break the pattern of war of the fae. The same war that has been going on for millions of years?"

"Billions," Ikta corrected me.

"Great, because that makes it so much more feasible," I sighed. "What would Faerie become?"

"I'd hope it would one day become what it was always meant to be: a place to practice and love the arts. Fighting might remain, but hopefully not chief among the hobbies." There was a faint spark of longing and hope in Summer's eyes.

The look made me think she was reminded of her daughter, twisted by the constant war and the stories she had told me of her father who had been happy as a carpenter.

I could see how ending war and turning to the arts would be meaningful for Summer. But desire didn't exactly make it more feasible. Even if I would break the great patterns, this one seemed like a monumental task.

"What of Maeve?" I asked.

"She'd love an end to the wars," Summer replied with certainty.

I didn't doubt that for a second. "Yet she's still not queen."

Ikta pursed her lips. "She will be. If you offer the winter fae peace in return for the throne, you'd find Winter dead in a snow drift by the end of the hour."

I wondered how Maeve would take me getting her mother killed.

"How do you propose all of this?" I still didn't know how I was supposed to fix everything.

"Hold court. Make yourself officially a fae king when you get back. We'll sit as nobles." Summer made her plan sound so simple.

"If we can agree that war is bad, why do we need to have a court session?"

"It's symbolic," Ikta replied. "Our own holding court is part of being a fae queen. It is there that we reconnect with the power we've shared and renew those bonds."

"Like the power you shared with me?" I asked.

"You what?!" Summer turned to Ikta, her eyes turning into two angry suns.

Ikta whistled and looked away, a smile on her face. "I gave him a chunk of my territory already. He's wielding my wild fae magic well already. So, really, my power was a good test."

"Test?" I fixated on the word.

"We were fairly sure it would work, but Ikta was not supposed to be first." Summer's eyes were two baleful suns threatening to scorch the spider queen into a shriveled pest.

I had a feeling that Summer was supposed to be first. Based on when she had tempted me in the past after her court sessions, I realized that her idea of a good time involved a lot of magic.

"It worked. Everything is fine. He gave it all back. But it is true that I'm the first member of his court now." Ikta stuck her tongue out at Summer, and I started to get concerned the two were about to fight it out right there in Hell.

I rolled my eyes. "If it's such a big deal, why don't we do it now? Besides, Ikta kind of surprised me with it. I didn't get to savor the feeling." The statement was mostly bullshit, but I knew it would make Summer feel better.

"Oh. Then good. With me, you'll be able to feel it properly. I have plans to make sure it is a memorable experience." Summer held her chin aloft.

One of the behemoth's heads flew over the hill, crashing not far from us.

"You don't think the dragons are going to eat that monster full of lust mana, do you?" Ikta frowned at the head.

I remembered the overwhelming lust that had taken me before, and my eyes went wide as I rushed forward, using my fae magic to pop open a portal to the top of the hill.

CHAPTER 13

I appeared on top of the hill to see the behemoth lying in a heap while Amira and Regina tore into its torso.

"Stop. Don't eat that," I shouted as another portal opened beside me.

Amira swallowed in shock. "My king?" There was a strange moment where Amira's dragon eyes went from a blank expression to one smoldering with lust. "Share the kill with us." She nudged the behemoth's corpse.

Ah fuck.

"The behemoth is full of lust because of where we are. There's a lot of mana in that thing. It's going to mess with your emotions," I pointed out to both dragons.

Regina raised a scaly brow ridge. "There's a solution to that."

I felt myself flush a little. "A way to get some of it out of your system. Yes."

Amira only smiled. "Yes, there is, my king."

Neither seemed particularly concerned, but I was fairly certain they weren't that far gone yet.

Ikta giggled as she placed a hand on my shoulder. "Go. Join them and have fun. Seems like they knew what they were doing. It is a good opportunity for your black dragon to get some bulk to her. But you might have to satiate her a bit, at least until her own mana flushes the lust out."

"We'll keep watch," Summer agreed with a smirk. She'd followed along and caught up with me at the top of the hill.

Regina had taken some of the behemoth but quickly realized the problem. "My king. What do you want?"

I thought about it for a moment and threw caution aside. Helping both of them grow stronger was fair, and I wasn't opposed to what would come of the situation.

"Eat it if you want. I'll help you deal with the repercussions. When you are done, I'll... I'll be over here. You know what you are getting into, correct? Oh, and clean yourselves before you come over here." I'd been covered in my share of blood, but I wasn't about to sleep with either dragon covered in blood, or in the middle of the field where they had a kill.

Instead, I stepped back over the hill and reached into my bracer, grabbing hold of a mattress and pulling hard to jerk the thing out of the bracer. I grunted; it had been hard to stuff into the space as well.

The spatial magic around the bracer was odd. Fitting something rigid and large like a bed frame was impossible, but something malleable like a mattress wasn't a problem. It just required a lot of shoving.

"Oh wow. She's really going at it." Ikta called from the top of the hill.

"She wanted the repercussions more than the size I think," Summer commented. "I think it's going to be a fun show. Besides, we could stand to learn a few things from the dragons."

"Are you two going to comment the entire time?" I glared up at the fae queens.

They looked at each other for a moment.

"Yes," Ikta replied with a smile. "Besides, your two dragons have been strung along for long enough. They are the last?"

"They are the last. Poor girls. Rest of them are sporting a mark." Summer nodded.

I rolled my eyes. "You two. Do me a favor at least and make sure they are clean?" I was a little nervous that one or both were going to come charging over the hill with more lust than sense.

"Sure." Ikta waved away my concern, only half paying attention to me. "Summy, what do you think about shoving some lust beast into the Fae Emperor before we let him ravish us?"

Summer snorted with no small amount of pride. "I don't need the help of Lust to drive him wild." She glanced at me out of the corner of her eye, her eyes full of promise for our next time together.

Her look faltered as something nearby caught her attention. She sent out rays of blinding light down on the other side while Ikta started to jump up and down excitedly, her fingers sparking with magic.

Amira was first over the hill. Her green eyes found me instantly and devoured me like a hungry beast. She had on a scandalous set of white lingerie that looked to be made out of spider webs. I knew instantly who had chosen her outfit, glancing over at an Ikta who was very pleased with herself.

Regina was next, wearing a bright green set of lingerie, a glamor from Summer. She had the look of a hunter who had finally found her prey, but it was barely held back by a strand of sanity.

"My king." Amira's breath came out ragged before she leapt the remaining distance, crashing onto me and making the mattress bounce among the pink grass.

I wasn't so surprised that I couldn't catch her. Up close, her green eyes held an intensity only matched by the way her short hair swayed forward on either side of her face like a pair of daggers.

Rather than let her lead the show, I grabbed her roughly and pulled her down for a passionate kiss. Her tongue pushed past my lips immediately and tangled with my own. She sucked and kissed like she was trying to steal my tongue.

I had to push her off and roll her over to enjoy the sight. It wasn't the first time I'd taken a dragon mate, but it would be the first time I'd taken two at once. A lot of the act of marking was about dominance.

I hovered over her, watching her breath. Her chest was heaving, the glamored lingerie not completely hiding her nipples underneath.

"Mine," I growled.

Amira was hungry for me, that much was clear, but she still growled back in challenge, snapping her teeth at me. My chest rumbled in response, the Dragon King in me angered by her daring to not bow down.

Before I could do more, a strong hand grabbed my face and turned it. Soon my vision was nothing but a tangle of red hair in my face as Regina pushed me off of Amira and slammed herself onto me, grinding her hip against mine.

"Yes. I'm going to mark you," Regina growled and the strand of sanity I'd seen earlier was gone. It had snapped.

Regina had been fairly well behaved on Earth lately, making it easy to forget that she had been raised among a more wild set of dragons, where females were in charge.

Amira's resistance might have been playing into some instincts, but Regina's was far more. And the red dragon was by far the strongest in sheer brute force, only losing to Polydora because of the difference in skill.

Regina pinned me to the mattress and kissed me hungrily. Another set of lips wandered my body as Amira pulled up my shirt and undid my pants with swift hands.

A rumble from my chest made Regina stop and toss her hair to see what Amira was doing. "Good girl. I promise to give you a share of my mate once I'm done."

Amira's eyes flashed dangerously, and she pounced on Regina, rolling off the mattress as the two of them fought for dominance.

Ikta let out a whistle. "Wow. This is eye opening. Need some help?"

I waved her off and rolled off the mattress to deal with my two unruly soon-to-be-mates. The two rolled over the ground while they grunted. Their tussle had knocked off the glamors; they were both perfectly naked.

I could see Regina's glistening slit, her rear positioned up in the air as she pinned Amira.

"I'm first," Amira growled.

"Not a chance." Regina was completely focused on the dragon under her and didn't see me before I grabbed her hips.

I tore my clothes off in one fluid motion and thrust myself into her. She let out a small groan and arched her back.

"You feel wonderful, my mate." I grabbed her hair and held her in the arched position as I slid completely into her.

The rough and tumble red dragon let out a mewling noise as I ground the two of us together.

"What was that?" I teased.

"Mine," she roared and tried to throw me off, but I held her still, holding tight to her bright red hair.

Her bucking created even more friction, bringing my dragon glee as I thrust deep inside of her over and over. It took a little bit, but soon her body submitted to me, and her movements were in rhythm with mine.

"Please," she begged.

I could feel her soaking my balls as each struggle painted them with more of her fluids. "Not so fast." I pulled her away from where she had Amira pinned to push her face into Amira's sex. "Lick."

Regina bucked, but I pushed her face into Amira's sex, holding her there. It wasn't long before Amira started to gasp and grabbed onto Regina's shoulders.

Smiling, I knew my cue and started back up, thrusting into Regina. She felt incredible, and I squared my stance so that I could support her weight and hold her legs still as I savored her depths.

"You feel incredible," I groaned and pumped into her.

With each thrust, I pushed Regina into Amira, and the black dragon sighed in pleasure and let out a cute little grunt. I was glad that they'd agreed to the moment before they'd eaten the monster. They were swimming in pure lust.

As if reading my mind, Regina pulled herself out of Amira and looked over her shoulder. Her eyes were shifted and she stared at me with a hunger I'd only seen in succubi.

"Don't be gentle, or I'm going to have to satisfy myself," she growled.

Knowing that more than a few of my mates liked it rough, I grabbed her hair again. I gripped close to the roots so that it was more about control and less about pain before shoving her into the pink grass and slamming my hips to hers, feeling just how wonderful she felt as I held her against the ground.

"Yes!" Regina shouted as I roughed her against the grass.

Little pink marks started to rub off on her shoulders as I pushed her into the grass. They looked like lipstick left from overly excited kisses.

Her excitement lit a new vigor in me, and I had to work to keep myself from releasing early. Pulling her hair back, I lifted her off the ground as I continued to thrust into her and nibbled on her neck, giving me something even more exciting to think about.

"Right here. I think I'll mark you right here." I rested my teeth against her shoulder.

She whimpered before letting out a roar of frustration as she tried to squirm, but I had her completely held off the ground. I used one of my hands in her hair to bend her backwards, while the other held her hips so I could continue to thrust into her.

"Harder."

I bit down harder and pushed myself roughly into her.

The dragon in me couldn't wait. I felt my jaw crackle as I raced against the clock. I needed to mark her just as badly as I needed to release inside of her.

"Harder!" she shouted.

Magic seared her shoulder as my teeth shifted, and I pumped like mad to finish inside of her as I branded her.

There was a palpable excitement between the two of us as she accepted my mark and I mated my red dragon.

Regina shuddered with a low growl, and I let the dam burst as I came inside of her.

"My mate," she whispered. There was a sense of defeat in her tone, but also a huge sense of relief.

I licked the wound as it healed over quickly, leaving a thin silver scar. "Mine."

I pulled out of her to see an overly excited Amira rush over and take my member, still slick with Regina's fluids, into her mouth in a single fluid motion.

Setting Regina down as carefully as I could, I sighed. Amira smirked around my cock as Regina kissed me fervently. Regina's lips were delicious as I let Amira suck my cock clean. The tall red dragon molded against me.

There was something special in the moments right after mating. It was a little period of peaceful bliss that was soon replaced with ravenous hunger from both of the other dragons.

Regina had more clarity in her eyes than she had before as she chuckled. "Let me help you with this one." She grabbed Amira and took control of the momentum. "Yes, that's it. You know who's in charge, don't you?"

I stood still and let the two of them work out their own pecking order. I was growing used to the dragons' need to assert power and figure out the hierarchy.

Amira let out a low moan. It wasn't even the slightest bit aggressive as she let Regina control her head.

"Now, be a good girl and draw his seed out. You have one minute," Regina instructed.

Amira's green eyes flicked up to me before she started going down on me with a frenzy.

I held onto the back of her head as she went as fast as she could, her tongue adding to the sensation as I drew deep breaths almost urging myself to cum for her.

"There, yes, right there." I tried to direct her as she hit a particularly sensitive spot, and she was quick to obey.

She curled her lip into the spot and went after it with a furious bobbing of her head.

I groaned in release.

Amira smiled as she slid off and opened her mouth to show Regina.

"Good. Swallow." Regina smiled, clearly pleased with her role.

Amira was still kneeling like a smitten puppy when I pushed her down onto the grass and settled over her. "Mine," I growled.

CHAPTER 14

"I mean, wow is all I can say. I didn't know dragon mating was so rough," Ikta laughed as we continued walking.

She hadn't stopped commenting since we'd started moving. It was growing dark and we'd been hoping to make it to the next town, but we were behind schedule for obvious reasons.

"Just the first time with a new mate." Amira blushed and touched the mark on her shoulder again as if trying to remind herself it was still there.

"Illuminating to say the least," Summer agreed.

Regina snorted. "Both of you already knew things about dragons. I've seen how you treat my mate." Regina tossed her hair and glared at Summer.

Both of the dragons were filled with confidence after getting their marks. It was as if they'd gone through something and came out the other side better for it.

I really needed to try to give them more attention. Yev was the only one of my dragon mates who really had as much access as the rest of my harem. Not that they were lesser in any sense, but their role in the harem was certainly more subdued. Larisa had been okay with it, and it seemed the rest of the dragons were as well.

I didn't know quite what to make of it, except that we'd have eternity together, and I'd just have to keep working on my relationship with them.

"Town ahead," Amira called out. Her eyes were shifted and staring into the distance.

"A bed would be nice. Some of us didn't spend most of the day on their backs," Ikta sighed wistfully.

"Quiet. We need a game plan for the town so that it doesn't end up like the last one." I really wanted a little sleep, and that wasn't going to happen if we entered with the same bang as before.

"Not turning into a giant dragon in the middle of town would be a start," Regina added dryly, a smile tugging at the corner of her lips.

"Funny. We'll stick out like sore thumbs, five non-demons in Hell," I said, my comment trailing off as Ikta snapped her fingers and became a succubus. She cracked a whip in the air for added effect.

I gave her a look. "Well, we can't all do that."

Summer pointed at me. "You should be able to put a glamor over all of us."

I started to argue and then sighed. "Fine."

Glamor was the biggest staple of fae magic. To produce glamor, it took layering the fae's perception of reality over the current reality. It was similar to making a portal, but I'd definitely practiced it far less. Which was the exact reason Summer was pushing me to try it.

I worked to imagine what I wanted to create, and then pushed my fae magic into that image. Finishing, I popped my eyes open to look at our group.

"Not bad." Summer glanced down at herself. "Is this what you imagine me wearing in your fantasies?" She raised an eyebrow.

I had enough shame to blush.

Summer had kept her general shape, but she was no longer wearing a perfectly fitting, flowing dress. Instead, she had on a pair of black stockings and nothing else.

"What? We are in the Pits of Lust. You've seen what these succubi wear," I tried to defend myself.

"At least you did better than Regina." Ikta glanced at the large dragon.

She had kept her stature but was stark naked with pasties over her sensitive areas.

"It seems that complex clothing is outside our mate's imagination." Amira glanced down at herself.

"He did just see us naked for a prolonged period of time," Regina pointed out.

Ikta pushed her magic out, and I let my magic embrace it, which wasn't too hard since part of her magic came from me now. She molded my glamors to include a little more clothing.

"Thanks." I smiled at Ikta.

"No problem, your majesty. This humble servant of yours just wanted to assist." She bowed low, her breasts hanging out of her outfit.

"Getting into the act?" I joked.

"Not at all. I'm your fae queen, you are my fae emperor." She bowed low and her hair dragged on the pink grass. "Besides, it's fun not to be in charge for once." She smiled while dragging her hair through the grass.

"Stop it, or you'll get pink grass stains in your hair," I observed.

Laughing, Ikta tossed her head back and forth, dragging it through the grass. "It's fine. Lots of the succubi have some pink in their hair. I think it's because they've been rutting in the grass." Ikta smiled and stood up, tossing her hair about. "Do I look like a well-fucked succubus now?"

"You look lovely," Summer was quick to reply and cut off further remarks in that direction.

"Thank you." Ikta played with her hair, inspecting the new pink marks.

"My mate. Maybe you should stay outside the city while we secure a room, then you can come join us with minimal interaction?" Amira offered.

I narrowed my eyes. "You think I'll cause trouble."

"You are kind of a magnet for it." Summer couldn't stop herself from smiling, but I could see that she agreed.

"Fine. Ikta go get us a place to stay. This town looks larger than the last. Regina, keep her out of trouble." I wanted the two of them paired up. Ikta was probably the best suited to go in and keep up my glamor if there were any issues, and Regina was dedicated enough to make sure the fae didn't cause trouble.

Amira would have worked too, but Regina had enough experience working with wild fae. I felt more confident she would be able to hold her own against Ikta's wiles.

"Of course, my king." Regina nodded and grabbed Ikta, both of them hurrying off in their succubus glamors.

I couldn't help but notice that the way Regina addressed me changed when I gave her orders.

"Well then." Summer dusted off her dress now that Ikta had fixed the glamor. "They'll be a minute. How about you take a rest?" She knelt down and patted her thighs, wanting me to use them like a pillow.

I rolled my eyes, but it did sound nice to take a rest.

***

"Did you mean what you said?" Regina asked as she hurried to the town with Ikta. The area was far larger than the little village they'd approached before.

"I say a lot of things, little dragon. You are going to have to be more specific," Ikta sighed. "I'm not a mind reader."

"About my king being your emperor." Regina didn't bother looking at the fae. Ikta had enough control of her emotions and body that she could easily falsify a facial expression.

"Of course." There wasn't an ounce of hesitation or deception in her voice.

"Why?"

"Change of course. There is pitifully little change in the grand scale of things, little dragon. My future husband brings great change. And that includes change that I want in the form of more dragons and more mana. But it also means change that none of us can predict. You have no idea how interesting that is. Finally, a bit of something new and exciting." Ikta's eyes shone with a brightness.

"You don't speak of anything like love," Regina pointed out.

"Oh. There is certainly the desire to be in his bed. I want to see what he'll do, and I want to be there to help him get to the next step so that he can show me more of what he'll change. Is not wanting to be with him over others yet another way to describe love?"

Now that Ikta was away from her mate, she spoke in the normal twisting ways of the fae. Even the nymphs had picked up the same mannerism, speaking more plainly around Zach.

It meant they cared enough about what he thought to change how they spoke, but it also made dealing with them when he wasn't around a little more frustrating after having gotten used to them speaking straight for once.

"You aren't wrong. But what would Zach think?" Regina asked.

Ikta scowled at her. "Don't try to use him to threaten me. I trust that he'd understand, though it might take him a moment. He understands my nature well enough. Choosing to be with him versus the array of all other options is love."

It was easy to forget how alien some of the ancient beings could be.

"Besides. We are here to find him a place to sleep before he can cause more trouble." Ikta waved away Regina's concern. "Let me deal with my relationship with my future husband. I've already given him the majority of my power."

"Did you really not have a way out of that?" Regina asked curiously.

"Trust cannot be taken. Only given. So, I gave him all of my trust and was rewarded with his in turn. Unlike you brutish dragons, I chose to submit to him already." Ikta licked her lips. "Sometimes giving in can be delicious."

Regina cleared her throat as she found herself watching Ikta's tongue. "Please. Focus on our task."

They were now fully in the midst of the bustling town. Demons were working all across the space, but not all of them were lust demons.

"Greed demons." Ikta wrinkled her nose at the sight of a few who looked almost human, but the parts of their bodies they'd haphazardly replaced with gold and jewels gave them away. The closer Regina looked, the more she realized it grew out of them almost like a tumor.

Ikta began to control her walk more, adding a swagger that mimicked the succubi. Regina frowned inside, but she did her best to follow Ikta's lead.

"Maybe when we return we should add a little more variety," Regina suggested.

"Not a bad idea. You walk more like one of the wrath demons." Ikta nodded to one down the street.

He was big, a nine-foot-tall wall of muscle scarred heavily from what looked like years of all-out war. The wrath demon was more red and less pink with black armor growing out of its body.

"Stop staring. Move." Ikta took a turn straight into a building. "Let me do the talking."

"Hello," a greed demon welcomed them. A diamond replaced one of his eyes, and chunks of his hair were gone. Little strands of gold and silver necklaces tried and failed to replace all of the hair. "You'll have to pay for a room tonight."

"No, we won't." Ikta focused instead on another demon who was sleeping against the counter. "Sleepy here is in charge. You just set up your spot to rip people off."

The greed demon scoffed and sized Regina up before backing down. "Big ass succubus."

"Some people like her thick, melon-crushing thighs," Ikta giggled quickly before waving him away. Then she sauntered over the counter and grabbed the hair of the sleeping demon. "Wake up." She smashed the demon's head into the counter several times before he stirred.

"Hmm?"

"We need a room, Sleepy." Ikta leaned down into his face.

"How'd you know my name?" The demon of sloth had black holes for eyes and started to hang his head, falling back asleep.

"Shut up. Room. Can we have one? I'll let you not do the paperwork," Ikta bargained.

The sloth demon managed a half wave before falling back asleep.

"Okay. We have a room. Easy." Ikta flashed her a smile.

"How did you know his name was Sleepy?" Regina asked.

"They are all named Sleepy because they are too lazy to come up with a decent name or remember their own." Ikta rolled her eyes and glared daggers at the greed demon. "Are you going to cause trouble when we come back?"

"Nope." The greed demon took up his perch and began shifting files and plants on the counter to hide the sloth demon further. He narrowed his eyes on Regina as she watched.

Regina stopped once they were out of earshot. "Thank you. Without your knowledge and help, I'd have not been able to navigate that so easily."

Ikta waved it away. "It was for him, not you. Besides, we are all a part of the Golden Plushie Society, no need to count favors. I'll help any of you."

Regina stood, baffled for a moment. There were different versions of Ikta, and it was hard to put them all together. Sometimes, Regina secretly thought that the ancient fae queen was lonely. Through all her words and excuses, she continued to help her mate and his harem. It was different than how she'd ever expected the queen of the wild fae to act.

And that in itself could be part of the trick. She could even be acting how Regina expected to try and slowly put her at ease.

A headache was forthcoming and Regina didn't care for it. Damned fae were always far too tricky. Regina knew she would tangle herself in knots trying to figure out what Ikta was really thinking.

"We have a problem," Ikta grumbled, stopping in the middle of the street.

"What?" Regina almost ran into the smaller woman.

Ikta pointed to a poster in the town and then tried to signal for Regina to look behind them quietly.

The poster had five silhouettes and a description of them, including the risk that they used magical disguises. And the most troublesome of all was the sizable bounty being offered by Beelzebub.

Regina glanced back to Ikta before letting her eyes rove the demons around them. A prickle of her senses came just in time for Regina to shove Ikta to the side and roll to the dirt.

A moment later, an ax passed through where they had been standing.

The big wrath demon that she'd spotted earlier was on the other end of the ax with eyes full of bloodlust. Unfortunately, he wasn't alone. A small group of demons had gathered to grab them.

With the added excitement of a fight, they were drawing more attention, and more were joining the circle.

"Ikta—" Regina wanted to warn her but then realized it wasn't them that was in danger.

Six spider limbs shot out of Ikta's back. Each of them had a little shimmer on the edge. Ikta's legs were like six scythes of the reaper. They moved quickly, each of Ikta's legs finding a target and cutting their head off with a single slash.

The wrath demon ignored the limbs, charging forward with Regina in his sights.

"Not so fast." Regina snapped a kick and buckled the demon's knee.

She'd expected that to slow him down, but all the demon did was roar and use its mass to slam her into the wall with the bounty poster.

"These fuckers." Ikta's spider limbs tore through the other demons. "Making a mess. What if I wanted to sneak into Zach's room tonight?! I can't do that covered in blood."

Regina wasn't in a position to reply, her air nearly cut off by the mass of the demon shoving her into a wall. She shifted her hands to claws before taking a chunk out of the wrath demon.

The wrath demon yelled again, his veins bulging as it gripped her shoulder, putting pressure down that reminded her of a dragon's jaw.

Regina let her horns grow out of her head and slammed them into the demon's face. There was a wet squish as she pulled her head back, waiting to see her mark.

But even missing half of his face, the wrath demon wasn't letting go. If anything, the demon was growing stronger.

"Oh, he's a tough one." Ikta's spider limbs skewered the demon's shoulders and pulled him up in the air before a third spider leg cut him in half from groin to head in a single go, emptying his entrails all over the ground.

"Uh... thank you?" Regina looked around them at the scene of wanton slaughter.

Ikta hadn't held back. Given how prone Ikta was to flirting and playing games, Regina had forgotten that she was in fact a terrifying fae queen.

"Thank me by cleaning this up. Then we need to lead our favorite dragon to the inn through another path." Ikta's limbs went back into her body.

"Wait, we are still going to stay in this town?" Regina thought it was better for them to move along.

"Of course. Now that we showed how terrifying we are, they won't touch us. At least, not until they send stronger people. We should be able to get some good sleep before then." Ikta waved over her shoulder.

CHAPTER 15

Ikta and Regina returned, finding me still laying in Summer's lap.

"Everything go okay?" I sat up, trying to interpret their faces.

"Perfectly fine. No real trouble." Ikta smiled wide enough to pinch her eyes together. Something about her smile and her words made me skeptical of her statement.

"You sure?"

"Yeah. Demons can be a little rowdy, but you just need to know how to handle them," Ikta continued.

Regina was purposefully keeping her face impassive, which was a telltale sign. But they were back, and neither looked like they needed major healing. I decided to let it all slide and not push.

"Okay. Lead on then." A yawn slipped out of my mouth. Summer's lap had been comfortable, but I hadn't been able to fall asleep.

"This way." Ikta waved us forward. "I got you a nice room to get some sleep."

"Nice is relative." Summer eyed the buildings while the nearby demons sized up our group.

I could pick out which type of demon each represented. It was clear based on their appearance. I was nearly sick with horror when I saw a female gluttony demon. Based on what Lilith had said, we would have turned Sabrina into something like the gross demon.

Gluttony demons were rotund, yet their skin was shriveled and sickly looking. It was odd how a being could look so starved and so fat at the same time.

"I'm not all about beauty, but I think it would be hard to love Sabrina if she looked like that," Ikta stated what we were all thinking out loud.

"Hush." I didn't want to antagonize the demons.

"They'll die if they so much as think about bothering me," Ikta snorted and tossed her pink-stained black hair.

I could tell that Regina was on edge, walking carefully at our side. My senses were tingling. Something more had happened earlier. Ikta led us straight to a building and past a counter where a greed demon leaned against the counter.

"That'll be half your soul, each, for a night."

One of Ikta's spider limbs shot out of her back and stabbed right into the demon's head before tearing straight through him and leaving a long gouge on the counter.

She huffed. "Some demons let their nature take over any common sense."

"Um. Is this how you pay?" I frowned.

"It's not his place. There's a sloth demon sleeping there." Ikta pushed some baubles off the counter and pointed to the sleeping demon.

I nodded, not exactly sure how lawless we could act before we caused real trouble and drew more demons down on us. "Okay. Then let's head up the stairs."

The brightly colored wood creaked like I'd expected underneath, and we climbed to the second floor, all slipping into a single room with two beds.

Ikta's spider limbs came out once more, and she drew silk from under her dress, making a small web over the door. While she worked on that, I started pulling food out of my bracer and handing it out to the others.

"So. Want to tell us more about what really happened?" I asked Regina while biting into my very meat-heavy sandwich. Based on the crunch of the pickles, I was fairly certain Nyske had made the food.

Regina glanced at Ikta who didn't react as she was busy with securing the door. "Well. We came, got the room. Then we were heading back to meet up with all of you, and we ran into a wanted poster describing all of us."

"Don't worry. The demons who thought they could take us are dead." Ikta smiled as she turned away from the door.

I stared at the webbed masterpiece. The door was thoroughly secured with webbing. I had no doubt that it was magically strong.

"You made that quickly." I was more interested in the webbing than anything to do with her killing demons.

"Of course. I can make lots of things with my silk." Ikta blushed.

I ignored her statement. "Do we need anyone to stay up and stand guard tonight?"

"Probably not the worst idea." Summer waved her sandwich around. "We are in Lilith's territory and working for her, but demons can be greedy. If there's a bounty for our heads, we should watch our back. Something tells me it will only grow worse as we continue."

"Beelzebub?" I asked.

"Sometimes the most obvious answer is the correct one," Summer agreed. "The question is how much resistance are we going up against and can we handle it?"

Amira looked at Summer like she'd gone mad. "We have two fae queens."

"Correct. And if they have a wanted poster of us, then they know that." I realized the problem. "Yet they are still sending people after us. You saw how powerful Lilith was."

"You cannot be worried. You are the Dragon King." Amira puffed herself up.

"I'm not worried," I refuted, but thoughts were still swirling in my head. Power could lead to blind spots. I wasn't going to underestimate cunning moves that could bring us down. "But they aren't worried either. If Lilith is on our side and she said she'd distract Lucifer, then that means we have Asmodia and Beelzebub to deal with. Two demons at Lilith's level very well might be a problem."

"Mammon will do anything for the right price," Ikta pointed out, sitting next to me and tore off the back half of my sandwich, eliciting a growl from me. "Hush. You have plenty of food. I watched your cute little nymphs shove it all in there."

"So, you think that Mammon will move in too." I thought back to the oddly sophisticated map she had drawn. We'd have to cross the Battlefields of Wrath before reaching the Hills of Greed and finally making it to the Pools of Gluttony.

If I were Beelzebub, and knew that Asmodia would make a move as well, I'd wait and see if the threat passed Asmodia before using whatever chip I was carrying to get Mammon to fight.

"Can we take flight?" I asked.

Ikta shook her head. "You'll travel faster, but not fast enough. It's better if we slip past Asmodia. Of the demon princes, she's very battle oriented. The demons in her domain are all going to be strong, and she's worse."

Regina nodded. "I fought a wrath demon in town. The more I hurt him, the stronger he became. I do not think fighting something like that on the scale of a demon prince is advisable, even for us."

"Okay, so we sneak through Wrath and then hurry the fuck through Greed. We can't teleport straight there, but we can teleport back the way we came." I frowned. "Tomorrow, we'll pick up the pace. We will use portals to jump forward as fast as we can."

"That's not a bad idea at all." Summer nodded. "If we get cut off, we can step back and find a new path."

"After we kill a few demons for daring to step in the Dragon King's path," Amira growled. It seemed that me being cautious bothered her.

"Sure," I murmured noncommittally. "Let's get some sleep. It sounds like today was a relaxing day compared to what is to come."

Regina nodded sharply and pulled Amira with her over onto one of the beds. Summer planted a hand firmly on my thigh to keep me in the bed I was already sitting on. She waved her hand as the two dragons nearly fell into bed, passing out promptly.

"Did you just knock them out?" I frowned.

"No. They were just that tired. All it took was a little nudge and a barrier to keep our conversation to ourselves." Summer's eyes pinched together with her smile.

Ikta joined us, sitting on my other side. "I would have just knocked them out. The black dragon is exhausted, even if she won't show it."

I rolled my eyes. "What did you want to talk about?" I asked Summer.

"About giving you a little of the summer fae. If Ikta has started, I'm afraid we must continue as well," Summer explained.

I frowned. "Why? I understand what you are all doing. You're trying to change a pattern in Faerie. That would mean ending the wars, ending the strife. But something's bothering me. The Dreamer seems motivated to also help us in this direction. What is her incentive?"

Ikta and Summer shared a look rife with meaning.

"How old do you think The Dreamer is?"

"Ancient old hag sounds about right," I grumbled a little too quickly. The Dreamer had manipulated me, and I held a grudge.

Ikta's eyebrow arched quickly as she dared me to answer the question she was about to ask wrong. "How old am I?"

"Beautiful," I answered like a smart man.

Ikta's eyes narrowed, but then she smiled. "He called me beautiful, Summy."

Summer rolled her eyes. "What about me?"

"Gorgeous." I couldn't reuse beautiful, and gorgeous fit Summer a little better.

"Which do you think is better?" Summer asked Ikta.

"Debatable. But gorgeous seems a little more thought out. I'll just have to accept that you win." Ikta shrugged.

"Back on topic," I tried to quickly move on. "Tell me about The Dreamer."

"She's a titan, Zach. Do you really think that her living as a giant flower that occasionally possesses a little blind nymph to speak to people is her normal form?" The look Ikta was giving me told me it very much was not.

"She's resting to conserve her strength," I realized, frowning. "She has been for a very long time. Nyske is one of the oldest fae, and it sounds like she rarely saw more than that."

"Long enough that her strength might not entirely be there." Ikta filled in. "Then she sees a pattern-breaking Dragon King who already has the heart of Maeve, the next Winter Queen, and demanded balance."

"So, she wants me to break patterns and free her?" I tried to piece everything I knew together.

"Freedom, in a sense." Ikta pursed her lips. "Why do you think none of us have been upset about her blessing? She's a nosy bitch, but what she did was for the good of all of Faerie. We think The Dreamer might be at the end of her life."

"What?!" I nearly shouted the statement, making me suddenly glad that Summer had erected the sound barrier. "She's going to die? But she holds Faerie together."

Summer nodded with pursed lips. "That she does. For now. But if there was a powerful force that she could use to anchor the pieces of Faerie, maybe there would be another option. Ikta, can you think of anything that could be that strong?"

Ikta put on a consternated expression. "Even some of the most powerful beings in the wilds are just that, powerful beings in the wild. They can't grow to the level of a titan to hold Faerie together. They certainly cannot do something about the whole mana situation that killed the titans in the first place. So even if they grew that powerful, they'd suffer the same fate. Oh! Oh! I can think of one."

I already had my head in my hands. "Me?" I looked up between my fingers.

"The son of two dragon gods, who's also the Dragon King and a pattern breaker. I mean, if I was a betting fae, I'd have to bet that of any options he would be the best to bear the burden. Bonus if he has lots of little dragons that stay in Faerie and solve the current mana starvation," Ikta continued.

"There's a very real problem with all of this though," I pointed out. "If what you are saying is true, then I let The Dreamer set it all into motion only to prevent Maeve from taking over Winter. I'm missing a third of what's needed."

"A setback," Summer agreed. "We are working with Maeve to remedy that. At worst, we'll need you to kill Winter."

I coughed. "Let's leave that as a last resort."

"Well, if Maeve fails, then her mother will likely kill her." Ikta shrugged.

"What?!" I roared and spun on Ikta.

"She's going to challenge her mother." Ikta shrugged. "That's sort of how it's done."

"While I'm away?" I narrowed my eyes.

"The Golden Plushie Society is behind her," Summer tried to talk me down, gently patting the air.

I was nearly wheezing, I was so worked up. I snorted several times trying to calm down.

"It was done on purpose while you weren't there. By the time we get back, Maeve should have challenged her mother," Ikta said. "She needs to do this herself. It is how it is done."

I was up and pacing by that point. "So. Maeve gets Winter under her control while I'm off helping Sabrina."

"And checking in on Hell. Lilith's comments all but confirmed the situation for me." Summer nodded. "The demons are starting to see the same issues as the Celestial Plane."

"The shrinking? That part of their plane collapses if the archangels leave?" I frowned. "If they haven't had a titan longer than Hell, why was the archangel that I fought so weak?" The situation seemed so different.

Summer shrugged. "He could have been a newly minted archangel, or justice could be one of the weaker attributes in heaven. That he was sent at all suggests he was the weakest. We are aware of Helena's mother and know she's likely to be more comparable to what we saw in Lilith."

"But to answer the question. Yes. Without a titan binding the Celestial plane, the void exerts pressure on the plane. It's like being in the middle of a grinder," Ikta explained. "A titan or something of comparable strength"— she pointedly focused on me—"could resist that grinding and ensure that nothing breaks down the plane."

"The archangels together are filling in for a titan?" I asked.

"Just so. They are probably more united than the demons." Summer nodded and patted the bed, encouraging me to stop my pacing and sit back down next to her.

I was going to refuse, but they both stopped talking, clearly waiting for me to follow the cue.

As soon as I sat down, Summer rested herself against me. "I apologize for not explaining it sooner. It was really only a theory between Ikta and me, but as things are progressing, we believe it is more likely."

"So, what of Heaven and Hell? What does Lilith want?"

"She is seeing that the death of sufficiently powerful demons is causing loss of territory in Hell," Summer explained. "It would be minor, but noticeable."

"Then what's going to happen if I kill Beelzebub?" I didn't want to collapse a huge chunk of Hell even if it was... well... Hell.

"A strategic loss," Ikta said. "The princes likely all know the situation, but Lucifer is too prideful to ask for help. Sloth doesn't care. They are the two strongest lords, from what we understand. Lilith comes in third, but she's using what is already in play to her advantage, which means you and your grudge against Beelzebub."

Summer picked up the explanation. "If you kill Beelzebub, a large part of his territory will likely be reclaimed by the void. It will show the rest of the demon lords, even the Prideful Lucifer, that there is a real problem that must be solved."

"The loss of a huge chunk of the plane should be pretty undeniable," I huffed. "So, you think I should bail or that I should keep going forward?"

"Push forward. Lilith gave you something you didn't know you needed." Summer put a hand on my chest where there was a lipstick mark that wouldn't go away. "I suspect she's playing her own games."

"Did she send Beelzebub to Earth to run amok?" I growled, wondering if Lilith was planning more than I'd realized.

"Unlikely," Ikta was quick to refute. "Each of the demon princes are playing their own game. She's just stealing their pieces to play to her own advantage."

"She's trying to make me do the same thing The Dreamer is, except here in Hell," I grumbled with a sudden understanding. "She wants me to hold Hell together?"

The fae queens shared a look.

"We are unsure. It is possible. But it is also possible she or Lucifer are going to try and take on the burden themselves. It could be Beelzebub is resistant and they need him removed."

I frowned. "But Lucifer is against me."

"So Lilith says," Ikta reminded me that demons didn't have the same compulsion not to lie. "We don't know if she speaks the truth or not, or if Lucifer is even involved."

I rubbed my forehead, feeling a headache growing with the potential for Hell's politics. But as I considered bailing, the reality of my lack of options hit me. I couldn't abandon Sabrina, and Lilith even took that option away by stealing her.

Yet, even if I had other options, I would have continued on this path. Saving Sabrina and killing Beelzebub were things I had come here to do long before Lilith and Hell politics came into play.

"We continue forward. This is how we save Sabrina. Anything else doesn't matter. But thank you for letting me know the score." There were beings that were thousands of years old playing a game that had been going on for ages. My own involvement was just the latest play by various beings far stronger than me.

I was catching up quickly, but I still had a lot to learn. "Heaven?" My mind made a few leaps of logic, and I wondered what they were going to do.

"Unknown," Summer said. "Helena's connection to her mother is tenuous at best. Love is a strong contender for the leader of Heaven as well." Summer sighed. "If she's hoping to use you, she's going about it in a very poor manner. Everyone knows you attract more dragons with gold." A hint of a smile tugged at her lips.

I went to roll my eyes but a yawn crept up on me.

"And it's time for our sleepy dragon to go to sleep." Summer pulled my head to her chest and then pulled us both down to the bed.

"Stupid big boobs," Ikta groaned. "Such a cheat."

"You are welcome to join us," Summer teased.

"Both of you shut it. I'm going to sleep." It had been a day, and their news had only made me more tired. I needed to be well rested for what was to come.

CHAPTER 16

I woke up comfortably snuggled, but as I tried to move, I found I was completely bound. My mind startled awake, and I began struggling like a bug trapped in a web as my brain tried to understand the situation.

It didn't take long to understand that spider webs had trapped me, my entire body bound in the magical web tough enough that, even as I strained, I couldn't break free.

From what I could tell, only my face and cock were free from the webs.

"You're awake. Perfect." Ikta crawled over me.

We were both suspended in the air on her webs.

"Summer finally fell asleep, so I get to have my way with you, little Dragon King." Ikta cackled and kissed my forehead. "You'll be nothing but a dry breeding husk by the time I'm done with you."

The manic glee in her eyes both chilled and excited me. Damnit.

"You like that." A soft hand cupped my cock. "You like that a lot." She pumped me a few times. "If you like it, then I'll just trap you here for eternity. Make a deal with Lilith to maybe let her share a little. Breed little dragons by the thousands."

"Ikta, what are you doing?" Summer blasted away the darkness and the magical shadows that had hidden the ceiling from my view.

"Roleplay. Am I doing it wrong?" Ikta's sinister gleam was gone, replaced by honest curiosity.

"No, you might have been doing it too right," Regina muttered from somewhere below us. "By the way my mate smells, he was at least a little afraid."

"No such thing as too right." Ikta rolled her eyes and focused on me. "This was fun though, right?" She pumped my cock again. "Unfortunately, they ruined the fun," she pouted.

"We need to get going," Summer reminded her. "Remember? Demon princes hunting us?"

"Fine." Ikta's spider limbs shot out and quickly peeled me out of the cocoon she'd created. "But I want to know, how'd you sleep?"

I blinked. "Surprisingly well. Wait, how long was I in that?"

"At least a couple hours," Summer replied for Ikta.

"Half the night." Ikta held a hand up and wiggled it. "Give or take half a night."

"So the whole night," I interpreted. "Well, we need to talk about consent soon. But then maybe we will try that again sometime."

"Really?" Ikta perked up. "Wonderful. Always fun to let out a little of my dark side."

"But that was roleplay," I clarified, eyeing the wild fae.

"Yeah. Roleplay." Ikta's smile wasn't entirely convincing as she fully freed me and the cocoon turned into a slide, placing me on my feet on the floor.

"You weren't going to work out a deal with Lilith and breed me for eternity." I frowned at her and picked off the last few wisps of spider silk.

"That was part of the roleplay." Ikta blinked in confusion.

"But you weren't actually going to do that," Regina asserted with a frown.

"Right..." Ikta trailed off and started walking away with a whistle.

Summer shook her head. "Either way, we need a portal out. There are a large number of demons watching the building. It'll be for the best if we can slip out of here as quietly as possible."

"Can do." I snapped my fingers and opened a portal back to the area where we'd been waiting for the ladies to check out the town last night.

Summer went through first, followed by Ikta, and I went with the dragons following behind me.

"Alright, let's start portaling. I'm hoping to speed this up." I took a breath to steady myself. It was going to take a lot of focus to travel by so many portals. "Ikta, we'll rotate."

In response, Ikta opened a portal as far as her line of sight could go. The other end of the portal was half a mile away. Using the portals, we were crossing great distances with only a few steps. I popped open a portal after going through hers. Each time we went through a portal, we jumped half a mile, and our march through Hell truly began.

***

"But that's roleplay," Ikta sighed, clearly frustrated.

"But the point of roleplay is that you wouldn't *actually* do it," Summer explained.

Ikta frowned. "That doesn't make sense. It would be far more real if I went through with the roleplay. Zach seemed happy enough."

"What makes it fun is the underpinning of safety that it isn't actually going to go too far." Summer had been trying to explain roleplay for a while.

I made another portal, and we all stepped through.

"How can you roleplay breeding him if you don't actually breed him?" Ikta's tone said she thought we were all the crazy ones.

"You just have sex with him, maybe a lot of sex. But it's made more fun with the roleplay," Summer tried to coach Ikta.

"Because he wants to be used as a breeding stud. So we should use him as a breeding stud. I bet Lilith would love that agreement. Lots of tasty lust mana in it too." Ikta made a slurping noise.

"But we don't actually involve Lilith," Summer said, checking to make sure the point was getting through.

"No. We use her. She'll help trap him here in Hell until there are enough dragons here to break the barrier." Ikta blinked as she stepped through her own portal confused.

"This is going nowhere," Regina grumbled. "Zach just wants the idea of being trapped in your sex dungeon spider webs, but not actually being trapped."

"Well, you kind of have to trap him to make it fun." Ikta rolled her eyes. "Otherwise, how is it fun if I just put a few spider webs on him and he pretends to be stuck?"

"No, wait. You're getting there. That's exactly it. Though, you can physically trap him to give him the sense of being stuck while talking about trapping him forever. But you can't actually involve Lilith and keep him imprisoned for eternity as a stud dragon." Summer looked optimistic she'd finally gotten through.

"Oh. So only keep him trapped for a little while to give the illusion." Ikta perked up, considering the idea. "A couple thousand years would be fine. That should give me plenty of dragons."

I groaned. "A few thousand years is not 'a little while'."

"Depends on your scale of time." Ikta stared at me like I was an idiot. "You're immortal. Once we use you as the glue to keep Faerie together, then you're going to be stupid immortal."

"Oh, right. I'll have the power of three fae queens, but I'll then be giving that power away," I reminded her.

"Still a lot of power. Not my fault you are going to give it all away, even if that's the smart thing to do. You still have the power of Faerie, which isn't nothing." Ikta frowned and stepped through another portal.

We had been going uphill for a while at that point. Only one group had tried to chase us, and they were soon left in our dust as we hopped through the next portal.

"Can we just get confirmation that if you get time with our king that he won't disappear for a thousand years?" Amira brought us back to the important topic.

"Mmm. I really don't think it's asking a lot. But fine, I'll only keep him for a few years. Surely that's fine." Ikta tossed her hair and charged through another portal.

"Days," Summer called out behind Ikta.

"Mmmhmm." Ikta's tone was non-committal.

"I promised her one week," I sighed. "When we get back, I think I'm going to end up fulfilling that. After checking on Maeve. So, you can all fetch me after a week if she tries to abscond with me."

"We do have that tracker now." Summer tapped her lips.

"Wait, what tracker?" I did a double take.

But none of the others seemed surprised.

"We had to have Nyske do it so that you'd never find it or be able to remove it." Ikta clapped her hands together. "It took a lot of haggling to get her to do it."

"Maybe I need to come to one of these society meetings." I frowned.

"No!" their chorus of voices rang out in unison.

"I mean. It's where we ladies discuss things. It wouldn't be a society meeting if you were there. It would just be a harem gathering that quickly turned into an orgy," Summer explained. "Besides, you'd derail our plans for world domination with your morals."

"All I hear are more reasons why I—" I cut off as I threw my body backwards and grabbed the edge of the portal. "Stop!"

"Oh. It's the end of the Pits of Lust." Ikta looked out. "You can fly. Why'd you stop?"

"Because I was suddenly hanging in midair. Make me another portal to the ground?" I asked.

Ikta winked and a portal opened underneath me. I let go and landed on the withered grass of the Battlefields of Wrath. Only then did I really take in the surroundings.

Ikta let out a whoop as she jumped through the portal, followed by the others. "It's ugly as shit." She stared around at the area.

And as I looked out, I had to agree. The Battlefields of Wrath were patchy spots of struggling grass with bare, hard-packed dirt everywhere. The colorful Pits of Lust had been far more appealing to the eyes. Above us, the sky shifted to angry red clouds that crackled with thunder.

"Eew we don't want to get caught up in a storm." Summer frowned at the clouds.

"Why?"

"It rains blood." She wrinkled her nose, quickly followed by everyone else.

"I vote we avoid the storm too." Regina was quick to cast her vote.

"I don't know, some blood rain could be kind of fun. There's roleplay we can do with that too, right, Summy?" Ikta smiled up at the blood-filled clouds.

"No. I am vetoing all roleplay that involves blood rain. Let's get moving and avoid that storm." I popped open another portal.

Ikta sighed. "Boring." But she joined me in continuing to portal hop away from the storm and didn't divert us.

"What's that?" I noticed a change up ahead on the plane. It was something different than the typical dying grass and hard-packed dirt. Shifting my eyes, I jumped through the next portal and got a better look.

I braced myself. Demons were marching in a large formation.

"We should avoid that." I made another portal to go around and stepped through, only to end up right in front of them. "What the..." Before I could go backwards, my group piled through the portal.

"You mess up?" Ikta teased. "Itching for a little fight?"

"No, they have that." I pointed, and the formation was carrying a large, enchanted pillar that I felt pulling at my portal. "It's drawing portals to them. That means Asmodia knows how we are moving faster. Doesn't look like we can ignore this one."

Summer's hand shone like she was holding a sun. She opened her hand and golden flames shot out to burn a chunk of the demons. Not to be outdone, Ikta's spider limbs shot out of her back, but rather than fighting like Summer or Winter with magic from behind, she charged into the demons.

I growled and threw my clothes into a pile before shifting into my hybrid form. The wrath demons were large enough that I needed to pack on a little mass. My form stopped growing at around nine feet tall, with gold scales covering me head to toe.

Goldie slid down my hand and formed a sword while I pulled out one of the silver swords from the archangel of justice. Properly armed, I charged into the demons, my dragon pleased at getting back into battle.

I figured the holy sword had to have some properties against demons. At the very least, it was enchanted to be effective against all manner of paranormals, which was mostly achieved by being able to slice through most anything.

"Zach!" someone shouted behind me, but I didn't pay it much attention as the howling of the demons filled the space between my ears.

Each of them was a huge seven-to-eight-foot wall of muscle, carrying an array of chipped and worn weapons. They barely wore any clothing, instead showing off their red flesh crisscrossed with gray scars, like they cared for nothing but battle.

I roared as I met the demons. Goldie and the celestial blade were suddenly locked in a competition over how many demons each could kill. My blades flashed silver and gold as demons fell before me.

Morgana's training kicked in and I stabbed, slashed, and mowed through the demons like a machine. Every time I killed one, it pissed me off. These ants dared to step into my path, to call me to them with that pillar like I was some sort of dog. I would exterminate all of them.

Ikta was fighting her way towards me as her six spider limbs tore through the big, scarred demons. There was the faint glow of her fae magic on the edge of each bladed leg. I realized it was similar to the edge of a portal that I'd used to cut before, but she'd focused it more precisely.

It was no wonder she tore through them.

I blocked a demon, breathing fire in his face before cutting him from head to groin with the silver celestial blade. My mind roared at the idea that he would challenge me. Soon the roar exited my mouth as I began to continue cutting through the demons in a frenzy.

Clearing through a few more, I spotted a bigger than normal wrath demon. It kicked its feet like a bull a few times before it charged through the other demons. I could feel that his strength was enough to scratch an itch and give me a challenge, and I eagerly waited for him to reach me.

He swung a maul high in the air, and the force actually launched him above his peers before he came hurtling down at me. Rather than use my swords, I roared and turned my dragon horns into a battering ram as I met his maul with my horns.

It hurt like hell, but this was battle!

Bloodlust ran through me as I skewered the demon with both swords. Then I ripped them out of his side, gore and guts spilling out around us. Pulling his body off my horns, I latched onto his head with my maw, ripping it free.

I roared around the head in my mouth before I melted it with death breath and returned to skewering demons. The larger demon hadn't been strong enough to be a worthy adversary. I went in search of a larger demon.

I fought through the masses, killing the lower order pest demons in my search. I desperately wanted to satiate the bloodlust filling my chest. My movements were frenzied until I spotted the largest wrath demon yet. She was leading a second army straight for us, and my eyes lit up with glee.

More! More battle!!

I roared and pointed my sword at the oncoming horde of demons, shouting and trying to get the rest of the demons riled up to fight the next army. With me leading them, it would be a slaughter, even with that giant demon leading the charge.

Nothing could stop me. These demons dared to think that I could be beaten?!

I'd slaughter all of them.

CHAPTER 17

S ummer clicked her tongue. She'd held Amira back while the other three charged into the mass of wrath demons, watching as they slowly lost themselves in the fight.

Although, Ikta was questionable. She may have retained as much sanity as she'd had before charging into the fray.

"Men and war. They love it a bit too much," Summer observed.

"What's wrong with my king?" Amira tensed up.

Zach was currently ripping heads off like a child with too many toys and not enough rules.

"He's fighting in the middle of a bunch of demons of wrath. Wrath has seeped into him, and he's going completely battle crazy," Summer sighed. "But we have options."

"He's killing all of them. They are too weak to stand before my king." Amira held her head aloft and Summer narrowed her eyes, wondering if the girl had picked up some emotional magic from watching the battle.

"They aren't the trap. They are just the bait." Summer pointed upfield, where the second army led by Asmodia was marching hard to reach them before Zach finished the rest of the bait army.

"Oh. That's a big demon." The black dragon deadpanned. "Very big."

"Zach will rise to meet her in battle. We'll see how it goes." Summer twirled her hair. "If Asmodia starts to pull ahead, we'll get Zach out of here. You and I will serve as backup. This fight might be more than our favorite dragon can chew, especially if he is not thinking rationally."

"What kind of odds do you think he has?" Amira paid attention to the battle fomenting in the distance.

"I'd give him 50/50. We aren't really sure how strong the demon princes are. And much of this fight will come down to that fact. But we do know Zach, and he is strong. It will be a good fight," Summer observed.

"And we'll be able to save him if it doesn't go well. Right?" Amira narrowed her eyes on Summer.

"We have a few plans." Summer smiled but didn't give away any more details.

Zach started enlarging his hybrid form until his weapons were nothing but little toothpicks as he rushed to fight Asmodia with a manic roar.

"You sure? Pretty sure there's nothing you can do to get him to walk away from that fight." Amira seemed less than sure.

"Oh. There are a few things that Zach likes more than violence."

**

The big demoness and her army were bearing down on me. Finally, I had a worthy adversary. The rest of the demons had proven themselves worthless, easily cut down by my blade. Ikta and Regina were next to me, both wearing identical smiles to mine.

I was vaguely aware of Summer and Amira nearby, each of them spotless from battle. I had a flash of anger seeing them not fighting alongside us, but it cut off quickly. I couldn't be angry at my mate.

Another wave of anger rippled over, this time coming from the giant demoness. My head snapped to meet her eyes.

"Fuck you," I spat and felt mass pack onto me, growing me into a glorious red and gold knight large enough to take on the giant demoness.

Somehow, her being bigger than me was an affront to everything I stood for. Growing so large was a strain, but rather than continuing the shift to my dragon form, I tried to stuff the mass all into my hybrid form, becoming bigger and bigger.

My silver sword became too small, so I put it back in my bracer before sending mental commands to Goldie. She struggled, and I could feel all she needed was more 'encouragement'.

"Grow dammit. You've eaten enough of my gold to grow!" I demanded of the elemental and squeezed it.

It responded by gurgling before growing into a golden short sword that fit my grip, but it felt like the little elemental was at its limit.

I roared in frustration, but there was nothing more to be done. The demon's army was upon us, and it was time to fight. My roar turned into a blasting fire that torched the front line of the demon army.

Some of the demons turned into charred crisps, but many of them weathered the fire, continuing their angry charge. I crushed the remaining demons with a stomp of my giant foot before throwing myself at the demoness.

Her ax was far too large for me to have any hesitation. I knew how to fight against an ax. Morgana had trained me, after all. Knowing the right tactic, I rushed inside the blade's range.

The giant demoness countered by opening her mouth, a rush of black flames filling my vision. They rushed over my face, failing to find a hold.

Grinning through the flames, I swung my sword to cleave into the demoness's side, but my blade moved through nothing but air, never finding any resistance. I stumbled forward and the demoness hit me from the side, picking me up and slamming me down on the army below us.

With a thought, Goldie turned into a much smaller knife, and I punched it repeatedly into the demoness' side as I held on with my other claw and rolled us over.

She was red in the eyes when I saw her next. She roared and gouged my face with her horns while her own claws started to tear into my side, ripping scales off by the giant fistful.

My teeth snapped down on the demoness's throat, and I tore a huge chunk off, only for the demoness to smile. Her fist crashed into my chest, throwing me off of her and up into the air.

The strength behind her fist had been startling. I hadn't met much that could match me in strength, and I was fairly certain at the moment that she was stronger. Just thinking about the force required to throw something my size was terrifying.

I crashed down onto the demon army and rolled to my feet as the giant's ax cleaved into the ground, creating a gouge in the landscape.

"Dragon King!" the demoness roared. "I am Asmodia, your opponent." She pointed her ax at me as her wounds turned into scars before my eyes.

I had my own healing, but it was nothing compared to what I watched her body manage. Not wanting to talk and let her wounds heal more, I charged. But I ended up having to stop short of her ax swing.

Pivoting my hips and twisting, I grabbed hold of the ax handle and pulled it away from her. Asmodia's eyes were a mixture of surprise and delight as I lifted her off the ground and slammed her body into the ground with her own momentum. Her ax went spinning off into the distance.

More of her army was smashed to bits with the hit, and I snapped a kick at her head. Seeing the hit coming, she rolled away, only getting a scratch that quickly became a scar.

Before I knew it, she was on me, and we traded blows like two giant boxers. Goldie wrapped around one of my fists, short golden spikes protruded out so that I could wound the demon prince with more than just bare knuckles.

Asmodia was skilled, and she knew that she'd regenerate a lot of the damage she took. It made her fighting style aggressively offensive.

It wasn't greatly different from fighting Morgana who also had incredible regeneration, except I couldn't overpower Asmodia. Instead, I snapped a kick at her thigh, letting my clawed feet destroy the inside of her leg and ruin her stance while it healed.

I followed up with my next hits. I got her with a right cross and a left hook, snapping her head back for the right haymaker that cracked the bones in her face and knocked her off her feet.

"Envoktus," I growled, summoning a storm of lightning. Not hesitating, I poured the lightning into the demoness the second it was harnessed.

Asmodia screamed under the pressure of the lightning but got to her feet, the burns healing and the soot falling off as she stood back up. But she wobbled slightly as Regina came crashing in, tackling Asmodia in her red dragon form. Regina locked her jaw around Asmodia's hand, thrashing her head and trying to rip it off.

Joining Regina, I jumped into the fray. Goldie became a butcher's cleaver as I slammed it down on the arm that Regina was working on.

One. Two. I hacked at the wrist until Regina ripped it off.

Asmodia stumbled back with a gushing wound but that didn't stop the battle maniac from smiling. "Die!" Asmodia shouted as she rushed us both.

Regina rushed ahead of me, bounding on all four. Asmodia's knee caught the dragon square in the head, cracking something and sending the red dragon sprawling on her side.

Watching Regina take the hit made me angrier as I slammed into Asmodia, bringing the cleaver to her shoulder. Her lighter wounds had healed quickly, but her arm wasn't growing back.

I could rip her to shreds, hack her into a thousand pieces for hurting my mate. Asmodia fought back, tearing through my scales, crushing them to dust with her ever-growing strength.

The warm blood ran down my side, but I couldn't feel a lick of pain through the anger that had overwhelmed me. My sole focus was hacking Asmodia to pieces. And based on her face, the demoness was taking sick pleasure in the entire fight.

I smashed my horns into her face and gored her before shoving her back, only for her handless arm to clamp down hard as she crushed me to her side. Asmodia held me fast in place, and for a second, I felt a panic rise up in me that I truly wouldn't be able to escape.

But a moment later, Ikta shot between the two of us, her spider limbs splayed out. Ikta cut down onto the shoulder of the arm holding me. She didn't completely sever it, but it was enough that Asmodia wasn't able to apply her full strength.

Using the weakness to my advantage, I clamped down on her arm with my maw and tore it the rest of the way off. As soon as I tossed her second arm aside, I bellowed in victory, warning the rest of the demons that I, the Dragon King, was not to be trifled with.

I looked down, noticing that even with both her arms completely removed, Asmodia was all smiles. Her arm I'd torn off was growing back slowly. I studied her. I didn't understand how she could be smiling in her current situation.

Black flames shot up into the air above us, quickly making an enchantment in the sky.

Fuck.

I opened a portal behind me and stepped into it, trusting Ikta to protect herself.

A moment later, a mile away, the enchantment finished and a giant ram made of black fire crashed down where I had been standing. Even from the distance the portal had moved me, I could feel the heat.

Summer stood out like a sore thumb, her gold flames shielding her and Amira. As for Regina and Ikta, I had no idea where the two had ended up. I just hoped it wasn't in the center of the raging fire.

"Zach. We are leaving." Ikta landed on my shoulder.

"No. I can win," I growled.

"You are bleeding everywhere, and we got what we came for," Ikta tsked on my shoulder.

"We did?" I frowned and turned back to Asmodia, who had a taunting smile that I could see from all the way from where I stood.

"Yes. We need to go." There was steel in Ikta's voice.

Despite her resolve, I paused. A wave of anger passed over me again and I wanted nothing more than to charge forward and lock myself in battle with Asmodia once again. If I just got angrier, I could kill the demoness and this would all be so much easier.

A low growl built up in my chest, and I heard Ikta sigh.

"Zach. Look! Gold!" A giant gold coin bounced on the ground with a jingle that was so loud and deep that it felt like it shook the whole world.

"Gold!" I shouted and jumped forward as a portal snapped in place in front of me. I fell through, landing on all four. My claws raked the dirt as I came to a stop next to Regina, still in her dragon form and torn to hell.

Her wounds pulled my attention away from Ikta and the gold. "Regina." I put a giant clawed hand on her and gently shook her.

She groaned and her eyes blinked open. "You look half dead, my king."

I glanced down, taking in my current state for the first time. Huge chunks were missing from my side, and even though I was red and gold, my blood had made me almost entirely crimson.

As my anger started to fade, it was replaced by a weariness that went far beyond the physical. I knelt on the ground and let myself shift back to my human form before I bled out.

***

"I can't believe that worked." Amira blinked as Ikta walked out of a portal next to her and Summer.

"Of course it did. He was being juiced with so much wrath that I just needed a momentary distraction." Ikta shrugged. "Besides, Asmodia was feeding pretty badly on him."

Summer snorted and stared out over the battlefield.

There had been so much death, with no real purpose. The demon prince had wanted to test the Dragon King. And Asmodia was still alive, eyeing them from afar with a crazed smile.

"Summy, want to let loose a little before we leave?" Ikta asked.

"I think it's about time that these demons stop underestimating us," Summer agreed and held her hand aloft.

Fae magic was simple in theory, but incredibly complex in practice. The fact that Zach had mastered portals so easily and was able to do visual glamor was impressive.

But what Summer was about to do had taken hundreds of years of practice.

Summer forced her will upon Hell and demanded reality be remade for her. "Get Amira out of here; our man likely needs healing."

"Jump," Ikta barked and Amira jumped, only to scream as she fell through a portal.

"Can you be serious for a moment?" Summer grumbled and focused back on her magic.

"No. There's nothing fun to be gained from being serious. Besides, she screamed," Ikta laughed and looked on at her magic. "Not bad."

Summer's mental image snapped into place and her golden flames poured out of her to form a giant avatar of burning gold. Zach had put up a strong fight against Asmodia. Summer wasn't going to let it all be for naught. And Summer had something for that. It wouldn't be fair for Asmodia to come back completely unscathed for their rematch.

Asmodia roared in challenge at the avatar and rushed it. Summer could trade blows with the demon lord, but that wasn't why she had come.

The avatar drew a sword, and Summer used her own body for it to mimic the motion, slashing out like she was holding a sword. The avatar mimicked her, slicing several shallow cuts in Asmodia. Then Summer poured everything that the avatar was through the sword, and golden flames leapt from the blade into Asmodia's severed arm.

The demon lord screamed. This time, the wail wasn't full of rage, it was full of true pain. The gold flames scoured every inch of the stump, searing and burning away any magic it found in the arm and withering it with the blistering heat of summer that not even the demon prince's healing could overcome in the short term.

A huge chunk of the skin turned into black, powerless charcoal, and Summer staggered back a step and wiped her brow. No matter what Asmodia had or did, she wasn't going to heal that stump for years to come.

Zach's fight mattered.

"It's time we go, unless you want to play a little more." Summer stood straight.

"No. I just really wanted to watch the giant dragon pounce on the giant coin," Ikta snickered. "Off we go."

Ikta made another portal on the ground. Summer rolled her eyes and fell through with a weak yell to satisfy Ikta.

***

After Summer fell through, Ikta was alone with the demon lord, who was still wailing from Summer's attack. And Ikta was not one to be outdone.

Ikta closed the portal for a moment. "You are good for my future husband, but only as a whetstone. You banged him up good, and I need you to be nursing your wounds for just as long, if not longer."

Ikta hadn't spent the whole battle killing nameless demons.

She grabbed the air in front of her, where she'd been leaving impossibly small threads of magic in the air and pulled. Flares of purple magic tore through the giant demoness, ripping off chunks of flesh. The magic cut off the demoness' other arm as well as both of her legs, causing her to topple over and come crashing down to the ground hard enough to make Hell shake.

Ikta stood close to the limbless torso and head before kicking the demoness in the forehead. "Be thankful that you are valuable for my future husband to use to grow stronger. It's the only reason I don't just kill you just to remind Hell that the Spider Queen once walked Hell and you all knelt to me."

"You have the young Dragon King in your web," Asmodia observed. "One day, he'll resent you for that."

Ikta snorted. "All I've ever done is play tricks. It's just that I'm playing tricks for my future husband now. He's still young and needs challenges like you to push him. You should fear the day that I stop playing tricks and stay at home knitting socks for all my children. Because that's the day he won't need my strength." She snapped open a portal and jumped.

"Catch me!" Ikta called out as she dropped with a giant smile on her face.

CHAPTER 18

Ikta fell on me with a giggle.

"Oof," I groaned.

"You were supposed to catch me," she pouted atop me.

I had seen Summer show up a moment before Ikta, who then had taken a moment to show up. "What did you two do?"

"Just threw a large attack at Asmodia to keep her from healing." Summer waved away my concern, glancing at Ikta with a question in her eyes.

"Oh, just some posturing and a little more damage." Ikta shrugged. "Cut off her legs so that she couldn't chase us. Doubt she's very fast without legs."

I snorted a laugh that then made my whole body hurt. Everything hurt.

"Could you have killed Asmodia?" I asked.

Ikta nodded her head. "Yes. After you softened her up, it would have been easier to mess with her when she wasn't paying attention. But I don't want to have the power of Wrath in me, nor do I want to finish your fight."

"Thank you for being honest," I grunted. "Should I take the power of Asmodia if I get the chance?"

"Yes," both fae queens replied at the same time.

Ikta smiled wide. "She's pretty powerful, and I think this is what Lilith secretly wants to happen. Otherwise, she'd be working harder to block them. There aren't even her agents working around here."

I sighed and nodded. There were more complex games being played around my disturbance of Hell than I'd like. But I'd get what I needed.

Amira got up from where Regina was laying naked in the pink grass, and my attention shifted over to the healer to get a report.

Amira met my eyes, knowing my question. "She'll be fine, but she needs rest. She's had her mana drained pretty badly, along with some heavy injuries in her dragon form." Amira walked over to me, once again studying my wounds. "That you are awake right now is actually pretty incredible. We saw Asmodia feeding on you that whole fight, and you were more wounded than whole by the time Ikta got you to pounce on the coin like a cat being teased by a laser pointer."

"I did not look like that," I grumbled.

"You kind of did," Ikta giggled and sat down next to me. "But I've been looking forward to using that trick to snap you out of a demon's emotional hold for a while."

"Been keeping that in your pocket?" I asked.

"You know, the demons were doing emotional manipulation to you and your dragon. I figured greed would snap you out of anything else if we had the chance." Ikta batted her lashes at me with false innocence.

I sighed and let go of my annoyance over being simplified down into some brainless, gold-obsessed simpleton. "Asmodia was getting stronger during that fight. Was that because she was feeding on me?"

"In part." Summer joined our little circle as Amira focused on me, putting her hands against my skin and then pulling away, like she was pulling something out of me. "Wrath demons gain power from anger, and getting injured is a good way to get angry."

I nodded and focused on Amira. "So, how does healing work for you? I can lob death magic, but not heal."

"That's because you don't use death magic exactly. For me, I see the death in your body in patches, and then I think of the death as gathering into a knife that I pull out of the wound." She frowned at my side and made another pulling motion. "You know, like pulling the knife out before the wound can heal on its own. Works well with paranormals who have their own enhanced healing."

It was a very simple way to think of healing magic. I thought it fit Amira well.

"Mind if I check over Regina?"

"Go for it." Amira shifted so that I could switch spots with her and focus on the unconscious Regina.

While Regina slept, her face was far softer than most of her awake time. I smiled, taking her in. Then I shifted my eyes and tried to look her over for death mana. "I don't see anything."

"Unless she's bad or hit with death magic, you won't see anything." Amira explained. "You'll have to focus and draw the death to a clump out of her."

Putting a hand over Regina, I focused, not really able to sense much. But from what Amira said, she'd made Regina stable, so it would probably be difficult to see the bits that remained.

So instead, I tried to breathe in death magic.

That was the best way I could describe it as I tried to suck any remaining death magic out of Regina. I took a deep breath that went on forever as I felt my aspects change to black and copper. I watched as little streams of faint dark-colored magic pulled out of Regina's body and into my mouth.

"Stop that." Amira hit the back of my head.

"What? I was drawing it out," I growled.

"Yeah. You were drawing death magic through her entire body!" Amira huffed. "Do you think we concentrate it before pulling it out for no reason?"

I felt properly chastised and focused again on Regina. "So, I should concentrate it and then draw it out," I muttered. Rather than breathing with my mouth, I tried to use my magic. I made a small ball in her body and then pulled it out.

"Better," Amira said. "Moving death around in a body is dangerous. Someone like Trina has knowledge and skills using her magic enough that she can draw it through pathways in the body to do the least amount of damage that she could."

"Meanwhile, I'm just a brute trying to heal with a sledge hammer approach to my magic?"

"At least you know it," Ikta laughed.

I pushed the comment aside and focused on Regina. I wanted to help, and I liked feeling useful. Time after time, I pulled death from Regina. It seemed like a smaller amount was accumulating between each time I tried to heal her.

As I let Amira work on me, I soon exhausted my ability to heal Regina and looked up, realizing I had no idea where we had portaled into.

"We are in the Pits of Lust. But where?" The pink grass was a dead giveaway, but we were in the middle of two hills.

"The boob mountains," Amira grumbled.

Ikta laughed. "It's the Pale Mounds."

"Same difference." Amira rolled her eyes and looked down at her own chest before glaring at the two fae.

"Maybe we should look around, to ensure there are no surprises." Summer grabbed Ikta and pulled her up to go for a walk.

Amira waited until they left before she spoke. "My king. Ikta could have killed Asmodia. Are you sure we can trust them?"

My head snapped up at the question. "Of course we can trust them."

"But she could ha—"

"Amira. Ikta and Summer are their own people with their own goals. They saved my life, and you are upset that they didn't do more?" I growled.

"They work for you. If she—"

"That's where you are very very wrong, Amira. They do not work for me. Both of them have my best interests at heart and have proven it time and time again. By not killing Asmodia, they left her for me."

"When they could have fought with you and defeated the demon prince." Amira was dead set that they were in the wrong; I wasn't sure what I could do to change her mind.

But I also knew that Amira's parents hadn't raised her to be independent. She was fiercely loyal and used to following orders. She was a soldier, so she might not ever understand Ikta and Summer.

"They want me to grow stronger. Both of them are heavily invested in me being powerful enough to hold together Faerie. Right now, they think Lilith wants me to help hold Hell together too."

The thought only piled more on my shoulders. "To make matters worse, those two are right. If they can't hold together these planes, how can I?" I pursed my lips and waited.

"But you are the Dragon King," Amira replied quickly and confidently. She really believed I could do anything I put my mind towards.

"I'm not a god, nor a titan," I told her calmly. "Both of those fae queens could probably take me if I forced a fight with them. Either way, all of us wouldn't be in a state to walk away. Same for these demon princes. What does that mean for the archangels and what happens when the titans come around for another pass at me?"

Amira frowned. "You are still a young Dragon King. In a few years, you'll tear them all to pieces for looking at you wrong."

I shook my head. "Not if I don't keep growing. And to grow, I need to fight and win against targets like Asmodia." As I spoke, I felt even more confident in my words and the actions of the two fae queens.

Unlike Amira, I was thankful that Ikta hadn't just solved my problems. There would be a point where she could not, and either I would be ready when that time came, or I wouldn't and we would all suffer.

"I do not like it, my king. But I do trust you." Amira found her own way to make peace with the situation.

"Good. Then since I'm in charge, keep watch. I'm about to pass out." The exhaustion was catching up with me quickly, and I lay down hoping that I would succumb to sleep.

But something kept nagging at the back of my mind, and I pet Goldie. "Sorry for being a jerk." I pulled from my exhausted mana stores and fed Goldie.

"Hurts. Hungry," Goldie said in a small voice.

"I'm sorry. There's no gold here, but I'll give you what mana I can right now." I said.

"Goldie weak." My bracer sniffled. "Goldie failed."

"You didn't fail," I said, looking over my shoulder at an Amira who watched me with a glare that told me I should be getting some sleep. "You did good, Goldie, I'll have to help you get stronger."

"Goldie won't fail next time you need a bigger weapon." The elemental had a stubborn tone that reminded me of a determined child.

"Sure you won't. I need to rest." I fed a trickle of mana to Goldie, but I couldn't spare much as my body was consuming most of it to help recover all the damage I'd received.

***

I wiggled my nose, smelling smokey, cooked meat.

"Oh, he's up," Ikta called out, and I could feel the smile in her voice.

I cracked open my eyes. "Smells good."

"Your hunter went hunting. Figured that'd be one way to get you up." Ikta pointed at Regina who had a giant slab of meat over a fire.

"What's that?" I asked, my instincts perking up.

"We are calling it demon boar," Regina answered. "There's a lot more where that came from. Lugging the thing back was hard, so I hope you enjoy it."

I glanced at the meat. "You realize what this is going to do to me, right?"

"We don't mind," Ikta piped up.

I rolled my eyes, but after the fight with Asmodia, I needed any nourishment I could get, even if it took away from future sleep. "By the way, how long did I sleep? Regina should have been out for a while."

Ikta paused. "A little over a day. Did you know you snored?"

"He doesn't snore," Summer sighed. "Stop trying to cause trouble." She turned her attention to me. "Your mana was severely depleted. But you should be well on your way to recovery. Dragons aren't too bothered by mana depletion."

"That's what killed most of the titans, yeah?" I asked, tearing into the meat and knowing that lust was going to wash over me. As I ate, I did my best to resist the pull of the lust and continue through the conversation as if everything was normal.

"Yes. But titans aren't dragons. They aren't just infinite fonts of mana."

"You are kind of a cheat," Ikta blurted.

"Don't you get mana from your land?" I asked.

"Every paranormal that 'makes' mana does it from something. Even phoenixes, the flaming pigeons that they are, just convert their previous life into mana. It's a net positive, but a long process." Summer seemed grumpy just thinking about phoenixes.

I knew that some had tricked her previously, escaping a fae deal by dying and being reborn.

"He's a cheat. It's okay." Ikta took some of the meat and delicately ate it while bouncing her brows at me.

"Careful there, Ikta," I warned. "Why are dragons cheats?"

"There are more theories than we could go over in a night. But suffice it to say, dragons are special and we don't fully understand why. Your parents might actually be the best people to ask one day if you really want to know." Summer shrugged.

I chewed the meat slowly, focusing on keeping myself in check. "Well, that aside. I slept for long enough. How hard was it to find the boar? I should probably do what I can to recover and train before heading back that direction. What are the chances that Asmodia is waiting for me?"

Ikta shrugged. "Probably pretty slim right now. But we have Mammon and Beelzebub ahead. If you are afraid of Asmodia, chasing down Beelzebub is probably not the best idea."

"Training?" Regina asked.

I pointed at the meat. "Trying to resist the emotional manipulation of lust. Half the reason I lost was because I let Asmodia draw me into her way of fighting."

The consequences of losing control to lust were far less severe compared to the other emotions of Hell. It made it a great tool to train.

"That's a wonderful idea. I could even do a striptease to increase the difficulty." Ikta smiled, jumping to her feet and starting to play with the shoulder straps of her dress.

I put my head in my hands. "Maybe we should start on easy."

"That's a great idea." Ikta thankfully stopped, but she turned to Summer. "You should do the striptease. He wants to start with the less tempting ladies."

Golden fire shot from Summers fingertips and chased Ikta as she fled through a portal.

"You and Ikta are getting along just fine." I smiled at Summer, knowing that the magic she had just used was her having fun. If she really wanted to hurt Ikta, she could have done far worse.

"She and I have come to an understanding. With Winter in denial that she is about to lose her throne, Ikta is the one who understands me best."

I nodded, saddened by Summer losing a rival and peer in Winter.

"Well. She's keeping you on your toes, but do me a favor and save the teasing. Jokes aside, I'm not sure I could handle it right now." I felt a warmth spreading through my abdomen and the feeling of a rising tingle in my pants.

I paused. I'd passed out naked. Somebody had dressed me.

"That she does. Ikta might not do things in a pre-dictable, or even consistently insane, manner. But she seems to always make everything work out in her favor," Summer spoke with a thoughtful frown, her brain seem-ing to process new information. "Anyway. If you are want-ing to get stronger before heading towards gluttony again, then what's the plan?"

"I was thinking that I would recover for another day here in the Pits of Lust. Once I'm back on my feet, we will head north again and try a different route. I was even consider-ing making the trip in my dragon form and devouring any demons or beasts I find as a way of training."

Summer raised an eyebrow at my statement. "And you risk fighting Asmodia again?" she asked.

"No. The goal this time will just be to expose myself to more wrath and see if I can build up a tolerance. Either that happens or we break through into greed. Anytime we see Asmodia, I either need to make a portal or Ikta can throw more fake gold coins ahead and move me along," I explained my plan.

"Oh, she would love that." Summer picked at the meat and teased me with her eyes. "Of course, there is another way you can increase your power in the short term." She let the offer hang in the air for me to figure out.

I frowned for a moment before realizing what she meant. "Taking more of Ikta's and your power?"

Summer only smiled and smacked her lips as she ate, a different kind of hunger in her eyes.

CHAPTER 19

I turned down Summer's offer that night. As I ate the meat, I had to focus on controlling my emotions, and it was proving difficult. I needed the training if I was to become the emperor of Faerie or whatever was happening.

After I recovered, we began hopping from portal to portal, and the next few days went by uneventfully as I worked on controlling my emotions and growing in strength. We moved around the Pits of Lust using portals, occasionally shifting into my dragon form and hunting some large beasts. Then we would return to the Pale Mounds and cook up the meat.

My two dragon mates joined me on the trips, and we hunted as a family. My dragon could not have been happier hunting in a pack. We kept our hunting away from the Pale Mounds to try to remain hidden for as long as possible. I wanted the advantage for when we finally took on our enemy.

"Today's the day." I stretched my body. "We'll portal into the Battlefields of Wrath and push north as quickly as we can. Our goal is to cover enough ground that I can portal back and forth with a little more freedom."

The women around me nodded.

"Besides, there aren't many monsters in Wrath's domain. They all get mobbed and eaten up," Ikta added.

I shrugged; the statement made sense.

Popping open a portal not far into Wrath's domain, I stepped through and looked around before waving for the others to join me. My clothes were stuffed into my bracer as the shift started, and I felt myself expand into my dragon form. I'd grown even larger with all the recent hunting.

"Get on," my voice boomed despite my attempt to be quiet.

Ikta scrambled up with her spider limbs and started working a web on my back.

"What are you doing?"

"Making seats," she answered as if the statement were obvious.

"Of course," I huffed.

"The seats look lovely," Summer added, climbing up and taking one of the seats that Ikta had rapidly made at the base of my neck.

"Oh, dragons would kill for seating." Regina climbed into another. "You really put these together quickly. They stretch a little at the edges too, so they won't hinder his movement. These are well thought out."

"I've been measuring," Ikta giggled. "Yet he keeps getting bigger."

After Amira clambered on, I took a loping run before catching enough wind in my wings to pull myself up off the ground. As I got bigger, it was getting harder to take off.

But I was soon in the air and flying over the Battlefields.

From above, the area looked pitiful. Unlike the Pits of Lust, there were no buildings, no apparent towns, just roving bands of demons looking for a fight. No wonder there were no monsters, the idiots probably went mad killing any that appeared.

The demons had already spotted me, so I flew low and poured death down from above, destroying them before I rose back into the air.

Demons were all sensitive to magic and would see right through any invisibility spell I cast, but that didn't matter. I'd taken to the air to get a better view of the area and map out more portal options. I wanted to work my way through Asmodia's territory without another fight with the big demoness.

"Wee!" Ikta stood up, using her limbs to hold her in place as she put her face into the wind.

"You are going to fall off," Summer warned like a mother scolding a child. But there was no real force behind it; she knew Ikta would do as she pleased.

"Nah. I'll just portal back if needed." Ikta paused and jumped off my back, screaming for a second before popping back in via portal and landing in her chair. "See?"

"Please tell me you aren't going to be doing that the whole time," I grumbled.

"Girls just wanna have fun," Ikta said with a giant knowing smile.

I let out a dragon-sized sigh. "Don't make me turn this dragon around."

"Boo!" Ikta shouted. "Oh look. I think that's another of those portal anchors." She stared out into the distance. "We should steal one."

"Or just destroy them," Summer corrected her. "They couldn't have been that easy to make."

I dipped low, strafing fire over the demons and their enchanted pillar and melting it. "Fixed. And I'm not carrying a giant pillar that disrupts portals. That sounds like a great way to fuck something up."

Ikta crossed her arms and pouted. "If I had that to study, I bet I could make one that drags any portals you make in the manor to a nymph pool. I'm sure they'd all get into roleplay for you."

"While we are all having fun, does one of those mean that Asmodia is near?" Regina asked. "She was using those to lure and bait you into a fight before."

"If our dear dragon can avoid being drawn into fighting like a madman again, he's faster than Asmodia with his dragon flight." Summer let out a light sigh as I dove on another warband of demons and smoked them to a demon.

"I'm not caught up. Just venting a little anger. A pissed off dragon goes full scorched earth. Get it?" I had a big grin on my face.

"If he can make jokes, he's fine." Ikta ignored Summer's concern. "How are you trying to control your emotions?"

"Oh. I'm just focusing on my greed and lust. I have my mates on my back. I can't let anything happen to them, and then when I'm done thinking about that, I think about the thing I'll do to each of you." I spiraled higher to see if Asmodia would be visible.

"Promises, promises." Ikta clicked her tongue. "Well, that's one way to keep the wrath in check. But that'll get hard as we cross Mammon's territory."

"Yeah, I won't lie. I'm scared shitless of that one." I spotted another army with one of the enchanted pillars and angled my wings to swoop down on them. "Let's be honest, I have a particular weakness for greed and gold."

"Doubt you would be the first dragon for Mammon to lure," Regina spoke up over the wind. "But he's not made himself your enemy."

"Yet. He hasn't made himself my enemy yet," I grumbled. "The temptation of a Dragon King's mana and any additional temptation that Beelzebub throws his way will certainly be a real problem." After giving it some thought, I was fairly certain that Mammon would get involved for the power that I held, if nothing else.

I strafed death over the demons, using the move to release some pent-up annoyance at having to leave the fight with Asmodia. A low growl built up in my chest as I swung back around and torched the pillar, leaving a giant burning gouge in the soil.

"You sure you are in control?" Regina asked. "Also, that's a lot of fire."

"I'm fine. Speaking of fire. Summer, I want to breathe some of your gold fae fire." I kept talking to distract myself as I climbed higher in search of more prey.

"Well then, you'll have to work on your summer fae magic and not just your wild fae magic." Summer sounded like a woman scorned.

"I want to, I just don't have as much access to summer fae magic." I wanted the damned gold fire. It was pretty and, from what I'd seen, very destructive. "Ikta gave me a bunch of her magic, so it's easier."

"I'm saving my magic for when we have our time together." I could nearly hear Summer crossing her arms in her statement.

"Well. If you want Ikta to be the only one to give me fae magic, I understand," I lamented with the best pout a dragon face could muster as I trudged through the air.

"Don't be like that," Summer sighed while Ikta cackled like a mad woman.

"He's got you, Summy," Ikta teased her.

"Somehow, I thought venturing through the perilous plane of Hell would be a little more serious," Amira muttered.

"This is very serious." Summer cleared her throat. "We are just being light to help Zach not go on a wrath-filled, murderous rampage."

"Thanks for that," I said. "Now about the golden fae fire."

"Well, we'll have to talk about terms and conditions before I let you license it. It is, after all, my signature power," Summer teased.

"Wow. Do you hear that, Ikta? I got yours for a steal."

"Oh. I only gave you part of it. I'm holding off on the rest because I know you'll want more. It's a more aggressive sales tactic." Ikta held her head high in triumph.

I zipped down and laid waste to another army of smaller demons.

This time, Asmodia showed herself, but she wasn't the same formidable force I'd fought. Scars crisscrossed her body as she shouted and lifted a nasty looking spear towards me. The tip was a jagged mess that looked more like a harpoon. At the very least, it would take a ton of flesh out with it.

As she wielded it, I realized that she only had that one arm. The other was still a charred lump.

"What are the chances she can hit me with that spear?" I asked, trying to climb up higher as quickly as I could.

"Hmmm... 100% give or take," Ikta estimated. "I bet she's pretty darn good with every weapon."

Asmodia launched the spear, and I spun to the right, closing my wings to make myself a smaller target as I dropped from the sky.

The demoness overshot high, and I cursed as I unfurled my wings while nearly getting hit by it on the way down.

"Damn she's good," Ikta admired the throw.

Before the spear hit the ground, Asmodia held out her hand and the spear shot back into her hand.

"Oh wow. That's cool." Regina watched on with interest. "You'd never lose your favorite hunting spear with an enchantment like that."

"Yes. That's what I'm most concerned about right now. Losing my favorite hunting spear. Definitely not losing my favorite wing," I grumbled, but I knew they were just trying to distract me. "Going to focus on the next one though. Hush."

Asmodia had gotten me to fly lower and was charging after me, the spear held back over her head as she tried to aim.

I zipped past her and wiggled my tail at her in a taunt.

The demoness launched the spear like it was being fired out of a cannon. This time, I was ready. I snapped open a portal hoping to catch the spear and have it drop down on Asmodia. However, it was too fast for me to try and catch it with the portal.

Asmodia was quick on her giant feet and dodged. She managed to get mostly out of the way, but the spear went through her back foot and nailed her to the ground.

I stared at her pinned down state, and my instincts were screaming. I couldn't give up the opportunity. I spun back around and dove as death breath built up in my throat.

"How are we feeling, my king?" Amira asked, concern lacing her tone.

"Like there's a chance to do some damage," I growled and recognized my anger, but it was a good tactic. This was a real chance to do some damage to Asmodia.

"My fire isn't fire born of flame. It's the withering summer heat concentrated into fire," Summer called out. "It doesn't just burn; it kills."

"Later." I was nearing the end of my dive and was focused as I banked hard to the left, my wing scraping the hard-packed dirt. As I banked, I let out a roar of death as the dark fog roiled out and over Asmodia. Then I leveled out and flapped hard enough to regain altitude.

The spear shot through the fog where I would have been if I hadn't banked hard.

"It was a trap," Regina said. "How'd you know?"

I circled back up. "Because she makes people angry and lures them into fights. Asmodia isn't fast, so she needs other tactics. She brings her opponents to her and defeats them in a battle of attrition. I have some logic, but I think I have to be done for now." The desire to go down and take another chunk out of Asmodia was like a red-hot poker in my mind.

"Good." Summer stroked the back of my neck as golden fire sparkled over my head. Then a large plume of the gold fire shot down into the fog, eliciting a strangled cry from the demon prince. "The reason she had a stump arm was because I burned your previous wound with my fire. It should be enough to stop her healing temporarily."

"Ah. Now I really need to learn how to use it." I continued to circle overhead for the fog to clear.

"My lord, do I need to start throwing gold coins to remind you not to stick around?" Ikta asked, and I could tell she would do so in a heartbeat.

"No. I'm going." I pushed my wings hard to fly away from Asmodia, feeling like a smug Dragon King having dealt with the demon prince in a manner far more fitting for a dragon.

"So, terms and conditions for the secret to your golden summery fire of death and gold? By the way, it is a very pretty gold. Have I told you that you are beautiful lately?" I buttered Summer up.

"Prettier than my golden fire?" she asked.

I hesitated just a moment too long. "You are far prettier."

"At least he knows the right answer, even if he takes a moment to get there," Ikta sold me out.

"The truth is the right answer!" I craned my neck around to stare at them and to check behind me as the death fog settled. It was surprising that Asmodia hadn't thrown another spear yet.

As I stared back, I noticed magic building up underneath the fog.

"Besides, I'm some fae king now. Can I even lie anymore?" I asked not just to them, but wondered aloud to myself.

"Why don't you say, 'You are far prettier than your gold fire,'" Summer demanded.

I focused on the bountiful chest of the beautiful fae on my back who would join my harem soon. "You are more beautiful than your gold fire."

And I meant it. The fire wasn't beautiful—it was glorious! My dragon brain didn't quite give the gold fire the term 'beautiful', so it was still the truth.

"That works. Now tell me I'm uglier than Ikta. We need to test your ability to lie," Summer added smoothly.

"Uh. Huh. Can't do that or even the other way around. There must be some fae mojo preventing me from comparing two fae queens," I lied, cheering in my head. I could still lie, or at least fib. That would be important as I tried to keep balance across my harem.

"There's no fae mojo preventing you." Ikta's glare had an almost physical force on the back of my head. "Are you saying that I *am* uglier than her?"

"Neither of you is any kind of ugly. It's like asking which red is more blue. Stupid question with no real answer. Thus, fae mojo is blocking me. Sorry, I can't answer that question." I put all my mental power into evading the question that was possibly more dangerous than the buildup of magic behind me.

"Not bad." Ikta studied me. "So what are you going to do about that spell behind us?"

"I was really hoping my sweet talk could save me there too. Want to pop me a portal when it's about to go off?" I asked Ikta with as much sweetness as I could put into my dragon's voice.

"I'll think about it. Let's talk about terms and conditions first," Ikta laughed like she'd won.

There was a rumble behind me as black fire shot out of the ground, racing after me.

A giant portal opened ahead of me, and I dove into it without another thought. I appeared above a group of demons carrying one of the enchanted pillars and burnt them to a crisp as I landed and watched the beam of black fire erupt into the sky.

"Okay. Just imagine me being so angry that I tried to take that head on." I shook my head. It looked like Asmodia had punched a hole in the sky with the power of the spell.

"Would be rather bad. Let's go hunt some lusty pigs and then have a barbeque." Ikta clapped her hands. "Then we can discuss the terms that you signed without reading."

"Huh?" I frowned at her. "You can't be serious."

"You used my portal. I consider that an acceptance of the agreement. Now, about the terms." Ikta pretended like she was writing on paper as she started listing out her terms.

CHAPTER 20

My giant dragon form had a possessive claw on the demon boar as I tore into it while listening to Ikta speak.

"So, first of all, you may refer to me as your 'favorite fae' or just 'favorite'. Or, maybe just 'favored'. Yeah that has a nice ring to it. You must let your Favored borrow gold from your hoard for making jewelry to wear," Ikta continued to list off demands.

"You don't get to steal my gold. Only wear it," I growled.

Ikta glared at me until I rolled my eyes.

"My Favored only gets to take as much gold as she can actually wear," I sighed, there was no fae magic to these terms, but it was amusing Ikta, and I didn't mind most of her demands.

"Good. Good. When you mark me, it can't be the left shoulder. That's where you mark everyone," Ikta huffed. "I want mine to be special."

Amira and Regina both looked at their marks and frowned.

"Yes. See? All of them are on the left shoulder. I want a special one on the right shoulder, or maybe somewhere more *personal*." She bounced her eyebrows.

"I can do that," I agreed. "But you'll have to help it happen. I get a little excitable around the marking."

Summer was sitting to the side by the fire which was roasting a hunk of meat on the spit for those that didn't have a dragon's constitution to eat raw meat. She was watching our negotiations with interest.

"Do you want your mark somewhere else?" I asked.

"On my breasts, preferably, so I can show it off with my cleavage," Summer said.

"OI I!" Ikta nodded excitedly before frowning. "Wait, no. I want mine to be unique. I get that. Summy gets somewhere else."

"Nope. She called dibs first." I snorted at the fae blowing smoke over her.

"Fine. Maybe we can do the thigh. Ass seems a little weird if I'm honest. But thighs could be sexy. Maybe I could show it off with a nice big slit down the side of my dress." Ikta held up her leg, studying it.

"It isn't that big of a deal." I regretted my words instantly when the entire group of women stared me down.

"Getting marked is a big deal, my king." Amira stood, her face clearly upset.

"It is permanent," Summer pointed out.

"Okay. Now we need to talk about after-court requirements for when you start holding sessions. I prefer a nice communal bath after court. It really bonds the members," Ikta said with a straight face.

Regina frowned for a moment. "But the court will just be you, Summer, and Maeve."

"Your point?" Ikta dared her to argue.

"Nothing," Regina clammed up. "Just making sure I have it straight. You three and our king in a bath or hot spring after every court session." Regina's voice dipped to a low murmur as she continued on. "Going to be pregnant a dozen times over before the end of the month."

"That's the plan!" Ikta clapped her hands excitedly before rubbing her flat stomach as if it would swell with her thoughts alone.

Suddenly, her stomach did grow larger.

"Won't I look lovely with a baby bump?" Ikta turned to me.

My eyes saw right through the glamor, yet the dragon in me let out a low, happy rumble.

"He likes that," Summer laughed. "Should we all do it?"

As soon as she said the words, Summer had a big baby bump. But then her joy came crashing down, and she dismissed the glamor with a wave of her hand, staring off into the distance. Her joy had evaporated so quickly.

"Yeah, he—" Ikta continued unaware, so I growled to stop her. "What?"

I stood from the boar and stomped over to Summer before blowing hot air over her. "Get on. We'll go for a night flight."

It took a lot to crack the control that the fae queens had over their emotion. I wanted to give Summer some space away from the others.

"That would be lovely." Summer climbed up on my back, the web chairs still in place.

Ikta watched with a thoughtful expression as I took off from the Pale Mounds and climbed high into the sky before shifting to my black dragon form to hide among the dark night sky of Hell.

Summer was quiet for the climb. She didn't speak until I was gliding high in the sky. "I am fine."

"It is okay not to be. Remember, I was there when it happened." I remembered how broken the fae queen had been after the death of her daughter. And not even two weeks had passed for her to grieve.

"I was prepared for it. She had been scheming for a while. It helps that Iapetus killed her; I only killed that possessed shell." Summer sounded calm, but she lay down on the webbing like she was exhausted.

"Doesn't mean that it has to be easy to lose your daughter. The thought of being pregnant again was too much of a trigger. I'll talk to Ikta when we get back." I growled a little, angry at Ikta for hurting Summer.

"Zach, I'm about to be surrounded by your pregnant wives. It wasn't the baby bump. When I made the glamor, I thought of my pregnancy with Aurora to make it." She let out a small sad sigh, and I turned my head around to see a single tear escaping her eyes.

"What can I do?" I asked, feeling helpless. I couldn't simply kill a demon or crush a political enemy. Those things I could do easily. I couldn't fix the hurt she was feeling.

"Just be here. Accept that I'm going through something and be here when I need it."

"Absolutely." I was almost angry that it wasn't a given. "Anytime, anywhere. We could be in the middle of Hell and I'll stop what I'm doing to help." I chuckled a little.

"You are taking Hell in stride." She rubbed my scales and pointedly changed the topic.

"Having the looming danger to Sabrina removed lightened this journey up a little. We still have important things to do, but at least we aren't lugging around a succubus who's losing herself. Silver lining in the middle of fighting demons."

"You are getting better with emotional manipulation. Better than the training with Sabrina and Helena beforehand," Summer pointed out.

I chuckled. "Maybe I had the wrong incentive in those training sessions." I cleared my throat. "Failure there wasn't really a loss for me."

Summer laughed and the sound was a huge relief. Somehow, I always worried that Summer wouldn't come back when she went down the dark path of thinking about her daughter.

"Thank you." Summer's laughter broke, and she took a deep breath. "You are good to me. I think my father would have liked you if the two of you had met."

"High praise." I glided through the night. Summer had put her father on a pedestal; saying he'd like me was monumental praise.

"Go down there," Summer pointed, and I turned to follow her direction.

She was pointing to rolling pink hills. I scanned with my enhanced vision and saw nothing troublesome. Not seeing any harm, I landed as softly as a giant dragon could. "What did you need?"

"Shift." She slid off my back.

I didn't hesitate, wondering what she had in store for me.

The second my bones were back in place, her lips pressed into mine. It was like fresh berries mixed with warm sunshine as my mind and body electrified.

She pulled away with half-lidded eyes that told me exactly what was about to happen.

"Summer, maybe now isn't—" I was stopped by a finger pressed against my lips.

"Sometimes a distraction with a man who takes care of you is exactly what a woman needs." She pulled her finger away once she finished her statement, and a wry grin spread on her beautiful face. "You can take care of me, can't you?"

Like all summer fae, she had sun-kissed skin and bright hair. Her hair was green like fresh leaves in the spring. Her features were sharp, which only contrasted with the generous soft curves of her body. She was impossibly curvy, yet thin and graceful as she was as tall as me.

"Then a distraction I can give." I kissed her again, the image of the beautiful woman seared into my mind.

My hands wandered down her soft dress, cupping her hips and holding her still as she hit me with a wave of magic that drowned my senses in everything sensual.

"Feel me," she whispered and pulled my hand up to feel her breasts. The mounds were impossibly soft, pliant, and warm as my fingers sank into them. "Do you like what you feel?"

"Yes," I growled, feeling my eyes shift.

"Where do you want to mark them? Here?" She used my hand to trace a curve. "Or here?" She pulled gently on my head down to her breasts and pushed me between them.

I was smothered by her chest and in heaven as she pulled her shoulders forward and squished them around me.

"Why don't you explore them a little more, my greedy dragon?"

I slipped an arm around her hips and picked her up to put her gently on the ground before I did just that, running my face all over her breasts, feeling every inch and covering them with kisses.

"Here." I kissed the top. "So everyone knows."

"I'd like that." Her hand wrapped around my cock and slowly stroked it. "But to mate with a fae, you need to put a child in her. Can you put a child in me?"

Her words were shocking enough that I broke from the trance and stared into her eyes before she nodded slowly, telling me it was okay. She was ready.

"I'll breed you like a nymph. You'd make a wonderful mother for my children. Dozens, maybe. I'll just keep you swollen." I kissed her and pressed her to the ground.

Summer's tongue tangled with mine, and I could feel her excitement before she pulled away. "Lay on your back, for you are my emperor and I shall serve you."

I rolled over with her, letting her move on top of me as she gracefully shifted her face between my legs. She teased me, just letting her warm breath tickle me for a moment.

I grabbed her hair, the crown woven into it becoming a firm place to grip and pulled her down over my cock. Watching the proud fae queen swallow me was delightful. I rumbled with pleasure that was more emotional than physical. Getting new mates was always exciting, but getting a fae queen was triumphant.

"Yes. Get me ready," I demanded, and I felt her smile as her magic dialed up to an eleven.

Pure pleasure ripped through me, like she was pouring sunshine down around my cock and into me. I tried to say something, but the words came out shuddered gasps. I picked up my head to see her smiling around me.

"Fuck." I only managed to get that one word out before my body began shuddering.

Her tongue ran up and down me, making my body go wild. As much as I wanted to hold back and not rush anything, I couldn't. Grabbing the back of her head, I thrust her down and came down her throat in spurt after spurt.

But Summer didn't stop. She continued going down on me and flooding me with the sensations that melted my mind and reformed it while I watched my beautiful fae queen please me.

Eventually, I'd had all I could take and pulled her off, gasping for air.

"Your majesty?" Summer feigned innocence as she batted her lashes at me. "I only wish to please you." She pretended to be an airhead nymph.

"On your back," I growled.

Smiling, she quickly rolled over and slowly spread her legs wide, a pair of bright green panties flying off. "As you wish."

I was on top of her in a flash, throwing my hips forward into her slick paradise. "You feel incredible."

Summer cupped the back of my head and pulled me down to her breasts. "No, you feel perfect. Now fuck me."

I thrust up into her, feeling her body give easily to me. Then she shifted, like she was riding me from below. Her moves were graceful and effortless as she watched me with golden eyes, a breathless gasp always on her lips.

She felt so good and was nearly glowing beneath me as I pounded into her, nearly melding our beings together. Golden, magical sunshine continued to fill me and make my entire body tingle with delight.

Summer rolled us on our side where my face was crushed between her breasts, and she curled around me while I thrust up into her with small jerking motions.

"I love you." I couldn't help myself.

She'd been helping me and teasing me along for some time now. At first, she had been beautiful and unobtainable, but somewhere along the line, that had changed. She was just my Summer, a love within my grasp. She teased me, keeping that spark alive until this moment.

Even at my wedding, she was slowly making me smitten with her.

"I know, and I love you, Zach Pendragon. You are truly a man worthy. Now, fill me with a child," she whispered in an airy voice.

I pumped into her with a new frenzy, and she rode each sway of my hips, clinging to my back and encouraging me with airy moans. My jaw cracked, and I tore down the front of her dress before biting the top of her breast and searing it with my mark.

Summer cried out in pleasure, and I felt her walls quiver around me as I emptied myself once more into her. When my jaw shifted back, I was panting above her. But when my eyes met hers, the gold in hers was gleaming with something new.

"Now, would you like to give me back some of my magic?" Summer teased.

I blinked, feeling more than satisfied. I was full in a very new way. "You gave me your territory," I realized.

"Only a small part. You seem full, and we'll have to spend all night for me to really give it all to you." She traced my jaw line with a finger. "We also need to be sure that you fulfill your promise and put a child in me. A dozen more rounds should work. You are up to that, aren't you? You promised me a distraction, and just once is a tease," she teased, her finger tracing down my chest.

I growled and nipped at her mark. "It would be my pleasure. Hold on."

I wrapped my arms around her and stood up in the middle of the hills, using my strength to pull her up and down on my cock as a smile lit up her face. She tilted her head back, moaning and relaxing into the moment.

CHAPTER 21

I portaled Summer and me back to the Pale Mounds, knowing the rest of our group would soon become worried. When we got back, I kept Summer in my arms, lying down with her pressed against my body. I was still feeling possessive after our mating.

Summer waved a little magic to give us privacy and wiggled herself into me. "That was a wonderful night." She rolled over and traced my chest as I lay on my back.

My eyes kept being drawn to the mark on her chest. "It's a gold scar."

"Yes, I think you put a little of my summer fae magic in it while you were doing it. You were brimming with my magic at the time." Summer traced the faint gold scar over her breast. "I like it."

"You'd better. It is permanent." I pulled her closer, just to feel her body. "Any regrets?" A part of me had worried Summer had gone too far with the 'distraction'.

"None. How does the summer fae magic feel? Better than the trashy wild fae magic, I hope." She narrowed her eyes in a playful warning.

"Much better. A lot of warmth and sunshine. Wild fae magic feels mysterious and elusive." I thought about it. "Wait, does this mean I get my gold fire now?"

Summer smiled and kissed my cheek. "Yes, we can work on the gold fire."

I started to get up, and she glared at me, putting a hand on my chest.

"But not right now." I interpreted the gesture.

"Tomorrow." She pulled me back into her. "Tonight, you are going to enjoy the embrace of a mature woman as you sleep. Said woman you put through her paces."

"How does the magic feel now that you've taken it back?" I was curious if it changed anything for her.

"Lovely. It is a little more fierce coming from you, almost like it has a little dragon flavor to it. But it is the same magic I've used for a long time. Better yet, how do you feel as a fae emperor?" she asked.

"Before, when my mana was filled up, I felt like a shaken soda bottle, pressured to explode whenever I used magic." I thought about the change. "Now I feel like a pool with so much more potential. I..." Feeling for my magic and realizing how full it was, I frowned. "I am not entirely sure, but I think I'm not giving off mana as much as I used to. Some of the overflow is going into my bond with Faerie, but it is so distant that it is hard to know how much."

"That would be very interesting and a welcome surprise." Summer was genuinely shocked. "We'll have to see when we get back."

I still had my eyes closed. "It feels like I'm growing stronger by putting some of my mana into Faerie."

"We'll take that anytime." Summer pressed me back into her bosom. "Now, rest your eyes. We have more trials ahead of us here in Hell."

***

"Sleep well, my husband?" Summer asked as I blinked into the bright morning sun, finding myself drooling on her chest.

"Oh. I think he slept wonderfully," Ikta laughed. "Sorry, I had to poke down the illusion to make sure the old witch hadn't turned you into a dried husk. Didn't realize how comfortable you found her pillows."

Regina was standing behind Ikta, weighing her own chest. Though I'd be the last to admit the reality, they weren't nearly as soft as Summer's. I was convinced Summer had done something to make them so pillowy soft. Even Pixie's chest didn't compare.

I was lost in my thoughts for a moment before I realized they were all waiting for a response.

"Can't remember a time when I slept that well before," I answered honestly, causing Ikta to roll her eyes. But I felt Summer smile.

"Well, it's time to start the day." I rolled off Summer who just lounged back with a smug expression pointed at Ikta.

"I knew she'd swoop in and steal you away." Ikta shook her head.

"You have a promise for a week in a pool of nymphs with him once we get out of here." Summer rolled her eyes and propped her head up. "So, don't try and get upset. I'm sure you'll mellow out after a little time with him. How long has it been? I bet you have the universe's longest dry spell."

A portal snapped open under Summer and sucked her in.

"Whoops." Ikta shrugged.

Summer glided down with the aid of her magic, while maintaining the relaxed pose. "Was that really necessary?"

"Yes." Ikta nodded repeatedly without an ounce of hesitation.

"Cut it out. We need to push back up into Wrath. Get ready to move out." Ikta and Summer were amusing, but I wasn't going to spend all morning on the two of them bantering. We needed to get moving; I wanted to finish my time in Hell, get Sabrina, and get back to my mates.

I had a plan; I just needed to push through it. And if I learned how to use Summer's gold fire in the meantime, that was okay by me.

***

I flew over the Battlefields of Wrath, spotting the edge of Mammon's domain.

The geography changed with the boundaries. The sparse plains turned into rolling hills of blinding silver and gold. Buildings cropped up everywhere, looking like gold bricks stacked on top of each other, like they were trying to see who could reach the sky first, before all of their building blocks inevitably came tumbling down. They were haphazardly stacked, like some sort of child's creation.

"Very different." I took in the city. The others had been simple.

"Why are they all building these... towers?" Regina asked.

"Because it has always been popular for the wealthy to live at the top." Ikta sounded almost sad as she stared at the domain. "All that glitter you see on the ground is real gold. It hides what's underneath. The land is a living fleshy mass, like a tumor."

"Eww." Amira made a gagging noise. "That's disgusting."

"Greed and tumors are a lot alike," Summer answered with a hint of disdain. "Both are the only things that grow continuously, and thus unchecked grow so aggressively."

As I stared at the buildings, there was a piece that still didn't make sense to me. "How do they make the towers without a mine or something?"

"The gold grows from the ground. Workers are forced to harvest it and smelt it. Many greed demons eat it, causing their body to change, growing precious metals and gems like the land. The souls... well, they are force-fed and become unending wealth in return. As they grow gold and gems from their skin, eventually, their body starts to transform. But the stronger demons just harvest their greed made physical." Ikta let out a sad shake of her head. "This is truly the worst Hell, at least for those poor souls."

I flew closer, but I made sure I never crossed the border.

But when I got close, Goldie quivered on my arm. "Huh?"

The elemental shot off my arm like a golden arrow.

"Goldie, come back here," I shouted and landed at the edge of the domain of greed.

But the gold elemental didn't listen, shooting into one of the towers and rapidly devouring a gold block.

"Uh, what's happening?" Regina asked.

I realized what we were seeing. "The gold is all very mana rich. I banned Goldie from eating my hoard. My guess is Goldie is very hungry right now."

Enough of the gold block was devoured by Goldie that the tower groaned before toppling like a set of dominoes. The tall tower managed to crash into another, and another, taking down a whole row of towers.

"Maybe we should get out of here before a huge number of angry demons come." Ikta pulled at my neck.

"Goldie! Goldie, come back here," I shouted as the elemental finished the block of gold. I expected Goldie to come back, but instead, the elemental shot itself further into Mammon's territory, splashing on the ground and devouring all of the gold, revealing the fleshy tumor that Ikta had spoken of earlier.

I growled as Goldie raced away from me. I wanted to charge after her, but by that point, demons were pouring out of the fallen towers, screaming.

"We need to go," I muttered. Greed was a particular weakness of mine and I couldn't risk the ladies on my back.

I let out jets of flame, hoping to melt the demons, but only their flesh melted. My fire revealed just how much of the demons had become precious metal. Even if it dripped, it hadn't melted completely.

"Go," Ikta urged, and I took a few more bounding steps before I was able to take to the air.

The demons threw chains at me, trying to catch me, but Ikta was quick. She scrambled along my side and cut the chains away with her spider limbs.

"What's the urgency?" Regina asked.

"Greed is going to be a hard emotion for Zach to resist," Summer explained. "The demons aren't as combative as wrath, but they might be more dangerous to him."

I looked over my shoulder, a pang of sadness ripping through my chest as I watched Goldie devouring the mana rich gold. "What's going to happen to Goldie?"

"I don't know if anyone's ever brought an elemental to Hell. They are already rare. And gold elementals? I've never heard of one. So I can't really tell you. But Goldie will eat all she can get until she is full, and I doubt the demons are going to be able to stop it," Ikta mused.

"She'll be safe?" I asked.

Goldie had been a silent companion for some time. I wasn't really sure what would happen. Even if Goldie had a penchant for my mana, I realized the elemental wasn't truly mine.

"She'll be all right." Summer patted my side.

I wanted Goldie back, but there wasn't much I could do at the moment. The elemental was sweeping through Mammon's domain like a swarm of locusts, and I needed to keep my distance.

"Of course it will. But I want to go find something to punch. Did you guys notice that there weren't that many war bands on the way up here?" I turned back towards the center of the Battlefields of Wrath. "Let's go see why Asmodia isn't hunting me today."

"And punch something," Ikta chirped. "We'll come back later and get your pet gold elemental. She will have grown up a lot. I'm sure she'll come back once she's had her fill."

"Yes, you've treated Goldie well. She'll be back," Amira agreed.

Not much time had passed since Goldie had become conscious. And at times, awareness was fleeting. Each time

Goldie had a thought, memories of all the time she spent with Zach came back like a flood.

She was his.

Born from flecks of gold that he had carefully found and collected when he was younger, Goldie was tied to him. And he kept Goldie even before she'd gained full consciousness, nurturing her with his mana.

The tastiest mana was Zach's mana. It was familiar, like the comfort of home. But he wouldn't let her eat his gold. He liked it like Goldie, and she understood that it wasn't food. It was Zach's; she couldn't take it.

Goldie still felt hungry. Always so hungry. Zach gave her mana, but he also forgot about her at times. Goldie was weak, too weak to help Zach too often. She slept, and if he didn't call, she didn't wake up. It frustrated her every time she did wake up.

When he had tried to fight the big demon, she didn't have enough strength to become a proper weapon, and Zach almost died! He was so wounded.

Then he brought her here.

So much tasty gold. Tasty gold that could help Goldie fix everything. Goldie would become stronger.

Goldie flowed over the fields, devouring all the gold she could find. Such delicious gold. To make things better, Zach had been worried about this place—it was dangerous to him. She had remembered what he had said with the scary one.

As Goldie devoured more of the gold, she grew larger and was able to devour more and more. She snorted. This time Goldie would be helpful. Even if it made Zach mad.

"Stop!" A demon flew into her path. This one was fast. "I am a knight of Mammon, and you must cease your devouring of Mammon's gold. They demand your presence."

Goldie flowed up from the ground, forming a shape similar to Yevvy. Yevvy was the best of Zach's wives. "I am Goldie, and I will destroy this place because it is in my... my... Zach's way."

She wasn't sure what she was to Zach exactly. As she'd been waking up further, she'd only grown more confused.

The demon moved quickly towards her, so with a thought, Goldie shot a spike out of her current form, catching the demon. As she poked into the demon, she found lots of tasty gold inside. Goldie devoured all of the gold, leaving behind scraps of gems and silver, but she didn't care for those and couldn't eat them.

She felt the life leave the demon. She'd taken too much of its being. But now she understood the demons around her more. The demon's mind had been partially made of gold, and while she didn't quite get its mind, she could pull its understandings from it. Pick through its knowledge and absorb some.

There was a lot for Goldie to understand, far too much. Like the memories from when she was asleep, it all washed on her at once. Immediately, she threw out some of the thoughts that were wrong, or at least wrong to her.

Zach was good, demons were bad.

Considering the memories, she shifted through them. The demon understood some basics, but its knowledge was incomplete. Or maybe the parts that she'd gotten were incomplete.

When she finished, she realized that other demons had crept up on her.

Goldie's eyes flashed, and liquid gold shot out from her in the form of needles. She jabbed out in every direction, piercing dozens of demons and draining the gold from them, searching for more among them for minds made up at least partially of gold.

After all but one of the demons died, she stared into the one remaining demon's emerald eyes.

"Where are more of Mammon's knights, or other stronger demons?" Her words were smooth and she smiled. She had learned! Pausing, Goldie wondered if the demon could talk.

Goldie had learned lots and lots from Mammon's knight, but she might have been hasty with throwing away parts. She needed more.

"That way." The demon held a shaking hand, and Goldie was pleased to see that he could speak. "If you follow the towers to where there are more and taller towers, you'll find stronger demons with Mammon at the center. Please don't kill me."

"Is Mammon like the knight? Are they all gold?" Goldie's eyes sparkled; she could devour more and understand things. She could become more powerful and understand her Zach even more!

"Yes, the stronger the demon, the more gold they've become." The demon nodded excitedly.

Goldie nodded in understanding, managing a smile.

Then she looked down at the demon. It was one of Zach's enemies. A spike of gold drilled into his head, and Goldie devoured all of his gold before she turned towards the direction he'd indicated.

"Mammon is a demon prince. Zach is scared of them, even if he isn't scared of the giant demon." Goldie frowned and held her chin up. The motion now made more sense to her and it made her smile. "I need to become stronger before facing Mammon. Just like Zach. Become stronger and then fight stronger people."

Rather than head straight for Mammon, Goldie became a pool of gold that expanded for over a hundred yards and swept over the land, continuously growing and devouring all of the gold she could so that Goldie would become the strongest she could before she met stronger demons.

And then she'd devour them too.

CHAPTER 22

I was worried about Goldie, but I managed to push the concern out of my mind as I flew over the Battlefields of Wrath.

"It's no fun when they all run away." I swooped down as another battalion of demons scattered as soon as I appeared on the horizon. "Aren't they supposed to be battle crazed?"

"Battle crazed, not suicidal. Besides, that one even had harpoons ready for you," Ikta pointed out.

"Not that it did much good." Summer tossed her hair, proud of her contribution.

"Melting them tends to make them ineffective," Ikta agreed.

"Don't pretend you didn't help. I saw those portals." Summer patted Ikta's head. "One day, you'll make a good harem member."

"Quit being so smug. You've been a harem member for less than a day."

"But I'm first," Summer pointed out. "Wonder if that means that I get to truly be the first in his court?" she pondered aloud.

"No. I gave him part of my power first. I'm first." Ikta narrowed her eyes.

"But I gave it all to him," Summer mused, as if she wasn't speaking to Ikta but having a philosophical conversation with herself. "I wonder who the Fae Emperor will pick... the one he's had his prick buried deep into for an entire night or some random woman who gave him a gift."

"Do you want to get thrown off?" Ikta ground her teeth. "Because this is how you get thrown off. Zach, who—"

"What's that? I can't hear anything over the wind!" I shouted loud enough to make the very air vibrate.

"Bullshit." Ikta narrowed her eyes and turned to Regina. "Is there really any difficulty in hearing while flying? He normally seems to know everything that happens on his back."

"Oh n— Yes, the wind can be very loud when he's in a dive." Regina nodded her head rapidly.

Ikta squinted at her. "You know I can spot a liar a million miles away."

"Good thing you are farsighted and can't spot a liar right under your nose," I grumbled. "Do not make me pick between my harem members. New rule."

"But it's fun to watch you squirm." Ikta blinked, her face instantly morphing into the definition of innocence.

"Oh. Okay. Then Maeve is first," I replied with extra cheer.

"What! No, that skank," Ikta shouted. "Summy, we can't stand for that, can we?"

"Absolutely not," Summer agreed. At least they agreed on something.

I sighed, already exhausted with the discussion, which made Ikta clap her hands.

"Why are you two jostling for this first position?" I asked.

"Because it's fun?" Ikta sounded genuinely confused. "Zach dear, I don't think you realize how long it has been since I've been in a friendly competition with anyone. There were so many years where I had nobody who could match me."

"As long as it stays a friendly competition," I warned.

"Perfectly friendly," Summer agreed. "I just want to be able to say I took the famous Spider Queen down a peg."

"You're going to peg me?" Ikta gasped before she broke her act and started laughing again while Summer rolled her eyes.

"These two." I shook my giant head.

"My king, I recommend we focus on our task. I see a structure up ahead." Amira had been quietly looking out as a scout. The woman didn't really have a humorous bone in her body.

And we needed that. While powerful, my team seemed to have the attention span of a goldfish.

"That looks like the colosseum." I focused on the structure in the distance.

"It's a lot bigger than that." Regina joined us, looking forward. "It's the only building we've seen in this whole land."

"Maybe it is where Asmodia stays?" I offered. "Hey, navigator, are we near where Asmodia's seat of power should be?"

"Oh. One moment." Ikta scrambled to get her map out. "Yes. Yes we are. There's a good chance that Asmodia is there."

I pushed myself flying faster towards the arena. So far, the armies carrying portal attractors had disappeared along with the demon prince. I had to wonder if Asmodia had given up, or if she was weakened from our previous encounters. There was a temptation to take care of Asmodia once and for all for interfering in my quest in Hell.

As I closed in on the arena, one thing became clear. The area was brimming with wrath and greed demons. They erupted in cheer loud enough to be heard miles away.

"Sounds like a party." Ikta's tone turned gleeful. "Let's crash it!"

"We are absolutely going to crash the party." I tucked my wings into a dive towards the arena.

Before I reached the arena, I unfurled my wings and zipped around in circles to reduce my speed and get a clearer view inside. All of the demons were turning away from the war games to see me circling overhead. From what I could tell, there was a war game being staged in the arena.

"Asmodia," I growled as I spotted the large demon, although she had shrank to a much more manageable size to sit in a big throne and was watching me with a smile.

"Dragon King. Join me. I have been waiting for you. I challenge you to a duel once these games are completed, or do you not have a dragon's honor?" The demoness's gaze flickered to the fae queens on my back before focusing on me again with a smile.

Knowing that all eyes were on me, I dove down, hoping I didn't fuck up what I wanted to be an epic landing. I flapped my wings hard to arrest my flight and hover as I started my shift, but I focused on losing mass first.

"I accept."

The ladies realized what was happening and slid off my back. The two dragons landed with a thud, but the fae queens made barely any noise as they gracefully touched down on the ground.

Continuing through my shift, I lowered myself as I shrank. I thought I did a pretty darn good job if I was honest, landing in my hybrid form so that I didn't have to be naked.

Demons around Asmodia fled, leaving the seats open.

Asmodia sized me up, we were a similar size. Both of us were at the top end of the wrath demons at close to nine feet tall. I took in her current shape. Several dark scars marred her blood red body, and her right arm was still missing. It wasn't her most impressive.

"A duel," Ikta mused. "Sounds like someone is afraid," she teased Asmodia.

The demoness glared at Ikta. "I am injured."

Her eyes flickered to all of the wrath demons lining the stadium. Some were still watching their group, others had shifted their focus to the bloodbath in the arena.

"Some see weakness. You will be my proof that I am not weak," she said.

I snorted, liking my chances. Both of us would be limited from external help and resources, but I could handle her. She had challenged me and this had been just what I'd been preparing for by training in the Pits of Lust.

"Killing you sounds fun. But if we have a moment, what do you know of what's happening in Hell?" I asked.

"You mean Lilith's schemes?" Asmodia grunted and sat back in a large throne where she picked up a hollowed-out demon horn and poured ruby red liquid down her throat. "The Lusty Bitch doesn't fight; she uses others."

I tamped down my excitement. Asmodia knew more than I had expected, and it seemed like she might be willing to share that information.

"I'm aware. I came here to kill Beelzebub, and she's decided to use that to try and reshape the power structure of Hell." I tried to sound like I knew and understood more than I actually did.

Asmodia snorted. "Lucifer has been trying to claim control of Hell and make himself a new titan."

"Are you sure you should be telling us all this?" Ikta laughed and pushed me into a chair before plopping herself down on my lap.

"It doesn't matter. The Dragon King has agreed to the duel. It cemented as a fae promise. The duel will happen regardless. He might as well know who he fights for." Asmodia kept her face towards the arena. "Lucifer has split Hell into two camps. Myself and Beelzebub follow him to raise the King of Hell into the next titan of Hell. The other four remain independent, but Sloth doesn't participate. And Mammon works for the highest bidder. That leaves Lilith and Levi. Levi will only work with Lilith as long as she doesn't take the power herself. Levi simply wants to prevent Lucifer from becoming stronger."

"Sounds like you three hold the advantage," I observed.

Asmodia turned to me. "We do. Yet it takes time to funnel enough strength into Lucifer that he can become the next titan, especially with interference from Lilith and Levi. You are Lilith's gambit now."

"I'm to break the stalemate by killing Beelzebub?" I surmised.

"If Lilith successfully recruits you as a being capable of defeating another demon prince, it will greatly shift the balance of power. Yet, when I saw you the first time and now with the fae promise between us, I see what she is aiming to accomplish. She could use your power to bind Hell together. And given your presence on Earth, she would bind Hell to the mortal plane as well," Asmodia spoke with bitterness.

"That's what we guessed," Ikta spoke up. "The question lingering in my mind is if Lilith will double cross us somehow?"

Asmodia's eyes flashed dangerously. "You won't make it that far."

"Ah, right. Because you are most certainly going to win the duel. But humor a fae queen asking innocent questions. If we pretend that Zach here is going to win, what's her plan exactly? If you die, and Beelzebub dies, that takes a huge chunk of power out of Hell. That can't be her real plan, can it?" Ikta asked from her perch on top of my lap.

"No. She wouldn't destroy that much of Hell, even if it means she has a chance at Lucifer. Right now, your presence alone is enough of an advantage for her." Asmodia narrowed her eyes. "The Dragon King and two fae queens in my territory and heading for Beelzebub prevents us from moving to protect Lucifer. She and Levi will likely attack at some point when they believe us to be unable to help. There are bound to be several layers to Lilith's plans."

Asmodia thought for a moment. "But if you think she'll let you take a chunk of Hell with you, you are wrong. More likely, she has done something to prevent that by either harming you or stealing the power for herself."

I wanted to speak up and deny the statement, but Ikta patted my arm, wanting to speak.

"Of course. I expect as much. But you must understand that it serves us to continue through and thrash you. We'll probably thrash Mammon for even considering attacking my majesty's group. Then we'll take Beelzebub for the bargain we made with Lilith. Do not try and turn us against her with your perspective. For us, we made the right choice. But I must commend your attempts at manipulation." Ikta clicked her tongue. "Even if they were at the level of sophistication of a child."

Asmodia's eyes glowed in anger for a moment before she turned and kept watch on the pits. "I think there is enough free room. Why don't we get started?"

"We agreed to go after, and a fae bond is enforcing that. But you are welcome to start," I spoke calmly, realizing that I felt the agreement rather tightly enforced.

Asmodia nodded to a nearby demon. "Clear the field out for us."

The demon shot into the pit, and like a storm of blood, passed through the two war bands, killing all of them.

"They ran out of time." Asmodia shrugged off the bloodshed and launched herself from her throne into the pit.

"Focus on the fight." Ikta rubbed my thigh and stood up. "You made a fae promise with Lilith to return Sabrina for Beelzebub's essence. She'll hold up to that end and if she tries to pull any other tricks... then I get to let loose. I have your back in all of this, but you've agreed to battle without help. So kill dumb dumb Asmodia for us."

I reached for Goldie to summon a sword, only to realize that she still wasn't there. Grunting, I pulled out one of the archangel's blades and jumped into the pit, landing with a thud.

"The terms. We duel to the death. Leaving the pit is forfeit, and by forfeit, that means forfeiting your head. No prizes. Just the other's head." Asmodia leveled her ax in my direction.

"Easy enough." I breathed slowly, thinking of what Summer had said about her golden fire. I felt the fae promise snapped into place between me and Asmodia, making the moment seem even more real.

The demoness shot forward, her ax chopping down like it was going to cut the world in two despite only having the strength of one arm.

My sword swung up to meet it while I smiled, feeling the heat of battle begin to settle throughout my body. Our weapons clashed and a shockwave ripped up the dirt around us, sending it flying along with any loose rocks.

The two of us blurred as we fought with the strength and speed of peak creatures of the paranormal world. I was amazed at the agility and strength she possessed within just her single arm.

Shockwave after shockwave washed over the first few rows of the stadium, and demons were scrambling to get higher as some were crushed by the pressure.

I nicked Asmodia repeatedly, but the damn demon regenerated any small wounds before we clashed again. She was happy to trade small cuts and try to whittle me down. Unfortunately, my scales weren't providing much protection from her ax.

My anger was well in check as my sword flowed through the forms that Morgana had taught me. The sword I held was meant for an archangel, and I could push magic through it, but simple flames wouldn't do much. So instead, I pushed summer fae magic into the blade, wanting the sword to not only cut, but to burn with withering heat.

Gold fire sprang up, and Asmodia's face broke the impassive mask she had on to one of surprise. "I knew I sensed fae magic. How? Have you eaten so many that it warped your magic?"

"I'm more than just the Dragon King." I smirked and lunged forward in a thrust that left a purposeful opening.

Asmodia saw the shot and blocked with her shoulder, taking a small cut and bringing her ax down low to fell me like a tree. Ready for the move, my sword stabbed into a portal the size of a fist over her shoulder and came out to block her ax.

Asmodia's eyes went wide before I kicked her in the gut and threw her backwards. She glanced at the wound on her one functional arm and let out a low, threatening growl. "Are you a dragon or a fucking fae?"

"Why not both?" I stabbed my sword into the ground, opening up a portal right below it as one opened right in front of her face.

Asmodia twisted out of the way, with only a scratch on her cheek, but Summer's gold fire burnt the wound. As a result, the cut wasn't healing with the same speed.

Asmodia touched the cut and came away with a little black soot on her fingers. "Abomination. You tricked me and hid your strength. How very fae-like."

"You should see Mammon's territory." I smiled, thinking of what Goldie had done in the short time we'd seen her let loose. Even if she didn't come back, Goldie was going to absolutely wreck the place.

"I see." Asmodia charged and locked me in an exchange of blocks and parries, keeping me using the side of my sword and not opening any opportunity for me to use the reach I needed for a thrust.

I shouldn't have been surprised that Asmodia was a skilled fighter. Her region of Hell required her to be the best. After the first few portals, she anticipated the move and was far better at dodging the strikes.

Changing up my strategy, I decided to use portals more defensively. Asmodia's next swing came towards me, and I popped open a portal in front of me to accept her ax. Then I deposited the weapon in her thigh as I took the opening to try and cleave her in two.

Asmodia dropped her ax and breathed black fire at me, forcing me to jump back as I tried to snap her ax with the portal. Unfortunately the slight delay to dodge the fire gave her enough time to jerk the weapon back out.

"Tricks are useless in the face of power." With a simple chop, Asmodia's strength soared and the arena was cleaved in two from the pressure as it landed.

I barely got out of the way as she took a deep breath and her eyes burned bright. All sense of reality fled her face as she became wrath incarnate.

CHAPTER 23

Asmodia swelled, her veins digging under her skin like earthworms and she grit her teeth hard enough that they chipped.

I barely saw any physical change. If she'd grown, it would have been less than a foot. But instinctively I knew she had gotten much stronger, using her pain.

Asmodia screamed, spittle flying from her foaming mouth as her scars rearranged. From the chaotic mess all over her body, the scars merged and intersected, like a cage over her skin.

Not wanting to give her any more time to put up a stronger defense, I thrust my sword forward, stabbing through a portal and into her face. But she anticipated my move, her arm coming up, her scars catching my blade and stopping it.

My sword scraped along Asmodia's scars like they were steel bands.

The demoness roared and shot around my portal as small spikes continued to grow out of her scars. It wasn't long before she looked like one hell of a pissed off porcupine.

Her fist came flying with speed that would make Morgana jealous, not that she would ever admit it. If Asmodia's movements hadn't been completely telegraphed, I wouldn't have been about to get out of the way.

The still growing spikes nearly caught my cheek as I dodged out of the way. Yet I could feel two small cuts that burned with pain and threatened to drown me in anger. The realization told me that the spikes were an even greater danger than I'd anticipated. Asmodia wanted me to lose myself in anger and fight less strategically.

I had to use the memories of my mates and the desire to find Goldie to ground me to the present and fight the wrath that was coursing through my blood and trying to turn me into a senseless brawler. That was exactly what she wanted. No doubt she could take anyone down in a straight up fight right now.

The entire stadium was screaming. Wrath demons were celebrating Asmodia's more formidable form, seeming to think the fight was over.

Knowing I needed to avoid her spikes, I moved and gave myself distance, trying to reformulate a plan. Before, I had been able to match Asmodia's offensive hits and play tricks to score cuts along her body. Summer's gold flames had helped make sure the wounds I was able to score counted.

But now, trying to match the rampaging pin cushion in front of me meant I needed a new strategy. Tricks wouldn't work against Asmodia's current form, which was exactly why she had chosen it. Asmodia needed me to come at her with strength not brains in order to best me, and filling me with pure rage could do that.

Running quickly through my options, I threw up a portal between me and her to test a theory. Asmodia stopped on a dime, not entering the portal. Instead, she spun around it, kicking off the ground and throwing herself at me.

I cursed as the giant pin cushion lunged at me, each spike threatening to send me into a wild rage.

All it took was one look into her mad eyes and frothing mouth to know it wasn't brilliance guiding her. Asmodia was operating on pure instincts honed from years and years of brutal battles in her domain.

Stepping out of her reach, I dropped through a portal to buy myself more time. There had to be a solution.

I wondered if I could wait her out. Maybe there was a period of time before the berserker state would end, and I could avoid her using portals. But if it didn't end, I didn't have a lot of options.

Death breath had worked on her in the past. Deciding to try it again, I breathed out a great, billowing cloud of death fog to see how she reacted as she charged forward.

Rather than dodge it, Asmodia blew her own fire in front of her to carve out a path.

Frustrated, I slipped away into a portal once more.

***

"My king is struggling." Amira frowned.

Ikta patted her shoulder. "No need to worry. My future husband has a brain up there somewhere. He just needs to use it." Ikta's voice was full of confidence, but she wasn't sure that her man was really going to come out of the battle.

She itched to jump down there and slay Asmodia, but her and Summy's meddling in the matters of fae had transformed him enough that he had begun making promises bound by fae magic.

A powerful demon leapt down to join their group. "Which one of you is the Dragon King?" the greed demon demanded.

Ikta wasn't in a good mood at that moment, so her spider limb cut off his legs before two more pinned his shoulders to the seat in front of her. "Watch your tongue. My future husband is in the pit fighting Asmodia."

"What?" The demon looked panicked, not by his loss of legs, but by the fact that Zach was in the pit. "We need him now. Mammon is summoning him. Err, Mammon is requesting his presence. It is very urgent."

"Can't. He's fae-bound to fight Asmodia to the death. But after he's wiped the floor with Asmodia, maybe you can talk to him." Ikta tossed the demon aside, his legs scooting slowly across the floor to try to reattach.

"Will his bound elemental die if he does?" the demon asked, a scared look on their face.

Ikta snorted, understanding what was happening. "No. Right now, it is under his limited control. If Zach died, the elemental would be wild," Ikta responded, keeping a little snicker from slipping out.

The demon, mostly made of gold, was the visage of a being experiencing pure terror.

Ikta chuckled to herself in her mind. Ikta had never been fond of an elemental, but she was now starting to like Goldie. The elemental was clearly wreaking havoc on Mammon and his demons.

The roar of the demons around her brought Ikta's attention back to the fight. Zach's use of fae magic was still weak, but it was his best option. He'd tried enough that he should be able to puzzle that out and use wild fae magic to cut through Asmodia's defenses.

It would be best if he wielded the magic from afar, but Ikta wasn't sure if Zach was strong enough in his use of the magic. The demoness's defenses were strong and she was operating as a fighter of pure instinct with incredible reaction times.

Her man launched all of his dragon magic at the demoness without so much as scratching her. Asmodia had prepared to fight the Dragon King. He had to fight as the Fae Emperor if he was going to win.

"Right. After he pummels Asmodia, where do we need to go to meet with Mammon? I'm afraid that I won't lead him into the heart of Mammon's territory while he's recovering."

The demon nodded. "I will rush to tell Mammon now. I suspect they will rush here." The demon hurried to get out of Ikta's presence.

"Goldie?" Summer asked.

"That's my guess. Does she have a plushie yet?"

All of the women present shook their heads.

"No. She's not very smart," Regina muttered.

Ikta decided not to comment that it felt like the pot calling the kettle black. But Ikta felt the need to defend Goldie. "No. She's like a just-born infant."

"Doesn't sound like she's acting like one." Summer drummed her fingers. "We'll see about a plushie if she's changed after this. Jadelyn gave me a few in case we had to bring a few succubi home."

Ikta snorted with laughter. "I could imagine that."

"Yes, well, they would have been nothing but concubines like the nymphs." Summer held her head aloft. "I am not letting any base succubi be a wife. We've done a good job at keeping them away. Thankfully, we don't have to worry too much about other demon types, and Goldie is getting rid of the second biggest problem."

Ikta laughed. "Oh yes, he'd love a golden greed demon. Probably stuff them in his hoard by the dozen if he had the opportunity. If we get the chance to talk to Mammon first, we need to draw a line there. What of Levi?"

"It sounds like she's working with Lilith, I hope that woman keeps Levi away if she knows what is good for her." Summer's attention snapped back to Zach. "Looks like he's finally understood. Crude, but not bad."

***

I had thrown everything I had at Asmodia, fire, lightning, death, ice, and poison. None of them did much of anything to her.

So far, only Summer's golden fire had any effect, and even then, it required too much mana to actually burn through Asmodia's skin. It was far more effective in cementing wounds. I could catch her in a portal, but she was prepared now for them to pop up and expertly dodged them.

That's when it came to me.

I clutched my hand and made a small portal, but a bad one, filled with cracks and fragmented to multiple locations.

When Asmodia got close, I threw it.

The closest thing I could compare it to was a magical spider web as Asmodia spun out of the way, but the web caught a cluster of her spines and I was able to shear them off. The spines had proved difficult when I'd tried to hit her earlier.

The spines were as hard as her scars, but I'd finally found something to get through them.

Jumping out of Asmodia's way, I slashed out, imagining a thin portal at the edge of my blade. Creating moving portals was far harder; they were supposed to be anchors between two spots.

I cut into Asmodia's shoulder before the portal locked into place. I smiled until the portal sheared right through my sword instead of her spines.

"Fuck," I screamed and wrath threatened to drown me in anger.

The multiple attempts and failures to injure her had been slowly eroding my patience. I was barely able to keep myself together, working to remind myself that I had another sword as Asmodia pushed her advantage and charged.

Part of me was glad that Goldie was gone. I still felt poorly about what I'd done to her during my first fight with Asmodia, and I was thankful she wasn't the sword I was using when I was testing new uses of my abilities.

With my new use of wild fae magic, I stopped running and fought Asmodia.

The two of us entered a strange dance. An enraged Asmodia dodged and squirmed away from my blade, moving quickly from side to side, trying to get inside my guard.

But with my fae magic, I was able to hold her off. But it did require a ton of focus to keep the razor thin portal on the edge of my new sword without breaking it. It was even harder to hit her, but I had a feeling that her own wrathful state came with its own set of flaws.

"I thought you said that power was everything? Meet my blade, you coward!" I roared and slashed forward.

Asmodia screamed, spittle flying between us as she charged and met my sword with her fist. My eyes grew large at the move.

My sword cut through her fist, sending fingers flying and straight through her wrists and cutting all the way down her forearm to her elbow before she jerked back. Her one good arm was split right down the middle as it started to heal.

I had to stop the healing process or I would never wear her down.

Switching tactics, I thought of the withering summer heat and blasted golden fire out of my mouth, washing Asmodia in the flames and preventing her healing. I wasn't nearly as precise as Summer, but I had fucking golden flames.

Even in the intensity of a battle to the death, I was pretty pleased with my new skill.

The flames passed, and Asmodia's split arm was hanging by her side where the cut was burnt black. My eyes met hers, and I saw pure, apocalyptic rage.

My feet slid apart, and I leveled my sword at her. "You challenged me. Now, let's see what happens when a demon prince dies."

Charging forward, I met her head on and cut through her waist. She managed to dodge enough to stick one spine into my shoulder.

I turned, my vision becoming red as I cleaved Asmodia's head from her shoulder. I panted as rage welled up in me, threatening to blow like a volcano.

"Yay! You won!" Ikta appeared, and a shower of coins and panties rained down on me. Her voice boomed over the entire arena. "Zach Pendragon killed Asmodia in a fair duel! Fear him!"

The jingling of the coins hitting each other caught my attention, and I looked around, realizing where I was and what had just happened.

I blinked as Ikta grabbed my hand and lifted it high, my senses returning to me. "Thank you."

"Figured you'd need a little wake up." She smiled. "Now, I have bad news, but..."

The ground rumbled, and a cracking noise roared through the stadium. The kiss print on my chest burned for a moment before a faint image of Lilith appeared.

She let out a long whistle. "Asmodia. Damn, really?" Lilith gave me a once over noticing that I was barely even wounded. "Good thing we are on the same side. Right?" She smiled prettily at me and waited for my response.

"We are right now." I eyed her, interested in making sure Sabrina was safe.

Lilith gave me a throaty chuckle. "Got it. Walking on thin ice. Well then, let me help you here. Want Asmodia's power?"

"Can you do it without making me an angry hedgehog? Preferably neither angry nor a hedgehog," I clarified.

Lilith nodded rapidly. "Of course, of course. Asmodia was born a wrath demon. She became more of what she was with strength. You are a dragon, that won't change. You'll just be a bigger, badder dragon."

I frowned thinking of what she said about Sabrina becoming a gluttony demon and wondered if she had been lying. But there was another problem.

"With a connection to Hell?" I asked.

"Well…" Lilith hesitated, and saw Ikta tapping her foot next to me.

"If you intend to use him to stabilize Hell, you should hurry." Ikta peered over at me, seeming to want to make sure she hadn't overstepped, which felt like a first. Maybe we were making progress.

Not waiting a moment longer, Lilith stabbed a sneaky little tail that I hadn't seen before into Asmodia before she jumped into my arms and kissed me passionately.

The kiss set me on fire, but at the same time, it was a familiar feeling that made me want to fall to my knees and do nothing but kiss her.

I kissed her while tasting rich delicious mana flow into me and make my cock hard. The power wasn't wrath but lust, pouring into me and drowning everything else out before I took hold of it and made it my own.

It wasn't wrath, nor lust. Just raw dragon power.

Lilith finished kissing me, and Asmodia's body had vanished. "Phew. How about that kiss?"

"How's Sabrina?" I asked, my mind returning to me.

Lilith stepped back like she'd been slapped. "A kiss like that and you ask about another girl?"

I waited for an answer.

"She's fine." Lilith puffed her cheeks out. "Men. She's acclimating to the essence I'm stuffing into her. You could say she's gone up four orders right now. I could use Asmodia's essence and bring her up to be my equal, but

Beelzebub would be better if you could manage it?" She raised a brow with the question.

"He stepped into my city and made a mess. I'm going to kill him for that," I replied calmly. The emotional manipulation on me had eased a great bit with whatever I got from Asmodia.

"Perfect." Lilith nodded. "So... you must have questions about being tied to Hell?" She twirled a strand of hair around her finger.

"No. It's fairly clear. Hell is at risk with how it is drifting from Earth's plane, and without a titan, it's getting harder to stabilize..." I paused, hearing another crackling, and the ground rumbled underneath me.

With the power and connection to Hell, I felt more confident in what was happening. Asmodia wasn't just the ruler of this chunk of land; she had been connected to a central piece where we stood. Her power radiated out until it butted up against the neighboring territories.

Now, even the void of her absence was pushing in. I stomped my foot, causing another quake before pushing back on the void and Lilith's territory. Surprisingly, Mammon's territory gave way, and I felt my territory expand in that direction.

I hadn't been to Faerie since the two queens had given me their territory, but I wondered if it would feel similar.

"There. Stable. You're welcome." I frowned.

Lilith clapped excitedly. "Wonderful. Now, I must know, are you going to kill Mammon?"

"Well, that all depends. Care to tell me your end game?" I asked, tired of games.

Lilith smiled. "Sorry, you are breaking up. Crshh. Sorry, I didn't catch that. Crshh." With a little wave, Lilith faded out.

Ikta just burst into laughter, clapping her hands. "Let's go kill everyone!"

Chapter 24

"We are not killing everyone." I put my head in my hands as Summer and my two dragon mates joined me on the floor of the arena.

"Now that you are in charge, it is kind of counterproductive to kill everyone." Amira shrugged. "Just kill the leaders."

I eyed Amira, not sure she was getting the point of what I was saying. "Probably not killing all of the leaders either. Beelzebub, yes. Mammon, maybe. The rest can live."

"It's because Lilith and Levi are cute, isn't it?" Ikta pursed her lips.

"I haven't even seen Levi," I protested.

"She's the Prince of Envy. Trust me, anyone who sees her wants her." Ikta cursed under her breath, muttering something about water or tails.

I ignored her objections, focusing on Summer who seemed like she may have more helpful information to provide.

"Mammon sent a messenger. It sounds like Goldie stirred up a heap of trouble, and Mammon requested your help. We told the messenger that you weren't coming." Summer glanced at Ikta who appeared to be still complaining about Levi under her breath.

I managed to make out 'stuck up bitch', making me wonder if there was history between Ikta and Levi.

"Anyway." I stopped trying to make sense of Ikta's mumbles. "So, what do we have to lose if we let Goldie weaken Mammon's forces and then we kill him?"

"Them," Ikta corrected me. "Mammon is androgynous. All the fun bits are long gone. Most of the greed demons start replacing everything with gold, silver, and gems. The stronger ones are almost entirely gold and gems, which is why Goldie is such a terror to them. If she can touch them, she can fuck 'em up bad."

"Damn. So greedy they gave up their fun bits?" I was shocked. "That's a damn shame."

"Yep! No golden bitches for you." Ikta smiled, a little too happy about that fact.

"Back on task. Mammon. What are you going to do?" Summer asked.

I glanced around at all the wrath demons that seemed to be holding their breath, waiting to see if I was going to start going on a rampage. "How long do you think Mammon's messenger will take?"

"Maybe a few hours?" Ikta guessed.

"I want to catch up to Goldie. So, that's what I'm going to do." I looked at the rest of my group. "Any objections?"

"No. Let's go get Goldie. And maybe stab Mammon in the face while we are at it just so that nothing bad happens to you with the whole greed thing," Ikta unapologetically declared that she'd kill someone.

My bones crackled, and I stretched out on all fours, arching my back as I grew into a giant dragon. When I thought I'd stop, I just kept growing bigger and bigger. I could stop, but I wanted to see just how big I could get.

Asmodia had been quite the boost. I'd make Brom look like a whelp in my current size, and maybe even begin to compare to my mother. I was starting to question just how strong my mother had become.

"Uh." Regina craned her head up, staring at my sheer size. "How am I supposed to get on that?"

Ikta was already scrambling up while Summer started to float.

Amira was throwing her clothes to the ground.

"What are you—" Regina frowned as Amira shifted into her hybrid form, picked up her clothes with her mouth, and clambered up my side. "Fuck it." Regina followed her example, shifting wings to fly her way up.

I chuckled at how small the remaining demons seemed. "You are in my territory, little demons. Continue as you have been. I'm sure things will shift slowly." This was no longer the territory of Wrath, but I wasn't sure what it would become.

My wings beat and blew away the wrath demons as I lifted myself slowly into the air.

"Whoa. I'm making seats back here. It takes time now that you are this giant," Ikta called from my back.

"Just getting out of the arena." I did a little hop with the help of my wings and set down before I started to walk faster than most shitty little mopeds. It was a leisurely pace, but I had giant legs.

"Not better," Ikta muttered, but I could see that she was making progress and would be done shortly.

Assuming she could figure it out, I leaned into the wind and picked up speed, fanning my wings out.

"Fine! I'm done," Ikta shouted as I flapped powerfully, throwing myself into the sky and flying towards Mammon's territory. I was ready to go find Goldie.

***

Goldie tossed the scraps of the latest of Mammon's knights to the side.

It hadn't been long, but it felt like eons had passed since she'd left Zach's arm. Goldie remembered the taste of Zach's mana like a favorite childhood meal. Memories of all of the demons Goldie had consumed threatened to drown out her entire life. But Goldie remembered Zach, and Yevvy with her egg.

But as Zach would say, Goldie had seen some shit.

"There she is." A demon pointed at Goldie and she frowned, devouring the rest of the memories of the demon in front of her. She was smarter and could parse out the nonsense a lot better.

Who cared what demons thought about Zach, she already knew what she thought about Zach or the rest of his people.

"You are small fries, of no interest to me." Goldie let spikes snag the demons, picking them up and bringing them closer so that they could hear her clearly. "But you are worth being messengers. Find me Zach Pendragon, and I'll think about sparing your miserable land."

She flung the demons away and stopped at a toppled block of silver from their spires. Pausing, she looked at herself in the reflection of the polished silver.

Goldie ran hands down her curves, molding her body slightly in the process. She had changed. No longer was she just a gold mimicry of Yev. She'd taken some of the traits of the demons and her former self.

Goldie twirled in front of the silver block. Her hair was pulled tight against her head and came off in large chunks that sort of looked like hair, but it wasn't. It made her look severe, only enhanced further by her higher cheekbones leading to a gaunter looking face. She'd make a wonderful villainess in a movie.

Yet she knew this was her. She was her own person now, with plenty of memories, but few of her own experiences.

Her dress shaped itself as she spun and she adjusted everything, trying to find what she liked while in the back of her mind she couldn't help but wonder what Zach would think.

Would he like what she'd done or what she'd become?

At first, she had started out with a simple motivation, but she was smart enough to know things weren't simple. She tapped her lip. The demon memories inside of her told her that subterfuge would work best. She could stay stupid and bound back to Zach like a happy little elemental.

He might buy it for a short while, but someone would figure it out and then she'd be in a hot mess. She'd lose Zach's trust.

The flicker of thought that was the old, simpler Goldie went past her mind. When Yevvy did something wrong, she rolled with Zach in the gold having sex until he was happy again.

It couldn't be that easy, could it? Part of her mind told her men were simple creatures, yet another told her that they could be just as devious as women.

Goldie frowned and started sorting through all the memories, tossing some out that made too many assumptions and focused on who had memories of a man similar to Zach.

That was the key.

Goldie needed concrete examples, not over simplistic and skewed sentiments of greedy demons. Zach was a good man. He would stick to what he thought was right and wrong. A strong sense of who he was.

Yes, maybe that was the best route to reunite with her Zach.

A powerful demon, possibly another knight, moved past Goldie and she stopped analyzing the memories. She jumped into action and followed him as a giant wave of gold that devoured the land. The demon was fast and also one of the strongest she'd seen. That demon had to have a wealth of experience.

Goldie flowed over the icky lumpy ground. The gold was all gone; she had devoured it all. The demon didn't sense her if she didn't want it to. She flowed quickly, seeing the demon heading for the central pillars, the one place that Goldie hadn't yet devoured for fear of this Mammon.

Spikes of her gold stabbed into the demon, and she sucked his gold out, stripping his mind.

Ah! This one had seen Zach recently. Goldie pushed the rest of his memories to the side only to learn that Zach wasn't coming. He was scared of Mammon.

Goldie's form rippled in anger.

Stupid Mammon keeping Zach away.

It was time that Goldie did something about Mammon, she was strong enough.

***

I flew through the air and my jaw hung open as I saw Mammon's territory.

"Holy shit," Ikta whistled. "No wonder Mammon sent for help."

There were scattered blocks of silver, but all of the golden grass was gone. The entire landscape was bare, fleshy tumor-like hills with the remaining silver scattered.

I could see down below remnants of demons, like they had been hollowed out and disassembled in a chop shop.

"There's not going to be any side effects to Goldie, is there? I mean, she ate all these greed demons and everything."

"Oh there's going to be side effects." Summer shook her head. "This is a lot of greed mana for that little gold elemental."

I kept my head up, focusing on where there were taller, more clustered spires of gold and silver blocks that still stood in the distance. "That's where Mammon is?"

"Should be," Summer said as a tower toppled. "Might be where Goldie is too."

I pumped my wings at the idea of seeing Goldie again. It hadn't been long, but I still felt like it was partially my fault for how I had treated her during the first battle with Asmodia. "Hang on."

"The seats work perfectly well." Ikta sounded offended. "No need to hang on. We'll be fine here."

"Seat belts would be nice," Regina called out.

"You didn't even know what seat belts were a few months ago. Give a wild fae dragon just a little bit of security and they are clinging to it like a baby with its blanket. Where is your sense of fun?" Ikta huffed.

"Ikta." There was a hint of warning in my tone.

"Yes, your majesty? What do you require?"

"Give them seat belts," I told her.

She sighed. "Hate to tell you all this, but seat belts on this ride are about as pointless as ones on an airplane. I mean, do you really think a strip of cloth is going to survive a fiery crash at those speeds? Hell, they might just chop you in half."

"I assume Zach would try to slow down when crashing," Amira pointed out.

Ikta's voice was all confusion. "Why would you slow down? That defeats the point of crashing."

Regina raised her hand. "I wish to never be on a plane with Ikta."

"Seconded," Amira was quick to agree.

"Thirded? Is that a word?" I frowned.

"It is now," Amira replied in a hurry. "No traveling with Ikta on a plane, certainly never with her piloting."

"Well, with Zach having mastered his invisibility spell to hide from the normals, I suspect you'll never need a plane again," Summer pointed out.

Ikta was perilously quiet, and I craned my head around to get a look at her.

She had her arms crossed and was pouting. "You are all picking on me. I'd fly a plane great. Bet I could do lots of loop de loops and dive continuously through portals."

"If you ever do fly a plane, stock up on barf bags," I advised her.

"Can I fly you?" Ikta asked hopefully.

"I fly me. Though, I have no doubt that you have ways to take control. But I would ask that you don't use them."

"None of you are any fun." Ikta jumped off my back with a giggle and a whoop before portaling back and tousling her messy hair. "Sometimes you just have to live a little."

"Maybe when I'm your age, I'll have similar feelings. But I'm too young," I told her as she reappeared through another portal.

Ikta only shrugged and started knitting small socks. "I guess I'll have to slow down soon anyway. Too many kids will be running around, and I'll be busy teaching them to have fun. I bet the kids will be tons of fun."

"Small children have no sense of self preservation. You'll fit right in," Summer snorted.

"At least she can stop them from falling on hard surfaces with her portals," Amira pointed out.

"Oh yes. Children love falling through portals. I have played with many nymph children. Make a slide out of silk and then put a portal on each end and watch the kids shoot through the slide on repeat." Ikta sounded proud, but somehow, I could only imagine her finding some way to overdo it.

"That and you have six extra limbs for them to climb on." I realized that Ikta would make the perfect jungle gym for a bunch of toddlers.

Another of the towers caught my attention as it toppled. I was getting close enough that I could see a wave of gold spilling through the land.

No doubt every demon down there could see me approaching now. A golden flea jumped from one tower to another, heading in my direction.

I knew who it was before they reached me, but I angled low with my body tense. "If Mammon manipulates me, you are all free to do what you need so that I do not hurt any of you or Goldie. Family first."

"Family first." Summer's voice was hard.

"I'll have you chasing gold coins until it wears off," Ikta promised in a sweet voice. "And then murder all of the greed demons into extinction so it doesn't happen again. No other warning is quite as effective at removing all threats."

Wait, was she saying genocide was a threat... but then there wouldn't be anyone... oh that's the point.

"Uh... Sure." I didn't quite know what to say to that nor the manner that she delivered her statement.

But regardless, I felt secure in flying low and landing on a hill that still had the golden grass on it. With several powerful beats of my wings, I landed gently, blowing some of the golden grass aside and making another tower sway in front of me.

Mammon landed down in front of me.

I wasn't sure what I was expecting, but it was not a featureless gold humanoid. Mammon sort of reminded me of the androids that often appeared in sci fi movies, a human shape that held no remarkable traits. Their entire being was gold, with a few sparkles of diamonds embedded along its body.

"Ah. Dragon King. It is a pleasure to meet you. There is a problem in my land." They glanced over their shoulder to see a giant wave of liquid gold coming our way.

"I can see that. My elemental went rogue upon seeing your land."

Goldie rose up and swallowed one of the towers that had to be over a dozen stories high and then spat out the silver cubes like cherry pits before hitting the hills and forming into an unfamiliar woman a dozen yards away.

Mammon moved closer to me, as if using me as a shield. "Please call your elemental off."

"Goldie." I watched the elemental, a little worried about the influence the greed demons would have had on her. "Are you okay?"

The gold elemental knelt on the ground. Her dress turned into a puddle of liquid gold where it touched and flowed over the surface. "Zach. I am your Goldie. I have changed, but I want nothing more than to return to you."

Mammon let out a shuddered breath. "Wonderful. So it's settled. Please take your elemental with you and leave my territory. I will completely withdraw from all of this conflict that threatens to reshape Hell. As you can see, my territory is all but wiped out."

I turned to take in the demon, not quite sure what was the right response to their offer.

CHAPTER 25

As Mammon spoke, I could feel a little trickle of greed flowing through me. The demon was trying to manipulate me. A low growl rumbled from my chest, which everybody around me seemed to interpret differently.

Mammon grinned like a fool who'd won the lottery.

Goldie jumped back, fear of rejection painted across her face.

"I can feel your manipulations," I growled, wanting to make it clear that Mammon was the one who offended me.

Goldie jerked forward and then paused, not sure if she should attack Mammon.

"I was doing nothing." Mammon held their hands up. "I am the embodiment of greed. There's just a passive effect around me. No need to harm me. Just tell your elemental to halt."

I looked over at Goldie. She'd certainly changed, but she still felt loyal. Not to mention that deferral towards me was pretty obvious. Mammon, on the other hand, would have joined Beelzebub in a heartbeat if it meant gaining more territory and power.

There was no reason to leave a dagger at my back.

"Weaken him, Goldie."

Mammon was quick to react to my words, slamming me with all his greed before he tried to go for my throat.

I held myself still, not even reacting as Goldie shot forward even faster. It was like she'd been fired out of a cannon, with spikes coming out of her body to intercept the demon prince.

As soon as Goldie touched Mammon, they stopped dead.

"No. Please," Mammon begged before his mouth was closed off by a tendril of gold. His body locked up and twisted in on itself.

Goldie slowly drew the demon back to her. "What do you wish for me to do?" She held Mammon to the side, immobilizing him as she not so subtly inched towards my left wrist.

I took a few deep breaths, laying down onto my stomach so that those on my back could get off if they wanted. "I want to know what happened?"

Goldie took a deep breath. She'd clearly thought about what she wanted to say. "I'm so very sorry for leaving you rashly. When I failed you during the Asmodia fight, I had a lot of guilt. I wasn't powerful enough. And then when we passed over Mammon's territory, I saw an opportunity. I was a juvenile at that point, but while I was killing demons, I was able to see their minds and take parts of their memories."

She prostrated herself as she continued, it all came out in one big rush. "Through consuming their memories, I have made myself smarter while throwing away tarnished aspects of their personalities. In doing so, I understand that my actions may have worried, or even hurt you. But I want your forgiveness, even if I don't deserve it."

I rumbled in thought; the temptation to take the gold elemental back was overwhelming, and I was trying to determine if that instinct was simply the overwhelming greed coursing through my body. It was hard to trust my own thoughts, knowing the sense of greed I was pushing back against.

Goldie cowered and shook before me as she waited.

Summer jumped off my back and put her arms around the woman. It was hard to think of Goldie as simply an elemental anymore. "Calm down. My husband is a little confused at present. Mammon just hit him with a lot of greed, and you must know that dragons are famously greedy."

Goldie looked up at Summer. "Husband?"

"Yes. Now, even if he doesn't take you back, I will. And I will give you the opportunity to continue trying to win him back," Summer assured Goldie.

I shook my head. "Weaken Mammon, and I will consume him. Lilith, are you going to appear again?"

Sure enough, the demoness appeared. This time, she was wearing a slinky little black dress with all of her succubus nature hidden. "You don't technically need my help this time." She glanced at Goldie warily. "Besides, your elemental is giving me bad vibes. Worse than when Levi is jealous."

Goldie turned herself into a golden version of Lilith. "Zach, do you like this form better?"

"No. I like your normal self," I replied quickly. My harem had grown large enough that I knew that answer very quickly.

Goldie shifted back to her normal form, still glaring at Lilith. "What is she still doing here if she doesn't need to be?"

Summer's hand on Goldie might have been the only thing stopping her from trying to kill Lilith. But I couldn't quite piece together why Goldie hated her so much.

"I can just eat him?" I asked.

"Yep. You are officially a Hell-Faerie-Dragon-King-Emperor thing. It's not going to make Lucifer happy when you claim three territories though."

"What if I only take two?" I asked.

"We could probably still lie to him and say he has the biggest territory so he gets to keep the crown. Wait, are you—"

"Goldie, eat Mammon," I interrupted Lilith.

It happened in an instant.

Goldie sucked Mammon into her body as the demon prince tried and failed to scream, his two diamond eyes disappearing into Goldie and then spat right back out like cherry pits.

"It is done." She smiled up at me.

"Return to my wrist; we will talk about the rest later," I commanded.

Goldie was on my wrist in an instant, hugging my arm fiercely and making my bones, even in my dragon form, ache.

Lilith watched the gold elemental carefully. "Okay. Well shit. That happened. Poor Mammon found his natural predator. By the way, your succubus is almost done. She'll wake up soon. As soon as she's awake, I'm going to let you know. Do you want me to send her your way?"

I had a feeling I had completely broken through layers of Lilith's plans with Goldie leveling all of Mammon's territory. Goldie had thrown everything out the window.

"Keep her for now. I would ask that not a hair on her head be out of place." I narrowed my eyes in thought. "She's going to ask for some things after she comes out of the transformation. Can you help her with that?"

"If that's what you want, big boy," Lilith replied in a hurry. "Is there a reason? Just looking to help you finish up and get out of Hell."

I wondered if there was a harm in telling her my plans, but she seemed like she had a healthy interest in us all getting out safely. "Sabrina is my ticket out of here. We have a setup back home. She's going to send a signal with instructions for her new summoning ritual, and we'll ride back with her."

"I will most certainly help with that, but you don't need that anymore." Lilith poked my chest. "You are bound to three planes. I'm pretty sure the Spider Queen here could help you jump between them now."

"The summoning is easier." Ikta shrugged when I glanced at her.

"Well. There you have it." I trusted Ikta. Even if she was crazy, she was on my side completely.

Lilith watched the two of us nervously and nodded. "Wonderful. I'm going to ditch. Have fun. See you soon." She faded out.

"Goldie, how does the land feel to you?" I asked.

"Sick. I am making it my own. From Mammon's memories, I understand much of it. This will be an elemental territory by the time I'm done with it." Goldie made a small mouth on the edge of the bracer. "But I shall not remain here. Instead, I will remain at your side. It is where I belong."

"You'll fill it with gold elementals?"

"No. Lots of metal, maybe some earth." Goldie made a grunt, and there was a ripple that came from the center of the territory.

The fleshy ground under me became harder and had a little more gloss to it.

"It will take time. May I... never mind."

Summer smirked. "Give her some of your mana."

"No. That's not...," Goldie protested.

I did it anyway, giving her a trickle of my mana.

Rather than greedily slurping it up like before, she seemed to reverently collect it and take small sips, savoring my mana. A part of me was relieved to see that she wasn't going to drain me like she had the other demons. While I trusted Goldie, I knew that power could be addictive.

"Is everything okay?" Goldie felt my apprehension.

"I expected more greed. Given that you've eaten all of these demons, including Mammon," I told her honestly.

Goldie paused in thought for a moment. "I am greedy. I want you, but I want to stay by you. Immune isn't the word, but I'm differently affected by the greed of these demons." She trailed off. "I am a very different Goldie than I was a few days ago. Suffice to say, I never want to leave you again."

"Guess she gets one," Ikta called out, pulling an object out of a portal.

I couldn't see it as Goldie shot part of herself off of the bracer and collected whatever Ikta had gotten her. Then she retracted back to the bracer.

It was all done so quickly that I could have missed it if I blinked.

"What was that?" I asked.

"Nothing," the voices around me sounded in unison.

"We should get going," Goldie changed the subject, and a part of her broke off and flowed over my arm up to my back before tearing away Ikta's spider webs and replacing them with gold thrones on my back.

"Hey!" Ikta shouted. "I worked hard on those."

"Didn't look that way." A Goldie appeared in one of the seats, but she was still on my arm.

"You can split yourself?" I asked.

"Sort of. Your bracer will always be my core. If something happened to it, the rest would disappear. These are just... clone bodies that I can control remotely. I have a lot of mass, but it is still difficult for me to split while keeping focus. And long distances become problematic." Goldie frowned as if thinking of a sudden concern.

"Wait, can you tell where your main body is?" Ikta asked suddenly.

Summer's eyes lit up as she mounted me and got into one of the thrones. "That would be very useful. But we'd just want a small piece."

Goldie seemed to understand and make a flicking motion with her fingers before a gold coin spun in the air and Ikta snatched it. "I won't actively listen to that fragment. You'll have to yell at me a few times to get my attention."

"It's only for emergencies." Ikta stuffed it into her bra.

I growled in understanding. "I thought you already had a tracker."

"But this is even better. Goldie can relay information to us now." Ikta smiled.

I huffed and Goldie patted my arm under the bracer.

"If you tell me not to, that coin will never speak," Goldie proclaimed.

"Emergencies only." I glared at Ikta. "No snooping."

"It will be done," Goldie promised. "Now, I want to feel the wind in my face. Are we going to kill Beelzebub?"

"Hell yeah." I got a running start and launched myself into the air. "By the way, Goldie, just how much mass do you have?"

"I could drown you in a pile of gold that you'd be unable to move despite your strength," Goldie preened. "But my mass is variable. Sort of like a shifter, I have access to all of it, but it isn't all with me at any point in time. Even then, I don't seem to have a fixed weight. Otherwise, these thrones might actually be cumbersome."

"They feel fine." I flew through the air, noticing how part of them shifted with my flight so that it wasn't a big stiff piece on my back either.

"Good. Let me know if they need more adjustments. I am so very happy to be back." Goldie hummed to herself as we flew, and I could feel her slowly munch on my mana, shivering on my arm with delight. "You are much bigger, and your mana is even richer than before."

"He ate Asmodia," Ikta explained.

"Oh." Goldie sighed. "You didn't need me?"

"It would have been a thousand times easier with you, but I had to risk it without you. Don't worry, you'll get a chance to stab Beelzebub when we get there," I promised her.

"Good. I will be of use this time. Against the two of us, Beelzebub will be far easier." Goldie nodded up on her throne.

I soared through Goldie's new territory, noticing just how much destruction she had wreaked. Dismantled demons were everywhere. What little survived were fragments of their former selves or the weakest of demons, not having any gold in them.

"Damn, Goldie." Ikta watched over the side. "Remind me not to get on your bad side."

"I have no bad side," Goldie refuted, a smile teasing at her lips. "Unless you harm Zach. I must remove all threats to Zach. As one of the Golden Plushic holders, I'll have to do it quietly, so as to not cause a stir."

Ikta turned back to Goldie slowly. "Damn. I LOVE THE NEW GOLDIE! We are going to be the best of friends. If you see anyone in the harem or the nymphs cause trouble for Zach, let me know and I'll set up their deaths."

"Agreed," Goldie nodded.

"Umm…" I hesitated. "I'd ask that you two don't plot to murder my harem."

"Of course not, your majesty." Ikta's voice was as sweet as could be. "But are they really part of your harem if they betray you? I don't think so."

"This is all hypothetical," Summer pointed out, but she didn't try and dissuade them.

"Promise to keep an eye on those two and not let it get out of hand?" I asked the more responsible member of our team.

"I can try," Summer agreed. "Now, Goldie, we'll need to catch you up tonight."

"I would love nothing more." Goldie bobbed her head. "I remember things and can see them through a new lens now, but it would be helpful to have your experience with matters explaining things."

"If I didn't know better, I'd say she was trying to butter you up, Summy," Ikta laughed. "I love this new Goldie. Future husband, hurry up to Gluttony so that we can find some tasty food and bring it back to the boob mountains for dinner."

"Tasty food?" I grumbled.

"Gluttony is full of monsters. Smaller than the ones we fought in Lust, but lots of them. Most of the demons are some form of animal-human hybrid as they become more human the stronger they become. But they all start out as big monsters for people to hunt and eat. They are all super tasty too," Ikta explained.

"Will I find them tasty?" Goldie asked.

"Eh. Probably not. But as an elemental, you don't really need to eat. You just need ambient mana. Or you can go dormant and feed off my future husband when you need to." Ikta shrugged.

"No need," Goldie said hurriedly. "Zach's mana is tasty, but I can sustain myself off of my territory of Hell. Mammon's memories suggest it is similar to holding territory in Faerie, only less rules around acquisition."

"Why do I feel like, as the person who holds the most territory, I know the least about it?" I frowned.

"Because that is absolutely true!" Ikta laughed. "Don't worry. We'll get you there, eventually."

CHAPTER 26

"This is amazing," Regina murmured around a mouthful of tiger.

I still couldn't figure out why a tiger had been in a swamp, but I had to admit that it was tasty.

Gluttony had turned out to be dense swampland teeming with life. We confirmed that mosquitoes did indeed come from Hell, and the ones still around were worse than those on Earth.

I hadn't stuck around, taking a giant tiger carcass back through a portal, and we were cooking it up as Summer and Ikta inducted Goldie into the Golden Plushie society.

At least, that was what Summer and Ikta had told me they were doing as they'd pulled her away. So I sat with my dragons around the fire.

"There is a tribe of weretigers in Faerie that we hunt sometimes. Tiger meat is wonderful, but this is better," Regina continued to talk around her food.

"I'm glad you like it so much. I never really considered tiger a potential staple of my diet." I shrugged and handed her another piece off the spit.

"I knew I loved you." She downed what she had been eating and took the next piece from me.

"Save some for our mate." Amira glared at Regina.

"He hunted for us. We should be respectful and enjoy it." Regina punctuated her statement by tearing into the meat.

Amira sighed.

"Don't worry. We can always get more," I reassured Amira. "You've grown quite a bit on this trip. What do you think your parents are going to think?"

The question seemed to catch Amira off guard.

"Do you think I'm bigger than my parents?" Amira asked.

Regina shrugged and waited for my assessment.

"It's probably close. I've seen Herm shift, but not your mother." I wasn't honestly sure how they would all compare.

"Mother is bigger," Amira blurted.

"Then maybe not bigger than your mother," I answered honestly.

Amira took a piece of meat off the spit and tore into it, her face lost in thought. "Do you think I could get bigger than her by the end of this trip?"

"Probably, if you take the lead for at least part of Gluttony," I replied after a moment of thought. She didn't have that much further to go, and the meat was mana rich.

And we could use the extra strength. Asmodia fought head first and Mammon had been countered completely by Goldie. But Beelzebub would be different. The demon was far more cunning, and he wouldn't fight unless he made the rules and was sure of his success.

We could use more strength.

Amira tore into the piece of meat. "Give me more."

I happily cut off more with a shifted claw and handed it to her.

"Mommy issues?" Regina asked, totally missing the empathy part of the question.

Amira just grunted and tore into her meat, so I answered for her, "Her mother is fairly controlling."

Amira nodded along and spoke around the meat. "My father is fairly cowed by her. She is one of the dragon leaders now, and that only makes her more insistent that her ideas are the correct ideas."

"You are my mate now," I declared, trying to give her more support. "Your mother's opinions of what you should and shouldn't do are downgraded. Hell, the Golden Plushie Society should get more of a say."

Amira sucked in the last of the hunk of meat that I'd given her. "Mother won't like that."

"Tell her to take it up with me, or stand behind Yev and let your mother experience the wrath of a nesting dragon."

The more we talked, the more I was sure that I wanted to cut off Amara's influence over her daughter. Maybe with time, Amira would become more independent.

Regina chuckled. "I don't know how strong your mother is, but pissing off Yev is a wonderful way to get taken down a peg. The entire Plushie Society would crush your mother under their boots if she laid a hand on Yev. For that matter, the Plushies would do the same for you."

"I don't get to join the Plushie meetings, but I'm well aware of all my mates. They look out for each other," I piled on.

Amira just nodded, and held her hand out for more tiger meat. "Either way, I want to be stronger. Does it bother you that this tiger was someone's soul once upon a time?"

I frowned at it. "Sort of. If there was a way to bring them back, maybe I'd feel compelled to save them. As I understand it though, it is just an inhuman beast now with never ending hunger." I glanced at Regina, curious how she would feel.

Regina shrugged. "They are tasty. Besides, what would be the point of saving them? Giving them humanity so they can see how shitty their situation is? It isn't like you could stuff them back into a body on Earth without a huge problem. At best, you could send them through Tartarus to get reborn, but then chances are they'd get eaten anyway."

She dug into another piece of meat, shrugging as juices ran down her face.

"Why torture yourself over things you can't affect?" she mumbled around her bite of food.

"I'm going to control two territories here. Maybe I can affect the outcomes," I countered.

"Systems can be changed, but it'll still be a system of some sort. People will live and die. You can't exactly put a farming commune next to Lucifer's territory. There will be death and fighting." Regina shrugged as if it was a foregone conclusion. "Look at humanity. It is always fighting with itself. Are you going to break into politics and try to solve everything there?"

I grunted. "Politics are useless. We would just use Jadelyn to pay for anything we wanted changed. You have a point, though. I'm not jumping to save everyone. I'm operating on the scale of saving planes of existence rather than individuals."

"As you should. You are the Dragon King and the Fae Emperor and whatever you are now to Hell," Amira agreed. "Just don't turn the whole system upside down to benefit yourself, and don't feel bad about eating a stupid beast living in a territory controlled by someone who wants to kill you."

She wasn't wrong.

I glanced over where Ikta popped the little bubble that was keeping their conversation private. "Ready to start planning for an attack on Beelzebub?" I asked.

"Is there a part in it where I get to go on a murder spree? First you hogged Asmodia, then Goldie hogged all of Mammon and his demons. I want to go on a murder spree!" Ikta stomped her foot, a slightly crazed gleam in her eyes.

She was a piece of work, but she was my crazy.

"Sure. I bet we can work in an Ikta murder spree." I couldn't help but shake my head.

"Yay!" Ikta bounded over to the campfire as I took one spit off and started to make another.

Goldie melted over to me and her clone tethered to my bracer as she sat close enough to press her hips into mine. She even melted herself up against me when I shifted. "I'm here to help, however I can."

Summer nodded at her. "Well, we need to take on Beelzebub. But I'm sure you realize he won't be as straightforward as Asmodia."

"No, he won't. Which is why I was thinking we'd lure him out by using me as bait." I glanced at Goldie. "Goldie here can protect me from an ambush."

"Yes, I can." The Goldie next to me spoke as my bracer expanded so quickly that it looked more like an explosion rather than a controlled expansion. The bracer soon wrapped me from head to toe in Goldie armor.

"No one will touch you." She retracted herself back to the bracer just as quickly.

"Impressive." Summer's face showed a moment of shock before she schooled her features. Ikta didn't worry about appearances, practically drooling over Goldie's latest move.

"What?" Goldie frowned at the wild fae.

"Could you make me a gold glitter bodysuit? God, I bet it would make my future husband go crazy. We should pick up some lust boar on the way out of Hell." Ikta sighed.

Goldie frowned. "I could, but I am remaining with Zach."

"But one of the clones? I mean, if we put all of his mates in Goldie dresses or bodysuits, they'd all be super protected." Ikta had set her sights on a new goal, and I knew the manipulations were only beginning.

"Don't give in to her pressure. She just wants you for your body, Goldie. Don't listen to her." Regina grew protective of Goldie.

Ikta gaped. "That's not true."

"You asked for one of my clones. That's my body," Goldie pointed out.

"Don't you dare team up on me." Ikta pointed a warning finger at Summer who was about to speak. "Always teaming up on poor Ikta. I'm just too beautiful. It's like a curse." She tossed her hair.

"I was going to get us back on topic for Beelzebub?" Summer smirked. "And your upcoming murder spree."

"Murder spree!" Ikta bounced in her seat for a moment before settling. "So, what's the plan, big man?"

"From what I have learned, Beelzebub hunts in those marshes. And is an expert hunter, given that is the main mode of growth and strength in Gluttony." I glanced at

Regina. "So, what are my chances of finding Beelzebub in his territory?"

"Zero. He can avoid you until he believes he is at an advantage." Regina had a thoughtful look on her face. "But your goal is to lure him out? Lure him to hunt you?"

I nodded. "Which I suspect he won't do if Ikta and Summer are with me. Possibly not if you are with me either." I tried to soften the introduction of my plan.

"Wait a second." Ikta frowned. "Where's the part where I go on a murder spree?"

I smirked. "We all go in and let Gluttony take over. You both will pair with a dragon. I'm 'alone'." I air-quoted the last part because Goldie would be with me. I was sure she could be a nasty surprise for Beelzebub or any other Gluttony demons.

Ikta's eyes went wide. "We get to pretend to be gluttonous hunters and kill and eat everything? Wait. I don't want to get fat, at least not until I'm pregnant. Then I get to eat as much as I want."

"It doesn't really work that way," Summer interjected.

"It does if I want it to," Ikta shot back, narrowing her eyes. "I bet you looked like a stupid supermodel while pregnant."

I glanced at Summer and tried to imagine her pregnant. If anything, she was probably even more glowing. I couldn't picture her losing an ounce of her charm.

"Maybe." Summer didn't refute the claim. "This plan sounds... interesting. But is it really the best? There's no guarantee that Beelzebub goes for you."

"That's why you and Ikta are in the other two groups. You can hold him off, at least until help arrives." I tapped

Goldie. "Can you make another coin for Summer? We'll use them to keep in touch if we need to."

Goldie flicked another coin off, and Summer caught it before stuffing it down the front of her dress.

"Great. Use the coin if you come into danger. The goal is to have three rampaging dragons be bait."

"Burninating the countryside," Ikta sang for a moment before she got strange looks from the rest of the group and rolled her eyes. "It's a song about a dragon."

"Who kills all the peasants and burns thatched roofs. I like to think I'm a nicer Dragon King than that," I clarified, and Ikta's eyes shone bright as she realized I knew the song. "You can go with Regina. She's a red dragon, and you can live out your dream."

"Yes!" Ikta shouted. "Regina we have to burninate the whole place. Don't worry, I'll show you how."

Regina blinked a few times before she finally nodded slowly. "I'm in your hands."

"I'll take care of Amira. Don't worry, dear, we'll see how much bigger we can get you in a short period so that you don't get bullied by your mate," Summer told Amira.

"I would never bully her," I refuted.

"You can be a little rough and bitey." Summer deadpanned. "We watched you mark both of them, remember?"

"I like the marking though," Amira said. "But more size would be nice so that I can deal with my mother."

"Poor woman is smitten. She likes the biting." Ikta put her head in her hand and sighed. "Dragons, am I right?"

Summer laughed and continued. "So, we'll let the dragons loose. Ikta can find some time to go on a murder spree, and Goldie is going to keep communication lines open. The goal is to get Beelzebub to spring a trap on us?"

"Sums it up pretty well." I nodded.

"That's a terrible plan," Summer sighed. "You are just putting yourself out on a hook waiting for that ugly bastard to bite."

I knew it wasn't exactly the most elegant plan, but if what we'd learned about Beelzebub was right, then we were walking into an apex predator's territory. Trying to flush him out through force was going to be difficult, and would drain us of too much energy.

"Do you have a better plan?" Ikta asked.

Summer crossed her arms. "We could take your plan, and just what did you call it? 'Burninate' the whole place until he has no choice but to come out."

"It's a swamp." I deadpanned. "Even a dragon is going to have a hell of a time setting a swamp on fire."

"Besides, that is very destructive to the environment. I expected his majesty to come up with a plan like that, not you." Ikta clicked her tongue in disappointment.

"See, my Favored is right." I smirked, knowing that Ikta would be pleased at the use of the term. Sure enough, she preened immediately.

"That is a very dangerous name for her." Summer nearly choked laughing as she continued. "Please use it for her around Morgana."

I paled at the thought. "Just when we are alone. How about that, Ikta?"

"No! I want it more than that. Maybe just in fae settings?" She tapped her lips in thought. "But regardless, we need to get this plan into action. How about when you tromp through the swamp, you just destroy it as you go?"

"Pretty sure that's going to happen anyway," Regina muttered. "Have you seen how big he is? It might be hard for him to burn the swamp, but he can certainly flatten the place."

"Squish it all. I wonder if you can accidentally squash that ugly toad Beelzebub. What a way to go." Ikta clapped her hands.

"If only we could be so lucky," I sighed before tearing off a piece of the meat in front of me.

"That's a problem for tomorrow. We'll enjoy each other as a family tonight." Summer moved behind me and rubbed my shoulders. "Ikta, you can keep watch, oh favored one."

Chapter 27

We had set off early in the morning as a group and tried to mimic organically splitting up as Ikta and Summer tried and 'failed' to wrangle Regina and Amira.

Then I set off on my own, devouring a path through the swamp as the morning turned into afternoon.

I tore through the corpse of a large bird, pulling it apart and swallowing the small morsel in one bite like an hors d'oeuvre. None of the creatures were really enough to do more than fill the gaps between my teeth for a moment.

"Zach," Goldie burbled on my arm.

"What?" I growled before remembering myself. "How are the others?"

"Fine," Goldie reported. "Just making sure I don't need to start throwing gold coins yet. I sense something up ahead."

"That vibration sense you have?" I asked. At some point, Goldie would need to explain to me how she could sense more than I could.

"Eight. They are creeping forward to get in your path," Goldie whispered.

I held my head up, playing the act of being consumed by gluttony. But in all honesty, I was stuffed. "More food," I growled loudly and stomped forward."

"I am ready," Goldie confirmed, and I felt her bleed across my body, filling the space between my scales. Large balls of her formed hidden at the base of each folded wing, ready to spread across and protect the thin membrane.

We had not had much time to practice it, but Goldie had already shown how well she could protect me. Multiple times throughout our trip, she'd made a golden wall over my scales. Even though they probably would have held, she was protective of me.

The swamp grew quiet around me as I stomped and stormed through it with abandon, snapping branches and kicking up slimy water.

I didn't have to go far before demons burst out, attempting to surround me. One even shot out of the water; the algae floating on the surface wrapped around him, revealing it actually to be his cape. Spears seemed to be the weapon of choice among the group as they rushed me from all directions. Their attacks focused on my wings.

In the time it took for them to leap onto me, Goldie shot over my wings and encased my entire dragon body with gold armor. Their weapons scraped along my hardened wings. It hurt, but my wings would be fine. It didn't take the demons long to figure out that something was wrong as they tried to flee their failed hunt.

But Goldie was not about to let them be free after attacking me. Golden tendrils shot out, lashing onto the demons before they could flee, and drew them back to my body as more of Goldie shot out, encasing each of them in a cage until I had a dozen caged demons hanging from my wings.

Damn, Goldie was scary.

"There were more than ten," I noted, knowing it would irk her and finding that amusing.

Goldie huffed. "I am not perfect. Some of them must have held really really still."

I glanced through them and frowned. "None of these are Beelzebub."

The demons fought against Goldie's cages, but she formed spikes on the inside bands of the cages and stabbed the demons until they stopped resisting.

"Who are all of you, and where is Beelzebub?" I growled at the caged demons hanging from my wings.

One of the demons, a hound-looking creature grunted. "We don't snitch."

Goldie slowly crushed the demon in the cage, filling the swamp with his screams for a minute before it all went quiet.

"Anyone else feel like not talking? I can make it permanent for the low low price of feeding my Zach." She shifted the cage so that it rippled along my body, and I devoured the demon, who had actually been decently powerful based on his mana.

"We were just supposed to slow you down," another demon whimpered. "The goal was to ground you by tearing your wings and then retreat for a formal hunt. You are the biggest hunt here in centuries. Beelzebub has promised us the hunt."

I didn't like the sound of that at all. If Beelzebub was mobilizing the demons of his territory to hunt me and my mates, it would take forever for me to get to him. And he would likely wear us down in the process.

"Oh. That should be fun," I growled and breathed fire into the cages until all of them were dead. "Goldie, check in with the other groups."

I didn't like that Beelzebub had decided not to show. He was biding his time, and it sounded like he'd mobilized a hunting army.

***

Ikta rode on the dumb giant red dragon's forehead like a surfboard. "Burn it!"

Regina obliged and torched the section of swamp Ikta had pointed towards.

"Yes!" Ikta jumped up and down clapping. "More! More fire!"

Regina snorted smoke up into her face. "Quiet, you. I'm hungry."

"Of course you are. You've eaten like a thousand pounds of gluttony demons. They make you hungrier than diet coke." Ikta laughed before the dragon underneath her tossed her head and tried to throw her off. "I didn't call you fat."

"I'm pretty sure you did." Regina ground her head into a tree as Ikta scampered along her horns.

"Stop trying to squish me!"

"I don't like spiders." Regina dunked her head in the water, trying to dislodge Ikta. "Spiders taste like shit."

"Rude." Ikta jumped along the dragon's spine. The dragon had become quite easy to aggravate now that she was hopped up on gluttony.

Someone was a hangry dragon, and the constant feeling of starvation from gluttony wasn't helping, despite having eaten her weight in demonic beasts.

Unfortunately, this hangry dragon was her future husband's mate and important to him, so Ikta couldn't do anything too drastic with the dragon's temper tantrums.

"Look! More food." Ikta pointed to an alligator in the water.

Regina crushed it with a paw, only to frown. "Another illusion! They must all be illusions because they don't fill me up one bit!"

"Oh. You are getting real testy with me. Careful, little whelp, or I will solve this problem in ways you don't like." It was mostly an empty threat; Ikta couldn't really do anything.

Regina went to roll, and Ikta jumped and swung from a tree to land back on the dragon's back.

"Look what you've done. My heels are wet now." Ikta grabbed onto the dragon's back and decided that a sleepy dragon would make better bait.

She snapped her fingers with a little magical flourish. Regina had been about to say something, but then dropped into the swamp, her nose well above the water line as she started to snore loud enough to alert all of Hell that she was here.

"Well, we were supposed to play bait." Ikta smiled at how well her move had gone.

Sure enough, several of the hunters had crept closer during their spat. Ikta had felt those moving through the trees through her threads. The ones underwater were always going to be the trickiest. Some could even go for Regina while she was playing dead.

An arrow whistled through the air, and Ikta side stepped it as if it was an accident.

"Oh my. Hunters! Wake up, stupid dragon." She stomped on Regina's head, only making the dragon snore louder.

More arrows peppered Ikta, and she playfully dodged them, if only barely. The hunters were being cautious. And Ikta was happy to play weaker than she was, letting an arrow catch her side and tear her dress.

Ikta feigned injury, clutching her side and crying out. The stupid dragon didn't even react, still snoring louder than an army of lumberjacks. "You got me!"

A gluttony demon stepped out from behind a tree, keeping his arrow pointed at her. Then another and another popped out from hiding. Ikta counted eight who had shown themselves. There were two more she thought in the water and another two hanging further back, like they were going to run if something happened.

With a smile, Ikta pulled at the threads near the far two and cut their heads off before they even realized something was wrong.

"The Spider Queen. I figured you'd be stronger." A crocodilian woman crept forward.

"Unfortunately not. I gave all of the fae wild's strength to my future husband, the man whose seed I will bear." Ikta sighed at the thought, and Regina snored even louder in response.

"Shame. We thought you'd be a better hunt." The crocodilian woman sneered as she spoke.

Ikta gasped while two tiny portals opened behind her feet and the lower two limbs stabbed down.

"What was that?" One of the hunters pointed at her feet.

"They are feet. Duh. Oh wait, do you have hooves? Was that offensive, feetist or something? You look kinda like a goat. I bet you have hooves. My bad." Ikta rambled on as she pulled two bloody spider limbs from the portals, fully aware the two demons in the water were now dead.

Their blood would soon fill the water and spoil her fun.

The hunter's response to Ikta's nonsense was an arrow to her face.

She rolled her eyes and popped open a portal so that the arrow took another hunter out, tearing right through his head. "Really, you should be more considerate to your fellow huntsmen."

Arrows flew from all of them. When the arrows were unsuccessful, they threw their bows to the side, pulling out nets and spears to chase her down. Two had stayed back, working on a larger spell.

Clearly, this group had fought together before with how they worked together with little communication.

Ikta danced excitedly on Regina's back. "This is going to be so much fun!"

None of the arrows hit her, and when the first hunter came up into range, a spider leg bisected him from shoulder to hip in an instant while she was still dancing and twirling.

The hunters came for her with the nets, trying to keep her in place while two had stopped and were starting to chant spells.

Ikta fell through a portal, only to pop out behind the two casting the spell, and hung upside down behind them. "So, what's the spell we are casting?"

They jerked around to see her, and one reached for his knife only to see the arm that had grabbed it to fall into the swamp. That hunter stared dumbly at its stump of an arm, seeming to not be able to process what had just happened.

"Rude. You should tell me the spell. That way I can at least appreciate your work before butchering you." Ikta finished the other with a few swipes and turned back to the one-armed caster. "So, what's the spell?"

"Inexorable doom," the demon said.

"Oh, that's a good one. Well done. But sorry, you didn't win. Better luck next time." Ikta stabbed through his chest and lifted him up before tearing him apart.

"Ouch!" Regina shot up, no longer pretending to sleep as one of the hunters cut into her wing badly.

She had totally been pretending. Yep. Pretending because they worked this out earlier, and Ikta one hundred percent did not put just a little juice in her fake sleep spell.

The demon jumped on Regina, trying to take her wings out of commission. Ikta jumped through another portal, killing two of the remaining hunters before Regina pulled her wings tight and rolled. The giant red dragoness crashed through the swamp, and three of the hunters disappeared under her giant red bulk.

Ikta stepped through a portal to pop back on Regina's head.

"You said you'd handle them," Regina shouted and snapped up one of the dead hunters, looking around for the others.

There was one left, and that demon was trying to flee.

Ikta jerked her hand in a motion like she was pulling something. Immediately after, the hunter fell into the swamp in pieces. "Really, such little faith. I had it all under control."

Regina unfolded a wing showing the big gash in the membrane. "They cut me badly."

"Given the size and experience of those demons, I think you came out rather well. The words you are looking for are 'thank you, oh great Ikta.'" Ikta made three little portals and stabbed through them in quick succession to make sure the three that Regina rolled over were dead dead and not playing dead.

"I can't fly for at least an hour," Regina whined.

There was a vibration against Ikta's skin. She grabbed the gold coin from her bra and flicked it in the air before catching it. "You need me, Goldie?"

"Zach has dealt with his ambushers expertly. He didn't even take a scratch fighting them," Goldie proudly reported.

Ikta frowned at Regina as if to say, 'see, he could do it.'

Regina huffed a cloud of smoke out of her nostrils. "We took out ours. Only a small cut to my wing, but I'll be grounded for a short period."

"Wonderful," Goldie replied through the coin. "Did you encounter Beelzebub?"

"Nope. No asshole frog among our demons. I'm guessing that means you didn't encounter him either. Which means he's hanging back, or more likely he's gone after Summy. Ooh, roasted frog legs tonight!" Ikta sighed. "Then we can get out of this Hell hole." She giggled. "And I can toss Zach into my pool of nymphs. Are you sure you can't be convinced to become gold dresses for me and my nymphs? Don't you want to please Zach?"

"I am not clothing for you to tempt Zach with," Goldie argued. "What do you mean we'll have roasted frog legs?" Goldie asked, changing the subject.

"Because Summy is a bad ass bitch when she wants to be. I mean, I feel a little bad for Beelzebub. He probably thought Amira and Summy were the weakest of the groups and went for the easier hunt." Ikta clicked her tongue. "Really, I'm disappointed he didn't come to play with me."

"We should go to Summer then," Goldie sounded concerned.

"Don't worry ab—" Ikta started before a giant gold plume of fire shot into the air. "Oh! Let's go find Summy. It looks like he's putting up a good fight. Maybe we can get there and join in the fun before it's over. Mush, Draggy!"

Regina turned around her giant red head. "You did not just call me 'draggy'."

Ikta mimed cracking a set of reins. Really, Regina should be honored to be ridden by her. "Mush, Draggy! We need to get there before the fun is all over."

Regina sat her giant red ass down in protest.

"Going to have to call you back, Goldie. A certain red dragon is being temperamental and needs to learn some manners." Ikta stuffed the coin back into her bra. "We can do this the easy way or the hard way." She stared at the red dragon who stared back at her for a long moment.

Regina snorted and stood up. "I can never tell when you are being serious." She turned back around and started to march through the swamp. "Stupid fae."

"Of course you can't tell. That's on purpose. You'll never know when I'm kidding or being serious because when someone finally figures out, they normally end up dead." Ikta laughed. "But don't worry. I can't actually hurt you or any of Zach's women."

"So then... I'll never figure it out, but I won't die?" Regina asked, sounding confused.

"Yep. Pretty much. Just keep going. We need to go help Summy. I have a feeling that things are going to get a little more complicated than Zach is ready to handle." Ikta frowned at the level of power that Summer had drawn out so quickly.

The woman didn't like to fight. If she was going all out, something was off.

CHAPTER 28

I craned my head to see the giant pillar of gold flames Summer was sending into the sky, concern growing inside of me.

"Nothing from Summer?" I asked Goldie.

"She didn't respond." Goldie's voice was soft, like she blamed herself.

"It isn't your fault. We head in that direction now. Their attack must be a much stronger group." I took two leaping strides before I tore through the trees with my wings and pulled myself up into the sky.

Gold fire still flickered at the edge of the area where Summer had blasted with her magic, pulling me forward like a beacon.

I pumped my wings making good time; we hadn't really been that far apart for this very reason.

"Zach. Ikta is en route, but Regina's wing is injured so they will be slow to arrive," Goldie reported.

"Doesn't matter. We can take care of Beelzebub." I was high enough to dive towards the burning hole that Summer had made in the swamp.

The situation came into view moments before I crashed into the water.

Summer was floating warily in the air, searching the water below her. Amira was lying on the ground, rolled onto her side and heaving from a wound.

I didn't hesitate. "Goldie, protect Amira."

The elemental shot a huge chunk of herself off my wrist. It hit Amira and encased the full-size dragon in an expanding gold egg.

I landed in the water below Summer, spraying water everywhere and pouring ice over the area away from Amira to give us space.

"Goldie, how much of your mass did that take?" I asked.

"Much of it, but I'm stitching Amira's side together," Goldie replied from my bracer.

Summer landed on my head. "Careful. Beelzebub is here. I failed to protect Amira; they attacked in three groups."

"Blame game later," I grunted and spun in a circle, looking for Beelzebub. "Where did he go?"

"If I knew that, I wouldn't be up here waiting. As a last resort, I threw enough power at the problem to push everyone away from Amira." Summer conjured a small ball of golden light and then used it to pierce the murky swamp water around us in a methodical grid.

"Do you fae really think you can waltz into Hell and run amok with no consequences? This is my territory." Beelzebub's voice seemed to come from everywhere.

"As a fae queen, I can do whatever I want. Including tear apart a demon prince who decided to send vampires into MY realm!" Summer whirled and fired off several blasts of golden fire. A demon, but not Beelzebub, caught fire and was incinerated on the spot.

I let out an appreciative whistle. Summer held a grudge. Even if the attack was on Winter, the demons had pushed the vampires to invade Faerie and if they had been successful it wouldn't have just been Winter who suffered for it.

"It seems you can't even protect the little dragons you brought with you," Beelzebub laughed.

Following his words, the sense of gluttony slammed into me and threatened to overwhelm me.

"Devour them!" Beelzebub shouted, and the idea penetrated my mind.

At one point in time, it would have been strong enough to influence my instincts. But I'd grown. I roared in frustration before blanketing the swamp with another round of freezing fog. "Get out here, toad, or are you afraid?"

"No, I'm just cautious," Beelzebub's voice floated over the swamp.

Movement caught my attention, and I spun to slap something out of the air, only to feel like I hit an immovable object.

"You aren't Beelzebub," I groaned stupidly just before pain shot through my other side.

The demon that had stopped my claw was a handsome, blond-haired man in a suit with two neat horns curling out from his forehead and looping into a black crown and locking it onto his head.

A blast of bright light over my shoulder told me that Summer was attacking Beelzebub, and I felt Goldie sliding over my skin and protecting the wound I'd received from the sneaky bastard.

"No. I'm not." The handsome demon slapped my hand away. "Most people just call me the Devil."

I cursed, shrinking back into my hybrid form as Lucifer pulled out a large, black crystal sword and swung for my head. I avoided his attack, but Summer wasn't paying attention to Lucifer and only turned at the last second to block with shimmering gold flames.

Beelzebub, the asshole, shot out of the water at the last second with a spear in hand, using the opportunity.

Seeing Beelzebub again brought me back. He was exactly like I remembered from the time in Helena's soul, only clear to see now that he was in the flesh. The demon prince vaguely looked like a frog, with a too-wide head and mouth along with a big swollen belly. Jowls hung from his face like he once was even bigger and now loose flesh hung off his face.

I wasn't going to let them double team Summer, so I shot forward, reaching for the fat bastard. Goldie became a golden claw that extended my reach and caught Beelzebub before he could reach Summer.

"Hold onto him," I growled and jerked Beelzebub back, bringing my other clawed hand around and taking a pound of flesh from his round form.

Goldie retracted even as Beelzebub tried to escape into the swamp. The gluttony demon jerked against Goldie's claw, and in a flash, bit through it as the world became nothing but bright light.

Summer clashed with Lucifer, and the result was blinding as Beelzebub escaped.

"Zach." Goldie's voice was filled with apology.

"It's fine." I didn't have time for her to feel poorly.

"I left some of myself on him. Cast a spell and I'll point you in the right direction," Goldie continued.

Throwing up my left hand, I shouted. "Envoktus!"

Ice magic launched out of my hand hitting a spot a dozen yards away, exploding into a giant tomb of ice. The spell expanded as the water froze, pushing Beelzebub out of the water, encased in ice. The demon was angry as he struggled in the icy prison, but Beelzebub quickly started cracking through the frozen confines.

I rushed forward. Goldie turned into a sword without prompting as I jumped to cut the demon in two before he escaped. My blade sheared the ice in two, and struck true to the demon, cutting him in half. I couldn't have smiled wider.

But my smile faltered as his two halves became two smaller demons that rushed me from either side. I was so caught by surprise that, if it wasn't for Goldie, he would have ran me through. Instead, I took two decently deep cuts and Goldie pushed the knives aside before they hit anything too important.

Both of the Beelzebubs dove into the swamp and disappeared once more.

I pointed my hand again, letting Goldie direct me as I shouted, "Envoktus!"

This time, I only froze one of them. Knowing better this time, I poured golden flames into my Goldie sword as I stabbed, letting the fire erupt inside the tricky demon's body.

"There's not even any mana in that body." I frowned as I pulled the sword out. It had given me almost no resistance.

A lump of Goldie slipped out of the ice and rejoined her body.

"The other wasn't marked by me," Goldie told me as I spun around in waist deep water with her in my hand as a sword.

Light exploded above again as Summer clashed with Lucifer. She landed in the water next to me, putting her back to mine. "You know, it was a lot more convenient when you were a dragon."

"Tell that to the stupid frog lurking in the water. How is Lucifer so strong?" I asked.

Summer groaned. "Lucifer has an ability to match the strength of anyone that attacks him."

I whistled. "Damn. That's some serious main character energy."

"Fitting. You'll find that he's quite convinced that he's the main character of the story," Summer chuckled. "Pride is a hell of a drug, and he leans into his sin fairly hard."

Lucifer floated above us, staring down with a bored expression. "Are you done talking? You are intruders making a mess of my Hell." He pointed his crystal sword at me and moved forward.

His charge was so fast that I barely got Goldie up in time to block and tear through the water as he knocked me back. Lucifer blurred and was before me again as I exchanged powerful blows in rapid succession with him.

He was fast, but his attacks were plain, without any flourish. Each attack met mine with incredible force. While he was merely mimicking my strength, that paired with his speed and black blade were enough to overwhelm me.

I dodged to the side and breathed death into his face to push him back, but Lucifer just pushed through the fog with a manic grin. I felt an impact on the back of my neck, and I twisted out of the way, feeling the burn of a cut and a warm trickle of blood down my back.

"For someone so full of pride, you sure like to fight dirty." I slammed my sword into Lucifer's.

"You aren't worthy of fighting fairly. No one can beat me." Lucifer tossed his hair in between his sword stroke with a satisfied grin.

"Oh. But you can't beat me, only match me." I pushed on Goldie to grow larger and chopped down on Lucifer as hard as I could.

He met my blade as I expected, but then I sent another request to Goldie.

Spikes shot from where our swords met and stabbed into Lucifer before he could jump out of the way. One of them went straight for his head. He had to slam his crown against the spike to prevent it from plunging into his eye.

The crown on his head cracked, and one of the pointed tips fell between us before Lucifer pulled himself off the spikes and his eyes went wide, turning a glowing red before two beams of pure mana from Hell tore out of them.

I brought Goldie up to block, but she screamed as the beams melted through her. Her protection faltered, and one of the beams punched a hole straight through my chest, missing my heart by inches.

Gasping for breath, I struggled to breathe as my healing kicked in and started to rapidly pull mass from my shifted form to repair my lungs. I threw myself through a portal to get out of the way as Lucifer tore through the swamp with his eye-beams towards me.

"He has laser vision!" I screamed as soon as I came out next to Summer.

Goldie whimpered and pulled her mass from Amira.

"Summer, get Amira to safety."

The black dragon had shifted back to her hybrid form under Goldie's protection and was only the size of an SUV. I snapped my fingers and opened a portal back to the Pale Mounds for Summer to use.

But rather than go through, she just tossed Amira and threw the Goldie coin in with her.

"You'll have to watch her for me," Summer instructed Goldie as a gold rapier formed in her hand. "My husband. Despite how much I love you, I must insist that you not fight Lucifer. He can clearly match you in strength and magical power. I would ask that you focus on Beelzebub and allow me to fight Lucifer."

"But he can only match me," I growled.

She gave me a look that said I knew better.

I hated to admit it, but among all the people present, I was younger by a far margin. Lucifer had my strength and a thousand extra years of practice. I couldn't let pride literally be the thing that let Lucifer take me down.

"Fine. But Beelzebub won't fight me straight up," I growled as Lucifer seemed to realize where I had gone.

"Then figure it out." Summer raced forward, rising up to the surface of the water. Her rapier met Lucifer before the two of them started to trade blows fast and furiously.

I spun, searching for mana with my dragon eyes to find Beelzebub.

"Now that my bulk is back here, I can protect you if you wish to feign weakness," Goldie whispered.

"That won't keep working forever." I spun her sword form in my hand as I watched and waited for Beelzebub to try and sneak attack me, only to realize it was Summer that he'd probably attack.

The waiting was the hardest part.

"Goldie, can you spread below the surface of the water like a giant web under me and Summer? I saw you take up a huge surface area back in Mammon's territory." I hoped my plan would work.

"I can, but then what?" Goldie asked.

It seemed that, while she had learned a lot, Goldie hadn't learned to think very creatively. "To work as a detection system for Beelzebub. He might even swim around, but he'll push off the ground to launch any attack. That's when you catch him," I explained.

"Oh." Goldie melted off my arm and plopped into the water. There was a brief shimmer under my feet as she expanded, then Goldie disappeared completely under the murky water.

My sense of connection to Goldie was still present. I felt her wrap part of herself around my ankle to stay connected, yet it didn't restrict my movement at all, fluidly shifting as I moved.

Summer danced with Lucifer, her swordwork swift, without a whole lot of power, a complete opposite of Lucifer, but that was the point. She danced around Lucifer's large black blade like he was a partner in the dance rather than her opponent.

It was impressive to watch and more than a little entertaining.

What made watching even better was that Lucifer was growing more frustrated by the moment. It seemed that Summer was actually the better fighter.

When he shot eye-beams at Summer, she dodged with a spin that I almost thought was going to turn into a pirouette. I wanted to keep watching, but I felt Goldie tense as an explosion of gold spikes shot up behind Summer to catch Beelzebub.

The large demon hit the spikes face first while Summer continued to fight Lucifer like the situation behind her had never happened. She clearly had massive trust in Goldie and me.

I raced forward while Beelzebub was still stuck on Goldie's spikes and grabbed both of his shoulders with my claws. This time, he wasn't going to perform any splitting tricks to escape.

Beelzebub was absolutely terrified. His frog-face of his was a mask of shock and despair as I latched down onto his shoulder. In the final moments, his look of horror shifted to a smug smile.

The second my jaws latched onto him, the scene around us changed.

CHAPTER 29

I woke up in biology class, blinking as I looked around and tried to figure out what I was seeing.

"What?" The word escaped my mouth as I tried to piece together reality.

Wasn't I...

I paused, unable to figure out what I had actually been doing. I knew I'd been on an adventure with my harem, but what we'd been going after was a mystery.

And somehow, I was now sitting in biology class, the entire class staring at me after my sudden outburst.

"Mr. Pendragon, while I recognize that you have paid to be here like everyone else, you have squandered the opportunity by sleeping. Do not then waste others' time and money by disrupting class. Is that understood?"

"Sorry, Professor. I'm just out of sorts today," I quickly apologized and glanced around class, recognizing Scarlett staring at me with a furrowed brow.

I hoped she'd be able to help clear the fog I felt in my head. Maybe tell me what we had been doing lately to jog my memory. I sat quietly through class that didn't make a lick of sense to me. When class ended, I tried to make my way over to Scarlett, half-wondering why she hadn't been sitting next to me.

"Hey, Scarlett." I slid up next to her and tried to grab her hand but she jerked away.

"What did you call me?" She scowled.

"Scarlett...?" Uncertainty crept through me.

"That sounds like a stripper's name, and it certainly isn't mine." She rushed ahead. "Leave me alone, creep, and stop staring during class."

I was stunned into silence as Scarlett rushed away, but I moved more quickly as I realized I was getting strange stares from everybody else in the class. Either something was wrong with me or something was wrong with Scarlett.

Was this a nightmare? I pinched myself hard, and it hurt enough for me to dismiss that idea.

My mind spun as I tried to remember the recent past. I had just discovered the paranormal, and Morgana had some theories as to what I could be, and Scarlett and I were going steady. Things were jumbled, out of order as I tried to focus and it wasn't clear.

No way, could it just have been a really detailed and long dream?

It had felt so real, so vivid. And a vampire dark elf would be a lot for my mind to make up on its own.

My stomach churned, and I nearly bent over with hunger. I stared down at my stomach, trying to remember if I'd eaten breakfast that day. I'd been hungrier ever since I'd found out I was a paranormal.

But the food could wait. I wanted to figure out what was happening, and the library felt like the best place to start. After classes, I could swing by Morgana's bar and see if she had any insight.

Psych was certainly not a major interest of mine, but the best theory I had was that all of the new information on the paranormal had caused some sort of short-term memory loss.

I knew magic was real, but I'd barely been a paranormal for long. I hadn't had time to make any enemies besides the asshole Chad, and he didn't seem like he'd be able to do anything to my memories.

As I walked down the hallway, I went through the cafeteria. I paused as I walked around. The space seemed larger than normal. My stomach growled, telling me to stop and give it food, but I pushed through.

And... into another cafeteria?

I was incredibly confused.

Grumbling under my breath, I charged through three cafeteria's in a row, stopping and staring around. I started to consider that I might be dealing with something magical and not mental.

Frowning, I moved more slowly, managing to step out of the building and walk across the yard to the library, only to be confronted with the cafe and the smells of cinnamon rolls.

My mouth watered like it was going to create a waterfall right there in the lobby.

"No," I spoke firmly, my voice booming out and causing a student to jump. "Sorry," I apologized and covered my ear like I was covering a Bluetooth earpiece.

I didn't want anybody to think I talked to myself.

I frowned, looking around and trying to decide the best next step. I refused to eat; I needed to get a grip on whatever was happening. Eating felt like a failure somehow—I couldn't explain it.

Rushing up the escalator, I passed several groups of chatting students and went straight through the stacks to where I knew the medical books would be. There would be a few psych books in there. I was sure there was something to help me understand what I might be going through.

Even if what was happening to me was magical, I was sure I could figure it out.

The draw was unmistakable.

I got to the section of the library and saw Jadelyn pulling out a book labeled 'business psychology'. I smiled, excited to have found Jadelyn and the area of books I needed.

She'd been helpful, if distant during my initiation to the paranormal. I went to speak, but then paused, wondering if it would be similar to Scarlett's reaction.

"Yes?" Jadelyn put on a simple, pretty smile that I knew was her just humoring her typical fans. My heart sank, but I tried not to show it on my face.

"Sorry. Just having some strange déjà vu." I tried to smile through the sudden pain of missing my Jadelyn. This one felt wrong.

"Yeah? Well I was hoping you'd finish that statement by apologizing for eye-fucking me every time you see me. By the way, how's the head? Chad beat the shit out of you yesterday after the bar. You should really keep your hands to yourself." Jadelyn crossed her arms, looking at me with absolute disinterest. Wrongness coursed through my body.

"Head?" I ran my hands through my hair and felt a painful swell.

What the absolute fuck.

I started to wonder if I was concussed. If Chad beat me up, then did I... was I a paranormal?

"Shit, you look terrible. Get something to eat and then maybe go hit up the nurse." Jadelyn's face changed, looking at me like someone would an injured puppy. I wasn't sure which was worse, her look of disinterest or her pity.

"I'm fine, just a little tired. Grabbing a book, then I'll be out of your hair." I hated apologizing to her. She should have been my Jadelyn, but something was wrong with the world.

Or something was wrong with me.

Suddenly, I wasn't quite so sure.

"Okay. But seriously, go get something to eat. You look like you are coming off a weekend bender of epic proportions." Jadelyn gave me a flat smile and moved away.

As she walked away, a book slammed into the top of my head and hit the knot. It was so painful, I fell down on my ass.

Oh god that hurt.

I rubbed my head and glanced down at the book. 'Lilith's Secret Tricks to Remember What Happened'.

I frowned, staring at the book as I held it in my hands.

A snarl sounded, and I looked up to see Jadelyn looking nearly feral as she dove for the book. My instincts flared, and I snatched it away, rolling away and down the aisle.

"What's the deal?" I asked.

"Drop the book. Now," Jadelyn demanded like some sort of deranged woman.

"I don't think I will." Clinging to the book, I used the bookshelf to get back to my feet as Jadelyn charged me, trying to tackle me.

Thankfully, she was not even half my weight sopping wet. I held onto the shelf with one hand and the book with the other, managing to stay upright.

Jadelyn leaned forward, trying to bite the hand that was holding the book. I wondered why she wasn't using any of her abilities to weaken me. Jadelyn didn't fight with her fists, unless they were full of cash.

When I didn't let go, she jerked back and forth like a rabid dog and actually started drawing blood. I felt terrible about it, but I clocked her in the head hard enough to daze her as she stopped biting me and fell to the ground.

I stared down at the deranged version of Jadelyn.

Something was very wrong, and I was starting to bet on the world I was in and not my own head.

"Sorry, Jadelyn. I didn't want to hurt you, but I'm not sure that's even really you," I spoke to the form on the ground. She started to move, her head slowly shaking, and I knew I had to get out of the library.

"Babe? What's wrong?" Chad came around the corner of the shelves. "What the fuck did you do to her? GUYS!" he shouted for help and both ends of the aisle were immediately stuffed with football players.

And if I'd ever needed assurance that the scene around me was being staged, I had what I needed looking at the entire football team in the library when they wouldn't be caught dead here.

Holding onto the strange book, I jumped and grabbed onto the shelves, working to climb my way out of the current situation. My stomach growled and gurgled, but I ignored it. I had bigger problems than food at the moment.

When I reached the top of the shelves, the football players had lined up on one side and were pressing the shelf like a lineman exercise, trying to knock it down.

"Fuck," I shouted as I jumped to another shelf as the previous one toppled.

It didn't stop them from pivoting and trying to take down the other shelf as Chad used the toppled shelf like a ramp to chase after me.

Running along the bookshelf, I tried to think of a way out. My brain latched onto a terrible idea as I raced down the shelves, but it was my best shot. So with a giant leap, I hurled myself out the nearby window and fell down a few yards.

In a rain of glass shards, I found myself rolling in the grass and getting to my feet, little cuts burned all over. I took a deep breath and then moved; I couldn't stop.

Adrenaline pumped through me, and I raced away as quickly as my feet could carry me. Thankfully, the football team hadn't been quite crazy enough to follow me through the window, giving me a moment to myself.

I didn't know much, but it was clear the book was important. I flipped the book open, frowning when the first few pages were blank.

Fanning the book, I checked the rest, my chest lightening when I spotted a page with some drawings. The page was pink, bright pink specifically, with little hearts and devil wings scrawled in black ink around the edges.

Sorry Zach,

A little subconscious trick, something you didn't know you needed.

Beelzebub has been doing this for centuries. It is actually how we killed the titan. We've all learned how to protect ourselves, but you haven't, and it isn't something taught easily.

You are the Dragon King, Fae Emperor, Demon Prince or something. You are powerful, and Beelzebub the demon prince has infected your mind and soul to take it over.

WAKE THE FUCK UP. Remember who you are. And if you can't, fake it until you make it.

Seriously, things are probably bad right now. Your mates are probably about to die.

I'd suggest you wake up.

P.S. When you finish your trip in Hell, don't kill me. I'm going out on a limb to help you here. Please keep that in mind. Besides, I'm too pretty to die. xoxo

I frowned as I read the note again, flipping through the book to make sure that there wasn't more that I had missed. What kind of book had text written in girly swirling handwriting?

I read the title of the book again. Lilith, as in the demon? Well, if werewolves and vampires were real, then why couldn't demons be?

Based on her note, I was fighting Beelzebub, and I might be a Dragon King, Fae Emperor, Demon Prince something. The thought was confusing. It was impossible to be all of that at once.

"There he is." A football player pointed at me.

I was out of time.

The whole football team had somehow recruited campus security, and they were all bearing down on me.

Going with the only explanation I had, I decided to believe that I wasn't having a mental break. And if that was true, then I was in the demon Beelzebub's trap. That bastard had dared to try to control me. I was a motherfucking dragon. He should have known better than to try to contain me.

The group charged me, and I went to meet them head on, charging into the mass.

But then I hit nothing and cracked open my eyes to find myself in a room filled with gold. Scattered throughout the gold were weapons stabbed into the piles, making ethereal blue and white mist.

Standing in the center was a fat ass toad named Beelzebub. He frowned, sitting on a gold throne.

My memories rushed back as I felt cold chains wrapped around me. I was the Dragon King, Fae Emperor, Hell something. We'd figure out the Hell part later, for now I needed to kill a damn ugly bastard who bit off more than he could chew.

"—that fucking lump of stupid gold." Beelzebub kicked a pile of gold, sending it cascading down the hill. "What the fuck does she think she is, restraining me. Fuck, wasn't she supposed to be controlled by him?!"

I smiled into the pile of gold coins. Goldie must not have taken kindly to Beelzebub trying to take over my mind.

"Fucking gold fucking elemental." Beelzebub was having a tantrum, and I slowly lifted my head to see that he was facing away.

Good.

Taking a link of the chain, I wrapped it around me in my hand. Then I pulled at the link softly to see if I could snap the chain. My test was a bit inconclusive. I was fairly sure I could break it, but I wouldn't know for sure without alerting Beelzebub that I was awake.

So instead, I waited for Beelzebub to go on another tirade. At the very least, it would offer me some surprise.

The demon prince had lurked in the swamp, attacking only when we were distracted. I couldn't wait to surprise him in turn. Given that he was a glutton, I didn't have to wait long.

A vein bulged so thick on his head that I thought it was about to burst before he started shouting again about the 'insufferable' elemental.

Throwing all of my strength into the single motion, I jerked both arms and got to a knee so that I could put my back into the move. The chain snapped as Beelzebub turned, but I was already moving, rushing up the pile of gold towards him.

The demon's eyes went wide. "What?!" His shout wasn't just for show; it gave him a reason to open his mouth.

I jerked to the side as a barbed tongue shot out, scratching me and then looping around and trying to catch me. I dodged and grabbed his slimy tongue, leaning back and pulling the fat bastard off his feet. I used his tongue to swing him around before slamming him down into another pile of gold.

"Fuck. You really are a frog."

"Toad. I was one, but no longer. Now I am a dragon!" Beelzebub's bones crackled, and he grew into my own dragon form. "Ha! You still have the pathetic soul of a human. Your dragon half, what did you call it? Your beast? It's mine now. I am the dragon, and you are nothing," Beelzebub gloated.

I was reminded of Lilith's note, and it gave me confidence.

So when Beelzebub snapped down with the terrifying jaws of a dragon, I calmly held my hands out and grabbed the teeth above me while I stepped into the teeth below me.

Both of them stopped against me as if they'd hit a wall.

"No. I am a dragon. You are a toad that's crawled into my hoard without permission!" Ripping apart the pair of jaws around me, they tore easily. They were like paper in my hands as I expanded, tearing down the dragon Beelzebub as I grew.

A little green flash darted out of the dragon as I tore it apart and dove into my hoard. I knew it was Beelzebub.

"Don't think you can hide here," I roared and my hoard split like an ocean before Moses, exposing the bastard even as he tried to run for the border of my mind, no doubt to escape.

Lunging forward, I caught his soul in my teeth, much like he had tried to catch me. But my power in my own soul was ten times greater than his now that I wasn't bound by him. I gnashed my teeth together, hearing a wet pop and feeling mana fill my body.

CHAPTER 30

With Beelzebub's death, my mind surfaced back to my body, and I found myself trapped in a golden ball.

"Goldie?" I called out.

"You will not trick me." Goldie's face popped out of the side of the ball.

"Thank you for preventing him from hurting the others with my body." I smiled at her.

She squinted for a moment, seeming to assess me before her eyes lit up. "You're back!"

"Before you release me, give me a little view into what's happening out there and then play along with me. I think there's an opportunity to use the fact that everybody thinks I'm incapacitated," I instructed.

Goldie nodded, and a ring around eye-level thinned out enough that I could see through it, even if the entire view had a gold tint.

The swamp was a wreck, but two more figures had joined the fight. One was clearly Lilith, and I could only assume the other was Levi.

Levi had long, blue hair and was fighting directly with Lucifer, taking his attacks head on without even bothering to block. Yet she was constantly being blown away, only to get back up without a scratch on her.

Meanwhile, Ikta and Summer stood by the golden shell. Regina was nowhere in sight. I expected that Ikta had sent her away to protect Amira while the two of them prepared to deal with me.

Reaching out, I felt my connection to Beelzebub's territory and took it as my own.

The battle between Lucifer, Lilith, and Levi continued to rock the land. I let Goldie's egg melt away and return to my bracer. Ikta's body didn't even twitch, but her spider limb caught the soft skin under my chin, and I knew I was a hair's breadth from death.

"What are the names of my breasts?" Ikta turned, her eyes lit with fire.

"Ikta," I grumbled, being very careful not to move my head at all. "I didn't even know they had names. Let's try an easier one."

"Ikta, do not bully Zach," Goldie demanded from my wrist.

"Fine," Ikta sighed and retracted her leg. "I knew it was you the second I saw your eyes. They have that good kind of lecherous expression, not the bad kind."

"There's a good kind of lecherous?" I asked.

"Yeah. It's like you find me hot and want to bend me over that log over there, plowing me into the swamp until I drown. But you are gentlemanly enough to not be too obvious about it." Ikta shrugged. "To catch you up, Levi showed up and started stalling Lucifer. I didn't even get to have any fun. If I'm honest, a part of me wanted Beelzebub to still have control of your body so I could have had a little fun."

"Would I have died?" I frowned and wondered what kind of 'fun' she'd have.

Ikta thought about it for a moment. "Not on purpose. I'd torture him out of you eventually."

"Well, care to help me with a plan, and maybe take a shot at Lucifer?" I asked. They were all so engrossed in the fight they hadn't noticed that I'd woken up.

Ikta narrowed her eyes and waited to hear the plan as Summer stepped up next to her.

"Let's hear it. Your bait plan worked." Summer waited.

"Well, pretty simple. I'm going to capture the two of you with Goldie and pretend to be Beelzebub to get close." My smile must have been unconvincing.

Both of them were quiet for a moment, as if waiting for more.

"Someone has to ask the important questions." Ikta grinned. "Will there be choking?"

I put my head in my hand, already knowing the correct answer to get her to agree quickly. "Yes."

"Alright, I'm all for this one. It's just some fun roleplay. Goldie, go ahead and get started."

Tendrils bound Ikta, and one looped around her neck squeezing her throat while more pieces of Goldie held her spider limbs back and a loop around her feet, pulling her hands up as if they were cuffed to her throat.

"That's weak. Okay, Goldie, because Zach is going to be too much of a softie for this part, if I tap twice that means I want it harder. Three means it's too much, and just random flailing means it's perfect and I'm just getting into it." Ikta tapped twice and Goldie constricted around her neck pulling at her skin until it was so tight that I had to believe it was hard for her to breathe.

"I'm concerned." I studied Ikta. "What if you can't tell the difference between taps and flailing?"

"It was your plan," Goldie spoke while Summer only shrugged along with us.

Summer was held with a loose noose around her neck and Goldie had loops on her wrists and ankles in a way that pulled her shoulders back and pressed her chest forward.

"A queen has to look superb, even when bound. Thanks for understanding, Goldie." Summer smiled. "Roleplay, right, Ikta?"

The Spider Queen made a series of choking noises I wasn't entirely sure were healthy, but then she tapped twice again on Goldie and the elemental squeezed tighter.

"Careful," I warned, trying not to roll my eyes.

"She knows her limits, and she's doing her part. Get your evil game face on," Goldie shot back. "You really are too much of a softie on your harem. It is sweet, but this will sell it. Beelzebub would not have cared about harming them."

I shook my head and sneered, staring at the fight happening in the distance and imagined them all dead, hanging before me to try and act like the murderous psychopath I had destroyed.

I'd heard once that acting was trying to mix the present with a reality you've made in your mind to really pull off a convincing act. It made me feel disgusting as I walked forward towards the fight with dead eyes, waiting for them to notice me.

Lilith was the first to pause, and she concentrated on me, her brows furrowing with doubt as she tried to judge if I was Beelzebub or Zach. By her continued frown, I guessed I was selling my act well enough.

I remembered her letter, knowing that there would be decisions to make in the future. I still wasn't sure of my choice, but the next step for me was clear.

Lucifer and Levi broke apart, watching me, but it was Lucifer who was the first to smile. "I see you were successful."

"Yes, and these two had more hope than sense. The elemental is truly powerful, and they don't want to damage him and hold onto hope that he can overcome this. We both know that isn't happening."

I held up the two fae queens and tried to imagine I was handling Frank's gym bag. That thing should have a hazmat team handling it, and it was the foulest image I could conjure to help me hide the love and care I had for the two bound women.

"I see that. But why leave them alive?" Lucifer asked with narrowed eyes.

Levi and Lilith stood together, watching with reserved caution. Lilith was whispering something to Levi and the two were distracted for a moment, arguing in hushed voices that I couldn't quite pick up, even in my hybrid form.

"Toys for later," I replied as Ikta double tapped her constraints and I could feel Goldie tense on my wrist.

I tried to suppress the grimace that would give away my act. Following through, I lifted a hand and squeezed as Goldie followed through on Ikta's double tap.

The fae queen started to thrash, and I secretly knew she was enjoying herself. It was hard not to smile.

I held my fist up as if I was the one squeezing Ikta until she slowed down and went limp. I tried not to stare, but I wasn't sure if she'd really passed out or was just faking. With Ikta, it was hard to tell.

But the move seemed to be enough to make Lilith double down in her argument with Levi.

"Well, I'm sure they will make fun toys." Lucifer turned so that he was including the other two demon princes in the conversation. "Now that the interlopers have been handled, we have to settle the matters of Hell. This is my kingdom and you two brought a heap of trouble into it. Lilith, dear, you overplayed your hand." Lucifer's eyes glowed red.

For a moment, I thought he was about to straight up eye-beam her, but then the glow settled. Now they just had an ominous molten look to them.

"You'll have to find a way to make it up to me," Lucifer sneered. "All of you will now kneel to your king. Beel, we'll have to talk about giving up some of your power to me. Now that you have the Dragon King's body, you have the power of three or four demon princes at your disposal. That is too much."

I hesitated, unsure how Beelzebub would act. Lucifer noticed the pause and tensed.

I glanced at the two fae queens in my grasp, trying to decide my next move. Summer looked bored and Ikta peeked open an eye and winked. I internally let out a sigh of relief, glad she hadn't been choked into passing out.

"Well, I was going to save it for later. But are you aware of how powerful the Spider Queen is?" I lowered my head, knowing that Goldie could protect me. "Her soul is yours. That should make up for the gap."

I motioned, and Goldie tossed her, causing her to splash in the swamp. She managed to keep her body limp as Lucifer pulled her out and examined her to see that she was still alive but 'unconscious'.

Ikta didn't move an inch, remaining in a limp unconscious form even as Lucifer roughly handled her. I was deeply impressed and terrified at how well she could play dead.

Lucifer threw Ikta over his shoulder. Her body flopped like she was truly unconscious, but then a millisecond later she came alive.

Her hand held what looked like a jagged piece of portal, like a fragment of a broken mirror as she stabbed Lucifer in the throat. She was able to stab him twice more before Lucifer managed to dodge out of a third stabbing. Unfortunately, the damage was done.

He staggered away and Ikta wouldn't be denied.

She jumped with those spider limbs splaying out even as Lucifer's eyes glowed, ready to turn and blast her. Lucifer's bloody head rolled off his shoulder and into the swamp. The glowing eyes faded out like a fading light.

Ikta landed on her feet as Lucifer's body fell. "That was fun! Tell me you got a picture. I really wish I had been in a position to see his face."

I just stared at her for a moment. "No. Sorry. No picture."

"How'd you know his weakness by the way?" Ikta picked up Lucifer's head and struggled with his horns for a moment.

"His weakness?" I frowned and Goldie set Summer down gently.

"Wait, you are Zach and not Beelzebub?" Lilith asked, her fighting stance turning more relaxed. "I wasn't sure, and then you were so rough with Ikta." Her eyes slid to the fae queen with a sudden realization.

"Go back. His weakness?" I asked.

"Lucifer is the betrayer. Betrayers always get betrayed; it's practically cosmic law." Ikta gave up and used a little of her magic to cut off the horns and work them out of the crown before she held up the ugly obsidian piece with triumph. Even with the one spire chipped from earlier, it was the crown of Hell.

"Really?" Lilith asked, frowning at Ikta.

"Pretty much how all betrayers go down is to get back-stabbed themselves. I don't make the rules. I just murder people when his majesty says it's okay." Ikta bowed to Lilith like a servant before skipping through the water towards me with the crown held high. She fully intended to put that disgusting thing on my head.

"No no. I don't want that." I backed away.

"But you killed the king. Now you get the crown." Ikta jumped up, trying to get to the top of my head, but I dodged her.

"I didn't take his power though," I pointed out.

"Wow. You choke a girl like that and you won't even take responsibility," Ikta pouted.

"Hey—" I paused to refute her and she pounced, slapping the crown on my head.

"That looks wonderful!" Ikta squealed.

"It really doesn't look bad at all," Levi addressed me for the first time.

I took a moment to look at the demon prince. She was tall, closer to Summer in height, with sapphire-blue hair that actually looked like thin, flowing gemstones rather than being blue. Despite the look, it was clear she was a demon. She had pale green skin and a pair of fin shaped horns protruding out the side of her head.

She was gorgeous though, and I could see why Ikta liked to curse her beauty. Her beauty was comparable to a fae, but with a strange desire to grab hold of her.

"I'm not sticking around, and I'm unsure if it is appropriate." Tilting my head to the side, I let it fall off and grabbed it.

"Keep it for now." Lilith waved her hands like she didn't want it. "Our gift to you. Besides, with Lucifer here, you have three territories. And your elemental has a fourth. You control more of Hell than Lucifer ever did."

Hell rumbled.

"You better eat him before Hell collapses. At present, there is a pretty big vacuum of power." Ikta pushed Lucifer's floating body towards me.

I glared at Ikta. She knew I'd take his power if it meant stopping the plane from being destroyed. It might be Hell, but it was full of living people, even if they might not have fit my definition of people a few years ago.

"If you are mad, you can choke me some more later. Goldie still wasn't as harsh as I'd like." Ikta held her throat towards me, and I picked up Lucifer just to move on from her comment.

"There's a much more pleasant way I can do this. Lilith, if you would? While you are at it, can you settle the debt I have with Beelzebub's essence?" I asked the demoness, knowing that she'd probably steal some of the power, but I was perfectly happy with that. I didn't know what I would do with all of the strength I'd gained. Nor was I sure if I really wanted to be the King of Hell.

Lilith skipped forward and jumped in my arms, kissing me as her tail stabbed into Lucifer, draining him dry.

My jaw crackled as soon as the kiss ended.

"Careful," Lilith teased. "I don't think you really want to mark me. Sticking to a single relationship isn't really my jam, and I really don't want you pissed off at me because I went cheating and kissing anyone who needs a little boost."

Her words had the desired effect and my jaw straightened back to normal. I couldn't help the look of disgust that marred it for a second.

"Yeah. That's a deal breaker. Good thing you know yourself. Sorry it won't work for you or Levi." Ikta worked her way between Lilith and me. "Now, let's get Sabrina and get out of here before you make any mistakes, yeah?"

Summer stepped up as well and hooked her arm in mine. "Absolutely. Portal, please?"

"Is there anything I need to know about Hell?" I asked the two demon princes before the fae swept me away.

"If you want to manage things, you can. But really, it's a big trap. Because of Lucifer and Asmodia, we've always had to stay here." Lilith created a pink straw hat and placed it on her head. "I'm going on a vacation. What are you doing, Levi?"

The stern woman narrowed her eyes at Lilith. "None of your business. Now that our mutual enemy is gone, so is our alliance. King." She bowed to me. "Please let me know if I can ever serve you better."

"No, that's okay." I didn't know what to say to that as the two fae queens successfully got me through the portal where Regina rested, watching over a sleeping Amira.

"Oh good, you are back." Regina looked up.

Ikta wrangled the crown out of my hand and plopped it back on my head. "Tada! He's the King of Hell now too!

So he's An Emperor, King, King, Prince, Prince, Prince." Ikta giggled.

"Never string those together again," I grumbled.

"I think you lose all the princes as you get the King of Hell, no?" Summer tapped her lips, considering the ridiculous string of titles more seriously than she should have been.

"So, what did you think of Levi?" Ikta asked.

"She's like a half-baked Summer Queen. Really, it's like someone was just jealous of Summer here and tried to look half as beautiful." I smiled at all of them.

"Smooth," Regina commented, earning herself a glare from me.

"I'm flattered. Now, I realize we left Lilith behind and we need to go fetch Sabrina and get out of here. Care to fly us there?" Summer pointed out.

My eyes shot open. I had been pushing that part of the trip down the road as we went after the next problem in Hell, but it had finally arrived. I would get my succubus wife back, and she wouldn't need to suppress herself anymore.

"We need to go. Wait, let me check on Amira, but get ready. We'll head out soon."

CHAPTER 31

I flew over the bustling city at the heart of the Pits of Lust and came hurtling down, only to stop before the massive black cathedral that fell far from the normal brightly colored buildings of the area. All of the stained glass were lewd depictions of debauchery.

Powerful flaps of my wings sent everyone scattering as I shrank back down to my hybrid form and landed. Goldie pulled everyone off my back, molding into her humanoid form and held onto Amira carefully. Amira was awake, but she was still weak.

A succubus met us at the entrance. "Are you here for your wife?"

"He is!" Lilith flew down on her own pair of wings. "I realized as soon as his ladies carted him off that I never fulfilled my end of the bargain, and that's quite dangerous with a fae." She was all smiles, but I could tell that she was nervous. "I was worried you'd beat me here and my ladies might come into conflict."

"Never," the other succubus replied and looked at me like a piece of meat. "This is the Dragon King?"

"And King of Hell," Ikta called out from behind me. "He killed Lucifer, Beelzebub and Asmodia. Ate them all. Then his elemental ate Mammon."

The succubus went from a teasing smile to a look of pure horror.

Lilith smiled and pushed her inside. "Please lead the way. Andariel, treat the king with as much respect as you can muster. No pain play. I don't think he'd react well to such experiences."

"Oh you'd be surprised what he's into," Ikta murmured before Summer hit her upside the head.

"Don't tempt the succubi unless you want to share your man with the succubi," Summer instructed.

Ikta rubbed her head and followed after Andariel. "We already share him plenty. What's one more? Besides, she looks like whips and chains. Maybe she'd be kind of fun and teach my future husband some new games." Ikta winked at me when I glared at her.

"I think you have your hands full, but I'm always happy to teach the King of Hell how to mix pleasure and pain," Andariel replied over her shoulder from the front of the group.

"She gets it." Ikta had to get the last word, and now even Goldie was glaring at her.

Andariel led us through gossamer sheets that broke up the inner sanctum of the succubi. Grunts, moans, and slapping of flesh seemed to rise up to the ceiling and fall down on our ears.

There was so much of it that it almost became a sort of strange torrid music.

"Sabrina is through here." Andariel pulled back a curtain and Lilith darted in first.

"Sabrina! Look who I brought! You must be so excited to be back to your normal self, and Zach is here to take you away." Lilith was all smiles as she pulled Sabrina off a couch.

My succubus wife blinked a few times before a brilliant smile blossomed on her face and she stepped up to me, forgetting the book she'd been reading. She wrapped her arms around my shoulders before pulling herself up to my lips and tasting me with a delicate kiss.

She was still very much her succubus nature at the moment, complete with eyes filled with little grains of golden sand. "Zach. I'm glad you are back."

Her jagged edges were smoother than when I'd left. She had a fluid, sensual grace in each of her movements now. It was a far cry from her normal timid behavior.

"And are you back?" I asked her, holding her face and searching her eyes.

"Yes, I am. Different, but I'm me. I'm not turning into a raw embodiment of lust," Sabrina answered me, and I could see the honesty in her eyes. She wasn't lust-crazed.

Yet it seemed she was more of what you'd expect from a succubus with a seductive twist in nearly everything she did.

"Drat. It'd be fun if you just revved up the dragon constantly." Ikta clicked her tongue before breaking into a smile. "Welcome back."

"Thank you." Sabrina broke from my hold and tipped her head to Summer and Ikta. "I'm sure that you two were a wonderful help to my husband. Maybe when we get back we can work on those magic lessons again. I'm sure he just punched everything."

"Oh. I don't know. He did pretty well on his own." Goldie peeked out from behind Regina, carrying Amira. Amira did not look pleased to need the extra help.

Sabrina's brow furrowed for a moment. "Goldie?"

"It is me." Goldie bowed.

Sabrina shot past me in an instant, quickly making a few glowing runes in the air around Goldie. "This is incredible. Elementals are so rare, and they aren't that well understood. Did you take some sort of leap in evolution? Your mass is HUGE! Holy crap. Where would you find so much gold? Wait, did you somehow multiply?"

Sabrina started drawing runes around Goldie to inspect her on a magical level.

"Ah. There's the nerdy succubus we love," I sighed, pleased to see that while she was certainly different, she was still very much Sabrina.

Lilith beamed at me. "I didn't take much of Beelzebub's power, but consider it a done deal?" She held out her hand.

I shook it. "Thank you. If we need to stay in contact—"

"We'll figure something out. I think you should contact Levi over me, though. You are just too tempting of a morsel for me, and I'm going to get myself in trouble if I spend much time with you." Lilith had a devious smile before she waved and popped her pink straw hat back on her head. It was clear she was ready to get out of my presence, but I suspected it was more than any sexual chemistry that might exist between us.

I turned back to Sabrina, who was still circling Goldie. Goldie looked unsure, twisting this way and that as she was instructed while glancing at me for help.

"Okay. Let's catch Sabrina up while we wait for our portal out of here. Send Pixie what she needs." I couldn't stop smiling. I was ready to be home.

***

A portal ripped open next to Sabrina not too long after, and Ikta jumped to her feet, her spider limbs splaying out and grabbing the edge of the portal. She got in place just in time for the portal to rip Sabrina away.

"In now!" Ikta screamed over the noise.

I shoved Amira and Regina in ahead as Goldie jumped back to my wrist and Summer marched through. The portal dumped us out in a messy room.

I frowned in confusion. The space felt like my study below the office, but the room was larger than I remembered. And I'd never seen any of the rooms so messy before. The bookshelf was definitely the one from the study, but everything was askew and on the floor.

"Zach." Nyske was on me before I could take in any more of the room. She pulled my arms up to help me up and then immediately started circling me, looking for any injuries.

"You look like you are in one piece." She clicked her tongue when she found a tear in my shirt before sticking a finger through it and prodding my skin to see if there was an injury.

Most of my harem was in the room, but I didn't have a chance to do an inventory of them all before Nyske rushed me. They were all watching with a wry smile as I was fussed over by Nyske.

"Am I okay, doctor?" I raised an eyebrow. I was the king of dragons. She should have more faith.

Nyske blushed. "Satisfactory. You came back in one piece."

I glanced around. "Did our portal make a tornado here or something?"

Pixie, who had been about to greet me, had her smile drop. "You fucker." She grabbed me by the collar as Fiona tried to hold her back and failed. "This is your fault."

"Hmm?" I paused and raised an eyebrow. "What did I do now?"

"The mansion is growing," Nyske explained. "So, things keep falling off as everything shifts, and the nymphs are getting a little testy at how often they have to clean everything up." Nyske put her hands on her hips. "Pixie might be a little tired of it."

"I will work on it, Pixie." I punctuated the statement by kissing her nose, and the move completely disarmed the nymph.

"As long as you know it is your fault." Pixie tossed her bouncy pink hair.

"Wow, you would think we were chopped liver," Summer jokingly grumbled to Ikta loud enough for the rest of the girls to notice.

"You aren't the important one. He is. You okay, Sabrina?" Kelly fished Sabrina out from where she had been sandwiched between the two fae queens.

"Hot damn. I think she got spicier." Taylor let out a wolf whistle at Sabrina, and grabbed her shoulders as if to show her off. "You look smoking hot now. I don't know if your bag shaped sweaters can hide it now."

Sabrina was blushing heavily before she waved her hand. Her succubus nature retreated under her magic, and she instead conjured herself a tight virgin killer sweater.

"Maybe I'm a little more confident in myself than I was before." She cast a smoldering look at me while I stared at her open back and the top of her ass that was peeking out.

"Wonderful." I smiled back, happy that she'd found some confidence with her transformation.

"While Pixie was doing her magic to summon you, the other nymphs were doing their magic in the kitchen. I think we'll have a riot on our hands if we don't go appreciate it soon." Jadelyn clapped her hands for everyone's attention. "So, how about we head to the dining room and talk about everything there where the nymphs can pretend to fill our drinks while they listen to your stories?"

"I'm a little concerned with the whole growing mansion thing. Is there a big mess outside?" I wanted to snoop around, but instead, I let Nyske and Scarlett grab my arms and lead me to the dining room.

"No, just the inside is growing," Nyske clarified. "Nothing on the exterior has changed."

"That's a relief. It would be really hard to explain to the national park district why the building seemed to suddenly grow to encompass their park." It didn't escape me as we walked through that each room had grown pretty substantially.

As we moved through the mansion, nymphs would spot me and giggle, swarming me to give me hugs that seemed to press their chests directly against me. One even grabbed my hands and pulled them away from a respectful clasp on her back down to cup her ass.

That nymph got a kiss, and then it opened up the floodgates.

"Ladies." Pixie stormed through. "Dinner first. I'm sure our mate will satisfy us all."

I was getting swept up being home. "Wait, where is Maeve? She has some questions to answer of her own."

Scarlett waved off my concern. "She's fine. The entire Plushie Society backed her. Let me tell you, the winter nobles caved immediately against a pregnant dragon and a gaggle of pregnant nymphs. Even Maeve is pregnant, which I think was a nice excuse for Winter to back down."

I sat down in my chair, trying to process all the new information.

As soon as my butt hit the seat, Morgana was in my lap, kissing me hotly before biting my neck and teasing the holes until there was a solid flow of blood.

"Shit, calm down." I laughed at her.

"More," Morgana growled around her nibbling of the wound trying to get more blood to flow.

I glanced at Trina for help.

"Oh. We are pretty sure she has a little whelp in there. She went through the eighteen barrels in less than a week and lost her super speed for a bit. The nymphs and dragons have been helping donate for her. Even then, her abilities have become spotty." The medically inclined dragon let out a little yawn at the end. "I'm pregnant too. You'll see lots of baby bumps here in the next month or so as their bodies start to prepare. Or in the case of your dragons, we'll be popping out some eggs."

"I want another egg," Yev demanded.

"And you'll have to be careful. I think Yev wants a whole clutch," Trina finished, eyeing the mother dragon.

Morgana finally pulled off me with a flourish as she wiped at her lips. "Mmm. So much better fresh. And glad to have you home."

"Uh huh. We'll have to work out some regular feeding if it is that bad." I kissed her lips, trying to hide my shock at all the news. "How's Kelly then?"

"I'm fine." Kelly sat at the table while Taylor hovered around her. "Pack says there is some strain though, so it might be a dragon. But I'm certainly not dealing with my abilities acting like spotty Wi-Fi. Werewolves are heartier creatures than Blueberry." Kelly smirked at Morgana, who was reluctantly extracting herself from my lap to give others some time.

"Hush, you won't even shift while you are pregnant," Morgana shot back.

"That's because it's bad luck!" Kelly hissed in return, and I got the clear feeling that it wasn't the first time they'd had this specific discussion.

"Wait, werewolves have superstitions?" I asked, bewildered to learn that werewolves, the creatures of superstitions, had their own.

"It isn't a superstition," Kelly argued and looked to Taylor for support.

"She's right. My uncle was first born, and supposedly, grandma liked to stay shifted. He still goes absolutely wild for tennis balls to this day. I hear he has a whole basement full of them." Taylor nodded with an absolute surety.

"What?" I frowned. "Tennis balls?"

"If you spend too much time shifted while bearing your pup, the babe will have some weird quirks. Like... obsessions with tennis balls, burying bones all the time, or some other stupid shit," Morgana explained. "They end up a little more wolf than human."

I snorted, finding it hilarious as I pictured the situation. But I managed to drop my smile based on the glares coming from the two wolves.

"I mean. Whatever you think is best for your baby," I corrected swiftly.

Kelly nodded and rubbed her belly. "Of course. If something happens, I'll shift. A small amount of time isn't a problem. A lot of bitches like to shift because it takes the strain off once you get nice and swollen. I have an entire pack of pregnant ladies to hang with though, and then the whole mansion is about to be swimming in pregnant nymphs. We can sit around and commiserate about what you've done to us."

"I'm sure they carry their pregnancy far too gracefully." Morgana eyed the nymphs as they paraded in and started setting out food.

"At least I can eat all I want." Kelly stabbed a slab of chicken right off the plate as the nymph walked past behind her. Kelly slapped the meat onto her plate and started to devour it as the nymph placed the remaining chicken on the table.

I looked around the table. Scarlett and Jadelyn took up the closest chairs on my right while my nymphs filed in on the left. Those that had been with me on the trip slid further down the table. Regina and Amira were showing off their marks while others pointedly looked at Summer's clear scar on her chest.

"So, how many succubi are coming to the manor?" Scarlett asked casually.

"Just Sabrina," I said with a roll of my eyes. "Do you really think that I'd cause that much trouble?"

"Yes," Jadelyn said without hesitation. "But I'm glad you held back."

"The base succubi are pretty... disturbing. And Lilith warned me that she doesn't stick to relationships well," I explained.

That answer seemed to garner a lot of attention from the table, and I could tell it was time to give them more details of my adventure.

Goldie popped up a miniature version of her new self on my shoulder. "I think those of us on the trip with him deserve some credit. He was eyeing Levi pretty heavily there at the end."

"Goldie's got a point. We need to be careful of that one. No plushie." Ikta pointed with a fork.

The rest of the table had gone quiet, staring at Goldie.

"Goldie?" Yev asked.

"Hi Yevvy!" Goldie smiled from my shoulder as a part of her budded off. A full-size Goldie ran around the table to give Yev a giant hug and whisper something to her before the two entered an excited chatter.

"What happened to Goldie?" Scarlett asked with a raised brow, staring at the elemental that had come back entirely different.

"Oh. Well, I guess I should start the story. So, we went into Hell and found this village of succubi in the Pits of Lust. Sabrina was pretending to be in charge—"

"Then Mr. Hero here interpreted what I said as an excuse to shift and fight a giant beast," Sabrina sighed. "Lilith noticed, and the whole secrecy thing went out the window." She smiled.

I rolled my eyes as the others started piling on, adding their details to the stories as I took the opportunity to bite into a big chunk of meat. The others were on the edge of their seats, throwing in commentary and cheering as we described everything.

At one point, Ikta created an illusion over the dinner table as she told the story of throwing a giant illusion coin through a portal to get me to stop fighting Asmodia. And she definitely embellished my obsession with the little coin. The illusion made me look like some sort of dog going after a squirrel.

Unlike my heroics, which were taken fairly casually, Goldie's story of wrecking Mammon's territory was a cacophony of gasps and praise.

I smiled as I sipped on my drink, my women around me chatting and laughing. It was good to be home.

CHAPTER 32

After dinner, the night had devolved into a torrid welcome home party that included a gaggle of excitable nymphs and my harem.

It was still dark out when I rolled out of bed, feeling energetic despite the hours of exertion.

Evelyn was wiggling her fingers at me and darted out the door with a giggle that just begged for me to come chase her down. Silk hung off her curves and danced behind her as she moved down the hallway. The winter nymph had soft, blue skin, and she'd chosen glittering silver silk to wrap her wonderful curves and show off plenty of skin.

Women were scattered everywhere as I moved through the manor. They were all sleeping in various states of undress on any remotely soft surface. There was even a trio of nymphs holding each other as they slept against the railing.

Evelyn made sure not to lose me as she moved, flashing a flirty smile before making sure I saw what door she ducked into.

I grunted and moved down the hallway, careful not to disturb the sleeping nymphs. One spotted me, cracking her eyes open and stifling a yawn as she tried to perform a wink and failed.

"Get some sleep," I whispered and moved to the room where Evelyn had just disappeared.

The second I stepped inside, the door closed behind me and Evelyn was on me, her supple blue skin pressed into my chest.

"Did you really replace me?" she teased.

I saw Maeve laying on the bed behind her, watching with rapt attention.

"You work for Maeve. We always knew that," I replied.

"Glad to hear I get to keep my job then." Fiona was in the room as well, sitting off to the side.

"Oh, hi, Fiona." I was caught off guard by her presence.

"Hi." She wiggled her fingers. "I've come to know Maeve and Evelyn better in the time you were away."

Evelyn slipped out of my arms, sinking to the floor and pulling my boxers down in one fluid motion. The next moment, my cock was in her mouth.

I groaned and held onto her head to stay still. "Glad you are making friends."

Fiona's eyes lit up watching Evelyn go down on me. "Evelyn, are we good enough friends to share?"

Evelyn came off me and kissed my cock between words. "Of course, dear. Assistants between the Fae Emperor and one of his queens will have to work together plenty. We should probably do some... what do you call them? Team-building exercises."

It was like she couldn't bear to have me out of her mouth as Evelyn swallowed me whole again and started to mewl in pleasure around me.

"He loved that." Fiona got to her feet, her body largely on display. The woman was all nymph curves as she smiled and came up to my side. "Do you love the feel of her mouth around you, your majesty?" Her breath was on my neck as soft touches went down my arm.

"Yes." I held onto Evelyn's head as she eagerly worked me. After my busy night, I knew it might take her a little while to work me into enough of a frenzy.

Fiona smiled and cupped my cheeks, gently pulling me to her lips and giving me soft sensual kisses that distracted me from Evelyn's efforts until she finished and pulled back, searching my eyes. "I haven't worked for you very long, but as a nymph, I understand families that I've worked for very well. Yours is beautiful. I hope I end up working for it for a very long time to come."

I kissed her back as Evelyn found a pace that excited me and locked into it, going crazy on me. "I don't casually pick up nymphs. Only the best for nymphs and mates."

"You'll get a mark if you want one," Maeve called out from the bed, watching with an excited look on her face. "Evelyn, do you want him this time?"

The nymph nearly screamed yes around me.

"I'm already pregnant, and we've neglected you. You've served me well, now get on your back." Maeve made room on the bed.

Fiona stepped back as Evelyn practically threw herself on her bed, spreading her legs and begging me with her eyes.

"Come, husband. I think Evelyn deserves a vigorous reward, and you need Winter to join your court." Maeve took my hands as I joined Evelyn on the bed.

Fiona was content to lean against the wall for the moment and watch.

"Not going to join?" I teased.

"Oh. I'm going to join, but I'm certainly not going to take the first round. That's no way to make friends." Fiona smirked.

Maeve cupped me and slid me into Evelyn as the newly minted Winter Queen kissed me. As her lips touched mine, my mind exploded as if someone had just shoved peppermint inside my very soul.

Evelyn mewled as I exploded from the start of the kiss and rolled straight into another with my dragon stamina. Meanwhile, Maeve continued to pump me with winter fae magic.

***

I fell into the bed, completely spent after a few hours with the three winter fae. But I had the distinct feeling that Fiona had held back. I knew it would take some time for her to fully get comfortable with me and the other winter fae.

The room felt filled with winter fae magic, I half-expected to see everything covered in frost. Maeve's magic had continually flooded me as I'd work to send it right back to her.

Ikta still had to give me the last half of her territory, but I had most of Faerie as my territory after my time with Maeve. Even though I had given the power back out, it felt like I was larger than life.

"I think we fried his brain," Evelyn giggled, sprawled nearby on the bed. "Good thing dragons heal quickly."

"I'm fine, just feeling the effects of all this Faerie magic," I replied, partially sitting up.

"Your majesty." Evelyn dramatically waved her hand where she laid next to me.

"He doesn't care much for that." Maeve reached across me and pushed her hand down, making me lay back down. "Besides, he's just our husband when we are in bed."

Fiona snorted. "She got enough of his seed to be wed." She slid off the bed and picked up her dress, slipping it on easily. "I will head back to work. My king? Emperor?" She frowned, unsure which term of address she should use.

"I think I'll stick with Dragon King as my predominant title for you guys. Emperor and 'majesty' feels a little much even if some of the fae insist on using it." It was what felt right to me, even if they wanted me to be called something more.

Evelyn made a funny noise, but I ignored it.

"Very well, my king. Do you need me to schedule time to rest?"

"I'm feeling fairly energetic still. No need." I wasn't sure if my body suddenly needed less sleep or if I was just wired from the fae magic, but I really did feel fine.

Fiona bowed low and nodded before slipping out of the room, leaving me with Maeve and Evelyn.

"Shame she didn't take your seed," Evelyn sighed. "I liked her."

"Slut," Maeve teased.

"Guilty as charged, officer. Please bring out the cuffs for your naughty naughty nymph slut." Evelyn held her hands out.

I snorted at her play.

"No, I guarantee there is a pair of cuffs in the nightstand. She always stocks them in my room." Maeve winked at me before turning back to Evelyn. "Are they red?"

Evelyn sighed. "I went looking for a gold pair, but I could only find cheap plastic ones painted like brass with yellow fuzz. Really, humans are so cheap. The Dragon King deserves gold handcuffs to lock me to his bed for an eternity of being ravished by his giant cock."

"Nymphs." I shook my head. "You seem to be feeling extra nymphy, Evelyn."

"Oh, we are all like this underneath. I know you have to have seen under that Pixie's professional facade. We just hide it in polite society." She shrugged and gestured to their two naked bodies. "This is the bedroom. I get to be as 'nymphy' as I want. I fucking love sex and am not ashamed to admit it. You do too. Everyone loves sex. I don't understand why humans are so shamed by doing something and enjoying something that is vital to the survival of their species."

"Sex is private," I replied.

Evelyn snorted. "Your sex life is not private. Hate to break it to you, but all your ladies gather up a few times a week and gossip about it."

Maeve slapped Evelyn playfully. "First rule of Plushies. Don't talk about the Plushies."

"It's literally his harem." Evelyn rolled her eyes. "But if you want to change the subject, I bet he wants the full story of you dethroning your mother."

"I would love to hear how you did it safely." I frowned, feeling protective of Maeve as I rubbed her pregnant stomach.

Maeve blushed and traced the scar on her shoulder. "Ikta and Summer explained their plans to give you their pieces of Faerie, and I wanted to give you winter too."

"But you decided to wait until I was gone to do something so dangerous," I growled and nuzzled her in closer, holding my Winter Queen tight. It helped to know she was okay, but I still was grumpy that she hadn't told me of her plans.

"My mother has had trouble holding a tight grip on her court since the Iapetus conflict. First, she was weakened. Then, when his involvement in Aurora's death spread, the court was terrified that Summer would retaliate for her bringing Iapetus to Faerie."

Evelyn cut in. "So, the court was ready to ditch. They just needed a strong reason. Enter my queen here confirming that she was pregnant with the Dragon King's child. Once we let those whispers spread through the nymphs, the court was primed for a takeover."

"She makes it sound so simple." Maeve rolled her eyes. "She spent about a week casually dropping hints."

"The nymphs talk while court is being held. It's a great place to pick up and pass on information. And we needed to do that given Maeve wasn't exactly welcome in court lately." Evelyn smiled innocently. "It was a little taboo that you marked both of us before putting a child in it. But then again, you are a dragon, and your kind aren't well known for their restraint."

I snorted. "I am a being of complete restraint."

"Oh yeah?" Evelyn pressed her chest in my face, and I happily played with her soft breasts, eliciting an excited gasp from her as I could feel her rev back up.

"Stop that. Can't we have a simple conversation?" Maeve pushed her back and my head out of her chest.

"It's difficult with him naked next to me." Evelyn had no shame. "Besides, I don't know if beds are for conversations, at least not for ones that involve so much talking."

"Anyway." Maeve could have stripped paint with the stare she gave Evelyn. "With the court primed, it was time to challenge my mother. And when I was about to challenge her, Jadelyn and Scarlett showed up with the rest of the Plushies. Even all the nymphs showed up. There is massive power across that group. Even without Ikta and Summer, the group is incredibly formidable."

"So, she walks in like a badass bitch with the Scalewrights, the first female Alpha, a pregnant and very frumpy vampire that might soon be a bloodlord, the heirs to the elven royalty along with enough dragons to start a war." Evelyn cracked into a big smile. "The look on her mother's face was priceless."

Maeve smiled and took my chin so that she had my full attention. "I have to admit, it was very satisfying." Her lips curled into a smile at the memory. "My mother was done for the second we stepped into her court. She knew she didn't stand a chance."

"Scarlett announced that you and your harem stood with Maeve before everything started, and that you wanted the throne for your child." Evelyn was all smiles as she recalled the scene.

"Then I owe my first mate a reward. She helped keep you safe when you went off and put yourself in danger while I was gone," I growled at Maeve.

"Hush." Maeve booped me on the nose. "I am the Winter Queen. Danger is a part of my life, and I do not need a growling husband hovering over my shoulder to protect me. This is what the Plushies are for anyway. We support each other in our own ventures. It helps keep the harem tight and reduce jealousy. We all have our own identities and pursuits."

I kissed the finger she'd poked my nose with, biting it after my kiss. "Still, wouldn't it have had more punch if I was standing behind you?"

"Unnecessary." Maeve waved my concern away. "The Dragon King is a busy man. Having a number of his wives there was already plenty. Few fae would risk your wrath. My mother knew she lost."

"All the fae respect a swelling belly," Evelyn replied, more serious than she'd been for most of the conversation. "For her mother to harm her unborn child would throw away her face in court, not to mention provoke you. It gave the court a solid reason to turn on Winter."

"True. I would torch all of the winter fae, eradicate them from the face of Faerie if she hurt you or our child." I could say it honestly, without an ounce of hesitation. Going through Hell had taught me a lot about myself and what I was willing to do.

"You are more aggressive," Maeve observed.

"Yes," I nuzzled her. "Now, tell me all about how it turned out perfect in the end."

"My mother knew that she was in a pinch and tried to outmaneuver me, but Ikta had coached me on some old customs. I was able to invoke them to challenge her to a duel," Maeve continued, and even though she was fine next to me, I still tensed at hearing that she challenged her mother to a duel.

Maeve noticed my stiffening. "It's cute that you care so much." Maeve kissed my cheek. "She ultimately was forced to accept and then surrender. She knew she couldn't touch me. It was a bloodless duel that the full court supported."

I nodded, a new question popping into my mind. "Where is Winter now?"

"In bed with you, have you gone blind?" Evelyn laughed. She'd clearly been holding onto that joke.

But I realized she was right. Maeve was now technically Winter.

"The old Winter. Your mother," I clarified, even though they both knew who I had meant.

"You wouldn't believe it," Maeve sighed. "My mother congratulated me after court that I had what it took to be a queen now. She had her stuff already removed from the queen's chambers and moved to a part of the castle that was more fitting for a high ranking noble." Maeve rubbed at her forehead. "She's laid claim to what she said was her family's original land, and last I saw her she was knitting little socks with a smile on her face."

Evelyn burst into laughter. "I wouldn't have believed it. Mab has never instilled anything but icy terror into her people. But her holding up two little knit socks was a sight I'll never forget."

Maeve sighed. "My mother has always pushed me to be ruthless, to fit her idea of what a Winter Queen should be. She was a good mother, but one with a fairly narrow view of what it took to be a queen for the winter fae."

"So, she gave you her approval and just backed down?" I frowned, not really understanding.

"Sort of. I think I'm going to understand her better now that she's not queen. It is hard to explain, but it is like she's thawed out and another woman is in her place." Maeve shook her head. "Maybe I never really understood just how much my mother sacrificed to try and be the perfect queen for the winter fae. Or at least, her idea of what was a perfect queen."

"But on the flip side, we now have a never-ending supply of knit goods." Evelyn was still laughing. "I think Winter knew more than the rest of us."

"According to the other two, my mother was extremely well versed in the prophecies and history records. I somewhat suspect she's been preparing for this day," Maeve pondered.

"She still made an enemy out of me when she left me alone with Nat'alet. She's not really my favorite person," I grumbled.

"Yes, that same 'mistake' that then caused her to forge a bond between you and her to protect her during your meteoric rise." Maeve gave me a small smile. "Who knows. She might have planned it all. Or she could be making it up as she goes. Either way, she's turned from my greatest enemy to my strongest supporter in the blink of an eye. Even if I'm left at a loss as to what to do with her." Maeve sighed.

"We could bend her over the Emperor's bed, let him get out all his anger," Evelyn suggested. "Who knows? They both might even like it, and you'll get that sister you always wanted."

"Not everything can be solved with sex," Maeve sighed, her face grimacing at the thought of me with her mother. Then a look of uncertainty crossed her face as she looked over at me. "You wouldn't want my mother would you?"

I was at a loss for words at the question before I realized she actually wanted an answer. "No. Never. I am somewhat curious to talk to this new W— Mab. Soon, I'd like to head back to Faerie. I need to see what's changed there."

Evelyn traced a finger down my stomach to the sleeping dragon between my legs and looped a finger around the head, rousing it from its slumber. "Well, we do want to make sure you like the nymphs as much as possible. It's good for an Emperor's servants to favor him from time to time."

With a thought, Goldie shot a lump off my wrist and caught Evelyn's wrist before chaining them to the corner post of the bed.

Goldie even tried to mimic golden fuzz. I smiled, stalking forward like the Dragon King I was. "You've been a bad nymph. Good thing Officer Goldie is here to hold you while my partner does a thorough inspection."

Evelyn let out a playful yelp. "I forgot she was here. Wait, Goldie! I need you to make something else for me."

"Prisoner's don't speak." Handcuff Goldie squeezed tighter on Evelyn's wrists.

"She's right. They only scream." I rolled her over and lined myself up for another round, smiling as the nymph let out a moan of pleasure.

CHAPTER 33

I was panting on the bed again when Fiona reappeared with a smirk. "My king, I apologize for interrupting. We weren't quite sure if you were here or had slinked off to another bedroom."

Maeve chuckled. "Have I been monopolizing him? I guess that might set a poor example for the other wives. They'll all be going out for big fights that scare the mighty dragon if it gains his undivided attention."

"Speak for yourself. I'm fairly sure his attention was divided between us equally." Evelyn lay next to me, her breasts shuddering with each breath. The sheen of sweat made her glisten.

Fiona smiled. "Ah. I see he enjoys it when the nymphs let loose. Good to know. But if you don't mind, Nyske and Pixie are gathered. We need to speak to you when you have a moment in your office. We would be more than happy to entertain you during the meeting if that would help."

"Blowjobs while getting reports?" Evelyn laughed. "You, sir, live a very blissful life. I don't know many who are as lucky to get this much nymph attention."

I kissed her on the forehead. "Well, if I want to focus, I'll have to turn them down." I glanced over to Fiona, running my hand through my hair while I looked around. "Any chance you know where my clothes ended up? I haven't stocked back up since coming back, and I know I'm out of pants."

"Pixie has a change of clothes ready in your office." Fiona smiled. "You'll unfortunately have to walk through a gauntlet of nymphs without them though."

I could at least put something on from my bracer, but I would play her game.

"Well, he's going to be late that way for sure. Take good care of him, Fiona." Evelyn waved and lay back down on the bed, grabbing the bedcover and wrapping it over herself as she settled into the bed.

"I think you wore her out," Maeve teased. "She's been very excited for another round, complaining that I spend too much time away from the mansion."

"Does your ascending the throne and then giving me the power mean I can rope you into hanging around more now?" I rolled off the bed, standing and waiting for her answer before I headed out.

"I have to attend your court, so I suppose that will depend on how frequently you hold court." She winked, knowing the idea of holding court would make me grumble.

"Damnit, now I'm going to have to hold court daily." I tried to play it off with a frown, but I couldn't hold the frown long when Maeve smiled back. "Alright, Fiona, lead the way." I snapped my fingers and put a glamor of clothes over me to at least seem decent.

"I think I liked you better when you couldn't use magic. I would have enjoyed watching you walk away naked." Maeve settled down in the bed next to Evelyn.

Shaking my head, I followed Fiona out of the room. Sure enough, we walked past plenty of nymphs that were getting the day going. As we walked, Fiona swirled a finger in the air, and suddenly, a fresh breeze dusted off all the grime and sweat covering my body. It felt quite refreshing against my lower body as well.

"Ah, my king!" A nymph in the kitchen waved at me, and I remembered her from the previous night. "We are making a feast for breakfast. What would you like delivered to your office?"

"Pancakes. It's always pancakes after a night like last night. Throw in plenty of bacon and sausage." Really, anyone who thought there was a better breakfast than bacon and pancakes had lived a troubled life. The nymphs made fantastic pancakes.

The gaggle of nymphs started giggling about sausages as I passed and then I heard them gossiping about their times with me.

"The nymphs here are some of the happiest I've seen in my career." Fiona was all business as she led me through the study.

The space was still a mess and the winding staircase had most definitely grown longer. Somehow, even after all of my changes, two flights of stairs still winded me. Apparently, that was simply a constant in life.

I opened the door to Pixie and Nyske having tea.

My pink-haired assistant looked up and frowned. "Darn. I had really hoped that you'd walk through the house naked. Not many of the nymphs can see through your glamors now."

"They are plenty good at imagining him without clothes anyway. The way they talk, I wouldn't be surprised if they only saw him naked now." Nyske put down her tea and smiled.

"Nymph vision," Fiona agreed. "It's only worse with how infatuated they all are."

I took the clothes from my desk and put on a pair of suit pants, frowning at Pixie. "Back to work already?"

"You are in high demand." Pixie shrugged.

"Screw all of that. What's the point of being an Emperor, King, and a King in three different societies if I don't get to pick and choose what I go to?" I rubbed at my chin. "Let's talk representatives. I'm not managing all this on my own."

My time in Hell had changed my perspective on some things. Being a leader was not about doing everything yourself.

"Sabrina is the easy pick for Hell." Nyske picked the low hanging fruit.

"Or you could group some of your activities," Pixie offered. "Manage Hell and Faerie in the same court session."

"I like that." I pointed at Pixie. "A lot. I like it a lot. What about Philly Council business? Thankfully, dragons don't meet this much." I put my head in my hands just thinking about all the different groups that now looked to me as their leader.

"The Philly Council is tricky. More political. Jadelyn or Scarlett might navigate it best. Then again, much of your interaction with them is through Silverwing Mercenaries, so Morgana will also be critical," Nyske thought aloud.

"All three of them," I answered quickly. "Send them together; let them iron things out. Oh, that means I need to meet with them on a regular basis. In terms of social calendar, Jadelyn can navigate all those invites to parties for me." Rubbing my hands together, I smiled, already feeling better.

"Any concern that people will think you are too close to the Scalewrights? That you favor them?" Fiona asked, playing devil's advocate.

"Don't care. I am close with the Scalewrights. If I'm going to start playing any council politics, I'll play it with my usual subtlety."

"Which means none at all." Pixie rolled her eyes and started to make some notes. "Elves?"

"The Highaen sisters. There's a little risk there, but it's also a big gateway for me into Europe. With Jadelyn's shipping ventures increasingly using Morgana's enchantments, I need to keep that lane open at all costs." I wondered if I could increase that network at all. The seven golden cities that Nyske had mentioned before might be an interesting avenue for South America.

"Faerie?" Pixie finished her notes and looked up, waiting for my answer.

"I'll hold a court session. All those mentioned so far attend, along with the three queens. Throw in Helena and Tills too. I took on a big risk by telling the FBI, and I need to keep on top of that."

"Oh. They have a few topics they want to cover with you already. There's a meeting later today with them, the Associate Director, and the new Special Agent in Charge for Philly." Pixie didn't look up from her notes.

"That's a mouthful," I observed.

"They just say 'SAC'. Though, I think it sounds kind of gross; a sac of what? Sacs are rarely pretty things." Fiona frowned at the word.

"Well, it's what we'll use. So, we got a new SAC. I hope Tills' new role is working out for her." I leaned against the desk. "So, do I need this suit?"

"Yes, keep putting it on. Besides, you look good in a suit." Nyske smiled over her cup of tea.

"I'll just have to start working on my glamor to fake it. Never really liked suits. They're too stiff and stuffy for me." I continued putting on the suit anyway. The last thing I needed was to suddenly become naked in a meeting.

My time was becoming too much of a bottleneck. Delegating a number of the groups I was supposed to coordinate with to my harem was the perfect answer. I'd far rather spend more time with my harem than with politically motivated strangers. Meetings with my harems were always more enjoyable.

"Ikta and her pool date?" I asked.

"Day after tomorrow," Pixie answered absently as she continued writing down notes to herself. "I beat her off with a stick when she demanded it happen today."

"That was the highlight of last night if you ask me. I've never seen Ikta put down quite so sharply before," Nyske giggled, enjoying Ikta not getting her way a little too much.

"I serve the Fae Emperor directly, just like her now. I even have his mark on me." Pixie traced the scar on her shoulder. "She does not. So I think I'm even a half a step ahead of her."

Fiona almost looked scared at Pixie's proclamation, glancing around the room like Ikta would just show up. To be fair, she had a habit of randomly popping in. "Don't say that to her face. The Spider Queen is not known for her tolerance."

"She can shove it. She can't touch me. Besides, I know she's too busy right now to be spying." Pixie had a big smile on her face. "And she knows that if she pisses me off too much, I'll schedule it such that she only sees him once a year."

I tried not to laugh and encourage her. Summer was right. The nymphs were starting to realize just how much power they had been given, they managed access to me.

"Don't go too harsh. If you need to push back, that's okay. But I'd rather you not start using my time as a threat," I cautioned her.

"Of course not. It's all theoretical, like how Ikta could kill me but won't. I won't really schedule her out of your life. Just let me and her posture a little. I need her respect if I'm to keep everything moving along." Pixie watched and waited to see how I'd react.

I threw on my suit jacket. "How do I look?" I expertly avoided continuing that conversation.

"You look fantastic." Pixie smiled. "And you'd have never even noticed the friction between me and Ikta if we hadn't said something. We have a council meeting now. Jadelyn, Scarlett, and Morgana will need to know that they should speak up more, and we'll let you fade into the background over the next few days before we remove you entirely."

She waited for my nod before continuing. "After that, you have a sparring session with Maddie while Morgana watches. She said you likely didn't keep up your exercises while you were out, and she wants to whip you back into shape. We are invested in making sure you can keep yourself alive." The last bit was met with a pointed look that told me I would be put through my paces in a few ways.

"You'll visit with Sabrina after that. You said you didn't really get much time with her on your trip, so we have magic lessons scheduled. She insisted that we continue them. Frank will join you for that," Nyske read off.

"We are going to have to start squeezing in my new court sessions, and I need to slip off to Faerie to see The Dreamer and check my powers." I had no idea how the nymphs would pull it all off.

Pixie clicked her tongue. "Move the assistant sex session to later tonight? We can send someone to check with The Dreamer, best not show up uninvited. Can you handle that Nyske?" she asked.

"I'll send one of the other wild nymphs. Can we cut Elena Wallachia shorter too?" Nyske glanced at me. "You didn't sleep last night. Is that a new, permanent thing?"

"No idea. But I don't really feel tired. Do any paranormals not sleep?" I asked.

"Vampires sleep less. Bloodlords only sleep to conserve energy, rather than because they need it. It is the healing factor, but the body still needs some time to sleep even if it does all its nighttime repairs quicker," Nyske explained. "You will want to try to sleep, but we can dial back the time until you start to have issues. That expands how much we can plan and squeeze in dates and such."

"Part of me wants to be really resistant to losing sleep. But I trust you all. Morgana seems to sleep decently when she's in bed with me."

"She's secretly a cuddle fiend." Pixie couldn't stop the sly smile. "Had you duped, didn't she? No, the vampire nocturnal myth started because they sleep less, and night is just better for shady shit like luring people into your home for their sweet sweet blood."

I nodded along. "Okay, we can try and cut a few hours of sleep out."

Pixie started to rework my schedule right then and there, pulling Fiona over to consult. Nyske got up off the couch and smiled at me as she reached my side and claimed my arm.

She played with my hand, spreading my fingers. It was something she used to do when we dated. She liked to touch me and casually examine me. "Hell wasn't too rough? Did you really not bring back a single succubus?"

"Huh? How are those two things even related?" I sat on the desk while the other nymphs worked on the schedule.

I pulled Nyske onto my lap, making Pixie glance up for a moment, share a look with Nyske and then go back to work.

"Because on a scale of zero to a hundred succubi coming back with you, zero means that it was rough down there and you didn't have time. A hundred meant that Hell was a cake walk and you enjoyed yourself," Nyske explained.

I blinked at how surprisingly logical that was. "No. It wasn't that bad. And I did mark everyone except Ikta while I was there. I had plenty of fun."

"No mark on Lilith or Levi we need to worry about?" She raised a brow and pursed her lips.

"Nope. Both are hot, but I had a house full of nymphs to return to. Just hot doesn't quite compare." I smiled and pulled her closer as she switched to my other hand, checking to make sure it was all working just right.

"Oh. It's all the nymphs that you cared about, is it?" Nyske's tone turned playful with just a hint of danger lurking beneath.

"You know, that's just an expression. I mean all of my harem and my assistants most of all. But you didn't participate in last night's endeavors." I didn't want to push her, but I wanted her to know that I'd noticed her absence.

Nyske and I had a much longer and strangely deep relationship. She'd been looking after me for most of my life, and we'd dated for almost a year before everything went off the rails.

"I'm waiting for the right time," Nyske sounded defensive. "I'll pencil in a date for the two of us when you are back from Ikta's pool."

"I'd like that." I snapped the hand she was playing with, closing it like a trap and holding onto her hand. "No thoughts about me and Ikta?"

"You are basically promised to her. This was a when, not an if. As for the woman herself, she's not so bad. The Spider Queen was always very loyal to her people. I'm more worried about you going back to see The Dreamer." Nyske frowned. "Do you have to do that?"

"Summer and Ikta think she's dying. I want to go get a few more answers before that happens. If she passes away, a lot of knowledge is lost."

Nyske wrinkled her nose. "Bitch can die. She used that oath to force me. I couldn't care less about her, even if she made me. But I'll come with you just so I can see her end."

Even when I'd dated Nyske, she wouldn't say a negative thing about anyone. That she held a grudge against The Dreamer was telling. But I understood. She'd been forced to go against what she believed was right.

"I'd love for you to come. Bonus points if you can help me get out of more boring meetings," I whispered the last part, covering my mouth so Pixie didn't see.

"I heard that," Pixie called from across the room. "These meetings are important, even if they are boring for you. They are vital for the running of the various worlds." She sighed. "Should we tell them all to bring scantily clad women to convey the information? Maybe make sure they are unattached in case we really need to hold your attention?" Her brow raised, and I knew a challenge when I heard one.

"No. I'm not that horny," I refuted.

"How many ladies was he with last night?" Fiona asked, tapping her chin.

"Countless," Nyske answered quickly.

"Betrayer," I gasped. "We were having a moment."

"And then you're planning on going to spend time with Ikta and a bounty of nymphs. You realize she's going to rotate them out the whole week?" Pixie piled on. "We've been reviewing the paperwork she made up."

"Well that just seems tiring." I let out a fake sigh.

"You'll have a blast. Now, chop chop. We need to get going. One boring Philly council meeting, coming right up." Pixie stood and dusted off her skirt even though it was always spotless. Then she stepped up to me and kissed me on the cheek. "Portal please. At least this way we can get around a lot faster. Imagine having to schedule for traffic in his calendar."

All three nymphs made a face as I snapped my finger and popped open a portal to one of Morgana's entrances to the Atrium, not wanting to push into her magical area unless it was required.

CHAPTER 34

"That wraps everything up." Rupert knocked on the arm of his chair in the Philly council chamber, and the murmurs and off topic chatter began at once.

Turning to me, Rupert had a teasing smile. "You barely squeaked in before the meeting. Glad to have you back."

"Glad to be back. Hell was... not the vacation I was looking for." I smiled. "I'm even more excited to see that Jadelyn worked with my nymphs to manage the council while I was away. Maybe that needs to be a more permanent thing?" I teased the idea.

"Nonsense. The Dragon King needs to be seen." Rupert was all jovial smiles, but the man could command a room.

"He's actually now the Dragon King, the King of Hell and the Emperor of Faerie. His life has gotten complicated and his schedule busier," Jadelyn pouted and rested her cheek on my shoulder.

"You wouldn't be ignoring my daughter, would you?" Rupert warned.

"He isn't, father. We spent plenty of time together last night." Jadelyn threw me a smoldering look.

Rupert winced. "Spare me the details. I suppose it wouldn't hurt to lead the council and have another Scalewright supporting me. Even if you are his now."

"Actually, I was thinking about her, Scarlett, and Morgana coming and working together," I replied.

Detective Fox snorted. "Just lump in a representative from the fae and Kelly. Then you can just singlehandedly be the majority vote."

I leaned my head to the side. "That's not the worst idea."

"Don't actually do that." The detective hung his head. "At least give Philly the illusion of democracy. Things are less problematic that way."

"Well, if I stuck around, Summer and Winter might just dump their role on the council on my shoulders anyway." I shrugged.

"Wait, you really are some sort of Fae Emperor?" Rupert blinked. "I never thought I'd see the day a man led the fae."

"Believe it." Maeve strolled over to my seat and smiled at Rupert. "With my ascension to Winter Queen, he now has Summer, Wild and Winter backing him."

Rupert let out a soft whistle and glanced at Detective Fox. "Remember when he started to date your daughter, and you were coming up with plans on how to get rid of different body types depending on what paranormal we figured out he'd be?"

"Nope. That doesn't ring a bell. And if any evidence ever shows up, I'm going to say I did it on your orders. It's best to be number two in an organization over being number one for that very reason. You are my fall guy." Detective Fox gave me a playful smile.

I believed that they'd likely built a few plans. Neither of them was thrilled when I started dating their daughters.

"How are Claire and Ruby?" I changed the subject, asking about their wives.

"Good. There's some sort of Mothers of the Dragon book club or something forming. I think it was Ruby's idea." Rupert shrugged.

"It was Claire's and you know it," Detective Fox sighed.

Kelly came over with Taylor hovering over her every inch of the way. "It really needs to be called Grandmothers of Dragons. Gosh, I wonder if the nymphs are going to get their mothers involved."

"Winter, err, Mab is coming over to our place tomorrow. We haven't hosted a fae in a while," Rupert stated.

"Of course she is." Scarlett wrinkled her nose distastefully. "She needs to have a word with the Plushies before she gets too comfortable."

"I'll pass that along. Who are the Plushies?" Detective Fox asked.

"Secret Organization dedicated to dominating the world and all known planes of existence," I replied off-handedly as if it was no big deal, causing both of my fathers-in-law to go wide eyed.

"It's Zach's harem. We have meetings. And we do not look to dominate the world, only hold it within our grasp so that we could if we ever needed to," Jadelyn sighed as if exasperated at the difference between the two.

"Wait, I thought Summer was joking?" I turned to her quickly.

Jadelyn's face snapped to an expression of pure innocence. "Would we ever really do anything bad?"

"Watch that one," Rupert warned. "I taught her too well."

"Anyway, let's go. You don't get out of training by gabbing with people." Morgana stood. She was always ready to leave the council chamber as soon as possible.

"Don't drain him dry. We do like him with his blood still in him," Kelly teased.

Morgana only smiled and clung to my arm to pull me away from the others. They eased back into casual conversation behind us as we headed for the door.

"So, how much have you been working with Maddie?" I asked to make conversation.

"A lot. She's started taking a few small jobs for Silverwing Mercenaries. Frank has been helpful too, but Maddie keeps him in the van. She makes him be lookout." Morgana stifled a laugh.

"Poor guy." I shook my head. "But she does need to keep a tight hold on him. It's only a matter of time before he tries to make his own harem."

"You've been a terrible influence in that regard. But Frank is coming along in his magic with his own creativity. With that comes more mana in his blood, and Maddie seems to be doing better." Morgana filled me in as we left the council chambers and wandered down her Atrium into the club and the twisting back halls of her own spatial dimension.

When we arrived at a crowded gym, vampires were working out around a big, matted area for people to spar. I noticed that the space had been upgraded since I had last trained, and vamps had blood in sports bottles taking sips while they exercised.

Maddie was in the matted area, stretching. "Oh, there you are. Was worried you'd make some excuse about not hitting girls again."

"Careful. If you keep that up, I might not go easy on you anymore," I teased.

"That's the plan." Morgana stepped over to the side. "Goldie, you aren't allowed to help Zach. Come here."

Goldie made a grumble before she shot off my wrist and formed a pair of large opulent golden thrones that did not belong in the middle of a gym. Goldie herself was already in one, her head leaning on her hand while she pouted. "I don't like being separate from him."

"Of course you don't. But I think you are doing more harm than good fighting for him. He must learn to handle all situations," Morgana instructed the elemental. "Now, you two. No holds barred. Go all out. Use what you want as long as it is yours. Zach, the mat and the walls here are enchanted to withstand you."

Goldie snorted. "You underestimate him." She twirled her hand, and gold spread out from the two thrones, entombing the room in golden walls. "Still don't go all out, but you can let loose some."

I grumbled, not liking putting too much effort against Maddie. I didn't want to actually hurt her.

"Go easy on me and I'll make you heal your balls back," Maddie warned.

"Consider the gauntlet thrown." Stepping back, I put my fists up and shifted into my hybrid form, ripping the suit to pieces. Suits were the worst clothing for any functional use. "Let's go."

"Nyske is going to be pissed. Do you know how long she took to make that suit?" Morgana laughed.

"Wait? Nyske made that?" I turned my head, and Maddie zipped across the mat, jumping to kick me in the face.

Seeing it coming, I popped open a portal and she flew through it straight into a wall.

"Why did no one tell me Nyske was making my clothes?" I growled at Morgana.

"She uses her magic for them. Calm down and pay attention." Morgana rolled her eyes at my antics. "You're fighting like a fucking fae."

Maddie flew at me again only for bright golden fire to blaze off me and force her back. "What is this? Fight me!" Maddie demanded.

"This is a good lesson for you, Maddie. Sometimes magic is badass." I had to admit the little bit of satisfaction as I breathed dragon fire over her.

A half-cooked vampire jumped through the flames and hit me in the face with her sword, but my golden scales caught the blade easily. I didn't even flinch before my hand swung up, catching her in a backhand and sending her flying.

"Don't underestimate even a baby vampire," Morgana warned. "You are fighting too confidently. Maddie, take the enchanted blades out if he's going to let you get free hits like that."

"Sorry, Zach. Hopefully, your harem forgives me when I disfigure you." Maddie stood up and her cooked skin flaked off as new, healthy skin replaced it. She stepped off the mat and grabbed a new pair of swords.

As soon as the weapons were in her hands, she shot forward.

I threw up a shield of lightning between us before shouting, "Envoktus!"

Lightning sprayed over the mat, catching her and flinging her back. But before she was swept away, she threw a little wooden block at me.

It didn't seem very threatening, but then it glowed for a moment. The glow faded as the block exploded into light and fire that did little more than scour the last scraps of cloth off me. By the time the blindness from the flash faded, Maddie was in my face and swinging for the fences.

Popping over a portal to save myself, I quickly moved into it.

As Maddie's swing came, I sank into the floor and popped back out in the air as I shifted a pair of wings and beat them hard to hover.

"Tricks are just that. Tricks. Maddie, this is what it is to fight the upper level of the paranormal." I took a deep breath and washed the mat area in lightning even as she tried to speed away.

Her vampire speed didn't matter as lightning blanketed the entire space. Maddie stopped dead, her body locking up from the electricity. I swooped down on her, landing hard enough to feel the crunch of her bones under me.

"Well, you actually use your fucking magic. Color me impressed. Maddie, he might be out of your weight class," Morgana commented, sounding actually impressed. I tried not to visibly preen as she continued. "Powerful beings like him or the fae queens are giant magical batteries. In a closed space like this mat, they will almost always win. They can just keep throwing their fat magical asses around, and there's not much you can do. Best bet is to kill these types when they aren't expecting it."

"Don't teach her to assassinate me," I grumbled.

"If I had a job to kill you, I certainly wouldn't even dare a straight up fight," Morgana considered the situation. "I'd just pretend to be an airhead, seduce you, and then slit your throat."

I suddenly felt the horror of when she had been surprising me with attacks at the beginning of our training. "Do not start doing weird attacks on me in the bathroom again."

"Of course not." Her words and her smile did not match. "Goldie, how about you get on the mat and fight Zach. It would do the two of you some good to understand each other's styles better."

Maddie picked herself up, holding her arm as it popped back into place. "Good fight. It is impressive how much you've grown in a short time." Then she turned to Goldie. "Give him hell for me, please?"

"I don't want to hurt Zach," Goldie grumbled and stepped onto the mat.

Goldie wasn't that big, maybe 5'5" and built more like Tyrande than Yev. But I knew she could weigh as much as she wanted.

"Zach, she's a good opponent. You can't really hurt her much either," Morgana instructed me.

"Really?" I frowned. I knew the new Goldie was strong, but maybe I didn't understand how strong.

"If you take a hunk of her gold out of her, she can just replace it or step on it and reabsorb it. Goldie is really a magical soul holding all that gold. So, physical attacks are fairly useless against elementals. You have to hurt their souls to really do any damage. For you, that really means all you can do is eat her unless you learned any soul tricks while you were out," Morgana explained. "But we won't do that. Instead, you two need to brawl it out and get used to each other's fighting so that you can work together better later."

Goldie put her hands up and jabbed at me from across the mat, her hand shifting with the movement. A golden pole shot forward a moment later, and I had to dodge even as it tried to wrap around me.

I made a fragment of a portal and severed the long limb before rushing Goldie, my fire breath blowing out ahead of me. Unfortunately, the move blinded both of us, not just Goldie.

By the time the fire cleared, Goldie had turned into a wave of gold that was crashing over my fire. Then she was on me, wrapping me in her soft golden embrace before her mass hit me like a tsunami. I rolled across the mat as she sank down onto me.

Goldie formed a golden straitjacket across my body, squeezing tight. "Got you."

I roared and pushed with my entire strength. Goldie bent and shifted as I forcibly ripped my arms apart and got my claws into Goldie, trying to tear the straitjacket off.

"Good, good. Goldie is strong, but she's gold. It's a soft but heavy metal. That's why she uses her weight like the tidal wave she made. It's going to be hard for her to keep an edge, use that," Morgana coached from the side.

Goldie reformed with a surly expression. "I just wanted to hug you."

"No hugs. Fight!" Morgana shouted at Goldie.

I went into melee with Goldie, using my claws to tear gold off of her as she turned her arms into two long blades and scratched me deep. I realized that Morgana was right. Goldie was using a lot of concentration to keep her blades sharp.

Trying a new tactic, I tried to head butt her with my horns. Unfortunately, Goldie met my headbutt, and it was like trying to hit a house. More specifically, a flying house. Her head had far more mass than mine.

I fell over backwards, dazed, and Goldie jumped on my hips, molding her form over me and pinning me with weight alone.

"What happened?" Maddie asked.

"Goldie is getting smarter. That's what happened. Good job. Use your variable weight against him like that. Pinning is going to work well." Morgana clapped.

"Who's side are you on?" I growled at Morgana.

"Everyone's. If you two fight enough, you'll both survive when I'm not there." She held her stomach for a moment. "Okay. Hold him still, Goldie, I'm coming in for a big drink."

I struggled just out of stubbornness, but Goldie sat on me, weighing at least twenty tons. Morgana came over, and I shifted a patch of my neck to not have scales as she bit down on me.

Morgana greedily slurped at my neck and pushed Goldie aside as she climbed onto me and started to tease the wound and suck like it was a sloppy make out session in the back of the bar.

"Get a room, you two." Maddie sighed.

"I feel something growing stiff," Goldie proclaimed.

"That's his dick." Maddie rolled her eyes. "Are you taking her into your harem too?"

"I know what a dick is," Goldie grumbled. "They gave me a plushie. I'm certainly on team Zach."

I felt her moldable form wrap around my reaction, and I managed to get a few mumbles out. "Goldie, not yet. Let's talk about it before we do anything."

"Fucks sake. Don't have sex in front of me." Maddie threw her hands up. "Goldie, let's fight while those two have their fun."

Goldie threw out a tendril of gold that tossed Maddie across the mat. "I won't even move. Try your worst."

Goldie did release me in order to focus, straightening up.

I picked up Morgana and walked to the edge of the mat, cradling my favorite vampire as she continued to lick and tease open the wounds she made. "You are really hungry."

Morgana didn't reply at first, sucking some more before she finally pulled off with a sigh of someone taking their first drink of the night.

"You have no idea how great your blood is. I have a very greedy baby, and it's your fault. You need to take responsibility." She lowered her voice. "Besides, pregnancy is making me crazy horny and these two will take a little time to wear themselves out."

She stood up and grabbed my hand, pulling me quickly into the nearby equipment closet.

CHAPTER 35

Frank left early from my lesson with Sabrina, using a weak excuse. I knew it was for my benefit, but we all played along. He might have picked up on the sexual chemistry between Sabrina and me, which had been on the verge of igniting the entire time we'd been working. And with his absence, that spark exploded.

The two of us had our own private reunion and celebration after he left.

"Do you like the new me?" Sabrina asked, her face vulnerable as she slipped back on a sweater that molded to her exquisite body.

"You are still you, even if you are a little more succubus now." I took a moment to really consider my answer, knowing she needed to understand how I viewed her now. "You are still the nerdy succubus. When I brought up the difference between two and three loops in a drawing, you lost all your desire for sex and had to correct me."

A smile reached Sabrina's eyes as she chuckled, and damn if I didn't react below the belt even as I put my jeans on. There was an effortless sexual attraction between us.

"Maybe we'll get used to the new me. I can't stuff it away with glasses like I had before, but I'm also a lot more comfortable with what I am. I *like* your eyes on me. I always have, but there was also some shame there that stopped me. I'm more comfortable in my own skin..." She trailed off.

"I get it. You aren't afraid of what being a succubus means now that you are a higher order. And your succubus isn't one of those things I saw in Hell," I filled in for her.

She nodded, pausing at my words. "You saw them?"

"And became even more determined to help you," I told her honestly.

"Sorry that I sort of bailed on the trip." She looked down at her feet.

"No. I'm sort of happy I didn't have to see you twist in on yourself and lose yourself along the way. That would have been... torture." There wasn't a better word to describe the situation she would have had to push through.

Watching her lose herself in her succubus nature would have been one of the worst possible outcomes I could imagine.

"Well, push that aside. I'm better than fine." She twirled a finger and her horns and pink skin disappeared, but her gold specks in her eyes stayed until she put on a pair of glasses that turned them blue.

Now she looked like the Sabrina that I had married, but somehow, there was something still very different. Confidence changed a lot about a person. She held herself up straight more and always seemed to have a smile just below her expression.

"You look hot as hell, you know that?" I pulled her up against me.

"Look all you want, touch all you want too, but know that if you touch too much, I'm not going to hold back," she teased.

I held my hands up. "We just got my pants back on."

Nyske came into the room on cue. She was the reason that we had stopped in the first place. "Oh good, you were able to disentangle from each other. Sabrina, I must say that you are absolutely ravishing. You are going to make a few nymphs jealous."

Sabrina smiled. "His nymphs are always welcome to join." A little devil tail poked out from behind her. "You do know what we can do with this, right?"

"Perfectly well. Though I prefer a little more one on one, if I'm honest. Pixie will take you up on it sooner or later." She shifted her focus as Pixie stepped in with a smile. Clearly, she'd followed the conversation and didn't disagree. "Time for the meeting with the FBI. Last meeting of the day and then we get dinner."

"And after dinner, it is assistant time," Pixie added before returning to the topic at hand. "I set up the room, and Sabrina is more than welcome."

"Where are we meeting the FBI?" I asked.

"They are coming to you this time. Helena sent a warning that the new SAC was being weird about the meeting. So, let's meet them outside the mansion," Pixie replied.

Rather than walk through the place, I snapped my fingers and opened a portal at the front door.

"You know the manor is too big when he just portals around," Pixie laughed.

"At least he's practicing magic more." Sabrina stepped through the portal and joined us at the door.

"Sticking around?" I asked.

"Yes, I am," Sabrina spoke with full confidence, and damn, I just wanted to push her up against the door.

"Down boy." Pixie put a finger against my chest. "Door. FBI. Don't fuck anyone."

Sabrina was all smiles as she opened the door just in time for two cars to pull up in my drive. "Good timing, ladies."

"We aim to impress," Fiona added, joining us by the door. "Are we hiding our natures for the start?" She turned into a stunning, dark-skinned woman.

"Yes, that would be best." I waved and hid the rest of the house from view. It would be easy for a nymph to walk past and spook the new SAC.

"Zach." The Associate Director stepped out of the car with a woman I hadn't seen before. When she stepped out, she scowled at me. "This is Georgia Gray, the new Special Agent in Charge for the Philly field office. Georgia, this is Zach Pendragon."

Georgia didn't like me from the start. That much was clear. And when she glanced at my glamored nymphs and Sabrina, she frowned even deeper. I tried not to let it get to me. I understood the stigma that had her viewpoint biased.

"Pleasure, come in. We'll sit down and talk this over," I welcomed them inside.

"The FBI coming to your place is already too much. Why are we treating this criminal so kindly?" Georgia spoke loud enough that she clearly intended for me to hear.

"Criminal?" I asked.

"You run a mercenary business. You are at least criminally adjacent. Even if we've closed the case that my predecessor opened up against you, I feel like there was something there." She had a slight northeastern accent, like she had grown up in a rough part of New York but had done her best to put it behind her.

The woman was of Hispanic descent and had plenty of rough edges. And with her new title, she clearly wasn't feeling the need to soften any of her tough spots.

"Zach is unique. You'll understand by the end of this discussion." The Associate Director gave me a small smile that said to put up with the other woman for a little longer.

I had no doubt Miss Gray would be tough on crime; I just didn't want her to be tough on me. I had enough to manage.

"The cloak and daggers show is pointless, but I'll go along with this." Georgia stomped into my house, followed by the Associate Director, Helena and Rebecca Tills.

Georgia stopped dead a few steps in and frowned, looking at the illusion I had to hide everything. For a moment, I thought she saw through it.

Rebecca understood better. "It's bigger than it looks on the outside. It got me the first time I stepped in too."

I tried not to laugh, realizing how desensitized I'd become since finding out I was a dragon. It didn't even occur to me that the spatial changes would throw somebody off.

Georgia just grunted as we followed Pixie to the dining room where Georgia had another complaint. "This table is massive. Do you sit on one end all alone pretending to be a brooding lord?"

"Watch your tongue," Fiona snapped.

The Associate Director gave Georgia a look that said 'calm your tits' in a more polite, professional way. "Sorry. Georgia is undoubtedly the best woman for the job, but she can be a bit abrasive. Good leaders often are; it takes bravado to handle the broader agency. Maybe we should do introductions? I see new faces from last time, or maybe I've forgotten."

"Pixie, Fiona, Sabrina, and I'm Nyske. You know the rest and we know all of you." Nyske hurried that part of the conversation along.

Georgia was about to say something, but Nyske held up a finger and gave her a look that shut her up.

"I'm sure you are wondering why the Associate Director has joined you in a house call, taking time from her busy schedule. And you also have two agents whose workload is a big black box that you haven't been allowed to look inside yet. Well, we are that black box. If you want to look inside of it, you are going to be polite to my man until he finishes explaining." Nyske finished her rant by snorting.

Georgia paused for a moment, considering Nyske before she nodded once. She was smart enough to stay quiet.

"Well, this is already going better than when I brought you in on this, Associate Director," I chuckled.

"Your nymphs really don't hold back. That's what I like about them." She smiled. "Don't run like I did, Georgia."

"Run?" Georgia raised an eyebrow.

At that moment, I snapped my fingers and made a set of portals covering the two exits to the room. "We planned a little better this time. Pixie, if you would?"

Georgia was staring at the two portals, a frown pressing deeper into her face before she turned back to the pink-haired nymph who started snapping her fingers every few seconds and putting a different glamor over herself.

"You see, Georgia, magic is very real. Vampires are real, and so are werewolves, but it gets so much stranger from there. Pixie here is a nymph, a type of person from Faerie. And Faerie is an attached plane of existence that is connected to Philadelphia, connecting this plane with the paranormal."

Georgia was clearly having trouble processing as her eyes flicked around the room, but she hadn't fainted yet.

"Now, Norton knew about us. He'd been contacted by a type of creature known as a titan and given powers. Then he shared them with some other law enforcement before he started using his powers to hunt paranormal. Those types of powers come with some heavy consequences; he basically served the titan. Then he came to Philly, my territory, and tried to do the same, particularly hunting me because this titan told him to do so.

"That didn't end well for him, not at all. So after he made a direct attack at some of my people, I killed him. It was messy, and there's a trail a mile wide that I'm sure someone of your intelligence could dig up given enough time. I'd rather not have to kill another FBI agent, so I brought the Associate Director here in on everything, and she formed a small task force led by these two agents." I pointed at Helena and Agent Tills. "Any questions so far?"

Pixie stopped snapping and returned to herself.

"Nymph?" Georgia studied Pixie.

"A type of fae. Yes, we like sex. And we have different priorities than humans or a number of other paranormals. Often we serve as close personal assistants to powerful paranormals," Nyske answered quickly.

"What do you mean 'your territory'?" Georgia turned to me, her eyes raked over the women behind me, and I could tell I hadn't made much progress moving up in her eyes.

"I'm the leader of a few things. But Philly is run by a council. I sit on that council. And I have a strong voice. I am one of the most powerful paranormal in..." I paused.

"The world," Sabrina added for me. "The only things that can really threaten him are either very old beings in Faerie, maybe a few of the archangels, and the titans in Tartarus. Oh, and I'm not a nymph. I'm a succubus."

Georgia snorted. "That doesn't make things better."

"Zach is a dragon. Like, a real fire breathing dragon. As I understand it, he is the king of all dragons in the world. They meet at irregular intervals and carve the world into territories because they are territorial and cause problems otherwise. They do their best to remain hidden," the Associate Director explained. "Dragons have large harems. You'll have to get used to a number of pretty women surrounding Zach. Both of these agents are among his harem, and thus able to work freely in the paranormal community."

"So it comes with a lot of perks?" Georgia asked.

"Immortality is a hell of a perk. Haven't gotten that far yet though," Rebecca replied and looked at me boldly, as if daring me to refute her.

"Among many other things," Nyske added. "For one, we have him at our back. In the paranormal community, that is a big deal. For another, the harem is very harmonious. We support each other."

Georgia somehow became more skeptical as she narrowed her eyes towards me. "So, when does this joke end?"

"When you start to believe it." I leaned forward. Scales rippled across my face and down my body. Then I turned my hands into dragon claws. "Want to touch? Sabrina,

Helena, would you care to show her your true selves? Nymphs, you as well."

The flutter of leather and feathered wings filled the room as Georgia's eyes went wide.

When she saw Fiona, she was truly startled. "You are blue!"

"That's what gets her?" Tills shook her head in disappointment. "You are going to have to get used to different colors. Especially hair. The summer nymphs have the kind of colors you can only find in bottles. Can we get some food served up?" She glanced at the portals.

"One thing first. Georgia, I need you to promise me three times that you will not discuss paranormal with another soul that doesn't already know about them," I said.

"Three times?" She frowned.

"It's a magic thing," the Associate Director added.

Georgia took a deep breath. "I will not break your secret of the paranormal." She repeated it twice more.

"Good." I let out a sigh as I brought down the portals.

Georgia immediately bolted.

"Ah shit. I thought she had been taking the information well. Goldie, get her," I called, and the gold elemental shot a cord of herself off of my wrist. I heard a scream followed by a slight thud down the hall.

"I think most people will run. You just had her in a cage until now." The Associate Director seemed a bit pleased she wasn't the only one to pull the move.

"You were just in a bigger cage," Helena pointed out. "But never mind." She looked up as her and Rebecca's nymph stepped in. "Can we get one of those drink carts and maybe a platter of food?"

"Coming right up." The nymph spun around, running off.

"Coffee!" Rebecca shouted after them and then turned to Georgia, who had been dragged back into her chair and held there by Goldie. "Their coffee is fucking magically delicious."

"I don't think she's interested in coffee right now," Goldie grumbled, forming her human shape behind Georgia.

The woman tilted her head back to look at Goldie. "It talks. And of course it is another gorgeous woman." She scowled at me.

"Thank you." Goldie grew far more cheerful. "I'm Zach's Goldie. I'm an elemental of gold. Zach used to keep a bottle of gold flakes under his bed, and since he is a Dragon King, all his magic eventually seeped into me and I gained sentience."

"It isn't Zach's fault that he's surrounded by beautiful women." Sabrina sounded defensive.

"He sure as hell isn't trying to fight it. It looks like he's enjoying this far too much." Georgia clearly had an issue with my harem. "A relationship should be between two people." She glanced at Helena. "I'm surprised an angel would stoop so low, or are you a fallen angel of some sort."

Helena blew out an explosive breath, and Goldie inched forward to protect Georgia. "No, I'm not some fallen angel. Fuck you. You must think you're religious."

Georgia crossed her arms. "Not something I have to share."

"Religious fanatics are always so weird about it." Helena rubbed her forehead. "Heaven is real, but they really just suck up your prayer for a form of energy it contains and eventually take your soul up there and let it live in a strange state of bliss while they feed on you. Or until you dissolve, and then they patch you together with other souls and make lower order angels called cherubs with the pieces of your soul."

Georgia was stunned into silence.

Helena continued, "I'm the daughter of the Archangel of Love. She's a right bitch, by the way. Not immune to the whole power corrupts concept. All the big ones are pricks."

Georgia blinked. "My abuela would be in heaven. She always believed in these sorts of things, but more shamans and such."

"Most wizards prefer an academic approach that started in Europe, but there are plenty of people you'd consider shamans in the southern hemisphere of the world," Sabrina inserted.

"Oh." Georgia didn't have much to say at that point. But looking to regain control, she focused back on the two agents that had information for her. "So, besides knowing that you all sleep with this guy. What have you two been working on? This has something to do with the agents that went native while investigating the cults?"

"Paranormal cult leaders actually brainwashed them," Helena replied with a twist of her lips. "Angels, actually. It's true they do hate free will, at least that part is right. Four of the agents are staying on and will join our section as we continue to go after some minor ones, but we are looking at the cults as they keep cropping up here in America."

A nymph came back with Tills' coffee, and she eagerly accepted it, taking a big drink and sighing.

"In other news, the guy who killed the Representative this spring is now dead. He was a demon from Hell, and Zach went there on other business, but tied up loose ends and killed him," Rebecca added.

Georgia frowned. "You killed them?"

"Locking up beings that can punch a hole in a battleship doesn't exactly work." The Associate Director stepped in. "In the case of the paranormals, we treat it as solved if they serve their own justice."

"This is going to take some getting used to." Georgia stared blankly at the coffee placed in front of her.

"I know, but I hope you can handle it."

The new SAC nodded. "I think I can. So, we hire Silverwing Mercenaries as an excuse to step back and let this guy handle it when it crosses paranormal lines we don't understand?"

"Pretty much. Otherwise, Helena and Rebecca are your best assets. There have been a few strange transfer requests lately. I would like all three of you to probe those agents," she replied.

Helena shrugged. "It's not a secret in the paranormal world that I work for the FBI. I can only imagine that now I have my own task force that at least a few paranormals in the bureau are curious."

"Going to run if I let you go?" Goldie asked Georgia.

"Even if I run, I don't think I'm escaping this mess. Might as well deal with it," Georgia grumbled.

I smiled. "Wonderful. Use my place as you like and let the nymphs know if you need anything."

At those words, a few nymphs poked their heads around the doorway.

"Just how many... wait, don't answer that." Georgia slammed back her coffee.

CHAPTER 36

The next day hadn't been quite as eventful as the last. Catching up with a number of major players in the Philly paranormal scene was almost becoming mundane as I adjusted to being home.

My nymphs were gathering up several of my harem for the next meeting. I had to get Jadelyn and Scarlett who had been back at their parents' house dealing with a few business items.

I stepped through a portal straight to the Scalewright's main hall.

"Ah. Zach, so nice of you to join us." Claire had to almost shout across the giant room. Jadelyn's mother was not subtle in the least.

"No, I—" The excuse fell from my lips as I saw the other women spread out across the room.

Oh fuck.

Amara, Mab, Claire, Ruby and so many more were present. It was mother-in-law hell.

"Ah. Thank you. Could someone get Jadelyn? I had an appointment to pick her up." I smiled. If I was going to navigate the current situation, I was going to need a little help.

"Oh. She'll be down in a few minutes, I heard her still in the shower a minute ago." Ruby smiled, knowing I was trapped as she patted the seat next to her, her five big fluffy fox tails moving aside to clear the space.

"Then I guess I'll just have to wait with you all. What do we call this group?" I sat down where Ruby had indicated, her tails instantly swooping in around me. It was a gesture that I associated with her daughter, and I was suddenly a little more uncomfortable at how relaxed it made me. She wasn't Scarlett.

"We have had some debates." Tyrande's mother sipped from her wine. "But someone suggested Grandmothers of Dragons."

"That would be Gods... for short. A little pretentious, if I might add." Claire was clearly not a proponent of the name.

"Not that I would go that far, but we do hold a certain amount of power." Amara was sitting up straight with a big smile on her face. She totally wanted to be a god.

Some might associate male dragons with being power hungry, but they'd be dead wrong. And they'd see that when they met Amara. The more I had met with Amira's mother, the more I had come to learn she craved power like none other.

And that fact made the coaching that Jadelyn was going to give Amira all the more necessary. And was part of why I really wanted to get out of the room.

"Well, you are all my mothers-in-law. It stands to reason that you should have enough strength to stand up to my actual mother on some topics," I reminded Amara that I was in fact the son of a Dragon God. Two actually.

The black dragon paled at the thought of my mother.

"She's not here, is she?" Amara asked, looking around.

"No. She still spends most of her time in the Fae Wilds. She's oathbound to The Dreamer. What little time she can get away, she spends stomping around my place and demanding to see her grandegg," I replied, but inwardly, I suddenly realized that she'd be free from her oath if The Dreamer died. That was a serious implication I had to consider if the others were right and The Dreamer's days were numbered.

"Soon to be many more eggs," another dragon I didn't recognize for a second spoke.

It took me a moment, but I was able to place her as Sarisha's mother. She saw the recognition and raised her glass in cheers.

"To more grandchildren!" Claire might as well have sounded the clarion call to start a royal hunt. The women around me all cheered excitedly and started talking about their daughters all getting pregnant.

"We have so many nymph mothers. I do hope you are ready for all the children." Ruby patted my leg consolingly. "One was trouble enough."

I swallowed. "Yes, well, this is what I wanted. There are plenty of hands at home to help out."

"You should do skin-to-skin contact with each of them. It's important," Ruby advised me.

"What if they all come at once?" I asked as the sudden imagery of myself buried under a pile of newborn babes entered my head.

"Then you do what you have to. Zach, your life is about to go through a big change. Most people do it one kid at a time." She smirked as the ladies around us were all gabbing about their daughters and how cute their kids would be.

The nymphs seemed especially excited about the prospect of becoming grandparents.

I shifted my focus to Mab, who had joined the nymphs in conversation with a big smile on her face that made me wonder if some sort of brain parasite existed in the paranormal world and could take over a previous fae queen's brain. The concept of a brain-controlling parasite seemed more plausible than the Winter Queen I had known to become the woman sitting in front of me.

My stare got her attention, and Mab looked up, smiling and excusing herself from the nymphs.

"Yes?" She stepped over, and Claire made room for the former Winter Queen on the couch.

"We were just discussing how Zach has chosen a unique route in becoming a father several dozen times over at once," Ruby laughed.

"My daughter among them," Mab spoke proudly. "Maeve has really grown into a strong woman. For a long time, I thought she'd turn out too soft."

"I think Maeve is perfect," I shot back a bit snippier than I'd intended, feeling defensive.

"She did quite well. I have to thank you for that. She had grown quite comfortable as the Fall Lady, never making any inroads for my throne. For a long time, I wondered if I had coddled her too much as a child and she'd become too comfortable in my shadow." A little of the Mab from before came out when she snorted. "But now she's learned when to be hard, and I am relieved of my duties. Instead, I get to spend time here with the other mothers-in-law."

"Show him your knitting," Claire encouraged from the other side of the couch. "I never knew you had such a hand with crafts."

Mab rolled her eyes and held out a hand. A nymph darted from the edge of the room, holding a covered basket. Even if Mab wasn't still queen, she still had servants.

"Well, even if I make the wrong colors for the first one, I'm sure there will be enough of them that they'll get used eventually." She blushed a little and pulled off the cloth to show a litany of knitted items. Many of them had a sort of flower pattern woven into the cloth.

I picked one of them up. "Wow, this is so soft." I had sort of been expecting the scratchy wool I was used to when I thought about grandmotherly knit goods.

"They've come a long way in yarn. It's all so soft now-a-days. When I was younger it was scratchy," Ruby commented, snatching a pair of little blue booties. "So cute." She put them on her fingers and mimed two little feet.

The nymphs almost collectively let out a cooing sigh. If I didn't know better, they all just ovulated.

I held a pair of little mittens that would barely fit on my fingers. "What are the mittens for?"

"So they don't claw their eyes out," Mab answered as if it was a normal concern.

"Wait, fae children try to claw their eyes out?!" What the hell had I signed up for?

"She's exaggerating." Claire smiled, reaching over to pat my shoulder. "All babies have a risk of scratching their faces with their sharp little nails. So you put mittens on them."

"That, and they help them stay warm. I had this all made from a species of fae goat that lives up in my territory. The softest wool is the bottom layer though, so we can only harvest it without killing the goats in the height of summer. It takes a lot of labor to separate that wool from the rest too. But it is the finest thread, and I will only allow the best to be placed on my grandchildren." Mab had a warm smile on her face as she picked out a knit hat.

I had been doubtful before, but seeing Mab now made me a believer that I didn't really know the real Mab before. The Winter Queen was almost a different person, one that had become hard to protect her people.

"It really is the softest I've ever felt." Ruby was petting the little booties. "We should really see if we can't help you harvest more of this."

"Unfortunately, the goats require harsh cold for them to grow their three layers of wool. We have tried for years to use magic to try and harvest the wool at other times in the year, but if you coddle them after you shear them, they stop growing the third layer because they don't need the protection. They have served as a lesson for me growing up that sometimes harsh conditions are required to bring out people's full potential." Mab glanced at me with a meaningful stare before going back to her knit goods.

"Can I just say that this stitching is also beautiful. I tried once when Jadelyn was young. But mine were so loose they were practically woolen lace. Is this the Jasmine stitch? It's so lovely, like a field of flowers." Claire held a blanket now and was just a font of compliments for Mab.

"Yes. It just takes practice. I'm sure you were just using the wrong stitch. This one is popular because it makes the fabric thicker for the cold," Mab explained.

Upon hearing talk of knitting, several of the nymphs moved over and surrounded me on the couch, preventing escape as they started to talk about the differences between knitting and crocheting with an excitement I didn't share.

It turned out that Mab was extremely knowledgeable on the topic. She started to explain the differences in the weaves for both, pulling out various tools and half-done projects from her basket. At one point, she even started to coach a nymph using one of her projects.

Considering how precious that wool was and that the nymph immediately messed it up without losing her head, I was impressed.

I was tightly packed in my seat, trying to figure out a way to politely extract myself. The only option I could come up with was to flip myself over the back of the couch and knock over a few of the nymph mothers, but it seemed difficult to do that subtly.

But as the women continued chatting, the backward flip started to feel like a real possibility. Maybe I could portal with the flip and escape their encirclement.

They started talking about two different colors of yarn that I couldn't see the difference between, yet they all seemed to see it. I was about to make the call to bail when Jadelyn came down the stairs and spotted me.

"Oh, Zach. I didn't realize you were here already." She kept a perfectly neutral smile on her face as she saw me.

Scarlett came down the stairs behind her and was less able to control herself. She curled her lips around her teeth to keep from laughing.

I stared at both of them, trying to transmit 'help' as much as I could with my eyes.

"Well, it seems you are busy. We can just take the Atrium to the mansion." Jadelyn was all soft smiles, as she started to wave. I narrowed my eyes at her, now trying to communicate threats.

"Don't we need him for the meeting?" Scarlett asked.

I was filled with love for my first wife at that moment. "Absolutely, I had come here to fetch you two." Using the excuse, I extracted myself from the circle of ladies with polite smiles. "Now that you are done, let's go."

A portal snapped open back to the mansion. We all stepped through, and the second the portal closed behind us, Scarlett and Jadelyn burst into laughter.

"He practically dove through!" Jadelyn was holding her stomach as she giggled.

"Can you really blame him? I have never seen the Dragon King in such danger before," Scarlett added.

Their words made the rest of the room look up with mixed levels of concern. My nymphs were furrowing their brows, wondering what sort of danger I had encountered at Jadelyn's place but knew that it couldn't have been too bad.

Meanwhile, Amira was highly concerned and stepped up, drawing on her death magic to heal me.

"It's fine." I patted her shoulder. "Sit."

"He got caught up in the gathering of mothers-in-law. They had him pinned in while they talked about knitting." Jadelyn was barely keeping it together.

"It's not funny. I have schedules to keep." I pointed at the nymphs for backup.

"No, you had some time. We thought you might enjoy a round with Scarlett, so we built in some padding," Pixie replied.

"Normally, I'd be sad that I missed the private time, but that picture of you surrounded by our mothers will make me laugh for days to come." Scarlett smiled. "You're welcome for me pulling you out before you start joining them in knitting."

"There's a kink for that," Fiona pointed out.

"There's a kink for everything. But some things like a knitting kink are just unconscionable." I shook my head. "That one is too far out of my comfort zone."

"Speaking of... I have a few consent forms for you to sign." Pixie handed me a folio with a few tabs sticking out the side, a familiar pattern for when she had documents for me to sign.

"Consent form?" I frowned and glanced at the title with wide eyes.

"I read through it. It's all fine. There's a release form that Scarlett and Jadelyn already read over and signed as well," Nyske added.

"We only changed one clause. She didn't try anything tricky," Jadelyn added.

I hesitated a moment but decided to trust my mates and scrawled my name as Pixie started to flip through the tabs she had marked for signatures. Before long, I was done and felt an odd sense of anticipation.

"Why did Scarlett have to sign a release form?" Amira asked, confused.

"Because I'm the first mate and ostensibly the leader of the harem. Jadelyn just signed because she was asked for her blessing. I think Zach made her promise to get it once upon a time." Scarlett shrugged, her eyes focusing on Amira more seriously. "On to the topic of today. Your mother. Zach was just talking to her actually."

Amira looked down at her hands. "I want to push back against her wishes. For a long time, she's determined my direction, and now that I am likely to bear an egg for my mate, I want to free myself to my own directions." She bit her lip, avoiding making eye contact with any of us.

I knew asking for help was hard for a proud dragon like Amira, especially after being under her mother's thumb for quite some time.

"Great. Then it's settled. We start by figuring out where you want to go, then move on from there." Jadelyn clapped her hands like she'd magically fixed the situation, but we had quite a lot more work to do.

CHAPTER 37

I'd been having dreams about The Dreamer, causing me some disorientation. I hadn't had the time to see her since I'd returned from Hell, and part of me was growing anxious that it would be too late soon. The Dreamer had answers I wanted to collect.

Waking up from yet another dream about The Dreamer, I tried to move and became even more confused.

"Huh?" I hung upside down, unable to move my arms.

"There you are. So nice of you to wake up." Ikta climbed over me and ran a sharp fingernail down my cheek. "Ah. They didn't find the hidden clauses in the forms. You are all mine now and forever."

She kissed me before hitting me with the mother of all glamors.

"Where am I?" The fog from waking up was only made worse by hanging upside down and being glamored.

"In my private lair." Ikta's voice was a promise of pleasure made physical.

She was gorgeous in a sinister beauty type of way. We always made the villains sexy, and she was certainly villainous in the dark room with a few spots of starry light that seemed off in the distance. Ikta herself wore scant pieces of black silk, expertly woven around her body to hide her sex and nipples, but somehow managed to exaggerate all of her creamy curves.

"That's nice," I murmured, feeling the glamor ripple down my spine. I couldn't help the silly smile that spread across my face.

"It is wonderful," she encouraged me to give her a little more. "You'll love it, find it comforting after a few years." She stroked my face. "Oh Dragon King, you'll be putty in my hands soon enough."

Ikta kissed me, and my head exploded with pleasure and passion that drowned out any other thoughts of resistance. "My darling, do you love me?"

"Yes," I responded without hesitation.

"Will you still love me when I keep you captive for years and years?" A warm hand cupped my cock and stroked me. "You'll breed me and some select nymphs until I have an army of dragons."

There was a slight protest in the back of my mind, wanting to resist, to fight the waves of comfort rolling over me. I couldn't help but feel that there was something I was supposed to remember tucked away, unable to be accessed.

As I tried and failed to think, Ikta spun around, placing her thighs hanging in my face. The slick warmth of her mouth engulfed me, and any semblance of thoughts I had vanished. She swayed, and the web I was in rocked slightly as it drove me deeper into Ikta's mouth.

Ikta's human legs wrapped around my head and pulled me close enough to lick her sex. I didn't hesitate, pushing aside a fold of silk with my nose and lapping at her. She was already practically dripping for me as I kissed her folds and licked at her fleshy pearl.

I was in heaven as she swallowed my full girth, from her soft lips all the way to her throat where she hummed around the head. I tried to thrust, push deeper into the pleasure, but she had me bound tightly in her web.

"Oh, Dragon King. I'm so happy that you want more," Ikta cooed and delivered soft kisses while she ran her fingers along my length. "Yes, right there, keep going."

My tongue was too busy with her clit for me to respond.

She pulled herself tightly against me before she shuddered, and I felt her warm fluids wash against my tongue. "Yes." She finished with a sibilant hiss. "I have been waiting for this day."

With my tongue free, I blinked in the darkness. "Maybe it's time you give me a little more mobility?"

"Nonsense. Where's the fun in that? But I will reposition you." Her spider limbs worked quickly, cutting free my cocoon while she spun another set of strands that held me almost horizontal; my head was a little higher than my hips. I had to admit, it was comfortable.

My face and my cock were still the only parts of my body not completely wrapped in her silk.

"There, much better, isn't it?" Ikta dangled above me and lowered herself down gently as her hips brushed against my cock, making it twitch. "So eager."

My entire body trembled with excitement at her touch. I hadn't had my release yet, and my body was begging to explode. But Ikta took her time, sliding back, the cleft of her ass perfectly cupping me and I felt the soft silk of her dress enfold me as she started to grind her ass into me.

I growled at her and strained in my silk bindings, but I couldn't break free. "Put it in."

"No." Ikta playfully tapped my nose. "I'm going to make you build up with such desire that your vision spots with the pressure. Even then, you are going to be begging me for the release. And when it comes, you will empty yourself into me, so delirious with pleasure you just want to do it over and over again."

Ikta curled her hand, and a touch of magic spun out around her. I felt my cock tingle, and I could swear I could feel every fiber of her fine silk dress as she ground against me.

I tensed, wanting to thrust, wanting release. "Fuck," I growled again, my voice filled with gravel.

"Not. Yet." She bent down and kissed me.

Her pillowy soft lips made me want to crush her against my chest while I rutted into her. I could barely stand it as she pleasured me and rubbed her silk clad ass against me, making my cock twitch and thrash.

"Please," I finally begged, deciding to try another tactic. Anything to get to bury myself inside of her.

Ikta clicked her tongue. "That's not good enough."

"Please, fuck me. I need to be inside of you," I embellished.

"Mmm better. I'll take it for now." Her hips rose and sank down over my member. She wanted it just as badly as I did.

I shuddered as warm syrupy pleasure poured itself over my cock and through my entire body. "You feel incredible."

"Not so bad yourself," Ikta whispered in an almost reverent tone, still trying to hide how much she needed this.

She was so tight, yet her body gave way to every inch of me as her sensual folds enveloped me. I wanted to cum so badly, pulling my body tight as I begged for it to release.

Ikta hummed as her hips shifted over mine, twisting and rising in ways I'd never felt before. She was using her spider limbs to hold onto the web, allowing her to move any way she wanted as she rose and fell onto my hips with a wet squish that seemed incredibly loud in the darkness.

"Oh Zach," Ikta whispered.

As she started to throw her hips into mine, the web bounced and threw me into her sex harder and harder in response to each thrust. My mind was drowned out in the bliss, and I could feel just how hard I was, knowing that just once in her wouldn't be enough.

I needed more. I wanted to stay buried inside of her.

"That's it. Keep going," I encouraged her. "I want it. I need it."

Ikta's spider limbs wrapped around me, and she pressed our bodies together as her web continued to rock them up and down. The web's rocking had gained enough momentum that she didn't have to do anything but ride me as I plunged in and out of her with the swaying of the web.

I felt the swelling of my cock for a moment before the dam burst inside of her, and true to her words, it was hard enough that my vision spotted. I let out a sigh of pleasure, relaxing in her web for the first time since we had begun.

"Yes." Ikta's walls were still shuddering. "The Dragon King is mine." She focused on me. "Am I yours, Dragon King?"

"Yes." I felt my jaws crackle with the desire to mark her.

Ikta was quick, moving along the cocoon and putting her thigh in my mouth as I bit down, searing her thigh with magic. "Mark me, my mate, my king, my emperor. I shall hold you forever, build you fortresses to conquer the world and keep you ensconced in so much pleasure that you'll never leave."

The Wild Fae Queen shuddered on top of me before going limp for a moment.

"We are not done. I need more. I'm still hard," I growled.

"Of course, your majesty. This poor servant just needed a moment to recover." Ikta spun back around. Her smile was beautiful as she cupped my chin and sank down onto me again.

This time, she kissed me with her pillowy lips while her spider limbs started bouncing the cocoon. Her kisses became more frenzied, and we made out as the web vibrated. Still inside of her, the rocking moved me in and out of her as well.

Never once did our lips stop touching as I greedily devoured hers until we came again.

"I believe a bath is necessary. We can come back to this later." Ikta popped a portal open under me, and I felt the air on my back for the first time as I fell out of the cocoon and through the portal. Ikta followed after me.

We both splashed into a hot spring, somewhere in Faerie.

The second I touched the ground, I felt overwhelming power swell inside of me. Ikta had given me the last of her piece of Faerie. In total, it was far larger than Winter or Summer's territory. Yet now I could feel there was a small piece missing that I could not access.

The Dreamer.

It made sense that she would hold onto the last piece, and I had to admit, knowing she was still alive gave me some relief.

"Your majesty, my queen." Lorina and Gresha bowed, a line of nymphs forming behind them.

"Hold her." I smiled as I rose from the pool, feeling so filled with power that I wanted to show Ikta who was really in charge.

Ikta shuddered as the nymphs rushed forward, grabbing each of her limbs, splaying her out on top of the water.

"You really had me going for a moment." I lined up her hips and then called on the ground beneath us to rise up and lock her limbs in place. "Nymphs, you have free reign to tease her as much as you can."

"You liked it." Ikta grinned.

"Oh, I love the feeling of you cumming around me. And I'll admit, the concept of being held for eternity did up the intensity. With the glamor you hit me with, I wasn't even able to remember the consent forms." I held Ikta as the nymphs started to kiss all over her body. "Hit her with your glamor, ladies, turnabout is fair play." I smiled wickedly at Ikta, her eyes sparkling as they met mine.

The nymphs giggled and didn't need any encouragement.

"But don't let her cum." I took satisfaction in the slight widening of Ikta's eyes.

"What?!" Ikta shouted. "I thought—"

"We have a whole week together, my mate. I see you like to tease, and I'm happy to oblige."

A nymph was between Ikta's legs, lapping my seed from her sex and making Ikta shudder as she tried to move, but Faerie had responded to my call and held her still.

"It was roleplay," Ikta gasped as the nymphs went to work on her.

"Yes, and now I'm going to make you cum every time I thrust myself into you." I smirked. "Keep it up, ladies. She really loves this and is still roleplaying. Your queen has always wanted a man that can hold her down. Isn't that right?"

"Yes," Ikta hissed and arched her back when she was close, trying to get the release, but the nymph backed off, leaving her on the edge.

***

Ikta and I were relaxing in the hot spring as nymphs started to deliver much needed refreshments. I snagged the pitcher of some sort of watered-down fruit wine and tipped the whole thing back, greedily trying to quench my thirst.

"Oh. You should put something fun in the next pitcher. This won't do anything to the Dragon King," Ikta pouted.

"No fun stuff." I put the pitcher down. "Well, not unless I say so. More, please." I handed off the pitcher as a nymph reclaimed my arm, massaging me again.

Another nymph pulled grapes off the vine, and I accepted them one by one. The gesture wasn't so much about eating as just accepting the luxury of the pool with the nymphs.

"How does it feel to be the complete ruler of Faerie?" Ikta asked, receiving similar treatment from a nymph next to me.

"Not complete. I need to talk to The Dreamer," I replied.

"Of course she held something back. This is sort of the plane she made," Ikta grumbled. "We'll see her another time."

"I can feel her life; it is waning. But I suspect it has been waning slowly for a very long time," I told her, now more in tune with the land.

"Will she last?" Ikta asked.

"I suspect she could hold on for centuries still, though in reduced capacity. Even now, she sleeps. I suspect that she spends very little time awake." Shaking my head, I realized just how weak The Dreamer had become.

Her power felt like a bottle that had been drained, with barely enough water to line the bottom. She survived by nursing that last bit of power. I even wondered if she had any real power beyond the fae oaths she used to make things happen.

It was probably best not to underestimate the last living titan.

"Good. I would hate to lose some of my week to her. We need another few dozen times to ensure I'm pregnant, then we can let the nymphs start to have their fill." Ikta lazily lounged next to me.

The nymphs started to giggle, and a warm mouth wrapped around me under the steamy water.

"Until then, just enjoy being Emperor and having my nymphs and me here to give you one week of sex-filled vacation." Ikta crawled over me and pushed the nymph aside. "You deserve a rest before you have all your dragons popping out eggs and taking over your hoard."

"What?" I sat up straight.

The nymphs giggled and pulled me back. "Your life is going to go through some drastic changes here soon," a nymph promised with smoldering eyes.

"I know, and I'm excited for it." And I meant those words.

I knew my life was going to change once more, but I couldn't help but feel the rightness in everything. And it helped at the present moment that I was surrounded by beautiful women, lounging in a pool for a week of relaxation. The rest of the world and my destiny could wait a week.

Afterword

Hey Everyone,

I'm happy to share with you Dragon's Justice 8! It was a fun ride and we are closing in on the end of the series. Our favorite dragon king is growing to epic proportions.

For DJ 9 I am going to work to bring back the 'case' structure to make it end in Urban Fantasy style with the classic investigation. Though it will likely take place in Brazil as Zach investigates the ongoing spread of cults.

Otherwise, things are going well. I bounced back from my month off. Life just caught up with me. My wrists are back in working order and I'm doing my exercises again! Some might say I spend too much time at the keyboard, but I just love writing.

I do have a Kickstarter as I explore other avenues for my series. I'm turning Saving Supervillains into a manga. It is a single manga volume of 200-220 comic pages. Please, check it out.

Please, if you enjoyed the book, leave a review.

I have a few places you can stay up to date on my latest.

Monthly Newsletter

Facebook Page

Patreon

ALSO BY

Legendary Rule:
Ajax Demos finds himself lost in society. Graduating shortly after artificial intelligence is allowed to enter the workforce; he can't get his career off the ground. But when one opportunity closes, another opens. Ajax gets a chance to play a brand new Immersive Reality game. Things aren't as they seem. Mega Corps hover over what appears to be a simple game. However, what he does in the game seems to effect his body outside.
But that isn't going to make Ajax pause when he finally might just get that shot at becoming a professional gamer. Join Ajax and Company as they enter the world of Legendary Rule.

Series Page

A Mage's Cultivation – Complete Series
In a world where mages and monster grow from cultivating mana. Isaac joins the class of humans known as mages who absorb mana to grow more powerful. To become a mage he must bind a mana beast to himself to access and control mana. But when his mana beast is far more human than he expected; Isaac struggles with the budding

relationship between the two of them as he prepares to enter his first dungeon.

Unfortunately for Isaac, he doesn't have time to ponder the questions of his relationship with Aurora. Because his sleepy town of Locksprings is in for a rude awakening, and he has to decide which side of the war he is going to stand on.

Series Page

The First Immortal – Complete Series

Darius Yigg was a wanderer, someone who's never quite found his place in the world, but maybe he's not supposed to be here...Ripped from our world, Dar finds himself in his past life's world, where his destiny was cut short. Reignited, the wick of Dar's destiny burns again with the hope of him saving Grandterra.

To do that, he'll have to do something no other human of Grandterra has done before, walk the dao path. That path requires mastering and controlling attributes of the world and merging them to greater and greater entities. In theory, if he progressed far enough, he could control all of reality and rival a god.

He won't be in this alone. As a beacon of hope for the world, those from the ancient races will rally around Dar to stave off the growing Devil horde.

Series Page

Saving Supervillains – Complete Series

A former villain is living a quiet life, hidden among the masses. Miles has one big secret: he might just be the most powerful super in existence.

Those days are behind him. But when a wounded young lady unable to control her superpower needs his help, she shatters his boring life, pulling him into the one place he least expected to be—the Bureau of Superheroes.

Now Miles has an opportunity to change the place he has always criticized as women flock to him, creating both opportunity and disaster.

He is about to do the strangest thing a Deputy Director of the Bureau has ever done: start saving Supervillains.

Series Page

Dragon's Justice

Have you ever felt like there was something inside of you pushing your actions? A dormant beast, so to speak. I know it sounds crazy.

But, that's the best way I could describe how I've felt for a long time. I thought it was normal, some animal part of the human brain that lingered from evolution. But this is the story of how I learned I wasn't exactly human, and there was a world underneath our own where all the things that go bump in the night live. And that my beast was very real indeed.

Of course, my first steps into this new unknown world are full of problems. I didn't know the rules, landing me on the wrong side of a werewolf pack and in a duel to the death with a smug elf.

But, at least, I have a few new friends in the form of a dark elf vampiress and a kitsune assassin as I try to figure out just what I am and, more importantly, learn to control it.

Series Page

Dungeon Diving

The Dungeon is a place of magic and mystery, a vast branching, underground labyrinth that has changed the world and the people who dare to enter its depths. Those who brave its challenges are rewarded with wealth, fame, and powerful classes that set them apart from the rest.

Ken was determined to follow the footsteps of his family and become one of the greatest adventurers the world has ever known. He knows that the only way to do that is to get into one of the esteemed Dungeon colleges, where the most promising young adventurers gather.

Despite doing fantastic on the entrance exam, when his class is revealed, everyone turns their backs on him, all except for one.

The most powerful adventurer, Crimson, invites him to the one college he never thought he'd enter. Haylon, an all girls college.

Ken sets out to put together a party and master the skills he'll need to brave the Dungeon's endless dangers. But he soon discovers that the path ahead is far more perilous than he could have ever imagined.

Series Page

There are of course a number of communities where you can find similar books.
https://www.facebook.com/groups/haremlit
https://www.facebook.com/groups/HaremGamelit
And other non-harem specific communities for Cultivation and LitRPG.
https://www.facebook.com/groups/WesternWuxia
https://www.facebook.com/groups/LitRPGsociety
https://www.facebook.com/groups/cultivationnovels

Made in the USA
Columbia, SC
03 January 2024

29804421R00224